I0583462

LISTEN, LISTEN

By Kate Wilhelm

Listen, Listen
A Sense of Shadow
Better than One (with Damon Knight)
Juniper Time
Somerset Dreams and Other Fictions
Fault Lines
Where Late the Sweet Birds Sang
The Clewiston Test
The Infinity Box: A Collection of Speculative Fiction
City of Cain
Margaret and I
Abyss: Two Novellas
The Year of the Cloud (with Theodore L. Thomas)
Let the Fire Fall
The Downstairs Room and Other Speculative Fiction
The Killer Thing
The Nevermore Affair
The Clone (with Theodore L. Thomas)
More Bitter than Death
The Mile-Long Spaceship

LISTEN, LISTEN

Kate Wilhelm

Houghton Mifflin Company Boston

1981

"The Winter Beach" was first published in *Redbook*. "Julian" was first published in *Analog Yearbook*, edited by Ben Bova and published by Condé Nast Publications, Inc., copyright © 1977 by The Condé Nast Publications, Inc. "With Thimbles, with Forks, and Hope" was first published in *Isaac Asimov's Science Fiction Magazine*. "Moongate" was first published in Damon Knight's *Orbit 20*, published by Harper & Row. "The Uncertain Edge of Reality" was first published in *Locus*.

Copyright © 1981 by Kate Wilhelm

All rights reserved. No part of this work may be reproduced or transmitted in any form or by any means, electronic or mechanical, including photocopying and recording, or by any information storage or retrieval system, except as may be expressly permitted by the 1976 Copyright Act or in writing from the publisher. Requests for permission should be addressed in writing to Houghton Mifflin Company, 2 Park Street, Boston, Massachusetts 02107.

Library of Congress Cataloging in Publication Data

Wilhelm, Kate.
  Listen, listen.

  Contents: The Winter beach — Julian — With thimbles, with forks, and hope — [etc.]
  I. Title.
PS3573.I434L5   813'.54   81-4179
ISBN 0-395-31269-8   AACR2

Printed in the United States of America

V 10 9 8 7 6 5 4 3 2 1

For Doug, Marge,
Lisa, Reneé, and Tara.

With much love.

CONTENTS

THE WINTER BEACH

HUGH LASATER stood with his back to the
window watching Lloyd Pierson squirm. They were in Pierson's
office, a room furnished with university-issue desk and book
shelves, as devoid of personality as Pierson himself was. He was
one of those men no one after the fact could ever identify, so
neutral he could vanish in a mist, become one with a landscape,
and never be seen again.

Lloyd Pierson stopped fidgeting with his pencil and took a
deep breath. "I can't do it," he said primly, examining the pencil. "It would be unethical, and besides she would appeal. She
might even have a sex discrimination case."

"She won't appeal. Believe me, she won't make a stink."

Pierson shook his head. He glanced at his watch, then confirmed what he had learned by looking at the wall clock.

Lasater suppressed a laugh.

"You do it, or I go over your head," he said mildly. "It's a
funny thing how people hate having this kind of decision shoved
at them when it could have been handled on a lower level. You
know?"

"You have no right!" Pierson snapped. He looked at Lasater,
then quickly away again. "This is insufferable."

"Righto. Dean McCrory, isn't it? I just happen to have his number here somewhere. I suppose your secretary would place the call for me?" He searched his notebook, then stopped, holding it open.

"I want to talk to your supervisor, your boss, whoever that is."

Lasater shrugged. "Got a piece of paper? I'll write the number for you." Pierson handed him a note pad and he jotted down a number. "That's a Washington area code. Dial it yourself, if you don't mind. You have an outside line, don't you? And his is a direct line, it'll be his private secretary who answers. Just tell him it's about the bird-of-prey business. He'll put you through."

"Whose private secretary?"

"Secretary of Defense," Lasater said, as if surprised that Pierson had not recognized the number.

"I don't believe you." He dialed the number.

Lasater turned to look out the window. The campus was a collage of red brick buildings, dirty snow, and too many people of an age. God, how tired he would get of so many young people all the time with their mini-agonies and mini-crises, and mini-triumphs. Unisex reigned here; in their dark winter garments they all looked alike. The scene was like an exercise in perspective: same buildings, same snow, same vague figures repeated endlessly. He listened to Pierson parrot his message about bird of prey, and a moment later:

"Never mind. Sorry to bother you. I won't wait. It's all right."

Lasater smiled at the bleak landscape, but when he turned to the room there was no trace of humor on his face. He retrieved the note paper, put it in an ashtray, and set it afire. After it was burned he crushed the ashes thoroughly, then dumped them into the waste can. He held the pad aslant and studied the next piece of paper, then slipped the pad into a pocket. He kept his amusement out of his voice when he said, "You will never use that number again, or even remember that you saw such a number. In fact, this entire visit is classified, and everything about it. Right?"

Pierson nodded miserably.

Lasater felt only contempt for him now; he had not fought hard enough for anything else. "So, you just tell her no dice on a leave of absence. You have about an hour before she'll get here; you'll think of a dozen good reasons why your department can't do without her services."

He picked up his coat and hat from the chair where he had tossed them and left without looking back.

Lyle Taney would never know what happened, he thought with satisfaction, pausing to put his coat on at the stairs of the history department building. He went to the student union and had a malted milk shake, picked up a poetry review magazine, bought a pen, and then went to his car and waited. Most of the poetry was junk, but some of it was pretty good, better than he had expected. He reread one of the short pieces. Nice. Then he saw her getting out of her car. Lyle Taney was medium height, a bit heavy for his taste; he liked willowy women and she was curvy and dimply. Ten pounds, he estimated; she could lose ten pounds before she would start to look gaunt enough to suit him. He liked sharp cheekbones and the plane of a cheek without a suggestion of roundness. Her hair was short and almost frizzy it was so curly, dark brown with just a suggestion of gray, as if she had frosted it without enough bleach to do a thorough job. He knew so much about her that it would have given her a shock to realize anyone had recorded such information and that it could be retrieved. He knew her scars, her past illnesses, her college records, her income and expenses . . . She was bouncy: he grinned at her tripping nimbly through the slush at the curb before the building. That was nice, not too many women were still bouncy at her age: thirty-seven years, four months, sixteen days.

She vanished inside the building. He glanced at his watch and made a bet with himself. Eighteen minutes. It would take eighteen minutes. Actually it took twenty-two. When she reappeared, the bounce was gone. She marched down the stairs looking straight ahead, plowed through the slush, crossed the street without checking for traffic, daring anyone to touch her. She got to her car and yanked the door open, slid in, and drove off too fast.

He liked all that. No tears. No sentimental look around at the landscape. Just good old-fashioned determination. Hugh Lasater liked to know everything about the people he used. This was data about Lyle Taney that no one would have been able to tell him. He felt that he knew her a little better now than he had that morning. He was whistling tunelessly as he turned on his key, started the rented car, and left the university grounds. She would do, he told himself contentedly. She would do just fine.

✿

Lyle put on coffee and paced while she waited for it. On the table her book looked fragile suddenly, too nebulous to support her entire weight, and that was what it had to do. The book had a flying hawk on the cover; sunlight made the rufous tail look almost scarlet. The book was about hawks, about the word *hawk*, about hawklike people. It was not natural history, or ornithology, or anything in particular, but it had caught on, and it was having a moderate success. A fluke, of course, such a long shot it could never happen again. She was not a writer, and she really knew nothing about birds in general and hawks in particular, except what she had researched and observed over the five years it had taken her to do the book. The book was so far removed from her own field of history that it was not even counted as a publication by her department.

Her former department, she corrected herself, and poured coffee, then sat down at the table with it and stared at the book, and went over the luncheon one more time.

Bobby Conyers, her editor for the hawk book, and Mal Levinson from the magazine *Birds* had insisted that a follow-up book on eagles would be equally successful.

"Consider it, Lyle," Mal had said earnestly, on first-name basis instantly. "We want the article. I know ten thousand isn't a fortune, but we'll pick up your expenses, and it'll add up. And Bobby can guarantee fifteen thousand up front for the book. Don't say no before you think about it."

"But I don't know anything at all about eagles, nothing. And Oregon? Why there? There are eagles in other places, surely."

Mal pointed to the clipping he had brought with him: a letter to the editor of a rival magazine, it mentioned the bald eagles seen along a stretch of Oregon beach for two years in a row, suggesting they were nesting in the vicinity.

"That part of Oregon looks like the forest primeval," he said. "And eagles, bald eagles, are on the endangered list. That may be the last nesting site on the west coast. It'll make a terrific article and book. Believe us, we both agree, it'll be even better than *Hawks*. I'd like to call it *Bird of Prey*."

Bobby was nodding. "I agree, Lyle. It'll go."

She sipped her coffee, her gaze still on the book. In her briefcase were contracts, a map of Oregon, another one of that section of coast, and a Xerox copy of an article on eagles that Mal had dug out of back issues of his magazine.

"What if I can't find the nest?" she had asked, and with the question she had realized she was going to do it.

"It's pretty hard to hide an eagle's nest," Mal had said, grinning, knowing she had been persuaded. He began to talk about eagles then, and for the rest of the hour they spent together, it had been as if they all knew she would go to Oregon, search the jagged hills for the nest, set up a photography blind, start digging for facts, tidbits, myths, whatever else took her fancy to make up a full-length book.

And she did want to do it, she told herself again firmly, and tried not to think of what it would mean if the book failed, if she could not find the nest, if the eagles were not nesting there this year, if . . . if . . . if . . . She would have to face Pierson and ask for her job back, or go somewhere else and start over. She thought briefly of filing a claim of discrimination against Pierson and the university, but she put it out of mind again. Not her style. No one had forced her to quit, and no one guaranteed a leave of absence for a job unrelated to her field. Pierson had pointed this out to her in his most reasonable tone, the voice that

always made her want to hit him with a wet fish. The fleeting
thought about the statistics of women her age getting work in
their own fields went unheeded as she began to think seriously
about the difficulties of finding an eagle's nest in the wooded,
steep hills of the coast range of Oregon.

Presently she put the book on a chair and spread out the coastal
map and began to study it. The nest would be within a mile or
two of the water, and the exact places where the bird had been
seen were clearly marked. An area roughly five to eight miles by
two miles. It would be possible, with luck, and if the bird watcher had been right, and if the eagles came back this year . . .

✿

Lyle sat on the side of her bed talking on the phone. During the
past week she had packed up most of the things she would take
with her, and had moved into her study those things she did not
want her subleasers to use. She would lock that door and keep
the key. Almost magically the problems had been erased before
her eyes. She was listening to her friend Jackie plead for her to
reconsider her decision, and her mind was roaming over the
things yet to be done. A cashier's check to open an account with
in the village of Salmon Key, and more film and developer
paper . . .

"Jackie, it's not as if I were a child who never left home before," she said, trying to keep the edge off her voice. "And I tell
you I am sick and tired of teaching. I hadn't realized how tired
of it I was until I quit. My God! Those term papers!"

She was grateful a moment later when the doorbell cut the
phone call short. "Lunch? Sure. I'll be there," she said and hung
up, and then went to open the door.

The man was close to six feet, but stooped; he had a big face.
She seldom had seen features spread out quite as much as his
were: wide-spaced eyes with heavy long lashes and thick sable-
brown brows, a nose that would dominate a smaller face, and a
mouth that would fit on a jack-o'-lantern. The mouth widened
even more when he smiled.

"Mrs. Taney? Could I have a few minutes to talk to you? My name is Hugh Lasater, from the Drug Enforcement Administration." He handed her his identification and she started to open the door; he held it to the few inches the chain allowed.

"Ma'am, if you don't mind. You study the I.D. and the picture, compare it to my pan, and then if it seems okay, you open the door." He had a pained expression as he said this.

She did as he directed, then admitted him, thinking he must be looking for an informant or something. She thought of the half dozen vacant-eyed students in her classes; the thought was swiftly followed by relief that it no longer concerned her.

"What can I do for you, Mr. Lasater?" She motioned to a chair in a halfhearted way, hoping he would not accept the quasi-invitation.

"No one's here with you?"

She shook her head.

"Good." He took off his coat and hat and put them down on the sofa, then sank down into the chair she had indicated. "You almost ready to go?"

She started, but then, glancing about the apartment, decided anyone with an eye could tell she was going somewhere. "Yes. Next week I'm going on a trip."

"I know. Oregon. Salmon Key. The Donleavy house on Little Salmon Creek."

This time when she reacted with surprise, the chill was like a lump of ice deep within her. "What do you want, Mr. Lasater?"

"How'd you learn that trick?" he asked with genuine curiosity. "You never had any intelligence training."

"I don't know what you're talking about. If you'll just state your business. As you can see, I'm quite busy."

"It's a dandy thing to know. You just step back a little and watch from safety, in a manner of speaking. Useful. Damned offputting to anyone not familiar with it. And you're damned good at it."

She waited. He knew, she thought, that inside she was frozen: her way of handling anger, fear, indignation? Later she would analyze the different emotions. And Hugh Lasater, she realized, was also back a little, watching, calculating, appraising her all the way.

"Okay, I'll play it straight," he said then. "No games, no appeal to loyalty, or your sense of justice, or anything else. We, my department and I, request your help in a delicate matter. We want you to get fingerprints from a suspect for us."

She laughed in relief. "You aren't serious."

"Oh yes, deadly serious. The Donleavy house is just a hop away from another place that sits on the next cliff overlooking the ocean. And in that other house is a man we're after quite seriously. But we have to make certain. We can't tip him that we're on to him. We need someone so innocent, so unlikely that he'll never give her a second thought. You pass him a picture to look at; he gives it back and you put it away carefully in an envelope we provide. Finis. That's all we want. If he's our man, we put a tail on him and let him lead us to others even more important and nab them all. They're smuggling in two-thirds of all the coke and hash and opium being used in the States today."

He knew he had scored because her face became so expressionless that it might have been carved from wax. It was the color of something that had died a long time ago.

"That's contemptible," she said in a low voice.

"I'm sorry," he replied. "I truly am. But we are quite desperate."

She shook her head. "Please go," she said in a low voice. In a flash the lump of ice had spread; her frozen body was a thing apart. She had learned to do this in analysis, to step out of the picture to observe herself doing crazy things — groping for pills in an alcoholic fog, driving eighty miles an hour after an evening in a bar . . . It was a good trick, he was right. It had allowed her to survive then; it would get her through the next few minutes until he left.

"Mrs. Taney, your kid wasn't the only one, and every day there are more statistics to add to the mess. And they'll keep on being added day after day. Help us put a stop to it."

"You have enough agents. You don't need to drag in someone from outside."

"I told you, it has to be someone totally innocent, someone there with a reason beyond doubting. You'll get your pictures and your story, that's legitimate enough. The contracts are good. No one will ever know you helped us." He stood up and went to his overcoat and took a large insulated envelope from the inside pocket. "Mrs. Taney, we live in the best of times and the worst of times. We want to squash that ring of genteel importers. People like that are making these the worst of times. It's a dirty business; okay, I grant you that. But Mike's death was dirtier. Twelve years old, overdosed. That's pretty damned filthy." He put the envelope down on the end table by the sofa. "Let them make the first move. Don't try to force yourself on them in any way. There's Saul Werther, about sixty-two or three, cultured, kindly, probably lonesome as hell by now. And a kid he has with him, cook, driver, handyman, bodyguard, who knows? Twenty-one at the most, Chicano. They'll want to know who you are and why you're there. No secret about you, the magazine story, the eagles, it's all legitimate as hell. They'll buy it. You like music, so does Werther. You'll get the chance. Just wait for it and then take advantage of it. Don't make a big deal of not messing up his prints if he handles a picture, a glass, whatever. Don't handle it unnecessarily either. There's some wrapping in the envelope; put it around the object loosely first, then pop it in the envelope and put it away. We'll be in touch."

Now he put the coat on. At the door he looked back at her. "You'll do fine, Lyle. You really will. And maybe you'll be able to accept that you're getting back at them just a little bit. It might even help."

✷

Brilliant green moss covered the tree trunks; ferns grew in every cranny, on the lower dead limbs, on the moss, every inch of space between the trees. Nowhere was any ground visible, or any rock; all was hidden by the mosses and ferns. Evergreen bushes made impenetrable thickets in spots where the trees had been cut in the past, or a fire had raged. Logging had stopped years ago and now the trees were marching again, overtaking the shrubs, defeating them, reclaiming the steep hills. Raindrops glistened on every surface, shimmered on the tips of the emerald fronds; the air was blurred with mist. The rain made no sound, was absorbed by the mosses, transferred to the ground below efficiently, silently.

Lyle sat on a log and listened to the silence of the woods on this particular hill. The silences varied, she had learned; almost always the surf made the background noise, but here it was inaudible. This was like a holding-your-breath silence, she decided. No wind moved the trees, nothing stirred in the undergrowth, no birds called or flew. It was impossible to tell if the rain had stopped; often it continued under the trees long after the skies had cleared. She got up presently and climbed for another half-hour to the top of the hill. It had been a steep climb, but a protected one; here on the crest the wind hit her. Sea wind, salt wind, fresh yet filled with strange odors. The rain had stopped. She braced herself against the trunk of a tree twisted out of shape with sparse growth clinging to the tip ends of its branches. She was wearing a dark green poncho, rain pants of the same color over her woolen slacks, high boots, a woolen knit hat pulled low on her forehead and covered with the poncho hood. A pair of binoculars was clipped to her belt under the poncho. She took them out and began to study the surrounding trees, the other hilltops that now were visible, the rocks of a ledge with a drop of undetermined distance, because the gorge, or whatever it was, was bathed in mist. She did not spot the nest.

She turned the glasses toward the ocean and for a long time looked seaward. A new storm was building. A boat so distant that it remained a smudge, even with the full magnification, was stuck to the horizon. She hoped that if it was a fishing boat, it made port before the storm hit. There had been two storms so far in the sixteen days she had been in Oregon. It still thrilled and frightened her to think of the power, the uncontrollable rage of the sea under storm winds. It would terrify her to be out there during such a storm. As she watched, the sea and sky became one and swallowed the boat. She knew the front would be racing toward shore, and she knew she would be caught if she returned to her house the way she had come. She stepped back under the trees and mentally studied the map of this day's search. She could go back along the western slope of the hill, skirt the gorge (it was a gorge cut by a tiny fierce stream), follow it until it met Little Salmon Creek, which would lead her home. It was rough, but no rougher than any other trail in these jagged hills that went up and down as if they had been designed by a first-grader.

The wind blew harder, its cutting edge sharp and cold. Her face had been chapped ever since day one here, and she knew today would not improve matters. She started down the rugged hillside, heading toward the creek gorge. The elevation of this peak was one thousand feet; her cabin was one hundred feet above sea level. She began to slide on wet mosses, and finally stopped when she reached out to grasp a tree trunk. Going down would be faster than getting up had been, she thought grimly, clutching the tree until she got her breath back. The little creek plunged over a ledge to a pool fifteen or twenty feet below; she had to detour to find a place to get down the same distance. "A person could get killed," she muttered, inching down on her buttocks, digging in her heels as hard as she could, sliding a foot or so at a time.

The trees were fir, pine, an occasional alder, an even rarer oak, and at the margins of the woods huckleberries, blueberries, blackberries, Oregon grapes, raspberries, salmon berries, elderberries ... She could no longer remember the long list of wild plants. They grew so luxuriantly that they appeared to be growing on top of and out of each other, ten feet high, twenty feet. She never had seen such a profusion of vines.

Down, down, slipping, sliding, lowering herself from tree trunk to tree trunk, clinging to moss-covered rocks, feeling for a toehold below, sometimes walking gingerly on the scree at the edge of the creek when the berry bushes were impenetrable. Always downward. At last she reached a flat spot, and stopped to rest. She had come down almost all the way. She no longer had any chance of beating the storm; she would be caught and drenched. Now all she hoped was that she could be off the steep hill before it struck with full force. She looked seaward; there were only trees that were being erased by mist and clouds leaving suggestive shadows. Then she gasped. There was the nest!

As Mal Levinson had said, it was hard to hide an eagle's nest. It was some distance from her, down a ravine, up the other side, a quarter of a mile or perhaps a little more. The rolling mist was already blurring its outlines. Impossible to judge its size, but big. It had to be old, used year after year, added to each new season. Eight feet across? She knew any figures from this distance were meaningless, but she could not stop the calculations. Half as deep as it was wide, four by eight then. It crowned a dead pine tree. A gust of wind hit her, lifted her hood, and now she realized that for some time she had been hearing the roar of the surf. She got up and started to make the final descent. In a few moments she came to the place where the little creek joined the larger one, and together they crashed over a rocky outcropping. Now she knew exactly where she was. She stayed as close to the bank of the creek as she could, searching for a place where she could cross. Farther down, near her cabin, she knew it was possible, but difficult because in its final run to the sea the creek was cutting a deep channel through the cliffs.

How lucky, she was thinking, to find the nest this close to her own place. The two creeks came together at the two-hundred-foot altitude, child's play after scrambling up and down one-thousand-foot peaks. Less than a mile from the cabin; it would be nothing to go back and forth, pack in her gear . . . She stopped suddenly and now felt a chill that the wind had not been able to induce in her. There was the other house, Werther's house. The nest was almost in his back yard.

The boy appeared, coming from the garage carrying a grocery bag. He waved and, after a brief hesitation, she waved back, then continued to follow the creek down to the bridge where tons of boulders and rocks of all sizes had been dumped to stabilize the banks for the bridge supports.

The rain finally started as she approached the bridge, and she made her way down the boulders with the rain blinding and savaging her all the way. The creek was no more than a foot deep here, but very swift, white water all the way to the beach. Normally she would have picked her way across it on the exposed rocks, but this time she plunged in, trusting her boots to be as waterproof as the manufacturer claimed.

She had forgotten, she kept thinking in disbelief. She had forgotten about Werther and his young driver/cook/bodyguard. At first it had been all she had thought about, but then, with day after day spent in the wet woods, climbing, slipping, sliding, searching, it was as if she had developed amnesia and for a week or longer she had not thought of them at all. It was the same feeling she had had only a few days ago, she realized, when she had come upon a bottle of sleeping pills and had looked at it without recognition. Then, as now, it had taken an effort to remember.

She made her way up her side of the boulders; five hundred feet away was her cabin dwarfed by rhododendrons. Wearily she dragged herself toward it, turning once to glance briefly at the other house, knowing it was not visible from here, but looking anyway. The boy had walked to the edge of the creek, was watching her; he waved again, and then ran through the rain back toward his own house, disappearing among the trees and bushes that screened it.

Spying on her? That openly? Maybe he had been afraid she

would fall down in the shallow treacherous stream. Maybe he thought she had fallen many times already; she considered how she looked: muddy, bedraggled, dripping, red-faced from wind-burn and cold. She looked like a nut, she thought, a real nut.

She found the key under the planter box and let herself in. The cabin was cold and smelled of sea air and salt and decay. Before she undressed, she made up the fire in the wood stove and put water on to boil for coffee. She wished she had not seen the boy, that he had not spoiled this moment of triumph, that the nest was not in Werther's back yard almost, that Lasater had never ... She stopped herself. She wished for golden wings.

"Don't waste perfectly good wishes on mundane things," her father had said to her once when she had still been young enough to sit on his lap.

She was smiling slightly then as she pulled off her boots; her feet were wet and cold. Ah well, she had expected that, she thought sourly. She made the coffee, then showered, and examined new bruises acquired that day. She had not lost weight, she thought, surveying herself, but she was shifting it around a lot. Her waist was slimming down, while, she felt certain, her legs were growing at an alarming rate. She would have legs like a sumo wrestler after a few more weeks of uphill, downhill work. Or like a mountain goat. She pulled on her warmest robe and rubbed her hair briskly, then started to make her dinner.

She sniffed leftover soup, shrugged, and put it on to heat, scraped mold off a piece of cheese, toasted stale bread, quartered an apple, and sat down without another thought of food. As she ate, she studied her topographic map, then drew in a circle around the spot where she knew the nest was. As she had suspected, it was less than half a mile from Werther's house, but not visible from it because of the way the land went up and down. There was a steep hill, then a ravine, then a steeper hill, and it was the flanks of the second hill that the eagle had chosen for a building site.

She started in surprise when there was a knock on the door. No one had knocked on that door since her arrival. She looked down at herself, then shrugged. She was in a heavy flannel robe and fleece-lined moccasins. Her hair was still wet from the shower, and out every which way from her toweling it. Her wet and muddy clothes were steaming on chairs drawn close to the stove. Everywhere there were books, maps, notebooks; her typewriter was on an end table, plugged into an extension cord that snaked across the room. Mail was stacked on another end table; it had been stacked, now it was in an untidy heap, with a letter or two on the floor where they had fallen when the stack had leaned too far.

"What the hell," she muttered, stepping over the extension cord to open the door.

It was the boy from Werther's house. He grinned at her. He was a good-looking kid, she thought absently, trying to block his view of the room. It was no good, though, he was tall enough to see over her head. His grin deepened. He had black hair with a slight wave, deep brown eyes, beautiful young skin. A heart throb, she thought, remembering the phrase from her school years.

"I caught a lot of crabs today," he said, and she saw the package he was carrying. "Mr. Werther thought you might like some." He held out the package.

She knew he had seen the remains of her dinner, her clothes, everything. No point in pretending now. She held the door open and stepped back. "Would you like to come in? Have a cup of coffee?"

"Thanks," he said, shaking his head. "I have to go back and make our dinner now."

She took the package. "Thank you very much. I appreciate this."

He nodded and left in the rain. He had come through the creek, she realized, the same way she had come. Actually it was quicker than getting a car down the steep driveway, onto the road, up her equally steep driveway. Over a mile by road, less than half a mile by foot. She closed the door and took the package to the sink. The crabs, two of them, had been steamed and were still warm. Her mouth was watering suddenly, although she had eaten what she thought was enough at the time. She melted butter, then slowly ate again, savoring each bite of the succulent crab meat. Werther, or the boy, had cracked the legs just enough; she was able to get out every scrap. When she finished, she sat back sighing with contentment. She was exhausted, her room was a sty, but she had found the nest. It had been a good day.

And Lasater? She scowled, gathered up her garbage, and cleared it away. Damn Lasater.

*

For the next three days she studied the area of the nest minutely. There was no good vantage point actually for her to stake out as her own. The pine spur was at the end of a ravine that was filled with trees and bushes. Nowhere could she see through the dense greenery for a clear view of the nest. She had to climb one hill after another, circling the ravine, keeping the nest in sight, looking for a likely place to put her lean-to, to set up her tripod, to wait. She finally found a site, about four feet higher than the nest, on a hillside about one hundred feet from it, with a deep chasm between her and the nest. She unslung her backpack and took out the tarpaulin and nylon cords, all dark green, and erected the lean-to, fastening it securely to trees at all four corners. It would have to do, she decided, even though it stood out like a beer can in a mountain brook. She had learned, in photographing hawks, that most birds would accept a lean-to, or wooden blind even, if it was in place before they took up residence. During the next week or so the lean-to would weather, moss would cover it, ferns grow along the ropes, a tree or two sprout to hide the flap . . . She took a step back to survey her work, and nodded. Fine. It was fine and it would keep her dry, she decided, and then the rain started again.

Every three or four days a new front blew in from the Pacific bringing twenty-foot waves, thirty-foot waves, or even higher, crashing into the cliffs, tearing out great chunks of beach, battling savagely with the pillars, needles, stacks of rock that stood in the water as if the land were trying to sneak out to sea. In the thick rain forests the jagged hills broke up the wind; the trees broke up the rain, cushioned its impact, so that by the time it reached the mosses, it was almost gentle. The mosses glowed and bulged with the bounty. The greens intensified. It was like being in an underwater garden. Lyle made her way down the hillside with the cold rain in her face, and she hardly felt it. The blind was ready; she was ready; now it would be a waiting game. Every day she would photograph the nest, and compare the pictures each night. If one new feather was added she would know. The eagles could no more conceal their presence than they could conceal their nest.

When she reached her side of the bridge again, she crossed the road and went out to the edge of the bluff that overlooked the creek and the beach. The roar of surf was deafening; there was no beach to be seen. This storm had blown in at high tide and waves thundered against the cliffs. The bridge was seventy-five feet above the beach, but spray shot up and was blown across it again and again as the waves exploded below. Little Salmon Creek dropped seventy-five feet in its last mile to the beach, with most of the drop made in a waterfall below the bridge; now Little Salmon Creek was being driven backward and was rising. Lyle stood transfixed, watching the spectacular storm, until the light failed, and now the sounds of crashing waves, of driftwood logs twenty feet long being hurled into bridge pilings, of wind howling through the trees all became frightening and she turned and hurried toward her cabin. She caught a motion from the cliff on the other side of the bridge and she could make out the figure of a watcher there. He was as bundled up as she was, and the light was too feeble by then to be able to tell if it was the boy, or Werther.

The phone was ringing when she got inside and pushed the door closed against the wind that rushed through with her. Papers stirred with the passage, then settled again. She had to extract the telephone from under a pile of her sweaters she had brought out to air because things left in the bedroom tended to smell musty. The wood stove and a small electric heater in her darkroom were the only heat in the cabin.

"Yes," she said, certain it was a wrong number.

"Mrs. Taney, this is Saul Werther. I wonder if I can talk you into having dinner with me this evening. I'd be most happy if you will accept. Carmen will be glad to pick you up in an hour and take you home again later."

She felt a rush of fear that drained her. *Please*, she prayed silently, *not again. Don't start again.* She closed her eyes hard.

"Mrs. Taney, forgive me. We haven't really met, I'm your neighbor across the brook," he said, as if reminding her he was still on the line. "We watched the storm together."

"Yes, of course. I'd ... Thank you. I'll be ready in an hour."

For several minutes she stood with her hand on the phone. It had happened again, the first time in nearly four years. It had been Werther on the phone, but she had heard Mr. Hendrickson's voice. "Mrs. Taney, I'm afraid there's been an accident . . ." And she had known. It had been as if she had known even before the telephone rang that evening; she had been waiting for confirmation, nothing more. Fear, grief, shock, guilt: she had been waiting for a cause, for a reason for the terrible emotions that had gripped her, that had been amorphously present for an hour and finally settled out only with the phone call. No one had believed her, not Gregory, not the psychiatrist, and she would have been willing to disbelieve, yearned to be able to disbelieve, but could not, because now and then, always with a meaningless call, that moment had swept over her again. She had come to recognize the rush of emotions that left her feeling hollowed out, as the event was repeated during the next year and a half after Mike's death. And then it had stopped, until now. "Mrs. Taney, I'm afraid there's been an accident. Your son . . ."

She began to shiver, and was able to move again. She had to get out of her wet clothes, build up the fire, shower ... This was Lasater's doing. He had made the connection in her mind between Werther, drugs, Mike's death. He had reached inside her head with his words and revived the grief and guilt she had thought was banished. Clever Mr. Lasater, she thought grimly. He had known she would react, not precisely how, that was expecting too much even of him. He had known Werther would make the opening move. If Werther was involved with drug smuggling, she wanted him dead, just as dead as her child was, and she would do all she could to make him dead. Even as she thought it, she knew Lasater had counted on this too.

○

Hugh Lasater drove through the town of Salmon Key late that afternoon, before the storm hit. He and a companion, Milton Follett, had been driving since early morning, up from San Francisco in a comfortable, spacious motor home.

"It's the hills that slowed us down," Hugh Lasater said. "The freeway was great, and then we hit the coastal range. Should have been there by now."

Milton Follett was slouched down low in his seat; he did not glance at the town as they went through. "Could have called," he grumbled, as he had done several times in the past hour or so. He was in his mid-thirties, a blond former linebacker whose muscles were turning to flab.

"Thought of that," Hugh Lasater said. "Decided against it. Little place like this, who knows how the lines are connected, who might be listening? Anyway I might have to apply a little pressure."

"I think it's a bust, she's stringing you along."

"I think you're right. That's the reason I might have to apply a little pressure."

He drove slowly, collecting information: Standard Gas, attached gift shop; Salmon Key Restaurant and Post Office, a frame building painted red; Reichert's Groceries, having a canned food sale — corn 3/$1.00, tomatoes, beans, peas 4/$1.00; Thom's

Motel, closed; a sign for a lapidary shop; farmers' market and fish stand, closed . . . Tourist town, closed for the season. There were a few fishing boats docked behind the farmers' market, and space at the dock for four times as many, unused for a long time apparently. A dying fishing town, surviving now with tourist trade a few months out of the year. Lasater had seen numberless towns like this one; he touched the accelerator and left the dismal place behind and started up another hill.

"Sure could have used a road engineer and a few loads of dynamite," he said cheerfully, shifting down for the second time on the steep incline. The hill rose five hundred feet above sea level, reached a crest, and plunged down the other side. He did not shift into higher gear as he went down. The wind was starting to shake the monster, forcing him to hold the steering wheel around at an unnatural position for a straight road. The wind let up, and the vehicle rebounded. He slowed down more.

"Another mile's all," he said. "We'll be in camp in time to see the storm hit."

"Terrific," Milton growled.

Lasater made the turn off the highway onto a narrow gravel road that was steeper than anything he had driven that day. The trees had been shaped here by the nearly constant wind and sea spray; there were stunted pines and dense thickets of low, contorted spruces. The motor home was vibrating with the roar of the ocean and the explosive crashes of waves on cliffs. There were other people already in the state park; a couple of campers, a van, and even a tent. As they pulled into the camping area a sleek silver home-on-wheels pulled out. Lasater waved to the driver as they passed in the parking turn-around; he took the newly vacated spot.

Milton refused a walk with him, and he went alone to the ridge overlooking The Lagoon. That was its name, said so on the map, and there it was, a nearly perfect circle a mile across surrounded by cliffs with a narrow stretch of beach that gave way to a basalt terrace, which, at low tide, would be covered with tide pools. The lagoon was protected from the sea by a series of massive basalt rocks, like a coral reef barrier. Although they ranged from twenty to forty feet above water, the ocean was pouring over them now; the lagoon was flooded and was rising on the cliffs. Waves crashing into the barrier megaliths sent spray a hundred feet into the air.

He looked at the lagoon, then beyond it to the next hill. Over that one, down the other side was Werther's drive, then the bridge over Little Salmon Creek, and then her drive. Here we all are, he thought, hunching down in his coat as the wind intensity grew. Time to go to work, honey, he thought at Lyle Taney. You've had a nice vacation, now's time to knuckle down, make a buck, earn your keep.

He had no doubt that Lyle Taney would do as he ordered, eventually. She was at a time of life when she would be feeling insecure, he knew. She had chucked her job, and if he threatened to pull the rug from under her financially, she would stand on her head in any corner he pointed to. He knew how important security was to a woman like Lyle Taney. Even when she had had a reason to take a leave of absence, she had held on grimly, afraid not to hold on because she had no tenure, no guarantees about tomorrow. He had imagined her going over the figures again and again, planning to the day when her savings would be gone, if she had to start using that stash, trying to estimate royalties to the penny, stretching that money into infinity. He understood women like Taney, approaching middle age, alone, supporting themselves all the way. It was fortunate that she was nearing middle age. The kid was too young to interest her, and Werther too old; no sexual intrigues to mess up the scenario. He liked to keep things neat and simple. Money, security, revenge, those were things that were manipulable. They were real things, not abstracts, not like loyalty or faith. He did not believe a woman could be manipulated through appeals to loyalty or faith. They were incapable of making moral or ethical decisions. They did not believe in abstracts. Maternal devotion, security, money, revenge, that was what they understood, and this time it had worked out in such a way that those were the very things he could dangle before her, or threaten. Oh, she would do the job for him. He knew she would. He began to hum and stopped in surprise when he realized it was a tune from his boyhood, back in the forties. He grinned. Who would have thought a song would hang out in a mind all those years to pop out at just the right moment? He sang it to himself on his way back to the motor home: "They're either too young or too old/They're either too gray or too grassy green . . ."

❁

Werther's house was a surprise to Lyle. It was almost as messy as her own, and with the same kind of disorder: papers, books, notebooks, a typewriter. His was on a stand on wheels, not an end table, but that was a minor detail. Carmen was almost laughing at her reaction.

"I told Mr. Werther that I thought you would be very *simpatico*," he said, taking her coat.

Then Werther came from another room, shook her hand warmly, and led her to the fireplace.

"It's for a book I've wanted to do for a long time," he said, indicating the jumble of research materials. "A history of a single idea from the first time it's mentioned in literature, down to its present-day use, if any. Not just one idea, but half a dozen, a dozen. I'm afraid I keep expanding the original concept as I come across new and intriguing lines of inquiry." His face twisted in a wry expression. "I'd like to get rid of some of this stuff, but there's nowhere to start. I need it all."

He was five feet eight or nine, and stocky; not fat or even plump, but well-muscled and heavy-boned. He gave the impression of strength. His hair was gray, a bit too long, as if he usually forgot to have it cut, not as if he had intended it to be modish. His eyes were dark blue, so dark that at first glance she had thought them black. He had led her to a chair by the fireplace; there was an end table by it with a pile of books. He lifted the stack, looked about helplessly, then put it on the floor by the side of the table. *A History of Technology,* Plato's *Republic,* a volume of Plato's dialogues, Herodotus, Kepler . . . There was a mountainous stack of the *New York Times.*

Many of the books in the room were opened, some with rocks holding the pages down; others had strips of paper for bookmarks.

"My problem is that I'm not a writer," Werther said. "It's impossible to organize so much material. One wants to include it all. But you . . ." He rummaged through a pile of books near his own chair and brought out her book on hawks. "What a delightful book this is! I enjoyed it tremendously."

"I'm not a writer either," she said quickly. "I teach — taught — history."

"That's what the jacket says. Ancient history. But you used the past tense."

Although there was no inflection, no question mark following the statement, she found herself answering as if he had asked. She told him about the magazine, and the book contract, the nest.

"And you simply quit when you couldn't get time off to do the next book. Doing the book on eagles was more important to you than remaining in your own field. I wonder that more historians don't lose faith."

She started to deny that she had lost faith in history, but the words stalled; he had voiced what she had not wanted to know. She nodded. "And you, Mr. Werther, what is your field? History also?"

"No. That's why my research is so pleasurable. I'm discovering the past. That's what makes your hawk book such a joy. It sings with discovery. It's buoyant because you were finding out things that gave you pleasure; you in turn invested that pleasure in your words and thoughts and shared it with your readers."

She could feel her cheeks burn. Werther laughed gently.

"What capricious creatures we are. We are embarrassed by criticism, and no less embarrassed by praise. And you have found your eagle's nest after all those days of searching. Congratulations. At first, when you moved in next door, I thought you were a spy. But what a curious spy, spending every day getting drenched in a rain forest!"

"And I thought you were a smuggler," she said, laughing with him, but also watching, suddenly wary again.

"The lagoon would make a perfect spot for landing contraband, wouldn't it? Ah, Carmen, that looks delightful!"

Carmen carried two small trays; he put one down at Lyle's elbow on the end table, and the other one within Werther's reach, perched atop a stack of books. There was wheat-colored wine, a small bowl of pink Pacific shrimp, a dip, cheese, crackers . . .

"I've never tasted such good shrimp as these," Werther said, spearing one of the tidbits. "I could live on the seafood here."

"Me too," Lyle agreed. The wine was a very dry sherry, so good it made her want to close her eyes and savor it. The fire burned quietly, and Carmen made cooking noises that were obscured by a door. Werther had become silent now, enjoying the food; outside, the wind howled and shook the trees, rattled rhododendrons against the windows, whistled in the chimney. It was distant, no longer menacing; through it all, behind it, now and then overwhelming the other sounds, was the constant roar of the surf. She thought of the pair of eagles: where were they now? Were they starting to feel twitches that eventually would draw them back to the nest?

Presently Werther sighed. "Each of us may well be exactly what the other thought at first, but that's really secondary, isn't it? How did you, a history professor, become involved with hawks?"

She brought herself back to the room, back to the problem Lasater had dumped in her lap. Slowly she said, "Five years ago my son, he was twelve, took something one of the boys in his class had bought from a drug dealer. There were twenty boys involved; three of them died, several of them suffered serious brain damage. Mike died."

Her voice had gone very flat in the manner of one reading a passage in a foreign language without comprehension. She watched him as she talked. She could talk about it now; that was what she had accomplished under Dr. Himbert. She had learned how to divide herself into pieces, and let one of the pieces talk about it, about anything at all, while the rest of her stayed far away hidden in impenetrable ice.

Werther was shocked, she thought, then angry. One of his hands made a movement toward her, as if to touch her — to silence her? or share her grief? She could not tell.

"And you turned to the world of hawks where there is no good or evil, only necessity."

She felt bathed in the warmth of his words suddenly, as if his compassion were a physical, material substance that he had wrapped around her securely. He knew, she thought. He understood. That was exactly what she had looked for, had needed desperately, something beyond good and evil. Abruptly she looked away from his penetrating and too understanding gaze. She wanted to tell him everything, she realized in wonder, and she could tell him everything. He would not condemn her. Quickly then she continued her story, trying to keep her voice indifferent.

"I found I couldn't stay in our apartment over weekends and holidays after that. My husband and I had little reason to stay together and he left, went to California, where he's living now. I began to tramp through the woods, up and down the Appalachian Trail, things like that. One day I got a photograph of a hawk in flight, not the one on the cover, not that nice, but it made me want to get more. Over the next couple of years I spent all my spare time pursuing hawks. And I began to write the book."

Werther was nodding. "Therapy. And what good therapy it was for you. No doctor could have prescribed it. You are cured."

Again it was not exactly a question; it demanded no answer. And again she felt inclined to respond as if it had been. "I'm not sure," she said. "I had a breakdown, as you seem to have guessed. I hope I'm cured."

"You're cured," he said again. He got up and went to a sideboard where Carmen had left the decanter of wine. He refilled both their glasses, then said, "If you'll excuse me a moment, I'll see how dinner's coming along. Carmen's a good cook, but sometimes he dawdles."

She studied the living room; it was large, with a dining area, and beyond that a door to the kitchen. The west wall was heavily draped, but in daylight with the drapes open, it would overlook the sea, as her own living room did. Probably there was a deck; there was an outside door on that wall. One other door was closed, to the bedroom area, she guessed. The plan was very like the plan of her cabin, but the scale was bigger. Both were constructed of redwood, paneled inside, and had broad plank floors with scatter rugs. She began to look through the piles of magazines on tables: science magazines, both general and specialized. Molecular biology, psychology, physics . . . History journals — some probably had papers of hers. There was no clue here, or so many clues that they made no sense. It would be easy to pick up a digest magazine or two, slip them in her purse, put them in the envelope, and be done with it.

But he wasn't a smuggler, she thought clearly. Lasater had lied. She picked up a geology book dog-eared at a chapter about the coast range.

"Are you interested in geology?" Werther asked, coming up behind her.

"I don't know a thing about it," she admitted, replacing the book.

"According to the most recent theory, still accepted it's so recent, there are great tectonic plates underlying the rock masses on earth. These plates are in motion created by the thermal energy of the deeper layers. Here along the coast, they say, two plates come together, one moving in from the sea, the other moving northward. The one coming in from the west hits the other one and dives under it, and the lighter materials are scraped off and jumbled together to make the coast range. That accounts for the composition, they say. Andesite, basalt, garnetite, sandstone, and so on. Have you had a chance to do any beach combing yet?"

She shook her head. "Not yet. I'll have more time now that I've located the nest."

"Good. Let me take you to some of my favorite places. South of here. You have to be careful because some of those smaller beaches are cut off at high tide, and the cliffs are rather forbidding."

Carmen appeared then. "I thought you were going to sit down so I can serve the soup."

*

Carmen dined with them and his cooking was superb. When she complimented him, he said, "No, this is plain everyday family fare. I didn't know we were having company. Next time I'll know in advance. Just wait."

There was a clear broth with slices of water chestnut and bits of clam and scallions; a baked salmon stuffed with crab; crisp snow peas and tiny mushrooms; salad with a dressing that suggested olive oil and lime juice and garlic, but so faintly that she could not have said for certain that any or all of those ingredients had been used.

"And take Anaxagoras," Werther said sometime during that dinner, "nearly five hundred years before Christ! And he had formulated the scientific method, maybe not as precisely as Bacon was to do two thousand years later, and without the same dissemination, but there it was. He wrote that the sun was a vast mass of incandescent metal, that moonlight was reflected sunlight, that heavenly bodies were made incandescent by their rotational friction. He explained, in scientific terms, meteors, eclipses, rainbows . . ."

The ancient names rolled off his tongue freely, names, dates, places, ideas. "Empedocles identified the four elements: air, earth, fire, and water, and even today we speak of a fiery temper, an airy disposition, blowing hot and cold, an earthy woman, the raging elements, battling the elements, elemental spirits . . . An idea, twenty-five hundred years old, and it's still in the language, in our heads, in our genes maybe."

Before dinner there had been the sherry, and with dinner there was a lovely Riesling, and then a sweet wine she did not know. She told herself that no one gets drunk on wine, especially along with excellent food, but, once again before the fire, she was having trouble following the conversation, and somewhere there was a soft guitar playing, and a savage wind blowing, and rain pounding the house rhythmically.

She realized she had been talking about herself, her lack of tenure and seeming inability to get tenure. "I'm not a hotshot scholar," she said, thinking carefully of the words, trying to avoid any that might twist her up too much. She thought: hot-shot scholar, and knew she could never say it again. She knew also that if she repeated it to herself, she would start to giggle. The thought of breaking into giggles sobered her slightly.

"You're interested in what people thought," she said almost primly, "but we teach great movements, invasions, wars, successions of reign, and it's all irrelevant. The students don't care; they need the credit. It doesn't make any difference today, none of it."

"Why don't you do it right?"

"I'd have to go back to Go and start over, relearn everything. Unlearn everything. I've always been afraid. I don't even know what I'm afraid of."

"So you bailed out at the first chance. But now I think Carmen had better take you home. You can hardly keep your eyes open. It's the fresh air and wind and climbing these steep hills, I suspect."

She nodded. It was true, she was falling asleep. Suddenly she felt awkward, as if she had overstayed a visit. She glanced at her watch and was startled to find that it was eleven-thirty.

"Ready?" Carmen asked. He had her coat over his arm, had already put on a long poncho.

Werther went to the door with them. "Come back soon, my dear. It's been one of the nicest evenings I've had in a very long time."

She mumbled something and hurried after Carmen to the car. The wind had died down now, but the rain was steady.

"He meant it," Carmen said. "It's been a good evening for both of us."

"I enjoyed it too," she said, staring ahead at the rain-blurred world. The drive was very curvy; it wound around trees, downward to the road, and only the last twenty-five feet or so straightened out. It would be very dangerous if the rain froze. Down this last straightaway, then onto the highway, across it and over the cliff to the rocks below. She shivered. Carmen had the car in low gear, and had no trouble at all in coming to a stop at the highway.

"Is he a doctor?" she asked. "Something he said tonight made me think he might be, or has been, a doctor." She shook her head in annoyance; she could not remember why she thought that.

"I think he studied medicine a while back, maybe even practiced. I don't know."

Of course, Carmen probably knew as little about his employer as she did. They had an easy relationship, and Carmen certainly had shown no fear or anxiety of any sort, but he was a hired man, hired to drive, to cook, to do odd jobs. They had arrived at her door.

"I'll come in and fix your fire," Carmen said, in exactly the same tone he had used to indicate that dinner was ready. There was nothing obsequious or subservient in him.

He added wood to the fire, brought in a few pieces from the porch, and then left, and she went to bed immediately and dreamed.

She was in a class, listening to a lecture. The professor was writing on the blackboard as he talked, and she was taking notes. She could not quite make out his diagrams, and she hitched her chair closer to the front of the room, but the other students hissed angrily at her and the teacher turned around to scowl. She squinted trying to see, but it was no use. And now she no longer could hear his words, the hissing still buzzed around her ears. The professor came to her chair and picked up her notebook; he looked at her notes, nodded, and patted her on the back. When he touched her, she screamed and fled.

She was on a narrow beach with a black shiny cliff behind her. She knew the tide had turned because the hissing had become a roar. She hurried toward a trail and stopped because Lasater was standing at the end of the beach where the rocks led upward like steps. She looked the opposite way and stopped again. Werther was there, dressed in tails and striped trousers, with a pale gray top hat on. She heard a guitar and, looking up, she saw Carmen on a ledge playing. Help me, she cried to him. He smiled at her and continued to play. She raised her arms pleading for him to give her a hand, and the eagle swooped low and caught her wrists in its talons and lifted her just as the first wave crashed into the black cliff. The eagle carried her higher and higher until she no longer could see Werther or Lasater or the beach, the road, anything at all recognizable. Then the eagle let go and she fell.

❁

Hugh Lasater waited until the Volvo came out of Werther's drive and turned north, heading for town, before he went up Lyle's driveway. There was a heavy fog that morning, but the air was

still and not very cold. The front of her house had a view of the
ocean that must be magnificent when the weather was clear, and
no doubt you had to be quick or you might miss it, he thought,
gazing into the sea of fog, waiting for her to answer his knock.

Lyle was dressed to go out, boots, sweater, heavy slacks. She
had cut her hair even shorter than it had been before. Now it
was like a fuzzy cap on her head. He wondered if it was as soft
as it looked. Silently she opened the door wider and moved aside
for him to enter.

"How's it going?" he asked, surveying the room quickly, mem-
orizing it in that one fast glance about. A real pig, he thought
with a touch of satisfaction. It figured.

"Fine. I've found the nest."

He laughed and pulled a chair out from the table and sat
down. "Got any coffee?"

She poured a cup for him; there was another cup on the table
still half-filled. She sat opposite him now, pushed a map out of
the way, closed a notebook. Her camera gear was on the table,
as if she had been checking it out before leaving with it.

"Pretty lousy weather for someone who has to get out and
work in it every day," he said. "Your face is really raw."

She shrugged and began to put the lenses in pockets of the
camera bag. Her hands were very steady. She could keep the
tension way down where it couldn't interfere with appearances.
Lasater admired that. But the tension was there, he could feel it;
it was revealed in the way that she had not looked at him once
since opening the door. She had looked at the coffee cup, at the
pot, at her stuff on the table. Now she was concentrating on
packing her camera bag.

"Met Werther yet?" he asked casually.

"Yes. Once."

"And?"

"And nothing."

"Tell me about him." The coffee was surprisingly good. He
got up and refilled his cup.

"You know more about him than I do."

"Not what he's like; how he talks, what he likes, what he's like inside. You know what I mean."

"He's educated, cultured, a scholar. He's gentle and kind."

"What did you talk about?"

He caught a momentary expression that flitted rapidly across her face. Something there, but what? He saved it for later.

"Ancient Greece."

"Lyle, loosen up, baby. I'm not going to bite or do anything nasty. Open up a little. Tell me something about the time you spent with him."

She shook her head. "I'm not working for you, or with you. I'm here doing a job for a magazine, and for my publisher. That's all."

"Uh-huh. It was the cover story, wasn't it? You don't buy it." He sighed and finished the last of the coffee. "Don't blame you. After seeing that state park I don't blame you a bit. Have to be an idiot to try to smuggle anything into that cove. Who'd've thought there'd be dopes camping out all winter. It's February for Christ sake!"

"You admit you lied to me?" She knew he was playing with her, keeping her off guard, but she could not suppress the note of incredulity that entered her voice. She knew he was a master at this game, also, and she was so naive that she didn't even know when the play started, or what the goals were.

"What'd you talk about?"

She started again. There was more than a touch of confusion in her mind about what they had talked about for nearly five hours, and somehow she had revealed something to Hugh Lasater. Almost sullenly she said, "Philosophy, cuisines, the coast, geology. Nothing. It was nothing of any importance." She finished packing her camera case and stood up. "I have to go out now. I'm sorry I can't help you."

"Oh, you'll help," he said almost absently, thinking about the changes in her voice, subtle as they were. Although she had learned to step back, her voice was revealing in the way it changed timbre, the quickness of her words. He had it now, the cue to watch for.

"Have you read your contracts for the article and the book?" She became silent again, frozen, waiting.

"You should. If you didn't bring copies with you, I have some. I'll drop them off later today, or send someone else with them."

"What are you threatening now?"

"You've got no job, kiddo, and the contracts have clauses in them that I doubt you'll be able to fulfill. I doubt seriously that you can get your story together within ninety days, starting nearly a month ago. And I doubt that you really meant you'd be willing to pay half your royalties to a ghostwriter. But you signed them, both of them. Honey, don't you ever read contracts before you sign them?"

"Get out of here," she said. "Just get out and leave me alone."

"People like you," he said, shaking his head sadly. "You are so ignorant it's painful. You don't know what's going on in the world you live in. You feel safe and secure, but, honey, you can feel safe and secure only because people like me are doing their jobs."

"Blackmailing others to do your jobs."

"But sometimes that's part of the job," he protested. "Look, Lyle, you must guess that this is an important piece of work, no matter what else you think. I mean, would anyone invest the kind of effort we've already put into it if it weren't important? We're counting on your loyalty — "

"Don't," she snapped. "Loyalty to what, to whom? In the Middle Ages the nobility all across Europe was loyal to nobility. The guilds were loyal to guilds. Peasants to peasants. Where's the loyalty of a multinational corporation executive? Or the Mafia? Loyal to what? What makes you think there's anything at all you can tell me that I'd believe?"

"I'm not telling you anything," he said. "I know you won't believe me. Except this. He's a killer, Lyle. I didn't want to scare you off before . . ."

She pressed her hands over her ears. "So let the police arrest him and take him in for fingerprinting and questioning, the way they do other suspects."

"Can't. He has something stashed away somewhere and we want it. We want him to lead us to it. If he's our man. First that. Is he our man? We can't go inside his house for prints. There are dozens of ways of booby-trapping a place to let you know if someone has entered. A hair in a door that falls when the door's opened. A bit of fluff that blows away if someone moves near it. An ash on a door handle. A spiderweb across a porch. He'd know. And he'd bolt, or kill himself. That's what we want to avoid. A dive off a cliff. A bullet through his brain. A lethal pill. We want him very badly. Alive, healthy, and in his own house where he keeps his stuff. We'll put a hundred agents on him, follow him ten years if it takes that long. If he's our man. And we expect you to furnish something that'll let us find out if he is our man. Soon, Lyle." He paused, and when she did not respond he said, "So you like the old fart. So what? Even the devil has admirers. There's never been a monster who didn't have someone appear as a character witness. You see it every day, the neighbors describing a homicidal psychopath as a nice, quiet, charming man, so kind to the children. Balls! Your pal is a killer resting between jobs. Period. You're in no danger, unless you blow it all in front of him. But I'll tell you this, I wouldn't underwrite life insurance on the kid with him."

She regarded him bitterly, not speaking.

He got up and went to the door. "I know, you're thinking why you? You didn't ask to get mixed up in something like this. Hell, I don't know why you. You were there. And you are mixed up in it. And I tell you this, Lyle baby. When it gets as big as this is, there's no middle ground. You're for us or against us. That simple. Be seeing you."

Hugh Lasater had known Werther/Rechetnik would turn up at the most recent molecular biologists' conference at U.C.L.A. this past fall. He had counted on it the way he counted on Christmas, or income tax day. And Werther had not let him down any more than Santa had done when he was a kid. Werther had been there and left in his white Volvo with the kid driving him as if he were a president or something. Since that day in November he had been under surveillance constantly. Twice they had tried ploys designed to get positive identification, and each time they had failed. The kid paid the bills, did the shopping, drove the car. Werther wore gloves when he went out, and the house was booby-trapped. Turk had spotted a silk thread across the porch the first day Werther had left, and Turk had backed off exactly as he had been ordered.

The first time they tried to get his prints indirectly, it had been through the old dog of a routine telephone maintenance visit. The kid had refused the man admittance, said they didn't want the phone in the first place and didn't care if it was out. Period. No one insisted. The next time a young woman had run into Werther on the beach. She had been wearing a vinyl cape, pristine, spotless, ready to receive prints. Werther had caught her reflexively, steadied her, then had gone on his way, and Milton Follett had received the cape. Nothing. Smudges. Just as reflexive as his catching the girl had been, his other act of smearing the prints must have been also.

There were two men in the Lagoon state park at all times, one of them on high enough ground to keep the driveway under observation through daylight hours, and close enough at night to see a mouse scamper across the drive. Farther south there were two more men in the next state park. He was bottled up tight, and they still did not have positive identification.

They could have picked him up on suspicion of murder, staging the arrest, mug shots, prints, interrogation, everything, but Mr. Forbisher had explained patiently that Werther without his papers was simply another lunatic killer. He would surely suicide if cornered. They wanted it all in a neat package undamaged by rough handling. They wanted his papers.

It irked him that no one would lay it all out, explain exactly what it was that Werther had. But Christ, he thought, it had to

be big. Bigger than a new headache capsule. He suspected it wa.
a cancer cure; the Nazis had used Werther's/Rechetnik's mother
for cancer experiments, and he was getting his revenge. It had
to be that, he sometimes thought, because what could be bigger
than that? The pharmaceutical company that owned that secret
would move right into the castle and be top of the heap for a
long time to come. When he thought of the money they were already spending to get this thing, that they were willing to keep
spending, it made his palms sweat. He did not really blame them
for not telling him all of it; that was not how the game was
played. All he needed to know, Mr. Forbisher had said primly,
was that they wanted Werther, if he was actually Rechetnik; they
wanted him intact with his papers. And Hugh Lasater had gone
off looking for exactly the right person to put inside the house
next door. Step one. He had come up with Lyle Taney.

*

She sat with her knees drawn to her chin, staring moodily at
the nest. She did not believe Lasater and she knew it didn't matter if she did or not. She never would know the truth, and that
didn't matter either. How many people ever learned truth in a
single lifetime? she asked herself, still bitter and angry with Lasater, with herself for stepping into this affair.

She had read the contracts, and she had asked Bobby about
the time, about other things Lasater hadn't brought up yet, but
no doubt would if he felt he had to. Formalities, Bobby had said,
don't worry about them. Basically, he had said, it was the same
contract as her first one, with a few changes because the work
was not even started yet. And she had signed. She was dipping
into her savings to pay for this trip, for the three months' rental
on the house, for the car she had leased. It takes a month to six
weeks to get money loose from the company, Mal had said. You
know how bureaucracies are. And she did know.

They must have investigated her thoroughly. They knew her
financial situation, the bills she had accumulated during those
wasted, lost years; they knew about Mike; they knew she would

be willing and even eager to leave her job. She remembered one thing Werther had said, about historians losing faith in what they taught. He was perceptive, Lasater was perceptive, only she had been blind. She put her forehead down on her knees and pressed hard. She wanted to weep. Furiously she lifted her head and stared at the nest again.

The sun had come out and the day was still and warm. Down on the beach there would be a breeze, but up here, sheltered by hills and trees, the air was calm and so clear she could see the bark on the pine spur that bore the eagles' nest.

"Mrs. Taney?" It was Carmen's voice in a hushed whisper.

She looked for him; he was standing near a tree as if ready to duck behind it quickly. "It's all right," she said. "The nest is still empty."

He climbed the rest of the way up and sat down by her, not all the way under the tarp. The sun lightened his hair, made it look russet. "You said last night that I could join you, see the nest. I hope you meant now, today. I brought you some coffee."

She thanked him as he took off a small pack and pulled a thermos from it. The coffee was steaming. He wore binoculars around his neck. She pointed and he aimed them at the nest and studied it for the next few minutes.

She had forgotten that he had asked if he could join her. She frowned at the coffee, trying to remember more of the conversation. Nothing more came.

"It's big, isn't it? How soon do you expect the eagles to come?"

"I'm not sure. They'll hang around, fixing up the nest, just fooling around for several weeks before they mate. Sometime in the next week or two, I should think."

He nodded. "Mr. Werther asked if you have to stay up here this afternoon. There's a place down the beach a few miles he'd like to show you. Beach-combing's great after a storm, and there's gold dust on the beach there."

She laughed. "I don't have to stay at all. I took a few pictures, I was just . . . thinking." She started to check around her to make sure she had everything. "Have you been with him long?"

"Sometimes it seems a lifetime, then again like no time at all. Why do you ask?"

"Curious. You seem to understand him rather well."

"Yes. He's like a father. Someone you understand and accept and even love without questioning it or how you know so much about him. You know what I mean?"

"I think so. It's a package deal. You accept all or nothing."

"He's very wise," Carmen said, standing, reaching out to pull her to her feet. He was much stronger than his slender figure indicated. He looked at her and said, "I would trust him with my life, my honor, my future without any hesitation." Then he turned and started down the hillside before her.

Just like Werther, she thought, following him down. He side-stepped questions just as Werther did, making it seem momentarily that he was answering, but giving nothing with any substance.

Lyle left her camera bag at Werther's house; they all got in the Volvo and Carmen drove down the coast a few miles. Here the road was nearly at sea level; water had covered it during the storm and there was still a mud slick on the surface. Carmen parked on a gravel turn-off, and they walked to the sandy beach. In some places the beach on this section of the coast was half a mile wide with pale soft sand, then again it was covered with smooth round black rocks, or a sliver of sand gave way to the bony skeleton of ancient mountains; here the beach was wide and level, and it was littered with storm refuse.

"We'll make our way toward those rocks," Werther said, pointing south. The outline of the rocks was softened by mist, making it hard to tell how far away they were.

It took them five hours to get to the rocks and back. All along the way the storm detritus invited investigation. There were strands of seaweed, eighteen feet long, as strong as ropes; there were anemones and starfish and crabs in tide pools, all of them colored pink or purple, blue, green, red . . . ; there was a swath of black sand where Werther said there was probably gold also.

It was often found among the heavy black sand; washed from the same deposits, it made its way downstream along with the dense black grains. They found no gold, but they might have, Lyle thought happily. She spied a blue ball and retrieved it. It was a Japanese fishing float, Werther said, examining it and handing it back. He talked about the fishing fleets, their lights like will-o'-the-wisps at sea. They had not used glass floats for thirty years, he said; the one she had found could have been floating all that time, finally making it to shore.

At one point Carmen produced sandwiches and a bottle of wine from his backpack, along with three plastic glasses. They sat on rocks, protected from a freshening breeze, and gazed at the blue waters of the Pacific. A flock of sea gulls drifted past and vanished around the outcropping of granite boulders.

"It's a beautiful world," Werther said quietly. "Such a beautiful world."

Carmen stood up abruptly and stalked away. He picked up something white and brought it back, flung it down at Werther's feet. It was half a Styrofoam cup.

"For how long?" he said in a hard furious voice. He picked up the wine bottle and glasses and replaced them in his backpack, then turned and left.

"You could bury it, but the next high tide will just uncover it again," Werther said, nudging the Styrofoam with his foot. He picked it up and put it in his pocket. "Speaking of high tides, we have to start back. The tide's turning now, I think."

They watched the sunset from the edge of the beach, near the car. The water covered their footprints, cleaning up the beach again of traces of human usage. It was dark by the time they got back to Werther's house.

"You must have dinner with us," he insisted. "You're too tired to go cook. You'll settle for a peanut butter sandwich and a glass of milk. I feel guilty just thinking about dinner while you snack. Sit by the fire and nurse your images of the perfect day and presently we'll eat."

Lyle looked at Carmen who nodded, smiling at her. It was he who knew what she would eat if she went home now. She thought of what he had said about understanding and accepting Werther, and she had the feeling that he understood and accepted her also, exactly as she was, nearing middle age, red-faced, frizzy hair going gray. None of that mattered a damn bit to him, not the way it mattered to Lasater whose eyes held scorn and contempt no matter how he tried to disguise it. She nodded, and Carmen reached out to take her coat; Werther said something about checking the wine supply, and needing more wood. She sank into the chair that she thought of as hers and sighed.

Perhaps she could say to Werther, please just give me a set of good fingerprints and let's be done with that. She could explain why she needed them, tell him about the hook Lasater had baited for her and her eagerness to snatch it. He would understand, even be sympathetic with her reasons. And if he was the man Lasater was after, he would forgive her. She snapped her eyes open as a shudder passed over her. Lasater was sure, and she was too. She felt only certainty that Werther lived under a fearsome shadow. She felt that he was a gentle man, whose gentleness arose from a terrible understanding of pain and fear; that underlying his open love of the ocean, the beach, the gulls, everything he had seen that day, there was a sadness with a depth she could not comprehend. She believed that his compassion, humanity, love, warmth, all observable qualities, overlay a core as rigid and unweathered and unassailable as the rocky skeletons of the mountains that endured over the eons while everything about them was worn away. He was a man whose convictions would lead him to action, had already led him to act, she thought, and admitted to herself that she believed he was wanted for something very important, not what Lasater said, because he was a congenital liar, but something that justified the manhunt that evidently was in progress. And she knew with the same certainty that she had been caught up in the middle of it, that already it was too late for her to exclude herself from whatever happened here on the coast. Unless she left immediately, she thought then.

"You're cold," Carmen said, as if he had been standing behind her for some time. He was carrying wood. "These places really get cold as soon as the sun goes down." He added a log to the fire, tossed in a handful of chips, and in a moment it was blazing. "You're in for a treat. He's going to make a famous old recipe for you. Fish soup, I call it. He says bouillabaisse." He stood up, dusting his hands together. "Be back instantly with wine. Do you want a blanket or something?"

She shook her head. The shiver had not been from any external chill. Presently, with Carmen on the floor before the fire, and her in her chair, they sipped the pale sherry in a companionable silence.

Carmen broke it: "Let's play a game. Pretend you're suddenly supreme dictator with unlimited power and wealth, what would you do?"

"Dictator of what?"

"Everything, the entire earth."

"You mean God."

"Okay. You're God. What now?"

She laughed. Freshmen games out of Philosophy 101. "Oh, I'd give everyone enough money to live on comfortably, and I'd put a whammy on all weapons, make them inoperative, and I'd cure the sick, heal the wounded. Little things like that."

He shook his head. "Specifically. And seriously." He looked up at her without a trace of a smile. "I mean if everyone had X dollars, then it would take XY dollars to buy limited things, and it would simply be a regression of the value of money, wouldn't it?"

"Okay, I'd redistribute the money and the goods so that everyone had an equal amount, and if that wasn't enough, I'd add to both until it was enough."

"How long before a handful of people would have enormous amounts again, and many people would be hungry again simply because human nature seems to drive some people to power through wealth?"

She regarded him sourly. He was at an age when his idealism should make it seem quite simple to adjust the world equitably. She said, "God, with any sense at all, would wash her hands of the whole thing and go somewhere else."

"But you, as God, would not be that sensible?"

"No. I'd try. I would think for a very long time about the real problems — too many people, for instance — and I'd try to find a way to help. But without any real hope of success."

He nodded, and a curious intensity seemed to leave him. She had not realized how tense he had become until he now relaxed again.

Very deliberately she said, "Of course, solving the population problems doesn't mean it would be a peaceful world. Sometimes I think history was invented simply to record war, and before records, there were oral traditions. Even when the world was un-inhabited except for a few fertile valleys, they fought over those valleys. There will always be people who want what others have, who have a need to control others, who have a need for power. Population control won't change that."

"As God you could pick your population," Carmen said carelessly. "Select for nonaggressiveness."

"How? With what test? But, as God, I would know, wouldn't I?"

"There would be problems," he said, looking into the fire now. "That's why I started this game saying dictator; you said God. Where does asssertiveness end off and aggressiveness start? There are real problems."

She was tiring of the adolescent game that he wanted to treat too seriously. She finished her wine and went to the sideboard to refill her glass. There was a mirror over the cupboard. She stared at herself in dismay. Her hair was impossible, like dark dandelion fluff; her cheeks and nose were peeling; her lips were chapped. She thought with envy of Carmen's beautiful skin. At twenty you seemed immune to wind damage. Sunburn on Saturday became a lovely glow by Sunday. She thought of Werther's skin, also untouched by the elements, too tough to change any more by now. Only she, in the middle, was ravaged-looking. She hoped dinner would be early; she had to go back to her house, take a long soaking bath, cream her skin, then get out her checkbook and savings passbook and do some figuring. She could do the book somewhere else, but if Bobby didn't take it, would anyone else? She remembered her own doubts about a second one so closely following the first, and she was afraid of the question.

The real fear, she thought, was economic. Whoever controlled your economic life controlled you. Overnight she could become another nonperson to be manipulated along with the countless other statistics. Her dread was very real and pervasive, and not leavened at all by the thought that Hugh Lasater understood how to use this fear because he also harbored it. That simply increased his power because he too was driven by uncontrollable forces.

Carmen joined her at the sideboard, met her gaze in the mirror. "You said you would heal the sick, cure the wounded. What if you had a perfect immunology method? Would you give it to the drug manufacturers? The government?"

Slowly she shook her head, dragged back from the real to the surreal. "I don't know. Perfect? What does that mean?"

"Immune to disease, radiation, cellular breakdown or aging . . ."

She was watching the two faces in the mirror, hers with its lines at her eyes, a deepening line down each side of her nose, the unmistakable signs of midlife accentuated by the windburn; his face was beautiful, like an idealized Greek statue, clear elastic skin, eyes so bright they seemed to be lighted from behind. She knew nothing changed in her expression, she was watching too closely to have missed a change, but inside her, ice formed and spread, and she was apart from that body, safely away from it. Is that what Werther had? she wanted to ask, wanted to scream. Is that why they wanted him so badly?

She started to move away and he put his hands on her shoulders, held her in place before the mirror. At his touch the ice shattered and she was yanked back from her safe distance. Startled, she met his gaze again.

"Would you?"

She shook her head. "I don't know. No one person could make such a decision. It's too soul-killing." It came out as a whisper, almost too low to be audible.

He leaned over and kissed the top of her head. "I'd better see if Saul needs any help." He left her, shaken and defenseless. When she lifted her glass, her hand was trembling.

Saul? Saul Werther. He called him Saul so naturally and easily that it was evident that they were on first-name terms, had been for a long time. Had Saul Werther promised him that kind of immunity? Was that the bond? Slowly what little she had read of immunology came back to her, the problems, the reasons that, for example, there had not been a better flu vaccination developed. The viruses mutate, she thought clearly, and although we are immune to one type, there are always dozens of new types. Each virus is different from others, each disease different, what works against one is ineffective against the rest. But Carmen believed. Saul Werther had convinced him, probably with no difficulty at all, considering his persuasiveness and his wide-ranging knowledge of what must seem like everything to someone as young and naive as Carmen was.

He was crazy then, with a paranoid delusional system that told him he could save the world from disease, if he chose to. He was God in his own eyes, Carmen his disciple.

She went to stand close to the fire, knowing the warmth could not touch the chill that was in her.

She would leave very early the next day. There were other eagles in other places, Florida, or upper New York, or Maine. And she would start filling applications for a job, dig out her old résumé, update it . . . If she stayed, Lasater would somehow find a way to use her to get inside this house, get to Saul Werther. And she knew that Saul and she were curiously allied in a way she could not at all understand. She could not be the one to betray him, no matter what he had done.

She hardly tasted dinner and when Saul expressed his concern, she said only that she was very tired. She found to her dismay that she was thinking of him as Saul, and now Carmen did not even pretend the master/servant roles any longer. Saul left his place at the table and came up behind her. She stiffened, caught Carmen's amused glance, and tried to relax again. Saul felt her shoulders, ran his hands up her neck.

"You're like a woman made of steel," he said, and began to massage her shoulders and neck. "Tension causes more fatigue than any muscular activity. Remember that blue float? Think of it bobbing up and down through the years. Nosed now and then by a dolphin, being avoided by a shark made wise by the traps of mankind. A white bird swoops low to investigate, then wheels away again. Rain pounding on it, currents dragging it this way and that. And bobbing along, bright in the sunlight, gleaming softly in moonlight, year after year . . . Ah, that's better." She opened her eyes wide. "Let's just have a bite of cheese and a sip of wine while Carmen clears the table, and then he'll take you home. You've had a long day."

He had relaxed her; his touch had been like magic working out the stiffness, drawing out the unease that had come over her that night. His voice was the most soothing she had ever heard. Perhaps one day he would read aloud . . . She sipped her sweet wine and refused the cheese. He talked about the great vineyards of Europe.

"They know each vine the way a parent knows each child — every wart, every freckle, every nuance of temperament. And the vines live to be hundreds of years old . . ."

The flame was a transparent sheet of pale blue, like water flowing smoothly up and over the top of the log. Lyle looked through the flames; behind them was a pulsating red glow the entire length of the log. There was a knot, black against the sullen red. Her gaze followed the sheer blue flames upward, fol-

lowed the red glow from side to side, and Saul's voice went on
sonorously, easily . . .

"My dear, would you like to sleep in the spare room?"

She started. The fire was a bed of coals. She blinked, then
looked away from the dying embers. At her elbow was her glass
of wine, she could hear rain on the roof, nothing was changed.
She did not feel as if she had been sleeping, but rather as if she
had been far away, and only now had come back.

"We have a room that no one ever uses," Saul said.

She shook her head and stood up. "I want to go now," she
said carefully, and held the back of the chair until she knew
her legs were steady. She looked at her watch. Two? Everything seemed distant, unimportant. She yearned to be in bed
sleeping.

Carmen held her coat, then draped a raincoat over her. "I'll
bring the car to the porch," he said. She heard the rain again,
hard and pounding. She did not know if she swayed. Saul put
his arm about her shoulders and held her firmly until the car
arrived; she did not resist, but rather leaned against him a bit.
She was having trouble keeping her eyes open. Then Saul was
holding her by both shoulders, looking at her. He embraced her
and kissed her cheek, then led her down the stairs and saw her
into the car. He'll get awfully wet, she thought, and could not
find the words to tell him to go back inside, or even to tell him
good night.

"Good thing I know this driveway well," Carmen said cheerfully, and she looked. The rain was so hard on the windshield
the wipers could not keep it cleared, and beyond the headlights
a wall of fog moved with them. She closed her eyes again.

Then the cold air was on her face, and Carmen's hand was
firm on her arm as he led her up the stairs to her house, and
inside. "I'll pull those boots off for you," he said, and obediently
she sat down and let him. He built a fire and brought in more
wood, then stood over her. "You have to go to bed," he said gently. "You're really beat tonight, aren't you?"

She had closed her eyes again, she realized, and made an effort to keep them open, to stand up, to start walking toward the bedroom. She was surprised to find that her coat was off already, and the raincoat.

"Can you manage?" Carmen asked, standing in the bedroom doorway.

"Yes," she said, keeping her face averted so he could not see that her eyes were closing again.

"Okay. I'll look in on you in the morning. Good night, Lyle."

She got her sweater off, and the heavy wool slacks, but everything else was too much trouble, and finally she crawled into bed partially dressed.

                           °

The cabin was dark when she came awake. She could not think where she was for several minutes. She was very thirsty, and so tired she felt she could not move the cover away from her in order to get up. Her head pounded; she had a temperature, she thought crossly. In the beginning, the first several times she had come home soaked and shaking with cold, she had been certain she would come down with a cold, or flu, or something, but she had managed to stay healthy. Now it was hitting. Sluggishly she dragged herself from bed, went to the bathroom, relieved herself, and only then turned on the light to look for aspirin. She took the bottle to the kitchen; it would burn her stomach if she took it without milk or something. But when she poured a little milk into a glass, she could not bear the sight of it, and she settled for water after all. It was six o'clock. Too early to get up, too dark . . .

The cabin was cold and damp. She remembered how she had been chilled the day before and thought, that was when it started. She should have recognized the signals, should not have spent the day on the beach in the wind . . . She had been walking back toward the bedroom, now she stopped. How had she got home? There was no memory of coming home. She tried to remember the evening, and again there was nothing. They had gone to Saul's house, where she and Carmen had played a silly game, then dinner, then . . . Then nothing.

Like the night before, she thought distantly, the words spaced in time with the pounding of her head. Ah, she thought, that was it. And still distantly, she wondered why it was not frightening that she could not remember two evenings in a row. She knew she was not crazy, because being crazy was nothing like this. She could even say it now, when she had been crazy she had been frightened of the lapses, the gaps in her life. And suddenly she was frightened again, not of the loss of memory, but of her acceptance of it with such a calm detachment that she might have been thinking of a stranger. She turned abruptly away from the bedroom and sat down instead on a straight chair at the kitchen table.

What was happening to her? She forced herself to go over the previous day step by step. Carmen's hands on her shoulders, her realization that Saul was crazy, paranoid, and her own panicky decision to leave today. She nodded. Leave, now, immediately. But she had to wait for Carmen to come, she thought plaintively. Her hands tightened on the table, made fists. She saw herself walking toward Saul's open arms, felt warmth of them about her, the comfort of resting her cheek on his shoulder . . . Unsteadily she stood up and got another drink of water. Leave!

She sat down with the water, torn between two imperatives: she had to leave, and she had to wait for Carmen. If she stayed, she thought, sounding the words in her head, Lasater would use her somehow to get to Saul. Still she sat unmoving, wishing Carmen would come now, take the decision away from her. She pulled an open notebook close and with block letters drawn shakily she wrote *Leave*. She nodded and pushed herself away from the table.

Packing was too hard; she decided not to take some of her things — the typewriter, some of the books, one of her suitcases. Dully she thought of the refrigerator, of food turning bad. She shoved things into a bag and carried it to the car and blinked at the trunk already full. She put the food on the floor of the back seat and decided she had enough. It was eight o'clock when she left the house and started down the driveway. At the bottom, a large blond man waved to her. She made the stop, prepared to turn, and rolled her window open a crack.

"Yes?"

"Lasater wants to see you. He's in a camper in the park." He went around the car, keeping his hand on the hood; at the passenger side, he opened the door and got in.

She looked at him, feeling stupid. Her door was locked, she had thought of it, but not that side. Slowly she pulled out onto the highway, climbed the hill, went down the other side thinking of nothing at all.

"There's the turn-off," the blond man said.

She turned and drove carefully down the steep gravel road to the campsite. She stopped when he told her to. They both got out and he motioned toward the motor home at the end of the campgrounds. She walked to it.

"Lyle, what an early bird! I thought it would be later than this. Come on in. I'm making breakfast, Mexican eggs. You want some?"

The interior was exactly like the ads she had seen in magazines. There was a tiny living room area with a narrow sofa and two swivel chairs. There was a counter separating that part from the even smaller kitchen, and beyond that another curtained-off part. All very neat.

"Why did you send that man after me?"

"Afraid you'd be up and out early, and I wanted to talk to you." He was dicing a red pepper. "Look, I can add another egg, no trouble at all. Pretty good dish."

She shook her head.

He reached below the counter and brought out a coffee cup. "At least coffee," he said, pouring. He brought her the cup and put it on a swing-out table by the side of the sofa. "Sit down,

I'll be with you in a minute. You hung over?" His scrutiny was quick, but thorough. He grinned sympathetically. "Have you told them anything about me?"

"No. I'm sick, I'm going to buy juice and aspirin and go to bed."

He backed away. "Christ! What a break! You okay? If you don't feel like driving to the village, I can send for stuff for you."

She shook her head again. "I'll go."

"Okay, but then in the sack, and stay until you're tiptop again, right? It's the rain. Jesus, I never saw so much rain. Has it ever stopped since you got here?"

He went on cheerfully as he added onions to the chili pepper, then a tomato. He tossed them all into a small pan and put it on one of the two burners of the stove. He poured himself more coffee as he stirred the sauce, and through it he kept talking.

"You know, it might be a good ploy, your getting sick now. You pile up in bed and he comes to visit, right? I mean, he digs you or would he have spent all day and most of the night with you? So he comes to visit and you ask him for a drink, a glass of water or juice, and later we come collect the glass, finis. Not bad actually."

Wearily she leaned her head back and closed her eyes. "You've been so smart," she said. "If I did what you asked and no more, I was safe enough. Hand over the prints, get my story on the eagles, forget the whole thing. If I poked around and learned anything more than that, you could always point to my medical record and say I'm just a nut."

"A plum," he said, correcting her. "You're a plum. I reached in and pulled out a real plum. You know there aren't any plums in plum pudding? Boy, was I ever disillusioned when I found that out." He had broken his eggs into a frying pan; he watched them closely, turned them, and then flipped them onto a plate. He poured his sauce over them. "No tortillas," he said regretfully. "Toast just isn't the same, but them's the breaks." Toast popped up in the toaster and he buttered it quickly, then brought everything to the living area. He pulled out another table and put his breakfast down. "Look, are you sure you don't want something, toast, a plain egg?"

"No."

"Okay." He reached under the table and flipped something and extended another section. "Presto chango," he said. Then he pulled a briefcase toward him, rummaged in it, and brought out an envelope, put it on the table. "While I eat, take a look at the stuff in there."

There were photographs. Lyle glanced through them and stopped when she came to one that had Saul Werther along with several other men, all looking ahead, as if they were part of an audience.

"Start with the top one," Hugh Lasater said, with his mouth full.

She looked at it more closely. It was an audience, mostly men, all with an attentive look. She studied it, searching for Saul, and finally found him, one tiny face among the others. Two other photographs were similar, different audiences, but with Saul among the others. There was a photograph of four men walking; one of them was Saul. And there were two blown-up pictures of the larger audiences.

Lasater had finished eating by the time she pushed the photographs aside. "You recognize him without any trouble?"

"Of course."

"But in one his hair's almost white, and in another one it's dark brown. He has a mustache in one, didn't you notice it?"

"I assumed they're over a period of time. People change."

"Two years," Lasater said. He removed his plate and leaned back in his chair once more, holding coffee now. "One of those conferences was in Cold Spring Harbor, one's Vanderbilt, the last one's Cal Tech. He gets around to the scientific meetings. And at each of those conferences there was an incident. A young scientist either vanished or died mysteriously."

Lyle closed her eyes. Don't tell me, she wanted to plead, but no words came; she realized her head was pounding in time with the booming of the surf. The booms meant another storm was coming. When the waves changed from wind waves to the long swells that formed a thousand miles offshore, or at the distant Asian shores, and when the waves did not dash frantically at random intervals, but marched with a thunderous tread upon the land, there would be a gale or worse. Saul had told her about the difference, and her experience here had confirmed it, although she had not been aware of the difference before his mini-lecture.

"I'm leveling with you," Lasater said now. "I want to wrap this up and be done with it. You must want to be done with it too. Lyle, are you listening to me?"

"Yes. My eyes hurt, my head aches. I told you, I'm sick."

"Okay, okay. I'll make it short. Picture Berlin back in the thirties. You see *Cabaret?*" She shook her head slightly. "Oh. Well, Berlin's recovering from the worst economic slump in history, expanding in all directions under Hitler. At the university they're developing the first electron microscope. And at the university is Herr Professor Hermann Franck, who is one of the pioneers in biochemistry. He's using the prototypes of the electron microscope fifteen years before anyone else has it. Right? Franck has a Jewish graduate student working under him and the work is frenzied because Franck is tired, he wants to quit, go back to his family estate and write his memoirs. Only he can't because the work they're doing is too important. He's on the verge of something as big in his field as Einstein's work was in his, maybe bigger."

"How do you know any of this?" Lyle asked.

"There were Gestapo stooges throughout the university. One of them tried to keep up with Franck and his work, made weekly reports that are mostly garbage because he wasn't being cut in on any of the real secret stuff. But enough's there to know. And, of course, Franck was publishing regularly. Then, something happened, and, I admit, this part gets shady. His grad student was beaten and left for dead by a youth gang. The professor applied for permission to take the body home for burial, and that's the last anyone knows of either of them. Obviously the kid didn't die. He survived, maybe killed the professor, maybe just hung around long enough and the old guy died of natural causes. He had a bum heart. Anyway, the student ended up with the papers, the notes on the work, everything. We know that because it all vanished. Eventually when Franck didn't show up at work, the Gestapo got interested enough to make a search, and found nothing. The war thickened, things settled, and Franck was forgotten, another casualty. Then twenty years ago the Gestapo reports came to light and a mild flurry of activity was started, to see if there was anything worth going after. Nothing. About twelve years ago a bright young scientist working on his thesis dragged out Franck's articles, and there was an explosion that hasn't stopped sending out ripples yet. Bigger than Einstein, they're saying now."

"What is it?"

"I don't know. Maybe three people do know. But for twelve years we've been looking for that student, now an elderly gentleman, who makes it to various scientific conferences and kills young researchers. We want him, Lyle, in the worst way."

Lyle stood up. "It's the best story yet. They keep getting better."

"I know. I can't top this one, though. He's crazy, Lyle. Really crazy. His family was wiped out without a trace, it must have done something to him. Or the beating scrambled his brains. Whatever. But now he's crazy, he's systematically killing off anyone who comes near Franck's research. He's able to keep up with what's going on. He can pass at those conferences. Maybe some of the time he actually works in a university somewhere. But if we can get a set of prints, we'll know. The Gestapo had them on file, they fingered every Jew in the country. All we want to do is see if they match. Maybe they won't. We'll step out, go chase our tails somewhere else?"

"And if they do match?"

"Honey, we'll be as gentle as a May shower. Somewhere there are a lot of notebooks, working notes, models, God knows what all. He can't keep all that junk in his head, and besides, he was just a student. Franck had been on it for years. It's on paper somewhere. We want him to lead us to it, and then he'll be picked up ever so carefully. There's a real fear that he'll suicide if he suspects we're anywhere near him, and he's too important to let that happen. He'll be better treated than the Pea Princess, believe me."

She went to the door. Her eyes were burning so much it hurt to keep them open; she was having trouble focusing. She still did not believe him, but she no longer knew which part of the story she could not accept. It was all too complicated and difficult. She wanted desperately to sleep.

Lasater moved to her side, his hand on the door knob. "Honey, we're not the only ones looking for him. And we are probably the nicest ones. Science is pretty damned public, you know."

"Now you wave the Russian threat."

"And others," he said vaguely. "But also, there are pharmaceutical corporations that know no nationality. It's a real race and everyone in it is playing to win. Even if by default."

"What does that mean?"

"The ultimate sour grapes, Lyle. A really poor loser might decide if he can't have the prize neither can anyone else."

He opened the door. "Look, no rain. I must be in California. Go on, get your juice and aspirin, and then pile in the sack for a day or two. I'll be around, see you later."

He knew he had frightened her at last. It had taken the big guns, but there was a trick to knowing when to show strength and when to play it cozy. She was shaken. She had to have time now to let it sink in that her own position was not the safest possible. But she was a smart cookie, he thought with satisfaction, and it would sink in. She would get the point soon enough that this was too big for her to obstruct. The next time he saw her, she would ask what assurance she had that once done, she would be truly out of it, and he would have to reassure her, pour a little oil on her conscience.

Hugh Lasater was fifty, and, he admitted once in a while to himself, he was tired. Watching Lyle walk to her car, he thought of what it would be like to have a woman like her, to sit by a fire when the wind blew, play gin, read, listen to music, cuddle in bed. There had been three women along the years that he had tried that scenario with, and each time what he got was not exactly what he had been after. The women he liked to cuddle in bed were not the sort who played gin by the fire, and, he said to himself, vicy vercy. Lyle drove up the gravel trail to the highway and he motioned to Milt Follett to come back inside.

Not Lyle, or anyone like her, he decided emphatically. Too old, too dumpy. He hoped she had not spread flu germs around.

"Get up there," he told Follett, "keep an eye on her place. Werther's sure to pay a sick call, and when he leaves, the house is yours. She won't get in the way." He did not believe Follett would find the prints, either. In his mind was a scene where Taney handed them to him; he believed in that scene.

Follett scowled. "It's going to rain again."

"Take an umbrella. Rain's good cover. They'll be in a hurry to get inside, you won't have to stay so far back."

Follett cursed and almost absently Hugh Lasater slapped him. "Get your gear together. You'd better take some sandwiches, coffee. He might not show until after dark."

Follett's fists were as large as sacks of potatoes, and as knobby. "Relax," Hugh Lasater said. "Someone has to teach you manners." He began to gather the photographs, dismissing Milton Follett, who was, after all, no more than a two-legged dog, trained in obedience and certain indispensable tricks, but who was inclined to yap too much.

Two days, he thought cheerfully. After all those years, two more days was not much. He had been in the Company when Cushman made the connection between Werther (or David Rechetnik) and Loren Oley's cancer research after Oley had vanished. Hugh Lasater had winkled out the details over a fourteen-month period, the Berlin connection, the old professor, everything he had told Lyle. Cushman had not then or ever grasped the implications and had shelved the investigation, but Lasater had stayed with it, working on it when he had time, keeping his own file. And four years ago Lasater had had enough to take his walk. He retired, pleading battle fatigue, nerves. He knew he had covered his traces so well that no one would ever be able to backtrack him. You're not going to write a book? they had asked, and he had laughed at the idea. A year later he had a new job, and was still on it. And in two days, he would know. But he already knew. He had known for over a year.

He sat with his long legs stretched across the motor home and made his plans while Follett grumbled as he began to put together sandwiches. Outside, the surf was booming like a cannon.

*

Inside Lyle's head the surf was booming also. She flinched from time to time, and she was squinting against the light even though the sky was solidly overcast now. Her legs ached and her arms felt leaden. A gust of wind shook her car and she knew the rising wind would make the coast road hazardous to drive. It was not too bad where the hills were high on the east side of the road, but every gap, every low spot, every bridge opened a wind channel, and it howled through, threatening to sweep anything on the road through with it. She came to the village and stopped at the supermarket. She had not had time to become very friendly with anyone in town, but they all accepted her by now with amiable good will. Most of the townspeople she dealt with seemed to know her name although she knew none of theirs. The woman at the checkout stand in the grocery nodded when Lyle entered.

"Morning. How're you, Mrs. Taney? That's a real storm blowing in this time. Got gale warnings up at Brookings already. We'll get it."

"Worse than last week's?"

"Last week?" The woman had to stop to think. "Oh, that wasn't much at all. This one's a Pacific gale. Better make sure you have kerosene for your lamp, and plenty of wood inside. Could lose the lights."

Lyle thanked her and moved down the aisle and began selecting her groceries. Juice, ginger ale. She remembered being sick as a little girl and her mother bringing her iced ginger ale with a bent straw. For a moment she was overcome with yearning for her mother's comforting presence. She saw straws and picked them up. Her pump was electric, she remembered, and picked up more juice. If the electric lines went down she would have no water until they were restored. She knew she had to drink a lot; she was parched right now in fact. When she got to the checkout she was surprised by the amount and variety of potables she had picked up. Irritably she regarded them; she should put some of the stuff back, but it was too much effort and she paid for them and wheeled the cart outside to put her bag in the back seat. The wind was stronger, the gusts took her breath away. And the pounding of the surf was like a physical blow to her head again and again and again.

Before she started her engine, she found the aspirin bottle and slipped it inside her pocket where she could get it easily. She put a can of Coke on the seat next to her and then turned on her key.

Salmon Key was on a bluff a hundred feet above sea level. On the streets running parallel to the coastline the wind blew fitfully, not too strong, but at each intersection and on the cross streets it was a steady forty miles an hour with gusts much stronger. Lyle went through an intersection, fought the steering wheel to keep her car in her lane, and then in the middle of the next block parked at the curb. She knew she could not drive up the coast against that wind.

She put her head down on the steering wheel and tried to think of someplace to go. The motel was closed for the season. She knew no one in town well enough to ask for a room for the night. Back to her house? She was afraid to go back. Saul would give her something to make her sleep again.

She jerked upright with the thought and knew it was right. He had given her something both nights. Why? She had no answer, only the question that kept slipping away as if she was not supposed to ask it, as if she had touched on a taboo that sent her mind skittering each time she came too close.

She remembered a gravel road that led from town up into the hills, following Salmon Creek to a picnic spot, going on upward past that. A logging road, dirt and rough, no doubt, but protected from the wind, and unused now since logging had stopped. She drove again, turned at the next corner, and headed back toward Salmon Creek. It churned under the wind, whitecaps slapped against the boats at anchor at the docks. No one was in sight as she turned onto the gravel road, and within seconds she was out of town with only the trees on both sides of the road. At the picnic grounds she stopped to take aspirin and drink the Coke. She was very feverish, she knew. This had been a good idea, she decided, waiting for the aspirin to dull her headache and ease the aches in her arms and legs. She would rest until the storm passed — they never lasted more than a few hours — and by the time it was quiet again, probably after dark, she would go on, drive to Portland, return the car to the agency, get a flight back home.

She had no home, she remembered. She had leased her apartment. But there were people she could go to, she argued. Jackie, Chloe, Mildred and Jake . . . Neither Lasater nor Saul could find her here, and tomorrow she would be safe. The aspirin was not helping very much; reluctantly she turned on the key and drove; the little park was too open, too accessible. Now the road deteriorated rapidly, from gravel to dirt, to little more than ruts. She should have stayed at the picnic area, she realized. No one would be there on a day like this, and she could not find a place to turn around, or to park, or . . . The road forked. Both sides began to climb steeply after this junction. Maybe she could turn around here. It took her a long time, and she knew she was scratching up the car, and scraping the bottom on rocks, but finally she had it pointing back down the dirt road and, exhausted, she turned off the key again and leaned back with her eyes closed.

The wind was distant, high in the trees, hardly noticeable at ground level. She could not hear the surf, and that surprised her because her head was still pounding with the same rhythm and urgency as before when she had thought the thunderous waves were causing her headache. The rain was starting finally, a pattering at first that eased up; soon it was falling harder. She had to get some things from the trunk. Warm clothes, her poncho, her afghan. It would get cold in the car. Still she sat quietly, wishing she did not have to move again for a long time. The rain let up and now she forced herself out. She was appalled by the mess in the trunk. She had tossed stuff in randomly. Her camera case was not there, she realized, and remembered she had left it at Saul's house when they had gone down the beach. She had no further memory of it. She found a long coat, her poncho, boots, the afghan, notebooks. She knew she would not want anything to read; her eyes were bothering her too much. There was a fire banked just behind them.

She arranged the car, put down both front seats all the way, made sure her bag of groceries was within reach, and the can opener she kept in the glove compartment, and only then allowed herself to lie down and pull the afghan over her and finally close her eyes. The rain on the car roof was too loud, but presently she grew used to it and found it soothing. She slept.

Her sleep was fitful and restless, beset by dreams. When she wakened, she was very thirsty; her lips were parched, and her eyes felt swollen. Her headache had intensified and her body hurt all over. She swallowed more aspirin and drank orange juice with it. She slept and dreamed:

Saul was her lover and they ran down the beach like children, hand in hand, laughing, tumbling in the surf, which was as warm as blood. They started to make love in the gentle surf, and she woke up suddenly, aching with desire.

She should drink again, she thought, but it seemed too much effort; she was too tired. She was curled in a tight ball, chilled throughout, and burning with fever. She would die, she thought then, and they would find her here one day and wonder what had happened to her. She dreamed they were finding her, poking at her body with sticks because no one wanted to touch her, and she woke up again. This time she rolled until she could reach a can of juice and she drank it all, and only then remembered she should have taken aspirin. She pushed herself up enough to reach the bottle, and she opened a second large can of juice and took aspirin again. It was nearly dark, the rain was hard and steady. She could not tell if the wind was blowing.

She dreamed she was telling her mother she had to go to the bathroom and her mother said not now, dear, wait. She woke up squatting near the car; the shock of icy rain on her back, face, arms, thighs brought her out of delirium. She was shaking so hard she could hardly get the car door open again, and, inside, her hands seemed uncontrollable as she pulled on her clothes. She could not remember undressing. Her hair was wet, ice water ran down her back, down her face. She found a dishtowel she kept in the car to wipe the windshield with and she dried her hair with it as much as she could. It was too dark to see her watch. She was so cold that she turned on the car engine and let it run long enough for the heater to warm the car. Then she was so hot that she began to tear off her clothes again.

She heard Carmen's voice: "Don't be scared. I'll come get you and take you home. We'll take care of you." She looked for him, but he did not come. He lied, she thought dully. Just like Lasater. Saul and Carmen examined her carefully; they looked at her throat, her eyes, listened to her heart, took a blood sample, and took her blood pressure reading. She answered Saul's questions about her medical history, her parents, everything. It was reasonable and thorough, and he wrote everything down.

"I'm dying," she said, and he nodded.

She woke up. She remembered hanging the dishtowel outside the window to get it wet and cold. She dragged it inside and wrapped it around her head. She could hardly move now because of weakness and pain. It was not the flu after all, she thought distantly, as if diagnosing someone else. He had poisoned her, she thought clearly. He was paranoid and he had known from the start that she was a spy. He told her so. He poisoned her and now she was dying from it. And they would find her body and prod it with sticks. She wept softly, then slept.

✻

At noon the wind was rising enough to shake the motor home from time to time. The trees around the campsite bowed even lower, and the air tasted of salt. The tent in the campsite collapsed, started to fly away. The kid who had been camping out rolled it up and stuffed it in the trunk of his car, and then he joined Lasater, who was standing at the railing of the park, overlooking the lagoon. The normally placid, protected waters were churning around and around; the wind-driven waves were meeting the outgoing tide in a free-for-all.

"Follett says something's wrong at Taney's house," the boy said, close to Lasater's ear.

"What?"

"Didn't say."

"Tell Turk to get his ass up there and find out."

The boy watched the water another second, then left, leaning against the wind. A few minutes later the rain started and Lasater went inside the motor home. Follett came in dripping a short time later.

"She never came back," he said, stripping off his wet clothes. "Werther's kid came over in the car at ten, carrying her camera gear. He went inside and came back out, still with the camera bag. He left. Been back twice on foot. Must wade the creek and come up the bank."

Lasater watched him with loathing. Follett's flesh shook when he moved; he had fatty flaps on his chest, like a woman who had been sucked dry.

"After he left the second time, I went to the house and looked around. She's flown. Half her stuff's still there, as if she wanted to fool you into thinking she'd be back. She left the refrigerator on, but she stripped it, and her toothpaste, deodorant, stuff like that, all gone."

Lasater could feel his fury grow and spread as if it were heartburn, and it scalded him just as heartburn did. She had sat there looking stupid, pretending she was sick, and all the time she had her car packed, her plans to skip out all made, everything go. And they were back at the starting post.

Wordlessly he got out a map and looked at the roads, the distances. She could be halfway to Portland by now. And he did not have a man in Portland. Or, if she was heading south, she would be in the Siskiyous approaching the California border.

"Okay, so we change plans," he said brusquely. "Take me up to her place and then you get down to the village and ask around, find out who saw her, which way she was going. Come back up to her place. And for God's sake, keep your mouth closed until we have a new play to run with. Let's go."

She had taken out maybe a third of the stuff she had brought in, he guessed, judging from the condition of the living room where there were still books and papers, and even mail. She had not bothered to open many of the letters. He did so and scanned them quickly. Nothing. He went through her drawers, and the darkroom, where there were many prints of the coast, trees, hills, and an empty nest. Nothing. She had started to make notes in a new large notebook, nothing. His search was very methodical and when he finished, everything was as she had left it, and everything had been examined. Nothing.

He built a fire in the stove and made coffee. She had cleaned the refrigerator but had not taken the coffee or sugar, or anything from the shelves. It looked to him as if she had left in a dead run. Why? Something had scared her out of here, what? Not his doing; she was already running by the time he had talked to her that morning. Werther? He heard his teeth grinding together and made himself stop. His dentist had warned him that unless he quit doing that he would be in dentures within a few years. He even did it in his sleep, he thought disgustedly. The thought of wearing dentures made him uneasy and irritable. It made him want to work his dentist over.

He sat facing the door and waited for Follett to come back, and prepared his story. By the time the soft tapping on the door stirred him, he had made a phone call, and he had the new play ready.

Carmen stood with the wind whipping his hair into his face. "Is Mrs. Taney here yet?" he asked, and the wind swept his words away.

Lasater stepped back and motioned him inside. "What? Are we going to have a hurricane or something?" He slammed the door as soon as Carmen was inside. "My God! It must be a hurricane!"

"I don't think it's that bad. Is Mrs. Taney back?"

"Oh, you're a friend of hers? Do you know where she is?"

Carmen shook his head. "Who are you?"

"Oh. But we do take turns, you understand. I'm Richard Vos, assistant editor at Rushman Publications. Your turn."

"Carmen Magone, just a friend. I got worried that she's out in this weather. She's sick with flu or something."

"When did you see her? Today?"

"Last night. How'd you get here?"

"I was just going to ask you that. I didn't see a car out there."

"I walked over from next door. You walk in from New York?"

Lasater didn't like him, too young, too flip, too bright-eyed. Mostly, too young. He had found his dislike of young men increasing exponentially during the last few years, and while he was prepared intellectually to admit it was jealousy, that did not prevent the feeling nor did it help once he recognized his antipathy had been roused yet again.

"I'm with a friend," he said. "Milt Follett, you ever see him play? We're doing his book on college football. He's gone to the village to buy some things. We thought Lyle would be here, she said she would be here. I brought her contracts to her." He indicated his briefcase, which he had brought in with him. Aggrievedly he went on, "I could have mailed them, but she said she'd be here, and Bobby, her editor, said it would be nice to visit and see how it's coming, since I had to be in Portland anyway to see why Follett's stalled. We'll end up with a ghostwriter," he confided. "I could have mailed them," he said again then. "You say you saw her last night? Did she say anything about going somewhere for a few days? Maybe she went somewhere to wait out the storm. Maybe she's scared of storms."

Carmen shrugged. "She didn't say, but she seemed pretty sick, running a fever. I've got to go. If she comes in will you ask her to give us a call?"

"Camping out with a buddy?"

"Not exactly. See you later, Mr. Vos." Carmen had not moved more than a few inches inside the door, and now he slipped out before Lasater could ask anything else.

That was a real bust, he admitted to himself. Briefly he had considered sapping the kid and giving the old man a call, tell him the punk fell and broke his leg, wait for him to drive over to pick him up and then grab him. How easy it could be, he mused. Grab him, make him tell us where the paperwork is, be done with it. He took a deep breath and went back to his seat on the couch. Maybe later it would come to that, but not yet. Taney would stay out a day or two, simmer down, but she would come back for her stuff. Someone like her wouldn't abandon a thousand-dollar camera. He'd twist her arm just a little and get what he needed that way. No suspicions, no fuss. And then, he thought coldly, Mrs. Taney, you and I have a little party coming up, just the two of us. First work, then play, right? Besides, he added to himself, the old man made a habit of killing off kids Carmen's age or a little older. No way could he believe Werther would lift a hand for this one. He made a bet with himself that

Follett would suggest they grab the kid and use him for bait.

All afternoon Carmen was out in the white Volvo during the height of the storm. There was a report that he had shown up at the park twenty miles down the road. He had checked it out, then had left, heading south. An hour later he had driven past again. He had checked out the Lagoon camp, and had gone north from there. Looking for Taney, Lasater knew. Why? It had to be something that had happened at their house. He was convinced the old man had said or done something that had scared her off. At dark the Volvo made its way back up the steep driveway next door, and stayed put the rest of the night. Early the next morning Carmen was at it again. The storm had blown itself out overnight.

At eleven Lasater could stand it no longer and he called Werther's house. After six rings the old man answered, and Lasater released the breath he had been holding. Belatedly it had occurred to him to wonder if Werther might sneak out in the trunk of the Volvo. He told his story about being an assistant to Lyle's New York editor, expressed his concern about her, suggested calling the police.

"I have done so," Werther said. "They obviously were not very impressed. You, however, have a vested interest in her, and you had an appointment with her that she missed. They would have to pay more attention if you voiced your fears."

Lasater had no intention of calling the police, and he was mildly surprised that Werther had been willing to bring them in, if he had. Hugh Lasater seldom expected the truth from anyone. Truth, he was convinced, was of such a nebulous nature that no one should expect it more than once or twice within a lifetime. You have to ferret out facts, data, scraps of information wherever you can find them and arrange them in a pattern that seems to make sense, always knowing that tomorrow you may have to rearrange the same bits and pieces to make a different pattern. That was sufficient, that was truth, always relative, always changeable, always manipulable.

Late in the afternoon the sun broke through the clouds and the air was spring-warm and fresh. The sea had turned a deep unwrinkled blue; it rose and fell slightly like a blanket over the chest of a sleeping woman moved by gentle breathing. Sunset was breathtakingly beautiful without a color left out. Carmen returned home an hour after sunset. He was alone in his Volvo. He looked exhausted, the report said, and mud was so high on the car that he must have been up and down logging roads all day.

At dark they all settled in to wait yet another day. Lasater felt he was caught up in a preordained configuration like the constellations of the zodiac, where each star is going at its own rate of speed in its own direction as a result of actions started long ago, which today resulted in this particular arrangement of parts. Although their motion might be imperceptible, they were all on the move; some of the stars were as close as they would ever get to one another and their destiny now was to separate, draw farther and farther apart. Others, he knew, were on a collision course that was equally determined and unavoidable.

He was nervous, and was keeping in very close contact with the watchers up and down the coast road. He had a man in Portland now, and another one on I-5. If anyone moved, he would be ready, and eventually someone had to move. Until then he had to wait. He had ordered Follett out to the motor home when he felt he would have to kill him if he remained in sight another minute, yawning, scratching, foot-tapping, too dumb to read, too restless to sit still. He wanted to go over and peek inside Werther's house, see what they were up to, and he knew there was no way. Heavy drapes, window shades; they were well hidden.

By late afternoon the next day fog moved in after a morning brilliant with sunshine. Carmen had gone out at dawn, and was back by two, and Lasater began pulling his watchers closer to the driveway. Fog was the most treacherous enemy of a surveillance job. The white car could move through it like a ghost, appearing to a watcher to be no more than a thicker drift, if it was spotted at all. The walkie-talkie unit remained silent through the long afternoon; no one was moving yet.

That afternoon Lasater felt like a chrysalis tightly wrapped in a white cocoon. The way the fog pressed on the windows gave him the illusion that the windows were giving, bowing inward slightly but inexorably. He half-expected to see tendrils of fog forced through small entrances here and there, writhing like snakes as they squeezed in, then flowing down to the floor where they would spread out like wide shallow rivers, join, become a solid white layer, and then begin to rise.

He got out the book on hawks, which he had started, then put aside. He did not like books on natural history, could not understand people who became rapturous over animals or scenery. From time to time he looked up swiftly from the book as if only by catching it unawares would he be able to detect the fog if it did start to penetrate the house.

He came to a chapter that dealt with Sir John Hawkwood, a fourteenth-century mercenary, and his interest quickened. Here was a man he could understand thoroughly. With no nonsense about loyalty to a state or church or any abstract principle, he had gone about his business of hiring himself out to the highest bidder, had done the job contracted for, then gone on to the next without looking back. He had used the weaknesses of others against them and in the end had been rich and honored. Taney was sharp, Lasater thought then; she had made her point that Hawkwood and those like him somehow had been bypassed by one aspect of the evolutionary growth of consciousness. They had not achieved the level of conscience that would necessarily act as a rein on their desires. Unlike the hawk, also without mercy, they were creatures whose needs were not immediate and inseparable from survival. Forever barred from the garden where the innocents still dwelled, and stalled on the ladder of evolution, they existed apart; symbol-making, dissembling, unrecognized before they acted and often after they acted, they were capable of incalculable evil.

Lasater snapped the book shut. She was going too far, talking as if those people had some kind of deficiency like a diabetic. And she contradicted herself, he thought angrily, first talking about all the stuff hawks grabbed for lunch: baby birds, rabbits, chicks, whatever they could lift, and then saying they could do no wrong. If he took something, she would be on his case fast. He despised people who were that unaware of their own double standards.

"Taney," he muttered, "deserves whatever she gets."

✿

Sunshine on her face awakened Lyle. She stirred, turned her head fretfully, and slowly drifted to full consciousness. Almost resentfully she pulled the afghan over her face and tried to go back to sleep, but she was fully awake. She did not move again for several minutes. She had not expected to wake up. She remembered snatches of consciousness, pain, fever, thirst, and she remembered that she had gone through the stages she had read about. She had felt self-pity, then anger, fury actually that this was happenning to her, alone in the wilderness. That had passed and she had felt only resignation, and finally anticipation. She had read about those stages preceding death, and when she realized she was looking forward to the end, she had thought with a start: it's true then. And now she was awake.

Her fever was gone, or at least way down, and she felt only a terrible weakness and thirst. Her mouth was parched, her throat felt raw, her lips were cracked. She raised herself to her elbow and looked for something to drink and saw a can of orange juice; she had not been able to open it the last time she had been awake. She reached for it and pulled it close to her but was too tired to find the opener and finish the task. She rested until her thirst drove her to renewed effort and this time she found the bottle opener and punctured the can with it, only to find she could not lift it to her mouth. Straws were scattered over the car; she groped for one and finally got it in the can and sipped the drink. She rested, drank again, then once more. By then she could pull herself up to a sitting position. Even propped up against the door, she found sitting too strenuous, and lay down again. She dozed, not for long; the sun was still on her when she opened her eyes the next time.

For the next several hours she sipped juice, dozed, sat up for seconds at a time, then minutes. She tried to remember what she had done through her ordeal, tried to remember her dreams. In one of them Lasater's face had grown so large it took up her entire field of vision; it had said, "Are you going to do it?" When the mouth opened, it became a terrible black pit.

"No."

"Honey, why can't you lie just a little?"

"Why can't you not lie just a little?"

"You make categorical statements and then feel obligated to live up to them. Now I have to get you out of here so I can bring in someone else." He shot her and while he was dragging her down the beach for the tide to take, he kept complaining, "You're nothing but a headache, you know? What would it have cost you?"

"Stop," she said then. He released her and she stood up laughing.

He stared at her aghast, then furiously stalked away.

She thought of the dream and could make no sense of it. It was either straightforward and meant exactly what it said, or it was so deep it eluded her. What would it have cost? she thought. She was not certain. Maybe she would have done a good thing even, but it was dirty; she felt certain of that, although she would have been unable to defend it if it were ever proven that Saul was a killer, or a smuggler, or whatever else they might claim.

She remembered a silver rain when all the fir trees had been transformed into Christmas trees heavily decorated with tinsel. She had been delighted with it, and if she had been able to get up and go out into it, she would have done so. That must have been when she was at her most feverish, her most delirious, she decided.

In a dream she had agonized over having to choose between Saul and Carmen, and they had waited patiently while she vacillated. She smiled; the rest of the dream was gone, forgotten, and probably it was just as well. Resting now she thought of the meaning of that dream: although she was almost ashamed of her admission, she was attracted to both of them. It was because they both accepted her unquestioningly, with approval, and either they were blind to her flaws, or thought them so unimportant that they actually became insignificant. She could not remember being treated exactly like this before. When she had been younger there had been the standard boyfriends, a proposal or two before she and Gregory had decided to make their arrangement permanent. All that, she thought decisively, had been biological, a burning in the groin, an itch between her legs, nothing more. Even at the height of passion, she had always known that Gregory was fantasizing someone else, someone made up of bits and pieces of movie stars and pictures in magazines. She never had talked about this with anyone because she had accepted it the way she accepted hunger and thirst and growing old, everything that was part of being human. But Saul and Carmen had not looked at her as if they were comparing her to an ideal who existed only in their heads. They had looked at her, had seen her as she was, and had accepted her. And she loved them both for it.

They were not afraid, she thought; everyone else she knew was afraid, at least most of the time. She remembered telling Saul she had been afraid all her life without ever knowing of what or why. Gregory was afraid. Mike's death had terrified him, as it had terrified her. She, blaming herself, had lived in dread of the day he would also blame her, because that would have justified her guilt. He must have felt the same way, she realized, and felt a rush of sympathy for him that she had not known before. He had needed to run all the way across the country, just as she had needed to run to the woods, to the hills.

She thought of Hugh Lasater, whose fear made him try to manipulate reality by manipulating truth, but the reality was always there, just out of sight, out of hearing, with its infinite terror.

Thinking about Hugh Lasater, she sat up again, this time without the accompanying dizziness she had felt before. She knew she needed food, her weakness was at least partly attributable to no food for . . . How long? It had not occurred to her to wonder until now. She tried the radio, nothing but static up here in the hills. She began to think of bread in milk, chicken broth steaming hot and fragrant. She settled for an overripe banana and ate almost half of it before she was too tired to bother with any more. She dozed, wakened, tried another banana, and later in the afternoon decided she had to try to get to the creek for water. She had stale bread, and wanted only some water to soften it in.

She was sticky from spilled juice, she felt grimier than she had been since childhood. The creek was no more than fifteen feet from her car but she had to stop to rest twice before she reached it. The dishtowel she had been using to cool herself with was muddy, filthy; she could imagine what her face looked like. The water was shockingly cold; she held the towel in it until some of the dirt was washed away, wrung it out slightly and then washed her face and neck. She was seized with a chill then. Shaking so hard that she spilled almost as much water as she had been able to get in the juice can, she started back to the car, thinking of the heater, of the afghan, of going back to sleep wrapped snugly in her poncho, covered from toe to head, sleeping deeply without dreams . . . And she knew she could not do that, not now. It was time to go home.

The heater took a long time to warm the car. She sat huddled in the afghan until then, leaning against the door, her eyes closed. She was afraid to lie down for fear she would fall asleep. She kept seeing her own bed, her covers, sheets, a hot bath, something hot to drink, coffee. She wanted to be home before dark, and she knew it would take her a long time to get there.

She ate a few bites of bread softened in water, and marveled at how hungry she was and how little she could eat at any one time. Two bites of this, three of that. She imagined her body as a giant sponge, absorbing water, juice, whatever she could pour into it, sucking it up greedily, dividing it fairly among her parched tissues. Her tongue felt more normal, and her throat hardly hurt now; she imagined her blood as sluggish as molasses from the refrigerator, demanding more and more of the fluids, stirring, starting to flow again, scolding . . .

She smiled at her nonsense and turned on the key, and this time she started down the dirt road. Within ten minutes she had to stop. Her arms were quivering with fatigue; her feet were leaden. And when Hugh Lasater turned up wih more threats, more demands, she thought, with her head resting on the steering wheel, she would tell him to get out and, if he did not go, she would call the police and complain.

And she would call Saul and tell him a man was asking strange questions about him. No more than that. If he knew he was guilty of something, it would be enough. And if he was guilty of murder, she asked herself, was she willing to be his accomplice? She couldn't judge him, she knew, and she turned on the key and started her lurching drive down the hill, down into fog.

She could remember nothing of this road, which was so steep and curvy it seemed now a miracle that she had driven up it. It twisted and turned and plummeted down, faithfully following the white-water creek. As she went down, the fog thickened until by the time she knew she had come far enough to have reached the picnic area, she could see no farther than a few feet in any direction. She knew she had missed the park when her wheels began to throw gravel. She stopped many times, sometimes turning off the motor, sometimes letting it run while she rested.

Then, with her front wheels almost on the coast highway she rested for the last time. She would not dare stop again on the highway. She closed her eyes visualizing the rest of her route. The steep climb straight up, over the crest, down again, straight all the way to the lagoon, then the sharp upward curve around the far side of the lagoon, down to the bridge and her own drive. She could leave the car in the driveway and walk the rest of the way. Not soon, but eventually. Reluctantly she started the last leg of her journey.

*

One more day, Lasater told himself, he'd give her one more day to show, and if she didn't . . . He had no other plan and his mind remained stubbornly blank when he tried to formulate one. He was certain she would be back before his self-imposed deadline.

He should have used a professional, he thought suddenly, as if stricken with terrible hindsight. If this fizzled it would be used against him that he had gone with an amateur when there were people available who could have done the job the first week. He worried about it, playing it this way and that, looking at the possibilities, and then he left it, just as a well-fed cat leaves a mouse corpse behind. He did not believe Werther would have let any professional inside his house. He had not stayed loose and on the prowl all these years, first eluding the Nazis, and then customs, whatever had come along, by being stupid. He had accepted Taney because she was an amateur, and Taney had to deliver. Lasater still held the image of Taney handing over the evidence he needed. It was a strong image, strong enough to keep him immobile in her house while he waited for her to return.

It was nearly five when he heard the car in the driveway. A minute passed, another, and finally he could wait no longer; he stamped out into the fog to see why she was stalling. He yanked open her car door to find her slumped forward against the steering wheel. He thought she was out, but at the sound of the door opening she stirred and raised her head. She looked like hell. He had not taken it seriously that she might be really sick; he had been convinced that she had run because her nerve had failed. But she was sick all right.

"Lyle, baby, you look like death warmed over. Come on, let's get you inside." He helped her out, then steadied her as she walked to the house. "Jesus, you had us all worried. Carmen's been all over the hills looking for you, they called the cops even." They had entered the house by then and he deposited her on the couch. "What can I get you? Are you okay sitting up like that?"

"Just get out," she said. Her voice was hoarse as if she had a sore throat. "I won't do anything for you. I don't care what you threaten. Get out."

"Okay, okay. I'll give Werther a call. I told him I would when you showed up. He's been worried." She started to get up and he pushed her back. She was too weak to resist his shove, which actually had been quite gentle. For the first time he wondered if she was going to get well, if she had pneumonia or something.

Carmen answered the first ring. "Mrs. Taney's back," Lasater said. "She's really sick, she might even be dying. I think she should be taken to a hospital, except there's no way you could get there through that fog. Is there a doctor anywhere nearby?" He knew there was no doctor closer than twenty-six miles. Carmen said she would tell Mr. Werther and hung up. "Do that, kiddo," Lasater murmured. He turned again to Lyle who had her head back, her eyes closed. "Listen, sweetie, they think I'm Richard Vos, a New York editor. I told them I had your contracts for you. They don't need to know more than that. Got it?"

Her nod was almost imperceptible.

"Okay. He'll probably send the kid over. When he gets here, I'm leaving. I'll be back at the park by the lagoon. You just get some rest now, take it easy for a couple of days. I'll see you later in the week."

Again she moved her head slightly. "I won't help you," she said.

"Okay, just don't worry about it for now. Get well first. And, Lyle, don't tell them anything. You're up to your pink little ears in this and it's classified. You blab, and, honey, they can put you away for a long time."

She started to take off her coat and when he touched her in order to help, she flinched involuntarily. He shrugged and moved away again. Her eyes were sunken, her face haggard, but her windburn was clearing up. She was pale as a corpse. "Honey, you look a hundred years old," he said softly. "I wouldn't lie down and stay still very long if I were you. Someone might want to shovel you under." She opened her eyes and for a moment he was startled. He had not noticed how very green they were before. Or now they looked greener against her pale skin. There was hatred in her gaze; when a woman is on the downhill slide of thirty-five, she doesn't want to be told she looks like hell, he thought maliciously. He regretted his own impulse to make her open her eyes and acknowledge his presence; now she looked more alive. Coolly he said, "I'm leaving your contracts on the table. I think he's coming. Remember, I'm Richard Vos."

He had heard steps on the porch, but no automobile noises in the driveway. It was the kid, come over to check first. He nodded, it was as he had expected. He opened the door and admitted Carmen who was carrying a paper sack.

"Mrs. Taney, how are you?" Carmen hurried to her and took her hand in both of his, studying her face. Lasater noticed that his fingers went to her pulse. Medical school dropout? Paramedic? He made a mental note to check it out.

"Don't try to talk," Carmen said, rising then. "I brought some soup. I'll just heat it up for you. Have you eaten anything at all since you left?"

"A little," she whispered in her hoarse voice.

"Soup is what you need," Carmen said and went to the kitchen where he shrugged off his coat and tossed it over a chair, and then rummaged for a pan.

"If you think you can manage," Lasater said, "I'll be going. I'm susceptible to viruses and bacteria and things like that. Get a sore throat if anyone within a mile coughs, you know. I tried to get a doctor, but there isn't any in Salmon Key. I'll be going back to the Lagoon Park." He was keeping his distance from Lyle, watching her as if afraid she might sneeze in his direction without warning. He snatched up his coat and tossed it over his shoulders and opened the door. "If you need me, you know. But I can't do anything. I don't know a thing about how to care for sick people."

Inside the motor home he snapped to Follett, "Let's go. Back to the park."

"What the hell's going on?"

"Never mind. We're leaving. At the first turn, I'm going to stop and you get out, go back up here and keep an eye on things. Werther's got to come over. The kid will either call him or go collect him when he thinks the coast is clear. She's really sick."

He drove slowly, unable to see more than two feet ahead through the fog. Grumbling, Follett left the motor home when he stopped, and Lasater continued down the highway. Visibility was so poor it would take him nearly an hour to get back to the park. If Taney could drive in it in her shape, he thought, so could he. He reached the bottom of the drive and stopped, trying to remember if the road had the white line on the side all the way, or only on curves, trying to remember if the road curved between here and the bridge.

✿

"This is silly," Lyle said, as Carmen held out a spoonful of the clear strong broth he had brought from the other house. "I can feed myself."

"I know," he said, smiling. "Open up. This is fun."

"Carmen, wait a second. I have to tell you something. That man who was here, he's an agent of some kind. He's after Saul. You have to warn him."

"We already know," Carmen said. "Open up, you're almost done."

She swallowed, then shook her head when he offered another spoonful. "You know?"

"Not who he's working for. But it's been pretty obvious that there are people watching us."

Lyle felt childishly disappointed, as if she had run a mile to warn of robbers only to find them already safely locked up.

Carmen looked at his watch, then said, "Now a hot bath for you, and then bed. Hold up your foot."

He pulled her boots off, as he had done another night, she remembered. She had forgotten that night. Again it alarmed her that she was not more fearful of the lapse, not at all fearful about it, in fact. He met her gaze and his face was somber.

"You'll gradually remember it all now. By morning when you wake up, it will all be there waiting for you to examine. You're not afraid?"

She shook her head.

"Good. I'll go fix the bath for you."

A few minutes later he said, at her bedroom door, "Yell when you get in bed. I'll tuck you in." His grin was back; he looked like a precocious child enjoying enormously this reversal of roles.

She didn't dare remain in the tub more than a few minutes; she had become so relaxed that she feared falling asleep and sinking forever under the water. Regretfully she got out, toweled herself, rubbed her hair briskly, and pulled on her gown. She was as eager now to be in bed as she had been to be in the tub. When she called Carmen her eyes were too heavy to keep them open. She was in a time-distorting presleep state that made it seem to take him a very long time to get to the bed, but when he was there, his voice close to her, she was startled that he had arrived so quickly.

"You're going to sleep like a baby," he murmured, and touched her shoulder lightly, drew the cover up closer to her neck. "You won't hear anything at all until morning. I'll be here tonight, no one will come in to bother you. Good night, Lyle." He kissed her forehead. She slept.

✿

Driving the motor home at any time was difficult for Lasater, who had never driven anything like it before this trip. He had trouble getting used to the rearview mirrors, which more often than not seemed focused on the sides of the monster itself instead of the road. And he did not like the feel of it on the highway; it was too high, the weight was in the wrong place, it felt skittery if there was a glaze of ice or a slick of water on the road, and that night fog was freezing to form black ice. He feared black ice more than an ice storm, because it was invisible; it formed in one place but not another that was equally exposed. The road surface of the bridge was already covered, and he skidded alarmingly. He shifted gears and slowed down even more, wondering if he would be able to pull the grade up to the top of the hill between here and the lagoon.

He had passed Werther's driveway and was starting up the hill, when he heard a car engine roaring somewhere in the fog. His first thought was that it was an idiot speeding on the coast road, driving blind. Then he heard a crash, and he knew someone had gone off the cliffs behind him. He yanked on the brake and got out, ran back on the white line at the edge of the road.

"Turk?" he called. "What the hell's going on?"

"Mr. Lasater? Where are you?"

The fog scrambled directional signals; it was impossible to say where any sound originated. Only the surf remained constant, and it was everywhere.

"Hey!" Turk yelled then. "Stop, where you think you're going?"

"Get out of the way! I'm going down to find him." Carmen's voice.

Lasater crossed the road; he could hear scuffling sounds now, then a sharp exclamation followed by harsh cursing.

"Turk, what's happening?" he called again.

"The old guy came down like a bat outta hell, picking up speed all the way, didn't even try to stop, but straight through and over the cliff. The kid's just gone down the trail. Must have radar."

"Call Follett. Tell him to meet you at Werther's house and give it a good dusting. Give me your flashlight. I'm going down there."

Turk began to signal to Milton Follett, then said softly, "Jesus H. Christ! Look!"

Up the hillside the fog was lighted from within as if by volcanic fires. There was a glow in the form of a mammoth aureole.

"That bastard! That goddamned fucking bastard," Lasater muttered. "Get up there with Follett, see if anything's left." He snatched the flashlight from Turk and looked for the trail down to the beach.

❁

By midnight the fire had burned itself out; the woods had not ignited; they were too wet and the moist fog had acted as a damper. The house had burned thoroughly, down to the foundation stones. Carmen sat huddled in a blanket near the stove in Lyle's house, his clothes drying on chairs. Lasater sat on the couch staring moodily at the exhausted boy, who had tried to find the car for over an hour until, retching and gagging, he had staggered from the pounding surf into Lasater's arms. The police had come and gone; they would be back at daybreak to look for the car and the body. Accidental death, they said.

Except, Lasater thought coldly, no one was dead yet. He did not believe Werther had been in the car when it went over the cliff, no matter what Turk thought he saw. Werther had to be waiting somewhere nearby, freezing his balls off in the woods, waiting for the coast to clear enough to show up here at this house. Taney wasn't out of it yet. Werther must be planning to use her to get him out of here.

Lasater slept on the couch that night; Carmen rolled up in the blanket and slept on the floor. At dawn he was up cleaning Taney's car with Lasater watching every movement, thinking she was more of a pig than he had realized. Carmen made coffee then, and presently said he was going shopping and would be happy to drop Lasater off at the park. When they went out, the trunk lid was still raised, airing out, and the back doors were open. Lasater felt a cold fury when the thought came to him that the boy was playing games with him, demonstrating that he was not hauling Werther out of the woods that morning.

❋

Lyle awakened slowly, first semi-aware that she was in her own bed again, that she was warm and dry and comfortable, and hungry; and slowly she began to remember the two evenings she had spent at Saul's house. She sat upright and pulled the blanket around her.

All those questions! He had examined her as thoroughly as any medical doctor had ever done. And she had permitted it! She closed her eyes hard, remembering. He had said she was to feel no fear or embarrassment, and she had felt neither; it had seemed the most natural thing in the world. She was startled by the memory of telling him all about Lasater, her involvement with him. Saul had known since that first night, and still had treated her with kindness and even love. The second night swam up in her consciousness and she shook her head almost in disbelief. He had injected her with something, and the rest of the night he had monitored her closely, her temperature, her pulse, her heart . . . She looked at her finger; he had taken a blood sample. Except for the physical examination, which had taken place in the bedroom, Carmen had watched it all, had participated.

As she remembered both evenings, snatches of conversations came back to her; they had talked seriously of so many things. She had been lucid, not doped or hypnotized, or unnatural in any way that she could recall now. But she had allowed it all to happen, and then she had forgotten, and had accepted not remembering. He had told her about that part of it: a drug in the sweet wine, suggestion. He had even said that if she truly objected to anything, she would refuse the suggestion. And she had refused nothing. Except, she amended, she had left the next morning although he had told her to wait for Carmen.

Slowly she got up and went to the bathroom. As she showered, more and more of that last evening came back to her. Just before telling her to wake up he had asked if she wanted to sleep there, in his house, and she had said no. She remembered thinking at the time that there was something she had to do the next morning, something she would not be able to do from his house. She had already made up her mind to leave so that Lasater could not use her to get to Saul. And she had to be home in order to carry out her intention. If he had asked even one question about her reasons, she would have told him, she knew, but he had not asked. He had suggested that she should wait for Carmen to come for her.

It was nine o'clock when she finished with her shower, dressed, and was ready to face Carmen. She was still weak, but she felt now that it was due to hunger, not illness. The house was empty. Coffee was on the hot plate. She poured herself a cup of it and sat down to read a note from Carmen on the table. He had gone shopping for breakfast. Back soon.

She was still sipping the strong coffee when he returned. He looked her over swiftly. "I'd say the patient is recovering," he announced. "What is prescribed for this morning is one of the biggest steaks you've ever tackled. Bet you finish it all."

"I've never had steak for breakfast in my life. Toast sounds like plenty." She wanted to challenge him, demand an explanation, but she was too hungry. After breakfast she would have her confrontation with Saul, not with Carmen who was simply a tool.

"Wait and see." He was unloading grocery bags and putting things away. When he unwrapped the steak, she almost laughed. Big enough for a party. While the steak was broiling, he opened a package of frozen peaches and sliced a banana into a bowl with them. She eyed it hungrily. He laughed and moved it out of reach. "Dessert," he said.

Then he brought two plates out of the oven where they had been warming, and they ate.

Lyle was on her second cup of coffee when Lasater arrived.

He scowled at the table. "Surprised you can eat on a morning like this."

"What does that mean?" Lyle asked. She had a dim memory that he was pretending to be someone from her publisher's office, and Carmen was pretending to believe that.

"They're searching up and down the beach for Werther's body," he said bluntly. "No luck so far."

She dropped her cup; it hit the saucer and toppled over, spilling coffee on the table. She turned to Carmen who nodded.

"He had an accident last night. He drove his car over the cliff."

Lyle did not move. She was trying to remove herself so far that she could see the house, the cliffs, the road, beach, forests, everything as she had seen it all in a dream once. So far back that nothing could touch her ever again. Faintly she could hear Lasater talking about a blood-stained car, one shoe, the wool-knit, navy-blue cap that Saul always wore. The distance seemed even greater when Lasater said something about leaving that afternoon. She was brought back when Carmen covered her hand with his.

"He's gone, Lyle. Are you okay?"

She nodded. He began to wipe up the spilled coffee.

"Why didn't you tell me?"

"You had to eat something. I knew you wouldn't afterward."

"What happened? Was it something I did?"

"No. There was a fire at the house and he went out in the car and the car went over the cliff. That's all they know about it."

"Is he really leaving?"

"I don't know. Maybe."

She nodded. They needed the body to make their identification. She started to speak again, but Carmen put his finger on her lips, silencing her.

Late in the afternoon she felt so restless that she could no longer stand the house and the waiting for something, anything to happen.

"Let's go for a short walk," Carmen said. "Are you up to it?"

She said yes. All day she had felt stronger and stronger until by now she felt almost normal. Her recovery was proceeding as rapidly as the illness had done. Carmen drove to the beach they had walked on before; he went closer to the black rocks to park this time.

Today the sky was gray and low, pressing on the tops of the coast range mountains, making the world seem very small, confined to this winter beach. The water was a shade darker gray, undulating with long swells, breaking up into white water where the wind waves rushed to shore. They walked slowly, not speaking.

That was where they had investigated the tide pools, exclaiming over the multicolored life forms there, the starfish, urchins, crabs . . . And over there she had found the blue float after its journey of many decades. And there they had eaten their lunch, and Saul had put the Styrofoam cup in his pocket to throw away later. And Saul had talked about the way the ocean savaged the winter beach when so few people were around to witness its maniacal fury.

"It seems lonesome," she had said, looking both ways on the deserted beach.

"It has presentiment of endings now," Saul had said. "Endings of life, of pleasure, of laughter in the sand. The winter beach is lonesome, but it fights back. Each grain of sand wrested from it is fought for, yielded finally, but never easily. And in the summer, very peacefully it all comes back, scoured clean by the mother ocean. But in the winter, that's always forgotten."

Gray, black, white; the winter beach was a charcoal drawing today, chiaroscuro colors that reflected her guilt, Lyle thought suddenly. And her guilt lay over every corner of her soul, every phase of her life. Her child, her ruined marriage, her failure as a teacher, her loss of faith both religious and secular . . . Her helplessness even. Had she told Saul why she had lost faith in history as it was taught? She could not remember. She hoped she had.

One day it had occurred to her that every great change brought about historically had been the result of a very few people, men usually, who were driven by the basest impulses: greed, the urge to ever more power, vengeance . . . The great majority of people had always been content to work their land, to mold their pots, weave cloth, do the life-sustaining things that were also soul-fulfilling; and the great majority of the people had always been manipulable by those few, ten percent or less, whose needs were so far removed from simple survival and personal salvation.

Saul had understood that, even if she had not explained her loss of faith. He had been interested in the other people, the ones with great ideas, the ones who created beauty, the ones who had tried to comprehend the mysteries.

Saul had been her natural ally, she thought dully, and by silence and inaction she had failed him, she had betrayed him; she had allowed herself to be used by Lasater who was a member of that minority.

And that was how they always succeeded, she went on, taking it to its conclusion, allowing herself no excuse, no possibility of deliverance from guilt; they found people who were too weak to resist, who were too afraid, too apathetic, too ignorant of their methods, and they wielded them like swords to strike down or capture the opposition. She had recognized Lasater immediately, had known his goals were not hers, were not even human, and she had done nothing. She had tried to ignore evil, deny its ability to influence her, and now Saul was dead and she would always know that she might have saved him if she had spoken early, before the trap was too tight, before Lasater and the blond man came. Just a few words in the beginning might have been enough. And she had done nothing.

And if Saul had been crazy, if he had killed people? She could not resolve the confusion in her mind about him, about how she had responded to him, about the grief and sense of loss she now suffered.

"You're crying," Carmen said, his hand on her arm.

She bowed her head and wept, and he held her for a long time until finally she tried to free herself. "I'm sorry," she said. "It's so pointless, isn't it? I didn't even know him. And he must have been very sick, he must have suffered terribly. No one like that can go around killing people and not suffer. He almost killed me. I know he almost killed me and yet, I can't help it, I'm crying for a madman who would have been put away if he hadn't killed himself, and I know he wanted it this way . . ." There was no way out of the contradictions and finally she stopped. When she looked at Carmen's face, she realized he was laughing silently.

Stiffly she drew away and started to walk toward the car. "You can't deny that he tried to kill me and almost succeeded. That injection of his, you were there, you know about it."

"It was a gamble," Carmen said, still smiling slightly. "But you were dying anyway."

"That's a lie. There wasn't a thing wrong with me before that shot. I had a life expectancy of at least thirty years."

"Exactly," Carmen said. "This walk has probably been too much for you so soon after your illness. Let's go home and have dinner."

She opened her mouth to respond, then clamped it shut again and got inside the car where she sat staring out the window all the way home. He was as crazy as Saul, she reminded herself.

*

Lyle saw a speck in the distance and knew the eagle was coming home finally. Every day there had been fresh evidence of the arrival of at least one of the pair, and now it was coming. She watched the speck gain definition, become separate parts. A wing dipped and the bird made a great sweeping curve, and she could see the tail feathers spread like a fan, rippling now and then as it made adjustments in its flight. She could see the white head, gleaming in the sun; it was looking at something below, turning its head slightly; it abandoned whatever had attracted it and looked ahead again. She was watching it through the view finder of her camera, snapping pictures as it came nearer. It cupped its wings, its feet reached out before it, and then it was on the spur, settling its wings down along its sides, stretching its neck. She snapped a few more shots of it as it preened, and then she sat back with her camera at her side and simply watched it. If the eagle was aware of her presence, it gave no indication of it. She was certain those sharp eyes had studied her blind, that they had seen her that day. There was a touch of majesty in its indifference to her.

Throughout the afternoon the eagle toiled at refurbishing the nest. It brought long strands of seaweed, and mosses, and sticks up to four feet long to expand the sides, and it worked the materials into place with an intentness and fastidiousness that was awesome.

Under the tree was a circle of litter; the eagle had picked out materials that had been good enough last year, but no longer pleased it. Old moss, old fern fronds, sticks. With an almost reckless abandon it tossed them over the side. When the light began to fade, Lyle picked her way back down the hillside, around the ruins of Saul's house, through the creek and to her own house, where Carmen was waiting for her.

She had not asked Carmen to stay, but neither had she asked him to leave; it was as if they both accepted that he would remain with her for now. The matter had come up only indirectly when she had said she couldn't pay him, and he had shrugged. For eight days he had been with her in the same relationship apparently that he had had with Saul. He did the shopping, a little cleaning, cooking; he prowled the beaches and brought home clams or scallops or crabs, sometimes a fish. Best of all they talked for hours in the evenings, never about Saul, or Carmen's past, but of history, current affairs, art, music . . . Lyle knew that one day he would get restless and drift on, but she refused to think about it and the hollow in her life that would result.

When she entered the house that day, the odors of cooking food and woodsmoke and the elusive scent of another person greeted her. She felt nearly overcome by contentment, she thought happily.

"Carmen! He's home. He's beautiful! A wing span over eight feet. All day he's been fixing up the nest, getting ready for his lady love to join him. Tomorrow you have to come up with me and see for yourself." She was pulling off her outer wear as she talked, unable to restrain the excitement she seemed filled to overflowing with. "I can't wait to see the pictures."

She stopped at the look on Carmen's face, a look of such tenderness and love it made her knees weak.

"I'll come up tomorrow. Maybe I can help you in the darkroom after dinner."

She nodded. And still they looked at one another and she wondered when she had stopped looking at him as if he were only a boy, when he had stopped looking at her as if she were untouchable.

Then she said, "I'm filthy. I'd better get washed up and change these muddy clothes." She fled. She was afraid he was laughing at her confusion.

They had dinner and worked in the darkroom for two hours. She felt like purring over the proof sheets; at least half a dozen of the pictures would go in, maybe more. Throughout the evening she avoided his gaze, and spoke only of eagles, her day in the blind, the dinner itself. She began to make notes to go with the pictures, and found herself writing a poem instead. When she finished, she felt almost exalted.

"May I read it?" Carmen asked.

She handed it to him silently.

He read it twice, then said, "I like it very much. It would make a good introduction to the book. I didn't know you wrote poetry."

"I don't. I mean I haven't before, not since college days." She took the sheet of paper back and reread her poem.

> *The dead tree flies an eagle on the wind,*
> *Then steadily reels it in,*
> *Dip, sway, soar, rise,*

All the time closer.
To the left, to the right,
Now too low, now too high,
But closer.
From nothing, to a speck
That could be a cloud,
To a being coming home,
It takes shape:
Sun on snow, the head,
Great wings without a waver,
White fan as graceful
And delicate as a black one
In a pale practiced hand.
From the tree's highest crotch,
From a nest of branches, sticks, twigs, moss,
Elaborate skyscraper room,
A silent summons was sent.
Now the dead tree reels the eagle home.

Abruptly she stood up. "I guess I'd better get to bed. I want to be up there early. I expect the other one will come in tomorrow or the next day."

○

In a scruffy camper in Lagoon Park Hugh Lasater played the tape over again, listening to their voices intently, following them through dinner, into the darkroom where their voices were almost too low to catch, back to the living room. He wished one of them had read the poem aloud. He heard their good nights, her door closing, Carmen's movements in the living room for another fifteen minutes; then the long silence of the night started. He turned off the tape player. Something, he kept thinking. There was something he should be catching. He rewound it and started over.

What he did not hear, because the device was activated by

sounds and this was done in silence, was the opening of Lyle's door at one-thirty. She stepped into the living room to look at Carmen sleeping on the couch, and when she saw him instead at the window that overlooked the sea, she did not retreat. Instead, after a slight hesitation, he came to her, barefoot, visible in the red glow from the glass door of the wood stove. He reached out his hand and she, after a slight hesitation, took it, and together they went back to her bedroom and softly closed the door.

Hugh Lasater listened again, and in the middle of the tape, he suddenly slapped the table top hard, waking up Milton Follett on the bunk bed.

"Son of a bitch!" Lasater said. "The camera bag. Where was it when the house burned down?"

Follett regarded him with hatred, rolled over, and went back to sleep.

Lasater had not been asking him; he already knew about the camera bag. Follett was good at certain jobs; he could watch and report movements down to a casual scratching of the head. And Follett had said that Carmen showed up with the bag at Taney's house when she was gone, and he had left with it. He had not been seen with it again. So Werther considerately put it on a stump out of danger before he set the house afire?

Lasater mused about the boy for a long time that night. He knew photography enough to help Taney in the darkroom. He remembered that sure way he had taken her pulse when she returned from her little jaunt. They had only his word that he had been hired by Werther in Los Angeles; if that was true what had made him jump into that crazy surf in an effort to find the old man. No one risked death for someone he had known only a couple of months, and that surf was a killer. Someone had to make sure that the car door had not jammed shut, Lasater said to himself. That would have screwed it up royally, if there had been no way Werther could have been thrown out. They had waited for the right kind of night with a pea-soup fog for their little charade; maybe the kid even had a rope guide to take him to where he had figured the car would land. No one paid much attention to him; he was always on the beach prowling around.

Lasater knew his foremost problem now was to convince Mr. Forbisher that his theory was right, that Werther had not been in that car, and that the boy would lead them back to him sooner or later. Turk was convinced that he had seen Werther go over the cliff; Follett believed him, but Follett would have bought anything to get him off this job. He hated the rain and wind and cold weather, and he hated the isolation here. He wanted a woman. When they got back to civilization, Follett would vanish a day or two. There would then be a news item about a woman's body being found . . . It was one of those things with Follett, a little weakness of his. Lasater could sympathize with his frustration even while his own frustration mounted to a dangerous level. Even Lasater had to admit that he no longer believed Werther was hiding out in the woods now. Not for eight days. In another day August Ranier would show up, listen to the arguments for continuing the hunt, make his evaluation, report to Forbisher by phone, and then render the decision. Lasater's mouth tightened as he repeated the phrases to himself, all so legal sounding, so proper and genteel.

He was certain they would not continue to pay the small army Lasater had brought to the coast to watch the old man and the kid. Maybe one operator, or two at the most. They might go for that. He would bring in someone who could get in close to Carmen, and stay close to him. A girl, he thought then, remembering Carmen's body as he had stripped in Taney's house. Even blue with cold and shaking almost uncontrollably, he had been good-looking, so young and unmarked it had been like a stab to Lasater. Hell, he thought, the kid was human, he must be almost as horny by now as Follett. If he could produce a girl who looked even younger, who looked hurt and vulnerable, who asked for nothing and apparently expected nothing, a runaway with a car of her own, a little money, Carmen would figure he could use her to get him to where he had to go. And where he had to go, Lasater had convinced himself, was home to Saul Werther.

✿

"Look," Lyle said softly. "She's pretending she hates it. That's stuff he just brought in yesterday." The female eagle was discarding seaweed vigorously; the male sat on a nearby tree watching her.

Carmen laughed. There was mist beyond the blind; it was too fine and too gentle to call rain, it was rather as if a cloud were being lowered very slowly to earth. Carmen had joined Lyle only minutes earlier; there were mist beads on his hair.

She had been afraid the morning might be awkward, but he had been up when she awakened, and when she had gone into the living room he had kissed her gently on the nose and had continued to make breakfast.

The female eagle reared up and half-opened her wings threateningly when the male approached the nest. He veered away and returned to his perch. "All in the genes," Carmen said in a hushed voice. "She's doing what nature programmed her to do."

Why this pretense of free will? Lyle wondered. She knew the female might pretend to become too disgusted with the nest, with the male; she might pretend to leave, might even go through some motions of starting a new nest. And in the end they would mate here and the fledglings would hatch out and learn to fly from that dead spur.

She found herself wondering about her own attempts to escape Lasater's plans, to free herself from the burden of betraying Saul, her own mock flight to freedom. From any distance at all, it now seemed as programmed as the eagles' behavior, at least her actions and Lasater's. Only Saul and Carmen had been unpredictable. Suddenly she felt that they had been from the start as alien to her as the eagles were, as strange and unknowable. And it had not mattered, she thought, and did not matter now.

"Why are you smiling like that?" Carmen asked.

"I was thinking that you and Saul came to Earth from a distant planet, that you're aliens. They won't find his body because he changed himself at the last moment into a great snowy owl and sailed away in the fog. He could come back as a butterfly, or an eagle, or whatever he chooses."

"I hope Lasater doesn't start believing that," Carmen said, laughing. "He might get the Marines out."

"Oh, no. He thinks that Saul was a Jewish student in Hitler's Germany and that he discovered something tremendous . . ."

She stopped at the change that came over Carmen's features. He leaned toward her and suddenly there was nothing boyish about him, nothing soft or tender.

"Tell me what he said."

"That last morning he stopped me as I was leaving, when I was ill . . ." She told him all of it. He did not move, but she felt more alone than she had felt in her life, as if a barrier that could never be scaled had come up between them.

"It's true, isn't it?" she whispered.

"Essentially. Some details are wrong. David's two younger brothers died young with Tay-Sachs Disease, and it nearly killed his mother. David and his older brother Daniel swore they would find a vaccine for it. But Daniel just couldn't make it in school. He dropped out, David went on. The professor was already into genetic research, and he allowed David to pursue his own studies because he saw that the two would come together at a later date. When the two lines did converge they realized they had something they had not counted on. The professor was terrified that the German government would get it, he was vehemently anti-fascist, and of course there was the danger that David would be picked up and forced to work in a government lab somewhere. So they kept it very secret, kept the papers on the farm the professor's family had owned for two centuries. David's brother knew what he was doing. When David was called up for registration, fingerprinting, the works, Daniel went. No one noticed. All those Jew boys looked alike after all. So David never was on file actually. David's parents and Daniel were hauled away one day. He found out — they always found out rather quickly — and he returned to the laboratory that night to destroy certain cultures. The Hitler Youth gang caught him there carrying a culture dish across the laboratory. The culture had to be maintained at blood heat or it perished. All he had planned to do was to put it in the refrigerator, because there was a danger of incriminating the professor if he actually destroyed anything in a way that could be proven. When the gang burst in on him, he dropped the dish. They threw him down on the mess and rubbed his face in it. Glass, culture, dirt . . . Then they took him outside the building and beat him to a pulp, and they dragged him back to the professor's house, and left him on the steps." He paused. "The rest of it is pretty much as Lasater suggested, except that the professor wasn't dead. They escaped together with the paperwork."

"If his fingerprints aren't on file, why did it matter if Lasater got a set? It would have ended there when they didn't match up."

"David's prints aren't in anyone's file," he said slowly, gazing at the eagles' nest. "But the professor's are. We simply couldn't be certain they wouldn't be available for comparison."

"You're saying that Saul is that professor. What about David?" Her voice sounded harsh and unfamiliar to her; she had to make a great effort to speak at all. She was caught up in a battle against disbelief and despair: Carmen was mad, as mad as Saul had been.

"You know I'm David," he said gently, as if only now becoming aware of her distress. "Don't look so scared. You really did know already. Watch the eagles this afternoon. I'm going down to the beach. See you for dinner." He leaned forward and kissed her lips lightly, and then was gone.

Dry-eyed, she stared at the eagles' nest. Crazy. Paranoid delusions. It had to be that. Gradually she found that she was accepting that he was mad and that she didn't care, it didn't matter. He had to be insane, or she had to accept something that had kept him twenty for all those years, that had stopped Saul at sixty-four and held him there. Something that had made them both immortal. And she could not accept immortality.

The female eagle returned with fresh seaweed to replace that which she had discarded; her token resistance was ended. The male followed with a long scrap of white material he had found somewhere. Together they rearranged the interior of their nest.

The sun came out and steam rose throughout the forest; the air was heavy with spring fragrances and fertile earth and unnamable sea smells.

And still Lyle sat staring, not taking pictures, trying to think of nothing at all. She would not think about tomorrow or the next day. She would do her job and if Carmen stayed, she would love him; when he left, she would miss him. Each day was its own beginning and ending. That was enough.

But she knew it was not enough. Carmen had pointed out the listening device on the underside of the table in her house. Lasater was still out there, listening, spying. Maybe he thought Carmen would lead him to the papers he so desperately wanted. Maybe Carmen could go to them. And, she thought suddenly, she was still here for Lasater to use. He had put her here, he thought of her as his instrument, his property to use when he got ready, to discard afterward, and so far she had not worked for him. The next time he would use her without trying to force cooperation, without her awareness or consent. When he started moving pieces again, he would turn to her and make use of her, she felt certain. Like the winter beach, she felt buffeted by forces she could not comprehend or thwart or dodge, and like the winter beach she felt a presentiment of endings, a loss of laughter in the sand.

o

August Ranier had come and gone and Lasater had been stripped of his army with a single word spoken very quietly. "Do I continue?" he had asked.

"No."

Ranier had handed Milton Follett and Lasater their termina-
tion checks — they had been hired as consultants — and he had
left in his dawn-gray Seville.

"Let's get out of here," Follett said.

"Aren't you willing to wait to pick up your bug in the house?"

"Yeah. I'm driving the camper up there. That little baby cost
me sixty-three bucks. Let's go."

"Milt, hold it a minue. Listen, I know that old man's alive and
well somewhere and the kid's going home to him one of these
days. I know it just like I know the back of my hand. Now that
Forbisher's out of it, we could double the price when we get the
stuff. You and I, Milt, just the two of us. A million, two million . . ."

Milt turned on the key and jerked the camper away from its
parking spot. He did not even bother to look at Lasater.

"Milt!" Lasater said softly. "Remember Karen?"

The camper shuddered to a stop and Milton Follett started
up from behind the driver's seat. His hands were clenched.

"Would you like another Karen?" Lasater asked, whispering
the words.

Follett was pale and his fists opened, the fingers spread wide,
then clenched again. "What do you mean?"

"I'll let you have Taney."

Follett sat down on the bunk bed. "Tell me," he said.

"What if the cops find her messed up, dead, her money, jewelry, car all gone? What do you suppose they'll think, especially
since the old guy disappeared so mysteriously such a short time
ago? They'll wonder why a good-looking kid like Carmen was
hanging around an old dame like her. But you can have her first,
as long as you want, whatever you want."

"Why?"

"I want that kid to run home to papa. He'll run when he finds
her. He'll know they'll be after him, he's not a dope. He'll run
and we'll be there. Who's the best team in the business, Milt?
Not Turk and that bunch of amateurs. You think there's any way

in the world the kid can shake us? I think he'll take us home
with him."

"When?"

"We need a car. One of us has to go up to Coos Bay and get
a car, and then we're all set."

"You," Follett said. "Too many people recognize me. You pay-
ing?"

"Yep. All the way. I pick up all expenses."

Milton Follett continued to study the idea. Lasater could tell
when he stopped considering it and let his mind drift to Lyle
Taney; a film of perspiration put a shine on his forehead.

Outside, the rain started again. It was like a drum beat on the
metal roof.

❖

Lasater was not even certain he had heard a knock on the door
until he opened it to see Lyle Taney there with rain running off
her. She was dressed in her down jacket and jeans, boots; her
hood was pulled low on her forehead. She looked like a commer-
cial for a hikers' club. He grinned at her and stepped aside to
allow her to enter. She pushed the hood back and stood dripping
on the rug.

"My God," Lasater said. "You look great! I've never seen you
look better!" Her lips were soft without any trace of chapping
now; her eyes were clear and bright, as green as sea water; her
face glowed, the windburn totally gone. She had swept Follett
with one quick glance, and now was looking at Lasater steadily.

"I think the lady wants to talk to me in private," he said to
Follett.

"Raining too hard," Follett said, not shifting his gaze from
Lyle Taney.

"What can I do?" Lasater asked helplessly. "He's bigger than
both of us. You want a cup of coffee? Let's get that jacket off,
dry out a little." He made no motion, but continued to study her,
the changes in her. Always before she had kept herself way back

where she thought she was safe, but now she was right out front, not hiding at all. Her eyes blazed at him, straight on. Then he thought, she was sleeping with the kid! He was fascinated and disgusted by the idea.

"Why are you still here?" she asked. "What else do you want? You drove Saul Werther to his death. What more can you do?"

"He isn't dead, Lyle. Let's not pretend. Werther, the kid, you, me, we're all in this together. We've come too far to try to kid each other."

"I'm warning you," she said, "if you don't get out of here and leave Carmen alone, and leave me alone, I'm going to call the sheriff's office and the nearest FBI office and anyone else I can think of and make a loud noise about an ex-agent and an ex-football player who keep threatening and harassing me."

"Baby, I'm on their side. National security takes precedence over local affairs every time."

"You're a liar, Mr. Lasater. I intend to make those calls if you don't get out of here and leave us alone."

Lasater laughed and reached past her to lean against the door. "Honey, what makes you think you'll be going anywhere to do any complaining?"

She did not move. "I asked everyone in the park which camper you and the football player were in," she said evenly. "Two tents, a motor home, two campers, and a trailer. Some of the boys thought it was neat to be camping out next to Milton Follett. They might even ask for an autograph."

Follett made a sound deep in his chest, a grunt, or a groan. Lyle continued to watch Lasater. "Just so there wouldn't be any excuse to delay," she said, "I brought you this." She took her hand from her pocket and tossed the bug onto the bunk bed.

"She's lying," Lasater said to Follett then. "She doesn't want cops asking that kid questions any more than we do."

"Let her go," Follett said. He had stopped watching her and now was looking at Lasater murderously. "She's been using my name around here. Let her go."

He was infuriated because the plum had been yanked out of reach, Lasater knew. There would be no way of getting him to cooperate again soon if she walked out the door. "Let's take off, go down the beach a ways and decide how to handle this."

"You'll have to move my car," Lyle said. "It's blocking you. One of you will have to go out and move it, and some of the people I talked to will be curious enough to be watching." Now she looked at Follett, as if she knew he was the one to work on. "I left a note for Carmen, telling him I was coming here. If he comes down, and he will, and finds all of us gone, he'll call the police fast."

"He put you up to this, didn't he?" Lasater demanded.

"You win because no one really opposes you," she said, and there was a new intensity in her voice. "I tried to close my eyes to what you were, what you were doing, trying to make me do. But I'm not afraid anymore, Mr. Lasater."

She was telling the truth; she was not afraid. He knew it, and he realized that Milton Follett knew it. For a moment the tableau held. Then, as if from a great distance, Lasater heard himself mutter, "Oh, my God!" and suddenly he knew what it was the old man had found. "It wasn't a cancer cure, was it?" he whispered. Wildly he turned from her toward Follett. "I know what it was! Look at her!"

Follett was moving the few steps that separated him from the other two. Savagely he jerked Lasater away from the door. "Get the hell out of here," he said to Lyle.

She left. She had not yet reached her car when the camper shook as if a heavy weight had been slammed against the side of it. She did not look back, but got inside her car and put the key in the ignition.

She started the car, left the camping area, climbed the steep gravel driveway.

He used it on me, she thought clearly, and it seemed as if the rain had come inside the car, was blurring her vision. She saw

Carmen on the road and stopped for him. He examined her face quickly.

"You could have been hurt!"

"But not killed?"

For a moment he was silent. She started the car again and drove south, toward the beach where they had walked with Saul.

"You could be killed," he said then. "But you could be hurt and hurt and hurt for a long time first."

She nodded. "Why did you do it to me?"

"We need help. We have to stay together in case one of us gets hurt. The other has to take care of him. No hospitals. No doctors. There are a few others, but they all have work to do, and some of us have to be able to travel here and there."

"To attend conferences, see who is getting too close."

"Yes. Lyle, who would you hand it over to? Our government? A church leader? Who should be given it? Eight hundred million Chinese? Two and a half billion Asians? Four and a half billion of all of us? A scientific elite? The military? Who, Lyle?"

She shook her head. "You're as bad as Lasater. Judge, jury, executioner."

"We know we are," he said very quietly.

She thought of the immensity of the sadness she had detected in Saul.

"Four people so far have followed that line of research," he said. "One of them was already spending his Nobel Prize money. I killed him and buried him." His voice was very flat now; she did not want to look at his face. "One of them died following the injection. Two of them are back at work, helping us keep it undiscovered."

They had reached the wide beach. Today the water was almost black under the low clouds and pounding rain. It was low tide, the waves were feeble. Lyle parked and they sat staring out at the endless sea. She thought of the story of the fisherman and his three wishes. This was her third trip to this winter beach. I wish . . . I wish . . . There was nothing to follow the words.

Golden wings, she thought. She could wish for golden wings
Why me? she had wanted to demand of Lasater. Why me?

"I don't want it," she said. "I didn't ask for it. You didn't ask
me if I agreed."

"I know. If you had wanted it, we wouldn't have chosen you."

"You can't make that decision for the rest of humanity. No
one can make such a decision for everyone."

"I know. We can't, but we have to, because if we don't someone else will. Who? You know the fears about an escaped genetic
experiment? If a mutated virus got loose, there wouldn't be any
way to stop it. There wouldn't be any way to stop this either.
We're carriers. You're a carrier now. It's in the blood, in every
cell of your body. A transfusion, sexual contact, that's all it takes.
Think of the malnutrition here now with our four-and-a-half-
billion population, and then start multiplying it endlessly. Parents, children, their children, all living forever until their metab-
olism stops because there's no food for them. They would hurt
for an awfully long time before that happened, Lyle, and they
would hurt very bad."

She thought of the look on Follett's face back in the camper.
She had recognized that look: cruelly possessive, hungry. Sexual
contact. And the Folletts and the Lasaters would be the ones to
get it. The others might all die, but not the Folletts and Lasaters
of the world. Lasater knew, but it did not matter. No one believed him, and soon he would grow old, die. She looked at the
sea, wishing for a sign, for a rainbow, a streak of gold at the
horizon, anything to take the decision away from her. There was
only the gray water rising and falling in slow swells, and the
steady rain.

"I don't know any science," she said finally. "What could I
possibly do?"

"First, write your eagle book. We'll stay here and go on just
as we've been doing. You'll become a rich reclusive woman.
You'll travel around the world, taking pictures, talking to people.
We need others, Lyle. You'll have to help me find the right ones,
recruit them, sometimes bury them."

Reclusive, she thought. Of course. Talk with many others, friends of none of them. No one could bear watching children age and die, watching friends suffer, grow old, die . . . "Others to do what?" she asked dully.

"At first we thought no one could ever have it, no one at all. It doesn't change you, you know. You don't gain wisdom, or courage, or anything else. You just keep living, exactly the way you are. But more recently we decided that if the world could change, if enough people could change . . . I don't know if it will work. Sometimes I know it can't. But we have to try. A few people here and there, people like you who don't want power or glory, who don't want to drive others to do their bidding. Unwilling recruits every one, the most reluctant elite the world has ever seen."

It was starting to get dark now; the clouds pressed closer against the ocean as if waiting for darkness to hide their possession of it. Lyle turned on the key. "We should get back before the fog comes in." She did not engage the gears yet, but sat with the motor idling. "Why are you here, at this place?"

There was a long pause before he answered. "Sometimes we have to go somewhere far away from people, where there are things that haven't been changed much, where no one talks to us very much. There are a few mountains, places in the desert, upper Maine, here. We need a place where we can just live without having to think for a while."

Lyle nodded. When the pain gets too great to bear, you try to escape, she thought: the bottle, pills, sex; and when none of them gives more than a momentary surcease, you go to the woods, or to the winter beach.

"Saul is well then. It was a trick to get him out of here."

"Yes. I had to wait to make certain you were with us. If your fever had gone too high, you might have killed off the genetic material we gave you. We couldn't know right away. Tomorrow I'll send a message to the *Times* personal column to let him know you're okay."

Now she shifted gears and started to back up. "I know what

the message should say. 'Blue float has come ashore safely.' "

"Welcome home," Carmen said in his most gentle voice.

She thought of the eagles, beyond good and evil, the winter beach entering a transition now, going into spring, and then summer when the ocean would bring back the scrubbed sand, make amends. All ordered, necessary, unavoidable. She started the drive home.

JULIAN

THE YEAR Julian was twelve he received a telescope for Christmas. A telescope in a great city is a particularly useless gift, he had learned. There had been three nights since the first of the year, and this was May, when he had been able to see the sky well enough to use it, and what little he had seen he might have observed just as easily with his own eyes. The moon was good, but he quickly became bored with looking at dark and light patches that could have been craters, or clouds, or smudges on his lens. What the telescope was good for was to observe the city.

The city climbed a hill in the section where Julian lived. His apartment building was high enough for him to be able to look out over the roofs of many buildings all the way to the river and up the hillside across it. He could see small boats, fishing boats, tugs laboring with barges, people on the bank walking, kissing, throwing stuff into the water.

In March a demolition crew had started to raze a tall gray office building a block from Julian's window. All spring Julian had been plagued with a series of minor complaints that had kept him out of school — sore throats, stomachaches, headaches. He had watched the destruction of the building from start to finish. Now it was no more than a pile of trash. On this day Julian had got up with a stomachache, and as soon as his parents had gone to work, and his younger sister had left for school, he had got out his telescope to watch the workmen with their bull-dozers and cranes clean up the mess they had made.

He swept the scene slowly, pausing to watch two men chug-a-lug from a thermos, moved on to where a grader was pushing the trash into a heap of different proportions. He raised the tele-scope to see what had been revealed by the removal of the last' wall, and there were tops of buildings, more windows to inves-tigate, the river, and on a hill across the river, revealed to him for the first time, was a motel. It was a grand location, with a view of the river below it and the city sprawling upward. He found the motel swimming pool with no difficulty; there were two children playing in it, and a woman nearby in a canvas chair. A man was cutting grass. A dog ran after him opening its mouth, probably barking. The man stopped to pick up a stone and throw it at the dog. There were seven cars in the parking area. Julian began to examine the building itself.

There were three black women with cleaning carts, and a man with a tool box who went into one of the rooms. He watched a maid run her vacuum cleaner in four passes and then leave a room. There were two doors with Do Not Disturb signs. He be-gan to go down the row of second-floor rooms. The third one had one side of the drapes opened in an irregular way, as if the fabric had caught on a chair or something and had remained like that, unnoticed by the occupant. Working carefully Julian fo-cused on the opening, then brought the room into sharp view. He could see little of it, the foot of the bed, a space, part of a dresser, the alcove where the bath was. As he studied it, a naked woman appeared. She came from the side of the bed, stopped at the dresser.

She was doing something in front of the mirror, her hands out of sight, only her back profile visible, from her head down to her calves. He couldn't see the floor. She was skinny, but his heart was pumping hard anyway, because a skinny naked lady was better than no naked lady at all. He wanted her to turn around and face him. Again and again he wiped his hands on his jeans, although his mouth was dry; his eyes were burning from not blinking. He had seen his sister, of course, but she was only eight and that was different. He had seen pictures of naked ladies, and that was different too. This was the real thing, this counted. He was afraid to touch the telescope now, for fear he would move it, lose her, and have trouble finding her again. Her hair was long and brown, lank, it looked oily; there was a hollow place on the side of her hip. She was almost as flat as he was. She moved back a step and he caught his breath as her breast in profile came into his range. It was like a small bag, not the high, nipple-pointed breast of the ladies in the magazines. She was old, he decided, and again, it was better to see an old naked lady than no naked lady at all. Now she turned and walked away from him, and he wiped his hands as he stared at the way her ass moved when she walked.

He leaned back weakly and became aware of his heart pounding, and the clamminess of his hands, and the dryness of his mouth. Also he had an erection, and he couldn't do anything about it, because what if there was someone out there in one of those rooms with a telescope watching his every movement?

He looked at the room, still empty, and wondered how long she would be in there, wondered if she was on the john or in the shower, wondered if she would reappear with a towel around her, or a robe on. The pounding in his chest and the pounding in his groin became one painful rhythmic beat. Maybe she had an accident, fell in the shower, was drowning. His head began to ache, and his eyes were tearing. When he felt he could stand it no longer, she stepped into view once more, dripping, her hair streaming water. She had hair on her lower belly, glistening wet, and little rivulets of water running down her smooth rounded stomach; her breasts were pink and . . .

Suddenly he ejaculated and involuntarily knocked the telescope askew. When he could train it on the motel window again, she was gone. Exhausted, he threw himself down on his bed, face down in the pillow, and he fell asleep.

He woke up in a paroxysm of terror, fighting the sheet, battling his pillow, gasping for air. He had been dreaming, had a nightmare, but there was no memory of it. He went to the bathroom and washed his face, then got on clean clothes — his others were sweat-soaked and smelled foul — and lay down again, this time with a comic book. He didn't read it, or even track the pictures. He dozed, woke with a jerk of fear, and got up, afraid of another nightmare. He noticed his telescope at the window and put it away without a glance outside. It was only twelve, but he felt that the day already had been endlessly long, as if he had a fever that was distorting his perceptions of time.

His mother called during her lunch hour.

"What are you doing?"

"Nothing. Reading comics."

"How do you feel?"

"Okay."

"Julian, is your stomach still hurting?" There was a new note of anxiety in her voice.

He made an effort to sound natural, but even to him his voice sounded strange, toneless. "I feel okay now, Mom."

After a silence while she considered, she said, "I'm calling Esther Manning to drop by. Let her in when she rings. And just lie around and take it easy."

"I don't need anyone to look at me, Mom. I'm okay now."

"Yes, I expect you are, but it won't hurt. Bye, honey. See you later."

Mrs. Manning was a tall heavy woman, not fat, but broad and big-boned. She could tell fortunes with playing cards, and knew many strange and esoteric things, like when and where to go out and find wild mushrooms, and if it was going to snow, and when to go out to hear migrating geese. One time when Julian had stayed home from school, she had dropped in, and when his mother had mentioned his complaint, she had turned to Julian and winked quite openly.

She arrived an hour after his mother's call.

"Ah, Julian, another headache? A sore throat? A singularly bad case of boredom?" She smiled widely and went ahead of him into the apartment. At the entrance he had been in shadows, but now in the light from a broad tall window, she paused to examine his face, and her manner changed. "Back into bed, my boy, and I'll read you a story."

He protested that he did not want to go to bed, that he did not want her or anyone to read to him now, because he was too old, that he wanted to finish his model plane, but in the end he lay down and listened to her begin "The Hound of the Baskervilles."

She read with expression that often was comical, sometimes chilling. Julian began to feel better, less dopey and strange, more relaxed. After half an hour she stopped to make tea, and he tagged along to the kitchen with her, talking about the moors. "It's just like that in real life," she was saying, washing her hands at the sink. She turned to find a towel, and he stared at her wet hands, and for a moment felt the room spin sickeningly. She took a step toward him, reaching for him with her wet hands, and he fainted.

❖

For the next week Julian was hustled from doctor to doctor, to laboratories where they took blood samples and x-rays of his head and made other tests. At the end of the time his doctor said they had found nothing.

"We want to talk to you," his father said that night, and Julian felt crushed by a sudden depression.

His father waited for him to sit down, his mother was already in her chair. "Julian, you have missed twelve days of school this spring. You say you're sick but no one can find any germs, or anything else they can point to. What have you to say about that?"

Julian shifted uncomfortably and stared at the beige carpeting. It was dirty under his feet, not bad, but grayer than the rest of the room.

"Julian! Look at me! If you are sick we want you to get well. If you aren't sick, we want to know why you pretend you are. Are you just too bored with school to sit through it every day? If that's it, for heaven's sake, say so. We can understand that."

Julian shrugged. When he said his head ached, it usually did; and if he stayed home with a stomachache, it really hurt for a while.

"Julian." His mother spoke now for the first time. "Is something else bothering you? Something on your mind? Something that puzzled you or frightened you?"

He stared at her uncomprehendingly, then shook his head.

"Honey, sometimes it isn't easy to tell parents if things are really bothering you. Sometimes it's much easier to tell someone new, someone who has studied kids, a child psychologist, someone like that. Is there anything you'd like to talk over with someone like that?"

Again he shook his head. "I guess I just don't like school too much. It's boring," he mumbled.

He could sense his father's relief. His mother leaned back in her chair and her face smoothed out again, and he knew he had said the right thing.

That night he had another nightmare, the third that week. He did not call anyone, or make any noise, and when he got up he did not turn on any lights for fear his mother would come to see what was wrong. He sat in a straight chair in his dark bedroom, shivering and wide-eyed. There was no memory of what the nightmare had been about. Only when he began to fall asleep in the chair, sitting upright, did he go back to bed.

*

He got by in high school, and his first years of college. He knew he was a constant source of disappointment to his parents, and he was a constant source of unhappiness to himself because of his own behavior that he realized was highly neurotic. He had irrational dislikes that set him apart from others. He would not shower or bathe. He washed all over, using as little water as possible. He refused to go swimming, or to participate in any water sport at all. If it rained he carried an umbrella and wore gloves, no matter what month or what the temperature was. He knew he was considered a prude because he did not like girlie magazines or nudie shows. People probably thought he was a latent homosexual because he avoided girls altogether. He knew he was afraid of them, and that this fear was as senseless as the others on the long list that made life hellish for him.

One day his psychology class discussed childhood fears. There were the usual things — menacing shadows of tree limbs on the bedroom floor; the creakings of houses that went unnoticed by daylight and became magnified after dark; a mother's illness and absence with its accompanying feeling of abandonment. Nothing very different from those discussed by the professor had been revealed. It was both reassuring and disturbing to find such predictable patterns. Then Kim spoke up.

"I came out of a deep sleep with fires blazing all around me and I thought I was in hell, that I had died and gone to hell. I had a bunch of nightmares after that, and to this day I have a pretty irrational fear of fire. What had happened was that our electricity had gone off during the night, and it was in the middle of winter, so my mother had taken me out to the living room to sleep in front of the fireplace. And I woke up."

Other more specific, more personal experiences came out then. One remembered early fears related to brakes squealing and metal clashing — a carryover from being in an accident when she was two. Another recalled awakening to find himself in a bathroom filled with steam, and the fear of being scalded in the tub of hot water — his mother's desperate attempt to relieve his croup as a baby had been to open his congested bronchial passages with steam.

Julian listened and tried to remember something from his own past that was similar. There had been a mild episode when he had been left alone at night once and the apartment had been filled with noises, but he knew that was not in the same category as the fears being discussed now. He had had nightmares off and on for years, but he had decided they were induced by a difficult passage over the threshold of puberty. He never had recalled any content of the nightmares anyway.

"How about your fear of water, Julian?" Rachel asked gently.

He hated her for bringing that up. It wasn't the same kind of thing, he felt certain. "I almost drowned once," he said shortly, harshly. There were some nods, and even a glimmer of sympathy here and there. Someone else began to talk.

Later he walked back to his dorm wondering why he had lied, why he had felt that rush of hatred for Rachel, the only girl on campus whom he thought he might be able to talk to, or ask out. Quickly there came the rationalization that he felt safe fantasizing about her because she was so unattainable.

Rachel caught up with him. "I'm sorry I brought that up," she said, putting her hand on his arm. "That was bitchy. I thought it might help you to talk about it while others were talking about the same kinds of things."

She was pretty, one of the best students on campus, and one of the most popular. He was amazed that she was aware of him enough to know he feared water. Kim must have told her. He felt certain her hand on his arm was an apology even more than her words. Brusquely he shook her off and strode ahead faster.

"It's all right. Forget it," he said, and turned in toward the nearest building.

The following year he was forced to take a health class to fulfill his requirements, and he sat through it glumly, bored, sometimes doing homework for other more demanding classes, sometimes simply brooding over his present life, his future, his past. All seemed equally hopeless. The teaching assistant was talking about various organs of the body, their relative size and importance.

"The largest organ of all, of course, is the skin. And probably it's the most complex. It's flexible, we can bend our joints and it gives, we can gain or lose weight. It has a one-way permeability. Perspiration can get out, but from the other direction it is totally waterproof . . ."

Julian clutched the desk top while the room spun. He saw the naked woman walking toward him, wet all over. He closed his eyes hard and put his head down on the desk and waited for the nausea and dizziness to pass; when he felt able, he got up and left the room.

Blindly he walked, then sat down, and again put his head down, his eyes closed.

His head ached, his eyes teared, and he stared through the eyepiece of the telescope fixedly, holding his breath until suddenly there she was. She was dripping wet, her hair was streaming water. He stared at the glistening pubic hair, and the little rivulets that ran down her smooth rounded belly. Her breasts were full and high, pink, with beads of water, one little stream running crazily down one side, vanishing in the crease below her breast. He looked at her face, glowing, beautiful, and her hair fluffing out, alive and soft, just a touch of wave in it, feathery about her face.

He had come then and never saw her again.

She had gone into the shower an old withered woman and had come out a beautiful girl gleaming with water on her body, in her hair. She had not dried herself. There had been no towel at all.

"She absorbed it!" he whispered. "She absorbed all the water!"

That was what his twelve-year-old self had rejected knowing. He had recognized it as impossible, as something grotesque and alien and too frightening to think about, and had buried it as deeply as he could.

The knowledge had lain in his mind like a snake in a bag, writhing, twisting, shooting out its venom now and then to poison his life, to bring him nightmares and make him afraid of girls and water and wet hands and rain on hair and a million other things that had separated him from everyone else.

He went over it again and again, recalling more details each time. There had been drops of water in her eyebrows, and he had seen them vanish, and beads of water on her upper lip . . . She had been smiling slightly, as if she felt extraordinarily good . . .

"Julian? Are you sleeping?"

He started at the voice close to his face and opened his eyes to see Rachel kneeling on the grass in front of him. Behind her there were two men from his health class, Kim and Robert.

"Are you okay?" Rachel moved back and held out her hand. "It's raining, you're getting awfully wet."

He stared at her hand for a long time, then looked at her face, back at her hand. Water was running off her finger, running along her wrist. He looked at her hair, cut so short that it was like a shiny black cap on her head; water ran down it onto her face, collected on her eyelashes. She blinked it away, watching him, waiting.

Suddenly Julian jumped up and pulled her to her feet also, grabbed her and swung her around and around, shouting, "It's all right! It's all right now!"

Rachel was laughing with him, gasping for breath, and Kim and Robert stood, uncomfortable and self-conscious, until Robert mumbled something about a term paper and they hurried off together with an air of relief.

"Tell me about it," Rachel demanded. "Let's walk in the rain, and you tell me what happened."

They walked, but Julian didn't want to talk yet. He wanted to watch the rain hitting grass, watch it roll off leaves and darken tree trunks, and bejewel flowers. He watched it collect in his palm, overflow, and run down like a miniature waterfall.

Two hours later they ended up in Rachel's apartment, which she shared with two other girls. "Let me change and get a raincoat and then we'll go let you change and then find someplace to talk," she said, toweling her head.

"How long would it take your hair to dry if you didn't do anything?" Julian asked, watching.

"In this weather? An hour, hour and a half. Why?"

"How long for hair down to your shoulders?"

"Three hours, unless you are out in the sun, or have a fan on it, or the wind. What are you driving at?"

And Julian told her, not all of it, but most. He finished saying, "I got so scared, or excited, that I knocked the telescope aside and by the time I got it focused again she was out of sight. I went to bed and fell asleep and had a nightmare that woke me up, and when I was really awake again, I had forgotten all about it, every bit of it, even using the telescope to snoop with. I never used it again for anything."

Rachel had become still as he talked, her eyes open wide, very dark blue, and, he thought, very disbelieving. Suddenly she shivered. "I'm freezing. Wait a minute while I change."

She hurried away and in a few moments came back in dry jeans and a sweater, carrying an umbrella. Her hair was still damp enough to cling to her head.

They didn't talk on the way to Julian's dorm, and she waited in the lounge while he went up and got dry clothes on, and then they went to The Caves, where they found a booth in the rear of the dark room well away from the pinball machines and the Foos Ball games and the tiny dance floor. Neither spoke until their pitcher of beer and bowl of peanuts had been delivered.

"It's too much, isn't it?" Julian said then. "You don't believe me."

She shook her head. "It isn't that I think you're lying or anything like that. But you could remember wrong."

He reached across the table and felt her hair, still slightly damp. "Her hair became absolutely dry within a minute or two, no more than that. She was dry all over within a minute."

"There could have been a fan on her, or maybe she dried her hair before she came out, or she wore a shower cap."

He shook his head.

"Julian, it has to be something like that, anything else is impossible. People can't simply dry off like that. You were a little kid. You could remember it wrong."

Again he shook his head. "Let's drop it. Hungry? I'm starved."

"Julian, wait . . ." But he had waved to the waitress, and she became silent, watching him.

"It's all right," Julian said. "Don't let it bug you. Okay?"

"Sure."

They ordered. Julian asked her about her summer plans and hardly listened to her answer, which seemed involved and complicated. He had to go back to Cincinnati, he knew, had to check out the people who had been there. When? He didn't know the date, just that it had been late in the school season, near the end of his sixth grade. There had been seven cars parked there, he remembered clearly, and recalled the man cutting grass, the dog running, children playing in the pool.

"Julian? Please, let's just eat and get out of here."

Rachel's voice was strained, and he realized that the waitress had brought their orders.

"Sorry," he said. Rachel looked at her soup. He did not know anything else to say. What he would have given last year to be sitting across the table from her, talking with her like this, he thought, and then, not only last year, last month even. Or yesterday. It never occurred to him to wonder why she was with him, why she was bothering. He felt only impatience. He wanted to eat and go back to his room and call his father for money. There had to be a decent reason, not just a little jaunt to Cincinnati. Special study course? Research project? He would think of something. He looked up to find Rachel studying him again.

"Will you do me a favor?" she asked quietly. "Will you talk to Dr. Yates?"

He shook his head. "No reason now," he said, smiling. "Yesterday there was, but not now."

"You know I switched my major from math to psychology. I

don't pretend to know much yet, but I think what you're doing is dangerous, more than repressing a memory even."

"Your quiche is getting cold," he said. "I'm okay. Just don't do the Jewish mother bit."

Carefully she put down her fork, gathered her purse and umbrella, and stood up. "I have to run, Julian. See you around."

He watched her go, then finished his French Dip sandwich, ate her quiche, which she had hardly touched, and went to his dorm to call home.

✲

The next morning, Saturday, he flew to Cincinnati, and went straight to the motel, which had been changed drastically by the addition of two new wings, and a much larger pool, and tennis courts. It was now owned by a chain, and the manager was unhelpful.

"I don't know anything about it back then," she said. She was in her forties, with hard brown eyes and polished white hair that looked like plaster. "The company bought it two years ago and remodeled, rebuilt, and I've been here almost the whole time. Before that I don't know."

He counted his money and knew he could not afford to hang around until the courthouse opened on Monday in order to check the record of sales of the motel. On the flight back he brooded about his naiveté in thinking that just like that he could find out anything. He needed time, all summer if necessary. He would find that woman who was not a woman, was not human at all. He would find her, or it.

✲

In Cincinnati he washed dishes and slept in a dormitory at the YMCA, and he learned that the motel had changed hands four times in the past ten years. The last owner lived in Atlanta.

In Atlanta the previous owner sent him to San Antonio where he was told about a tornado that had wrecked the business eight years ago and killed Mrs. Gunn, the wife of the owner then. Mr. Gunn had gone to a farm on the Ohio, near Waterton.

✻

"You were supposed to turn over the books when you sold the business," Julian said. "But you didn't. Where are your books, Mr. Gunn?"

The old man blinked lazily and shrugged. "Damned if I know. So water-soaked wasn't no reason to turn 'em over to no one. Roof got torn off, you know. Whole damn roof, whoosh right off."

"You must have them somewhere," Julian said desperately, glancing about the trailer where Timothy Gunn lived, on the rear of his son's property.

"Might be here somewheres," the old man agreed. "Wouldn't pay me to stir around, get excited and hot hunting for 'em."

"I'll buy them," Julian said quickly. "Ten dollars."

The old man smiled and shook his head.

"Twenty. It's all I have, Mr. Gunn. Please. I'm trying to find my mother. For ten years I thought she was dead until this summer when I learned my father had driven her away, and she went to your motel. I have to find her. She might be sick, need help." Julian blinked back tears of frustration at this senile old man and his complacent grin.

"Calm down, son. Just take it easy. Reckon them books ain't going to do me a hell of a lot of good, now are they? Ten dollars, you say?" He went to the bed and pulled out a storage drawer, drew out the books.

"I just need that one, for May," Julian said quickly.

"All or nothing," the old man said, as if driving a hard bargain. "Just keep cluttering up the place with all that old junk. All or nothing."

Julian almost snatched the books away from him, and yanked the right one to the top of the stack. There were watermarks on the cover, but inside the ink was legible. He flipped pages and found May. There it was, it had to be! May 29, 30, 31. Stella Johnson. Stella! He almost laughed.

"Reckon you found what you're looking for," the old man said genially. He sat down again, dismissing Julian. "Good luck, son. Ten years is a hell of a long time to be without someone you care anything for."

❀

"Hey, that's a pretty heavy foot you got there, kid." The man in the passenger seat stirred and sat upright yawning. Julian was driving his car, somewhere between Phoenix and Los Angeles.

"Sorry," Julian said. He slowed down to sixty. "She sure wants to run, doesn't she? Great car."

The man nodded and started talking cars. This was Julian's third ride since leaving Ohio, and this would take him home. Stella Johnson had given an address in Los Angeles, had auto tags from California. His parents had moved to Los Angeles three years ago; he could make that his base of operations, search records again — he was getting good at that — and he would find her.

"You in training for the Indy or something?" the man beside him growled. "Stop the car. I'd better drive awhile."

Julian had nudged it up to ninety again.

❀

At the address Stella Johnson had given there was a gas station that had gone out of business so long ago that it was boarded up with wood turned ashen with age; twelve-foot trees were growing from the cracks in the broken concrete, and many years' accumulation of dumped trash behind it made a hill as high as its roof. He was not surprised. The license number had been bogus also.

For three days he had scurried around town looking up women named Johnson, then he had given it up. There was no reason to believe her name was less phony than any other information she had given.

Julian sat by the pool in his parents' back yard, and although he heard his mother approach, he did not look up. He waited to see if she had found yet another way to ask the two questions they besieged him with every day: What is the matter? and What are your plans?

"Julian? You okay?"

"Sure, Mother."

They had been so happy to learn that he had lost his phobia about water. For a week his parents had been practically manic in their relief, only to have new apprehensions creep in that made them exchange worried glances, or, worse, avoid looking directly at each other when he was around. He could imagine their whispered conversations about him when they thought he was sleeping. *Is he crazy, I mean really crazy this time?* Or, *you have to try to get him to see a doctor. He's your son.* Strange how he was always someone else's son if there was trouble, and "my son" when either of them wanted to brag a little.

"Julian, you know how worried we are about you. You don't say anything. You sit here for hours brooding. You have letters you haven't even bothered to open. You're in trouble of some kind, aren't you? That girl who keeps writing? Rachel? Money? A bad drug experience? You see, I can't even narrow it down to a possible cause. Julian, please let us help you. If you need professional advice of any kind..."

That was it, professional advice. From the start he had thought that he alone had caught a glimpse of one of them, but maybe that was wrong. Others might have seen them, might have reported them. Maybe there was a growing dossier on them, with every tidbit welcomed.

That afternoon he told Sergeant Manuel Vargas what he had seen ten years earlier. The sergeant nodded and wrote it all down.

"Not much to go on, now is there?" he asked. "We'll put the license number through a routine check, but ten years is a long time, kid."

Julian knew the sergeant would do nothing. Another nut report, that was how he thought of it. He had not asked to see the motel registration book, or anything else, but simply had made notes while Julian talked and then soothed him enough to get rid of him.

At the FBI office he talked to a young man named Walter Montgomery who wore a sports shirt and no tie, which surprised Julian. He thought they always wore three-piece suits.

"Julian," the agent said soberly, "I think you should talk to a psychiatrist. You were twelve, right? She excited you sexually and you even had an orgasm. In your mind she became young and beautiful and desirable. You couldn't face the knowledge that an old woman might have excited you, so you altered her to suit your preconceived idea of what a beautiful girl should look like. She sounds pretty much like a centerfold cutie to me. The illusion you created, your excitement, and your guilt over spying all combined to give you a nightmare that's still with you. I can't help you, but a psychiatrist is trained to deal with this kind of thing. There's nothing shameful about it, or really very complex, it seems to me. It's a natural development."

"And her address, the phony license plate?"

"So she was hiding from someone or something. People do it all the time. Ran away from her old man, didn't want him to track her down. Must be a thousand reasons why people do a vanishing act. And ninety-nine point ninety-nine percent of the time it's harmless."

*

"Julian, you saved all my letters! And I thought you never even opened them!" Rachel sat on the floor emptying a box that he had packed hastily when he had moved out of the dorm to this apartment that they shared. "I wonder what your parents think of me. A pursuing bitch, I guess."

"Ha! You should have heard my mother's voice when I mentioned, rather obliquely I thought, that I might like to have my own apartment this year. She nearly shrieked with joy. Her very next words were, 'How's that nice girl, Rachel?'" He grinned at her, then went back to the term paper he was working on.

His grades had picked up this year, and it seemed likely he would make straight A's, something he had never done in his life. He thought the shock might kill off both parents. For the first time since his early childhood his parents felt good about him, and he was at peace with himself. He looked up a moment later; a light rain was falling, and for a second he had a feeling or fear, but it passed so quickly that it might not have existed at all. Sometimes he remembered like that, a passing rush of adrenalin, a fleeting memory. Finally he had accepted the FBI agent's theory that his prepubescent self had played a trick on him, accepted it out of desperation, he knew, but still there had been nothing else he could have done.

"What are you doing with all these?" Rachel asked. She had found the stack of motel registration books.

"The old man made me buy them all, or none. So there they are."

"Instincts of a pack rat," she muttered, and began leafing through one of the books.

He added a few lines to his paper, read a paragraph, made a note to consult his textbook, and started to write again.

"You were thirteen, not twelve," Rachel said. "It was ten years ago."

"Twelve," he said, not looking up, keeping his place in the book with one finger while he wrote. "I was in the sixth grade."

"Not according to this," she said firmly.

Irritably he closed his book with his pencil in it, and went to take the registration book from her. There were eight of them altogether, all the years Mr. and Mrs. Gunn had owned the motel. Rachel was right, Stella Johnson had registered ten years before. He snatched up another book and opened it to May — there she was again. And again.

Two books had been flooded until little in them was legible, but the other six all showed that year after year Stella Johnson had spent the last three days of May in that motel.

The rush of adrenalin was like a surf increasing before a

storm. He stared at the entries, compared the signatures, the license numbers, the addresses, and in his mind he saw the smiling young woman, hair fluffing out, skin glowing with health.

"Julian!"

Rachel's voice was almost too distant to be audible; he knew she was at his side, her hand shaking his arm, but when he turned toward her, that other face was still there. He blinked and shook his head, and although the vision faded, the surf pounded, pounded.

"Julian, are you all right? I thought you were going to pass out or something. Look, it's a coincidence. You just happened to pick a woman who has business in Cincinnati every year. Maybe she has a parent in a home there. Maybe she's having a lifelong affair with someone whom she meets each spring. Maybe she stays in the motel several different times each year. Have you looked through the other months?"

He had not thought of it, but now he went through them all. She was there only in May.

"Whatever the reason," Rachel said, "no doubt it is entirely harmless and innocent. None of your business. You have to let it drop, Julian. You're going to graduate in two weeks. You have finals and term papers to finish. You have to let it drop."

She had faded out again as she spoke. Stella Johnson would be there this May, he realized. He would find her.

He got through the rest of his term with no clear memory of what he did. His grades, steadily high all year, plummeted, and one professor called him for a conference and suggested a medical check-up. Mononucleosis, he suggested, could be the reason for the sudden lassitude.

Rachel insisted on going to Cincinnati with him. They drove her VW and arrived on the twenty-eighth. "Now what?" Rachel asked despondently, surveying the room. Everything in it was either brown or gold, even a picture on the wall. They were on the first floor, steps from the swimming pool area, and squeals and shouts were very audible.

"You take a swim. I want to look around. I'll meet you at the pool in half an hour."

She shook her head. "I'll come with you. The pool is solid kids, in case you didn't notice."

He shrugged, and together they strolled back to the lobby, a large open room with half a dozen vinyl-covered chairs, some dim lamps, a tiny newsstand to one side, doorways into two halls, and an arch that led to the elevators.

Julian nodded. It would be simple to sit here and watch anyone checking in. They looked over the dining room and the coffee shop, and he checked entrances and exits. There was no way Stella Johnson could avoid going through the main lobby.

That night he told Rachel that he was planning to stay in the lobby the following day until Stella Johnson appeared and he found out her room number.

"And what am I supposed to do while you do your private-eye act?"

"Whatever you want. I don't care."

"I know you don't care! You don't care about anything now, do you? You're too busy chasing a childhood illusion!"

"I didn't ask you to come, remember. I didn't even want you to come!"

"Well, maybe I won't stay very long! This is crazy! You know this is crazy, don't you?"

Furiously he stalked out of the room and sat by the pool glowering at the children in the water. Crazy, it kept coming back to that. In a little while Rachel came and sat by him.

"I'm sorry," she said in a low voice. "I'll go downtown tomorrow and do a little shopping, buy a couple of books. If she doesn't come tomorrow, can we go home? Will that satisfy you?"

He nodded. She would come.

*

Late in the afternoon the next day the manager of the motel asked him why he was loitering in the lobby. It was the same

woman he had talked to the year before, but obviously she
did not remember him at all. He mumbled something about his
wife visiting her family, and small rooms giving him claustro-
phobia, but after that he knew the desk clerk was keeping an
eye on him.

Stella Johnson showed up at four-thirty. He recognized her
instantly. She wore sunglasses that covered nearly half her face,
and her hair was hidden by a scarf, but he felt certain enough
to approach the desk and start examining the tourist brochures
as she registered. About mid to late thirties, he estimated, no-
ticing the small lines about her mouth, and the way her hand
was already starting to look bony. He stayed close enough to
hear her room number when the clerk gave her a key, and then
wandered to the window, ostentatiously checked his watch, and
left. She was on the second floor, number twenty-two.

"What are you going to do now?" Rachel asked. She was
subdued and looked frightened.

"Sometime before she has a chance to leave, I'm going to
grab her and keep her for a day or two and then put her in a
shower. You'll see. And then I'm going to deliver her to the
FBI."

Rachel paled. "That's kidnaping! You can't do that! Julian,
please, just call the police and tell them; let them take care of
it now."

"I went through that once," he said brusquely. "Not again."
He thought, then said, "I'll follow her tomorrow, see where she
goes. There might be a lot of them, maybe they meet here every
year."

The upper rooms all had two entrance doors, one from the
balcony that led down to the pool area, and an inside door
to the hallway and elevators inside. Julian missed Stella Johnson
when she left the motel. At ten-thirty he put in a call to her
room and no one answered the telephone. At eleven he watched
the cleaning woman enter and he knew he had lost her.

"I don't want to hang around here all day," Rachel said. "She won't be back until God knows when. Do you plan to sit and watch her door all day long?"

"Let's go to the zoo," Julian said. "Spend the afternoon there, have a nice dinner, see a movie if you want. Okay?"

She was right, Stella Johnson probably would be out all day, and on the next day, before eleven, she would check out and vanish again. On the way to the zoo he stopped at a supermarket and bought canned fruit, tuna fish, peanut butter and bread, lemonade mix, whatever else he could think of to last a few days. He knew where he could take Stella Johnson — to a duck-hunting camp his father had used regularly. No one would be there this time of year. Rachel watched him with large frightened eyes, but she said nothing.

All afternoon they wandered about the zoo. It was very hot, and the park was crowded. Gradually he worked his way toward a concession stand he remembered from his childhood, and was relieved to see that it still had the same assortment of junk for sale.

"Look," he said, pointing to a board covered with tin badges. "I had collection of them when I was a kid. Let's get one."

Rachel dragged back. She had been watchful and wary all afternoon, but had not questioned him, had not brought up Stella Johnson once. "I have a headache," she said now, tugging on his arm. "Let's go back and get some rest."

"In a minute." He made his way through the kids who pressed in on the stand. "One of those," he said, pointing to a Junior Detective Badge. Away from the crowd he carefully pinned it to the inside of his wallet while Rachel watched, tight-lipped.

She wanted to return to the motel, but he took her to dinner first, then walked her through the downtown area, pointing out places, stores, streets that held memories for him. It was nearly eleven when they got back to their room.

"What are you planning?" she asked then, standing at the door, pressed against it as if for support.

"I'll wait an hour, until no one's still wandering around, then

I'm going up to her room and pretend I'm a local detective investigating an accident she might have witnessed. I'll ask her to go with me to file a report. I know where I can take her for a couple of days."

Rachel shook her head. "You'll go to prison for kidnaping. You might even be shot."

Julian didn't reply. He went to the bathroom to wash his face and hands, comb his hair.

"Julian, you haven't slept since we found her name in those books, two weeks ago. You're too tired to be able to think clearly. We can just follow her when she leaves the motel, see where she goes, and then take time to make real plans, not this cobbled-up scheme that will get you killed."

He lay on the bed, his hands under his head, and tried to find a flaw in his reasoning.

Rachel sat by him. "You know I love you. And you love me. We can have so much together. This has been the best year of our lives. Everything's ahead of us, just waiting. And you're risking it all. This obsession will ruin everything for us."

Julian wished she would shut up. "Tomorrow," he said, "you should check out and get a cab to the airport and fly home. You have nothing to do with this. If anyone questions you, say we had a fight and I left in the car."

She bit her lip, got up and wandered to the mirror, back to the side of the bed where she regarded him for a moment. Then she sighed. "I'm going to the coffee shop. I'll bring some back for both of us."

When she was gone he went to the mirror and looked at himself carefully. It was true, he had not slept much in the past two weeks, and it showed; his eyes were deeply hollowed, his face, always slightly thin, now looked emaciated. Curious how he had not even thought about feeling tired, or jumpy from not sleeping. The pounding surf kept him alert, wide awake, ready to spring. He checked his pocket again to make certain he had keys to Rachel's car, counted his money again, and studied the map again to make certain he remembered the road to the hunting camp. He opened the door when he heard Rachel kick it. She came in holding two paper cups covered with plastic lids.

"Yours is the one with the cross, sugared," she said.

He was grateful that she did not start another scene. He sipped the coffee, sitting on the bed, leaning against the headboard.

"There's a party out by the pool," Rachel said. "You'd better wait until they break it up. There's no way you can avoid them."

He checked his watch. He would give them half an hour.

Rachel finished her coffee and came to the bed.

"Can we just lie quietly together," she said, "until it's time?"

Julian drained his cup and put it down and she lay beside him. He held her comfortably, not very hard, and she put one hand on his chest, the way they slept every night. Neither spoke. Once he wanted to look at his watch again, but his arm was under her and she was relaxed. He decided not to make her move. He felt himself drifting and he jerked.

"It's only ten after twelve," she murmured. "Try to rest a few more minutes. You're so tired."

He never knew when he fell asleep, or that he was falling asleep. He dreamed that he was wide awake, waiting for the clock hands to move, watching them fixedly in order to catch the motion.

He woke up with a pounding headache; his mouth was lined with rank rat fur. He pushed himself away from the bed groggily, still fully dressed. Rachel was sitting near the window. The room was very bright even with the drapes closed.

"What time is it?" he demanded.

"One, a little after."

"You put something in the coffee? You did that to me!"

She nodded. "Some of the sleeping pills I got last summer. I had to do something. It was all I could think of." She looked and sounded miserable.

"Get out!" he croaked. "Get the hell out of here, out of my apartment, out of my life! Just clear all the way out!"

He yanked the telephone up and dialed Room 22. No one answered. He called the desk and asked if she had checked out; she had.

Rachel did not move until he was finished. Then she came toward him, one hand outstretched, and he felt his own hands clenching. She stopped.

"Can't we even talk about it?"

"Right now I'd like to kill you," he said savagely.

She shook her head hard and closed the space between them in one flash of motion. He slapped her, knocking her backward. She stumbled over a pillow on the floor, caught herself on the foot of the bed, and hung there, gasping. Julian turned and went into the bathroom. He was shaking so hard he thought he might be having a seizure. He stripped and turned on the shower and stood under it until his hands stopped twitching, and he was able to breathe normally. When he returned to the room, Rachel was gone, her suitcase, her jacket, books, everything of hers was gone.

✿

Julian waited for his guests, ignoring the nervousness of the others in the apartment. John was unable to stay in any one place more than a few seconds. He flitted like a butterfly trying to decide which flower in a garden was best for his needs. Kim kept looking at Julian, then quickly away, as if afraid his own uncertainty might infect Julian. Julian smiled at him. He alone in the room was not nervous, not uncertain.

Near the windows Corinne was finishing annotating a manuscript. She brought it to Julian.

"I circled the statements you probably should refute," she said. "Like where they say you're copying Jesus. They have no understanding at all, and that will make people uneasy, and besides, it isn't true."

He nodded. He had read the article thoroughly and knew its every flaw. And he knew it did not really matter what they said; the fact that the article was scheduled for publication the first week in May was what was important.

Dolly Kearns was the photographer and Eric Mendel the writer, who showed up promptly at two. Dolly nodded in approval at the apartment. It was austere, with no ornamentation at all, except a white marble fountain with softly falling water. The fountain was simple, unadorned, four feet high. The only furniture in the room was a wooden bench with cushions, pillows on the floor, several lamps, and a large desk. Venetian blinds covered the windows.

The disciples bowed silently to the guests and filed out the door, leaving Julian, who was seated on the floor.

"Julian Grange?" Eric Mendel asked.

"Just Julian."

"Julian. You read the article? Is there anything you'd like to add, a statement maybe?"

Julian shook his head. "Many things will be printed about me, most of them untrue, some as true as the writer's understanding permits. It does not matter." He paid no attention to Dolly Kearns, who was moving about the room snapping pictures as he talked.

"It is true that you actually baptize people?"

"The act of baptism as a purification rite predates Christianity by thousands of years," Julian said. "It is so old that it fades into the oblivion of prehistory. It was revived in the time of Jesus as a symbol that is immediately understood by everyone who experiences it. Since then it has become perverted and has lost much of its meaning. It has become so closely associated with specific religious rites that it is no longer available to outsiders who do not share those particular beliefs."

"But you do baptize?"

Julian smiled. "You will print what you will. And people will read what they will. But I do have a statement, something you can add to your article. This spring I will show you a miracle."

"Some people say you've worked miracles already, getting kids off drugs, straightening out delinquents, things like that," Dolly Kearns said, snapping her pictures.

"Those are miracles only if you believe there is no human potential that can be awakened. People who come to know there is a higher life attainable within their grasp, not in a mysterious hereafter, have no further need for their addictions. They shed them with ease, without pangs or regrets. That is the human potential, and in itself is miraculous. That is not the kind of miracle I will show the world this spring."

"When will this miracle take place?" Eric Mendel asked, not writing now.

"Memorial Day."

❉

Julian's book was published in April. One reviewer said it was so simple that any schoolchild could have written it in a single page. Its message was: You are not a machine. Machines were invented to serve humanity. Human potential is as yet unimaginable because no one has demonstrably reached an upper limit. Human beings are so narcotized, sedated, polluted, conditioned, and lied to that only an outside force can shock them into wakefulness and awareness. And so on.

"He promises nothing," the reviewer complained, "and yet he has followers, people who must want to hear how foul life is, and that it can be better, because that is all that is in his book."

"In less than a year," another critic said, this time a psychologist, "Julian appeared out of nowhere with a message that has been stated repeatedly by scores of others, and yet he has found disciples. It is the mysterious rite of baptism that he employs that is irresistible," the psychologist went on. "Those people who flock to him do not want reason and logic, they want and need mysteries, and Julian is providing them."

Julian read all the reviews, the letters to editors complaining about his blasphemous usurpation of the Christian rites, the psychological analyses of his meteoric rise. When his followers urged him to reply to his critics, he shook his head, smiling. "One cannot respond with reason when it is the unreason of belief and faith that is questioned. Only those who experience the purification can understand its meaning. To all others it must remain illogical, a blasphemy, paganism revived, whatever they choose to call it."

The article that Eric Mendel had written was published early in May. Julian read: "It is his absolute belief in his own words that turns an audience of skeptics into a roomful of people who are shaken in their own beliefs, people who wonder why they have held to beliefs that suddenly seem so childish and even harmful. When Julian talks about the water cycle, how the rain cleanses as it falls, cleaning the air, then the land and the rivers, only to return to the ocean where the process starts again, one realizes that this is important. It is an elementary school lesson repeated by this remarkable man, and somehow it takes on a significance that was missing before. He tells his audience that the ancients knew about the powers of water to heal, to cleanse the body and the spirit, and they go away believing, or longing to believe so fiercely that they are drawn back again and again. Those who undergo the purification rite *are* changed, and whether it is subjective only matters little because the change they experience influences their lives . . ."

Julian put the magazine down and stared at the little fountain that never was turned off. A year, he thought, it had taken only a year to come to this. For three days and nights he had sat by a swimming pool studying the water in sunlight, under artificial lights, by starlight, the water churned by dozens of bodies, when it lay unmarred by a ripple, cratered by rain- drops . . . And it had come to him whole and complete, every- thing had appeared, nothing had been omitted, no detail that he later had to improvise. He felt that he had opened a gate that day and from then on had simply followed the path he had found. He seldom had to think about what he would say or do under any circumstances; the words came, the acts flowed of their own accord.

Kim and John entered the room and waited. He gazed at the fountain another few seconds, then went to his favorite cushion and sat down, motioning for them to seat themselves also.

"You have the hall rented?"

Kim nodded. He was Julian's age, not yet twenty-five; he had been the first disciple, and was still the one Julian turned to first.

"And the necessary stage is being prepared, the pool, everything?" Julian knew it was all going according to plan; the questions were ritualistic, they all accepted that. Kim and John were here for special instructions.

"You have rented the house for my meditations and seclusion?"

Again Kim nodded.

Without further questioning Julian told them what they were to do. Neither objected or asked for reasons. They listened attentively, and when he was finished he embraced them and they left. He returned to the fountain. After a moment he dipped his hands in the water and watched it run down the sides of his hands, down his fingers, off his finger tips.

*

"Who are you?" Stella Johnson demanded. She was about forty, he thought, with a hard voice, but frightened eyes.

"Julian. I have known you for twelve years, Stella Johnson. You destroyed my life."

She took a backward step, staring at him. "You're crazy. I've never seen you before."

"But I saw you." Julian turned the key in the lock and put the key inside his pocket.

"Why did you have them bring me here? My friends will call the police. You can't simply kidnap a person and get away with it." They were all the right words, but there was no conviction behind them. When he did not reply, she whispered, "What are you going to do to me?"

"Nothing. Keep you here for three days and then take you to a gathering where I am to speak. Nothing more than that, unless you desire it."

She was watching him fixedly. Now she sank down into a chair. "Why? It doesn't make any sense. Why me?"

Julian smiled at her. "We both know why. I don't know who or what you are, but I do know how to make you reveal that you are not human."

"You don't know anything about me," she said. "You can't."

He nodded. "There will be time. Perhaps you will tell me."

"I might kill you," she said desperately.

"I thought of that. My friends are outside in the camper they brought you in. They will take turns watching, and if you emerge they will catch you and take you to the police and charge you with murder. It might not stick, you might claim self-defense and get off, but during the interrogations, the days and nights under constant surveillance, I'm afraid your secret would be revealed."

She leaned back and closed her eyes.

Julian sat down with a book and started to read.

The second day she begged him to permit her to bathe, and he gave her a wash basin of warm water and watched as the water vanished. She looked nearer fifty than forty. He gave her fruit and vegetables to eat, and a glass of water late in the afternoon. She looked like a fifty-five-to-sixty-year-old woman.

Once she tried to attack him with a pan from the kitchen, but he overpowered her easily and took the pan from her. She was frail and weak.

"You'll kill me!" she cried. "Is that what you want, to kill me? I haven't done anything to you. I haven't harmed anyone."

"You destroyed my life," he said again. "For twelve years I've lived with a nightmare. You, or others like you, permeate our history. The witch hunters knew about you, didn't they?

They tried to find you by dunking suspects into water. The test was not who drowned, but who came out young and beautiful. How long have you been here? How many of you are there? Why are you here?"

She sat down again and closed her eyes.

That night she told him she was dying. She looked like a mummy. She was too weak to rise from the bed. Her hair was thin and lank, her arms withered, her face sunken in. Julian brought the basin and bathed her, then again, and still again.

"It is not enough!" she moaned. "Please, permit me to bathe."

"No! I will bring you water, all that you can have. It ends tomorrow night. For one more day I'll watch over you, keep you alive and well enough."

"And then?"

"It depends on you."

"I won't cooperate in any way!"

"But you will. Willingly or not, you will cooperate."

She turned away from him, forty again, or fifty.

"The Egyptians knew about you, didn't they? They knew mummies could be revived with water, brought back to glorious youth. In their worship of Isis, they ritualistically submerged celebrants, didn't they?"

She did not answer.

In the morning he gave her oranges and apples, but no water. At noon he offered her more fruit, and again late in the afternoon. Throughout the day while he aged minute by minute, she advanced by years.

"I will scream that you are forcing me, that you kidnaped me and starved me," she whispered hoarsely. "They won't let you half-drown a helpless old woman."

"If you make a scene," Julian said, "you will be thrown into the pool and kept there by my followers until the police arrive, fifteen minutes, half an hour, however long it takes. There will be cameras, video tapes, witnesses. I will denounce you as a witch, as the devil in human form."

She shuddered. "Again. There is no end to it."

"If you cooperate," Julian went on, ignoring her dread, "you will enter the water exactly like the others. You will allow the ceremony to proceed normally, and you will walk out of the water transformed. A miracle. My followers will take you to a dressing room where you will be helped into clothes. There is a back door. Your car will be waiting for you. No one will follow you."

"I don't believe you."

"As you choose."

She was a bent, shriveled woman when he led her to his car, seated her, and got in to drive into the city for the Memorial Day service. Kim and John followed closely in the camper.

"Where are you from?" Julian asked, gently now, no longer a victim of the pounding surf that had been with him most of his life. She was an old woman near death, not a threat.

"It does not matter where," she said after a long silence. "We developed a disease in space and came here hoping for aid, but we found primitive people, no help. We could not return home. We stayed." Her voice was hesitant, ancient.

"You personally, or your people?"

The silence was prolonged. He reached into the glove compartment and got out a thermos of water and handed it to her. She drank carefully, emptied it.

"You are immortal then?"

She laughed harshly. "We die every day. One by one we have been hunted, tortured, persecuted. We don't dare try to form alliances with your people. We don't dare try to stay in our own group for fear we will all be massacred together. Today there are so few of us."

"I used to try to understand why you were drawn to this city year after year," Julian said, keeping his tone light. He let amusement seep into it as he said, "I imagined you had a spaceship here somewhere and every year you all gathered for a ceremony of some sort."

She looked out the window. They were in the suburbs of the city.

"I stopped thinking that," he went on. "I began to think you were spies from another star, that you came here to transmit information out into space. It isn't anything like that, is it?"

Wearily she said, "In the beginning when we knew we were dying, our bioengineers transformed us, and they erred. There was not enough time to study the humans thoroughly. It was a desperate gamble. If we could become enough like the humans we found, perhaps we could escape the disease. Humans are immune, it does not attack carbon-based organisms..." She sighed and her words were slurring when she went on. "We acquired great wealth. It takes great wealth to pursue scientific study, and we waited until your technology developed to produce the equipment we need. We studied and learned much, and learning much, we found that our disease is incurable. So we die, minute by minute, day by day, and yet we live on and on." Now she looked at him, her mouth twisted in a death's-head grin. "It is a pity we cannot tell our people of our dilemma. They would appreciate the irony."

"Why do you come here every year?" Julian asked gently.

"Our time is not like yours," she said in her croaking voice. "A day, a year, neither is what you experience. In a day we can empty ourselves to each other, all we have learned, all we have gained. And we can fill ourselves, give each other hope enough to continue... A year, to you so long, is nothing; a blink, and it is gone. Only these shells keep time in a way our brains cannot fathom." She passed her hand over her chest, down her stomach, her thighs. Her hand shook as with palsy. She lifted it and watched it a moment, then let it fall. Suddenly she sat up straighter and her voice was louder and firmer when she exclaimed, "You put something in the water, didn't you?"

"Yes. A mild tranquilizer. You won't even fall asleep, but you won't worry and become upset. It won't hurt you, Stella. It will let you relax."

She moaned and made a grab toward the key.

"I thought you might try something on the way in," Julian said kindly, holding her away with one hand. "I thought you might wait until we got on a crowded street and then try to get the key, or try to jump from the car, or call for help. I thought you might tell me pretty stories to distract me, and then make the attempt. Just relax now, Stella. No one is going to hurt you." He talked almost crooningly as he drove, and she slumped back against the seat, her eyes open, but unfocused.

*

Julian took her to a dressing room where he helped her undress and then laid her on a cot. Gently he washed her, even her hair, and as he ministered to her, she revived, and regained some of her strength. He stopped bathing her when she appeared to be in her mid-sixties. He helped her don a tunic that tied at her shoulders and fell to her thighs in a straight line.

"Soon," he said, "you will feel completely normal. I'll leave two young women with you. They will accompany you to the stage when it is time. What happens then is your decision."

He went to the door and beckoned Corinne and Mary, who silently entered the room and took up their posts. Then he went to the stage.

He talked for an hour. He told his audience they were not machines, but thinking, rational human beings. They were not ciphers, or entries in a file clerk's ledger, or numbers in a computer, but feeling, perceiving human beings. He told them all past was prologue. There was nothing that was not in his book until the last ten minutes. Then he paused, and when he continued, his manner was changed. He had been intense from the start, but now he was like a wire that is charged and taut with suppressed energy.

"When I was a boy," he said, the words ringing, "I had a vision. I became frightened by it and my parents took me to doctors and psychiatrists. They could find nothing wrong with me, but I was changed, and they all knew it. My life was changed.

My dreams were changed. I had a vision that has persisted in my head from that day until this, and I have spent my life trying to bring understanding to that vision. I want to share it with you tonight."

He paused again, then went on in a low voice. "In my vision I saw an old woman who had come to realize that her whole life was a monstrous lie. They told her she was insignificant and she believed them. They told her she was a number, that everyone else was a number, that numbers are infinite and go on forever, that none of them matters. And she believed them . . ."

No one moved in the auditorium. It was so quiet the thousand people there might have been holding their breath. Julian could feel their power become his power and he was the surf, his voice rising and falling, an irresistible force, as he recounted the lies of their lives.

"I had a vision!" he cried. "This woman found the strength to say NO! This woman found herself. She shed her own past, repudiated the lies, refused the self she had become. In my vision this old woman was purified."

He smiled self-deprecatingly. "I was a boy," he said. "I did not understand . . ."

He spoke of his search for understanding through education, through religion, philosophy, psychology. "And in the spring last year I had a vision once more. In it a door opened onto a path, and I could see all the steps that would lead me to this place on this night. At the end of the path . . ." His voice fell to a near whisper. "At the end of the path is the light of understanding, the light of acceptance, the light of love, the light of glory. I say to you that tonight you will see that light with me!"

The chorus from a local Unitarian church began the "Ode To Joy" and he quickly left the stage. Kim met him, his cheeks wet with tears.

"How is she?" Julian asked.

"Fine. The tranquilizer has worn off, but she's calm. Will you see the celebrants now?"

It was customary for Julian to greet each person who had

come for the purification ceremony. He went from one curtained cubicle to the next, embracing each follower in turn, welcoming them. When he entered the room where Stella Johnson was being held, he stood by the door and did not approach her.

"Are you all right?" he asked.

She nodded. "I heard you, there are loud-speakers. Did you tell me the truth back in the car?"

"Yes. That is the door. Your clothes are here, your car is outside."

She bowed her head. "There are certain patterns," she murmured, "that recur. You are playing a very dangerous game. In the end it will cost you everything." She looked at him. "You will not search for me, for anyone else?"

"Never."

"I will do what you say. And we will part. I shall watch your career with great interest, Julian."

"Good-by, Stella Johnson," he said, and left her room. Outside her door he took a deep breath and started toward the stage to finish it.

"Julian!"

He stopped at the voice, and when he turned, Rachel was there. "I thought you might come," he said.

"You have her, don't you? Julian, there's an FBI man out there. He came to my apartment and asked me questions yesterday. He said she has vanished, that she checked into the motel and then vanished. He'll arrest you. He thinks you're crazy!"

"And you? Do you think that?"

"Julian, please, let her go now. If she's hiding from anything or anyone, she'll not make a scene or cause you trouble if you just let her go! If she is what you think she is, you have to surrender her to the government! Think what it would mean to everyone if we could learn what she can do. They won't let you have this secret all to yourself."

She was very pale and frightened.

"I can't. Don't be so afraid, Rachel."

"I have my car outside. I'll hide you. Please come with me now. I love you, Julian."

"I know. And I love you." He turned and continued to the stage where the curtains were now being drawn to reveal the pool. Three steps led up to it. There was a small platform around it, three steps down the other side. It was Spartan in its simplicity. He went up the three steps and down into the water, which came to his waist. It was body temperature.

The first one came from backstage. She was twenty, Candace. There was a rapt expression on her face, her eyes never left his as she approached, then held out her hand for him to take.

"Candace, you have been afraid and now you repudiate fear." He submerged her, one hand firm under her neck, still holding her hand. She stiffened, then relaxed, and he drew her up. "Candace, you have been lied to, and believing the lies, you have become the machine they said you are. You repudiate hypocrisy and lies." He submerged her again; this time she was perfectly relaxed. Then, "Candace, you have searched yourself for strength and found it. You have rejected the lie that evil is part of being human, and you have rejected evil. With this act you proclaim that purification is at hand, that the self can purify the self."

He smiled at her and submerged her a third time, and when he drew her up from the water, she was radiant. From the audience there was a collective sigh. Disappointment? Satisfaction? He could not tell.

William was next, a forty-year-old ex-policeman. At first he was more tense than Candace had been, but by the end, he too was obviously ecstatic.

Now Stella Johnson came up the steps, hesitated only a moment, then extended her hand. It was cold and shaking.

"There's no television," she whispered, hardly moving her lips.

"No." And he began the ceremony. When he tried to raise her, she resisted, and not until she squeezed his hand did he lift her from the water. Now he could feel the charge in the air, feel the hushed quality in the auditorium, as the air before an electrical storm is hushed. He said the words as if in a dream, staring into her face. Already she was younger, stronger, vibrant. He submerged her again, and again she signaled when she wanted to be raised. He was the surf, pounding, pounding, crashing on the shore, crashing against boulders.

". . . purification is at hand, that the self can purify the self." He lowered her into the water and watched her face. Her eyes were open, a faint smile curved her bright lips. Her hair streamed out about her face. She ran her free hand down her body, up again, felt her breasts, then her cheek, and she smiled at him. Then she signaled and he raised her.

He was blinded by a white light that filled the room, that burned his eyes and paralyzed him. She was with him in the light, smiling, still holding his hand. Nothing else existed. Slowly she raised his hand to her lips and kissed it lightly, then she turned and mounted the steps from the pool. The attendants were there with a robe, and she waved them away and walked off the stage, her hair feathery about her head, no water dripping from her body as she moved.

Someone in the audience screamed, and for a moment there was panic as people leaped up, started to surge toward the stage. Julian held up his hands. "Stop," he said quietly. He turned toward the side of the stage where Mildred was waiting. She looked like a person in deep shock, or ecstasy. Down in the audience his followers were getting the people back to their seats, and in a moment the ceremony continued.

*

When it was over Julian held up his hands once more. "Purification is at hand! The self can purify the self!" The curtain closed, and only then did he leave the pool. Kim met him with a robe. Beyond the stage there was a dead quiet that suddenly broke into a wild clamor.

"Where is she?" It was the FBI agent, Walter Montgomery.

"There are hundreds of people who aren't going to stay out there very long. Your people can't hold them back. And I want her before they break through. Where is she?"

"Who?" Kim asked, trying to push Julian forward. "You have to change before they get in," he said. "They all want to touch you, to gaze at you."

"You know damn well who I mean," Montgomery snapped. "That old lady. You snatched her after all, didn't you? And drugged her. She was glassy-eyed from dope. Where is she now?"

Kim stopped pushing and stared at Montgomery. He turned to Julian. "He didn't see."

Julian shook his head. "Mr. Montgomery, I don't know where she is. I have to change now." The noise was getting louder.

Rachel was beside Montgomery. She said, "Julian, what happened? Why are those people trying to break down the doors? What happened?" She was near hysteria.

"You didn't see either, did you?" he asked gently. "I'm sorry, Rachel. I'm truly sorry." He went past her to his dressing room. He was stopped one more time. Eric Mendel was standing by the door. He looked dazed. Hesitantly he reached out and touched Julian's robe, then touched his hand. Julian smiled at him, and went inside the room. Before the door closed he could hear Montgomery demanding to know what Mendel thought had happened, what the hell was going on.

Kim slipped into the dressing room, started to reach out to help Julian undress, and drew back his hand.

Julian looked at him wonderingly. "What is it?"

"I'm afraid to touch you. It *was* a miracle, wasn't it?"

"Yes," Julian said. "Yes, a true miracle." The clamor increased, then died down as the sound of many feet drew closer, and that too stopped as outside the door they gathered and waited silently.

WITH THIMBLES,
WITH FORKS,
AND HOPE

I

THE FARMHOUSE glowed in the late afternoon dusk, like an old-fashioned Christmas card scene. Low evergreens crowded the front porch, the sidewalk from the drive curved gracefully; it was all scrubbed-looking, the white clapboard freshened by rain that had started to fall. Charlie felt a twinge of guilt at the cleanliness and the comfort of it after spending most of the day in New York. He parked in the garage and entered a small side porch that led into the back of the house. The porch was a catchall for the bottles to be returned to the store, newspapers destined for a recycle center, some wooden seed flats that had got only that far on their way to the barn, an overflowing woodbox. When the clutter got so bad that he could no longer make his way through it, he cleaned it up, but not until then, and he never had finished cleaning everything — the seed flats had been there since June.

Inside the house the fragrance of soup was tantalizing; there were the odors of wood fires, of onions, of cats — three of them — cedar paneling, and other things he had not been able to identify, leftover things from when the house was built, or from the first seventy years of its occupancy.

"Hello," he called out, but he knew Constance was out. The

house felt empty when she was outside. Two of the three cats stalked over to sniff his shoes and legs, checking credentials before they accepted him. The third one, Brutus, glared at him from on top the upright freezer. It was Charlie's fault, obviously, that the rain had started again. Brutus turned his back and faced the wall.

Charlie went through a narrow hallway, through the utility room, all the time dancing to avoid squashing a cat. He heard the soft plop Brutus made when he left the freezer, and he knew the evil old tiger cat was following along, his tail rigid, daring either of the other two to get in his way. They would keep an eye on him and scamper if he got near. Brutus was a New York cat; he had not, would never approve of country life. In the kitchen there was a copper-colored electric range with a stove-top grill, a dishwasher, a disposal that had never been used since they had moved in — meat scraps went to cats, and everything else went on the compost; there were rows of hanging pots and pans, all gleaming copper-bottomed, seldom used. What was used every day for nine or even ten months of the year was a forty-year-old wood cookstove. On it now there was the iron kettle with soup simmering so low that a bubble broke the surface once every five minutes or so.

The orange cat rubbed against him and complained about things generally. He rubbed its ears for a moment, then said softly, "She's going to be mad as hell, Candy." Brutus swiped at the gray cat, Ashcan, in passing and settled himself on the rocking chair nearest the stove. His eyes gleamed yellow as he narrowed them in the way that made him look Mephistophelian. Candy went on detailing her awful day, Ashcan licked the place Brutus had nabbed him, and Charlie tried to think of a way to break the news to his wife that he had practically taken on a job for them both. She would be mad as hell, he said again under his breath, and he put down the briefcase filled with reports that he planned to read that night, and have her read.

On the slope overlooking the house and yard Constance was

on her knees planting daffodils under the half-dozen apple trees that made their orchard. Next year they should start bearing. Goddamned rain, she muttered, had to do it now, couldn't wait another fifteen minutes, had to be right now. Rain trickled down her neck, icy fingers that made her skin flinch, trying to turn itself inside out. She plunged the bulb planter into the yielding earth, twisted it viciously, lifted out the plug, and laid it down. With one hand she scooped up wood ashes and bone meal and sand and tossed the mixture into the hole; with the other she groped in her pail for another bulb and dropped it in, no longer taking the trouble to put it right side up. She returned the column of dirt topped with newly cut grass and jabbed at the ground a scant six inches away to repeat the process. It was impossible now for her to summon the vision of apple trees in bloom on a golden carpet.

She had heard the car and knew that Charlie was home. She had known when Charlie left that morning that when he got home he would hem and haw around for a while and finally blurt out that he had taken the job, that it would be a milk run, nothing to do, nothing dangerous, etc., etc. Her stomach would churn and her blood would chill, making her fingers cold, and she would nod silently and try to find words that would tell him she hated it, but she was willing for him to do it because she knew he couldn't just quit the business cold turkey. She knew that now and then he would go see Phil Stearns and come home to tell her that he had agreed to do just this one job, this one last time.

But it wasn't fair, she muttered. For twenty-five years Charlie had worked on the New York City police force, and he had come out scarred but intact, and it wasn't fair to risk everything again.

The worst scars were the ones that could not be seen. Invisible scar tissue had formed, protecting him where he had been hurt too often. In the beginning he had been possessed by zeal, a sense of mission, holy justice; over the years that had become cynicism and simple dedication to sharpening his skills of detection. Then he had become different again, had developed a cold fury because nothing changed, or if there were changes, they were for the worse. His rage at the criminal began to extend to the victim. Constance had known then it was time for him to get out. Surprisingly, he had agreed, and three years ago, at forty-seven, he had retired.

She looked with dismay at the pail, at least twenty more bulbs. The rain was coming down harder; there was a touch of ice in it. Her fingers were red and swollen-looking and her nose had started to run and she couldn't wipe it without smearing mud across her face. "It isn't fair!" she cried, looking at the house.

By the time she finished the job and put away her equipment, the rain was a downpour and the day was finished with the gray sky lowering to the ground. Charlie met her at the back door and drew her inside, pushed her gently into a chair, and brushed a kiss across her nose as he leaned over and pulled off her muddy boots. He helped her out of the sodden jacket and then took both her hands and pulled her across the kitchen through the hallway to the bathroom that was steamy and sweet-smelling from bubble bath.

She sighed and did not tell him she would have preferred a shower in order to wash her hair also. Since her fingers were stiff with cold he ended up undressing her and then held her elbow firmly until she was in the tub, only her flushed face and wet hair above water.

Charlie was perplexed about the hair; she was not the image he had anticipated with mud on her cheek, and her hair dripping and clinging to her cheeks and her forehead.

"Be right back," he said and left, taking her wet clothes with him.

As soon as he had vanished, she stood up and pulled a towel from the rack and tied up her hair. It was silly for Charlie to baby her, she was taller than he was, and almost as broad. Her face was wide, Slavic, her eyes pale blue, her hair almost white it was so blond. The gray that was already showing here and there blended in and no one but Charlie knew she was turning.

She knew she neither looked nor acted like the kind of woman a man would baby. She sank back into the suds and thought again it was silly for him to go through this to ease his conscience, but she was glad he did. Sometimes he babied her, sometimes she babied him; it worked out.

He came back carrying a tray with two frosted martini glasses, the shaker, a plate of garlic salami, the kind you could get only in a good New York deli, and strips of cheese. He sat down cross-legged on the floor so that his eyes and hers were level, poured the drinks, handed her a towel and then her drink, and began to tell her about the job. While he talked he ate the salami, and held out pieces for her to bite.

Constance watched him and listened and she thought: he was night to her day, all dark and brooding and secret. His hair was a mop of tight black curls, his eyebrows so heavy they made his face look out of proportion. There was a gleam of gold in his mouth when he laughed, one gold cap. His teeth were crooked, an orthodontist's nightmare, but they were the whitest teeth Constance had ever seen.

"Lou Bramley," Charlie said, eating cheese, "will be fifty-one November first. That's Saturday. He's got a wife that he cares for, two good kids, treasurer of Tyler and Sacks, Incorporated, no debts, everything going for him. And Phil's sure as sin that he's going to suicide before the end of the day Saturday. And leave him, Phil, holding a five-hundred-thousand-dollar insurance policy."

"So why doesn't he just not issue the policy?"

"Because it's too big to piss away without more than an itch to go by. And nothing's come up. He's had his best working on it for the last three weeks and they haven't come up with anything. No motive. No problem. No woman. Nothing."

"Why does Bramley say he wants that kind of insurance?"

"His story was that at a party a screwball astrologer told him the next six months are the most dangerous of his life, that unless he takes extreme care the odds are good that he will be killed in an accident." Charlie poured the last of the martinis and laughed. "Phil even hired an astrologer to do a horoscope for Bramley. Nothing to it. He's riding a high wave, nothing but good things ahead. Can you imagine Phil going to an astrologer?"

Constance laughed. They had known Phil Stearns since Charlie's college days. Phil believed in nothing but actuarial tables. "Charlie," she said then, "it's an impasse. In time a good psychologist or psychiatrist could give Phil his answers, but if his people couldn't find anything in three weeks, what does he think you can do in three days? He has to gamble, or cut loose."

Charlie nodded. "I more or less told him the same thing. Midnight Friday the policy goes through automatically if he doesn't reject it. By midnight Saturday we both think Mr. Lou Bramley will no longer be with us, and Mrs. Bramley will come into a sizable fortune. Phil is ready to cut him loose, but he wants a back-up opinion from a good psychologist. From you."

She shook her head. "I'm retired. And you are too, if you'd just remember it from time to time."

"Bramley's gone down to a flossy resort in Florida, in the Fort Myers area. That raises the possibility of a vanishing act instead of suicide. In either case it has to go down on the books as accidental death for the big payoff. All Phil wants you to do is go down there and observe him, talk to him, and on Friday give Phil a call. He needs something more than an itch to refuse a policy like that."

Constance glared at him. "You can't take jobs for me. I'm not an indentured servant or something."

"I didn't tell him anything definite," Charlie said reproachfully. "I did say that if we agreed, we'd want a week's vacation at the flossy resort after we finished this little job. On Phil, of course."

She shook her head. "Go stir the soup or something."

As soon as he was gone, she opened the drain, pulled the towel from her hair, and turned on the shower. She hated bubble bath; this was a gift from their daughter. Of course, Charlie would be hooked on Lou Bramley, they were the same age. He would never admit it, but the idea of stopping everything now when there was so much to do, time enough finally to do it, that would frighten him. He was not a coward, he had survived too many encounters with near death, and had gone back too many times, but he was cautious. He was not ready. His own unreadiness would make it impossible for him to sidestep Lou Bramley, who evidently was ready. Charlie would have to know why. He would have to stop him if he was stoppable.

✿

Constance had called Charlie late in the afternoon of her first day at the luxurious hotel. She had managed to talk briefly with Lou Bramley, she reported. "He's withdrawing, Charlie," she had said soberly. "Anyone with half an eye could spot it. He's not eating, not sleeping, doesn't finish sentences. He stares and stares without moving, and then jumps up and walks furiously on the beach. Nervous energy. He's so obsessed he doesn't even realize he's got two women pursuing him."

"Two? What do you mean?"

And she had told him about the woman who was openly stalking Lou Bramley. The bellboys and waiters were betting on when she would land him, it was so obvious.

Charlie did not like having a woman appear. It was possible they planned to skip out together.

He was going to like it even less, she thought. She had learned that the woman was June Oliveira, from Brazil, and Lou Bramley was the first man she had paid any attention to in the week she had been in the hotel. Wherever Lou Bramley went, she was so close that she might as well have been attached to him. Constance had watched her sit at a table next to his, and start edging her chair toward him. When she got within whispering distance, he apparently had become aware of her for the first time, and he had moved out to a beach chair in the sun. His action had been almost absentminded. The woman had continued to watch him intently, and moments later when he jumped up and started to walk, she had followed.

It would have been easy to miss, Constance knew. The terrace was usually a busy place, especially during the late afternoon happy hour. Waiters were rushing back and forth, groups forming, breaking up, re-forming. If she had not been watching closely, she might not have noticed, partly because the woman was so brazen about it; somehow that screened her intentions even more than secrecy would have done. When she first mentioned the woman to Charlie, Constance had realized she could not describe her beyond the most obvious features — long black hair and slender figure. Her face was smooth and unreadable, expressionless; she wore no jewelry, no makeup, no nail polish. Probably she was in her thirties; she was too self-assured to be younger, but there were no visible signs that she was older.

Up to this point Charlie would be willing to accept her assurance that Lou Bramley and the woman were strangers. And then she would tell him that last evening the woman had moved to a room next to Bramley.

The bellboy who was willing to sell information had rolled his eyes when he told her that. Later last night Constance had gone for a walk, and in the shadows of a sea grape bush, she had stopped and looked back at the hotel, studying it until she found her own room, counting up and over from it to Bramley's. On the balcony next to his, she had made out the dim figure of the woman as close to the joint rail as she could get.

Constance remembered the chill that had shaken her, and she felt it edging up her arms now. She looked at her watch; he should be home, she decided, and dialed the number.

Charlie sounded pleased; he was running down a good lead, he said, but the woman continued to worry him. She could be a complication, he admitted.

"I'll see if I can get anything from Bramley about her," Constance said. "I'm having a drink with him in a few minutes. I doubt that we'll be able to talk, though. That woman will be in his lap practically. Charlie, she . . . she really bothers me."

"Okay. Keep your distance from her. Don't get in her way.

She's probably got her own little racket going. Just watch the gazebo from a distance. Right?"

She agreed, and in a few minutes they hung up. She had not thought of the gazebo for a long time, but this didn't feel at all like that. There was something strange and mysterious going on, but she felt no danger; this was not the way she had felt when she had made the workmen move the little structure — hardly bigger than a playhouse. Nine years ago when they were in the country on weekends and part of the summer only, she had looked out the kitchen window one Saturday morning and had felt her skin crawl. She had to move the gazebo, she had said to herself sharply, and without another thought she had gone to the phone and called Willard Orme and had told him to bring someone out to do it. He had protested and tried to arrange a date a week away, and she had said she would get someone else to do it and remodel the house and build the garage and all the rest of the work he was figuring on doing for them. Reluctantly he had come out and moved the gazebo. That afternoon Jessica and two friends had been sitting in it drinking Cokes and eating hot dogs when a storm had blown down the walnut tree near the barn, and it had fallen on the newly bared spot of earth.

This was nothing like that, she told herself sharply. It was time to go down and meet Lou Bramley, see if they could find a place where she could get him to talk a little, a place where there would be no room for June Oliveira to be at his elbow.

The terrace was very large, and even though there were forty or more people on it, many tables were vacant. The hotel was between seasons now; after Thanksgiving, through spring, it would be jammed and then it would be impossible to wander out and find a table. She sat down, and shook her head at the waiter. She would order when Lou Bramley joined her. She spotted him as soon as he walked from the lobby through the wide doors. He hesitated, looking around, then nodded and started for her table. He had taken perhaps ten steps when he paused, looked past her, and changed his direction to go through the terrace, out to the beach chairs in the sand, where he sat down next to June Oliveira.

"For heaven's sake," Constance muttered to herself. "He's falling for her line." Bramley was facing the gulf, away from her. June Oliveira was at his left, talking to his profile. Constance watched them for several minutes and then decided not to let Oliveria get away with it so easily. She picked up her purse and put on her sunglasses; it was still very bright out on the sand. She hated going out in the sun because her nose was burned, her cheeks, her chin. She walked across the terrace, and down the three steps, turned toward them, and then veered away and headed toward the beach instead. She began to feel the heat of the sun on her nose and cheeks, and abruptly she turned and went back, without glancing at Lou Bramley and June Oliveira.

In her room again she began to shiver and started to adjust the air conditioner, but she had turned it off when she arrived and it had not been on since. She went to the balcony to let the late afternoon sun warm her. She realized that she was cursing under her breath and suddenly she laughed. A tug of war over a man! She had not played games like that since her teens. Now she began to look over the people on the sand below. Finally she found Lou Bramley and June Oliveira, exactly as before. She stood thinking and then went back inside and dialed Charlie again.

"I just want you to call her, and keep her on the line a few minutes."

He didn't like it, he said many times, until she said she would hire a bellboy to do it, and if she paid him ten, that woman would more than likely pay fifteen to learn the identity of the hoaxer.

"And if you get him out of her clutches, then what?"

"I'm going to try to get him drunk enough to sleep tonight. If he doesn't, he just might go through with it, no matter what you tell him. He's desperate for sleep."

Charlie grumbled some more, but he would make the call to

Oliveira in five minutes. "Honey," he said before hanging up, "just be damned careful."

Lou Bramley sat in the afternoon sun with June Oliveira and on her balcony Constance shivered. It was crazy, she told herself sternly, there were fifty people down there, and that many more on the beach, dozens of people swimming, or sunbathing. It was a mob scene down there.

Almost thirteen years ago Charlie had given her a present of one year of defense classes. He had insisted over her protests, saying further that as soon as Jessica was ten, he was going to enroll her also. Months later she had come home one afternoon upset and unwilling to continue. "Charlie, what Kim is teaching us now are lethal blows. I don't like it."

He had held her shoulders and regarded her soberly. "If anyone ever lays a hand on you, hurts you, you'd better kill him. Because if you don't, I will. You'll get off with self-defense, but it will be murder for me." They both knew he meant it.

What her classes had not prepared her to do, she thought decisively, was to stay in her den and shiver when she had agreed to do a job. She waited in the dark, cool bar for the bellboy to summon June Oliveira for her urgent long-distance call. The bar adjoined the terrace; it had ceiling-to-floor smoked-glass windows that let the patrons see out and kept those on the outside from seeing in.

The day the walnut tree fell was the day that Jessica had given up junk food, had in fact become a health-food fanatic. The girls had come running in talking shrilly, caught up in a nervous reaction to the storm and the crash of the tree, and the realization that they could so easily have been under it. Jessica had stopped at the door and looked at her mother across the kitchen. There had been beads of sweat on her upper lip. Wordlessly she had crossed the room and hugged Constance very hard, shaking, saything nothing. Strange, Constance thought as she watched, how memories like that one pop up, complete, every detail there, as if it were a little scene one could raise the curtain on at any time.

She was glad she had been with her daughter on the day she learned how short the distance was between life and death.

Presently June Oliveira appeared, walking fast toward the lobby. Constance left the bar through the terrace door and went straight to Lou Bramley. The woman had left her scarf on the chair; she did not intend to be delayed very long.

"Hi," Constance said. "Want to take a walk?"

Bramley jumped up and looked around swiftly. "I certainly do. Let's go."

They started for the beach, then he stopped. "It's no good. She'll just tag along."

"I've got a rental car in the lot," Constance said, taking his arm. "Let's go somewhere else to walk."

They went to a flagstone path that wound between the swimming pool area and the tennis courts, up past the terrace, to the street-front parking lot. Not until they were on the busy highway heading south did Lou Bramley relax.

"I really wanted to talk to you professionally, but Im not quite sure of the etiquette of the situation. And I owe you an apology," he said. "I'm sorry."

Constance laughed. "I'm retired. Any advice I give these days is just that, advice, like you might get from sweet old Aunt Maud."

She glanced at him as she spoke; his mouth twisted in an attempt to smile, then settled back into a tight line. His sunglasses were mirrors that completely hid his eyes. She turned her attention once more to the road. Incredibly busy, she thought, didn't those people know there was a gas shortage? Probably many of them were on their way down to the Tamiami Trail, through the swamps over to the east coast.

A straggly line of pelicans flew across the road; she admired pelicans more than all the other birds. They were scruffy-looking on land, ungainly, comical, but in flight they were supreme. So little effort seemed to go into it. They just opened their wings and sailed.

"I came down here to think through a problem," Lou Bramley

said after the silence had stretched out long enough to be almost unbreakable. "A business problem," he added quickly. He turned his head away, as if afraid that even with most of his face hidden behind the sunglasses, he might reveal too much. "Lucky, my wife, says that we constantly signal to each other, all people, and that we learn to read the signals as kids and get sharper at it as we grow up. She says that women don't make passes at me because I'm not signaling that I'd be receptive." He paused, waiting for her response.

"That's really very good," Constance said dutifully.

"Yes. And now especially, with this problem, I know I'm not hunting. So why is it that I can't turn around without having that woman at my side? Earlier, I wanted to have a talk with you and I went to her instead. I don't even like her. I actively dislike her, more than anyone I've met in a long time. And I can't stay away from her."

"I wonder what she wants," Constance said.

"That's the stumbling block for me too. There must be some kind of con game that she's going to pull when the time's right."

"She isn't right for a con artist, too blatant, too uncaring about appearances." She spied a good place to leave the highway at a small restaurant with beach access. "Finally, we can take our walk."

They walked on the hard-packed wet sand at the edge of the water. Lime-green waves rose knee high before they lost themselves in the froth. Flocks of sandpipers probed the sand, scattered at their approach, settled again as soon as they passed. Now and then a large white heron fluttered up out of their way, or a bunch of sea gulls screeched at them. Constance did not push the conversation or try to direct it as he talked about the woman, June Oliveira. She got little from it; he was not a good observer, not an attentive listener, not at this time in his life anyway.

They turned back as the sun was setting in a gaudy display of reds, golds, ivory, green . . . Offshore, a large yacht was moving south. They watched it.

"I don't swim," Lou Bramley said suddenly.

"My husband doesn't swim very well," Constance said. "He paddles a little."

"I saw you heading straight out into the gulf this morning; it gave me a sinking feeling in my stomach when I realized I couldn't see you any longer."

"I don't think June Oliveira swims either," Constance said. "At least I haven't seen her doing it."

"She thinks it's dangerous. She doesn't do anything dangerous. She thinks people are crazy who do."

He did not break the silence again until they were drawing near the tiny restaurant. "Would you like to have dinner here? I understand almost all the seafood restaurants are pretty good."

They got a booth by a window and she ordered a martini; they watched the end of the gaudy sunset while they waited for it.

"What happened after you published your articles?" he asked. He had not ordered a drink, and watched her sip her martini with poorly concealed desire for one just like it.

He was punishing himself, she thought, making himself live through every minute of this week without help of any sort. The hollows under his eyes were alarming.

"I had already quit the hospital when I began to write the articles," she said. "They brought a little pressure on the university. I had tenure and they couldn't have touched me, but it was uncomfortable. I finished the semester and dropped that too. It wasn't as if I sacrificed anything," she said easily. "I was busier than ever doing consulting."

"They made it look like a continuation of the old battle between the psychologists who aren't doctors, and the psychiatrists who are," he said thoughtfully.

She shrugged. "A plague on both their houses. I'm researching a book right now that will damn the psychologists just as much as those articles damned the holy psychiatrists."

"I'd like to see that," he said almost regretfully, and his eyes went distant as his fingers began to tap on the table top. He was back in his own hell.

"It's heady stuff," she said, "taking an opponent that much bigger than you are." His gaze remained fixed. She pulled the menu close to the candle and tried to make out the faint print.

When the waiter came to take their orders she asked to see the wine list and was disappointed by the selection. She did the best she could with it and said firmly, two glasses. Lou Bramley started to protest, then became silent again. For the first time he seemed to be uncomfortable with the silence.

"I'm surprised that they're still treating so many people with electroshock," he said.

"Several hundred thousand a year. For a while they thought they had a better solution with psychodrugs, but what happened was they ended up with addicts. Mostly women."

"And the difference in the treatments for men and women. That was shocking too."

"Shocking," she agreed. "That's the word."

Suddenly he smiled, the first time. "I'm not very good company. I'm sorry. Thanks for rescuing me, though. I'm glad we got out, away from that woman."

He ate little, but he drank the wine, and she kept refilling his glass; when the bottle was low, she signaled the waiter, who immediately brought a new one. The food was delicious. She was sorry he had not eaten.

They both ordered Key lime pie and while they waited for it, he said, "I really wanted to talk to you about a favor. You mentioned that your husband is joining you this weekend and you'll be around next week?"

She nodded.

He leaned back as the waiter came with their pie. For a minute Constance was afraid he would reconsider and withdraw again, but as soon as the waiter left, he went on.

"I thought I might miss you tomorrow. I have an important call I have to wait for in my room, and I thought you might have plans to go out. Anyway, that woman has made me jumpy, and I don't want to leave anything in my room. For all I know she might find a key somewhere, let herself in." He tried to laugh to show that he did not really mean it, but the effort was wasted. "It's something I want kept safe for me. I'm going deep-sea fishing, but I mentioned that already, didn't I?"

He knew he had not. The lie evidently made his mouth dry; he had to drink some of the awful water before he could continue. Constance was missing nothing: his sudden thirst, the way his fingers tightened and relaxed, tightened again, the way he avoided her gaze. He was still too dry to go on and he reached for the wine this time.

Constance took a bite of the pie and drew in a deep breath. It was sinfully good, made with real whipped cream, real lime juice.

"I don't want to leave confidential papers in the hotel safe," Lou Bramley said finally. "I know they have to turn things over to the police in case of accident or anything," he said in a rush.

He stopped again and this time Constance thought he would not go on. "This has to do with your business problem?"

"Yes. That's it. I would like to know that someone responsible has the papers, just in case."

"I'll be glad to hold anything for you."

"Thanks. And if, I mean there's always a chance that something could happen, and if it does, would you just drop the stuff in a mailbox for me? There will be two envelopes ready to mail. Inside a larger envelope."

She nodded.

"I can't tell you how that relieves my mind," he said. "I know it must sound crazy, but I've got a hunch that I should make sure that stuff is safe." He put his fork down and looked past her out the window and instantly his face was set in that distant look she had come to know.

"I believe very much in hunches," she said. "I used to wonder why everyone in my profession paid so little attention to intuitions, hunches, things that we all experience and no one wants to talk about. Some of those patients committed to years of institutional life, ordeals of drugs, shock treatments, hours of psychodrama, group therapies, the works, are there because they couldn't bring themselves to ignore their intuitions. They got out of control. Others, even sicker people on the outside, pretend there is no such thing. There has to be a middle ground, there has to be a handle to it, a way to look into it without being labeled crazy. I haven't found it yet," she admitted. "But I'm convinced that you can't treat neurotics, psychotics, psychopaths, any of them unless you admit that part of the psyche is still uncharted, unknown, and powerful."

She had brought him back; he was regarding her with interest.

"They'll crucify you," he said softly.

"They might try. I'm hammering my nails as hard and fast as they are hammering theirs."

He smiled with her.

She made a waving motion. "Enough of that. Why is your wife nicknamed Lucky?"

It was a silly story — her father had won a daily double the day she was born — but it started Lou Bramley talking. It was all about his wife and two children now, the trips they had taken, the strange and wonderful things the children had done. Nothing current, nothing about the future, nothing more recent than a couple of years ago. When he paused, she told a story about Jessica, or about Charlie.

They were the only customers still in the restaurant when it closed. He was yawning widely. At the car he stopped and looked back at the small dining room, the beach beyond it pale under a new moon. He nodded, then got in.

It was shortly after twelve when they walked into the hotel lobby and saw June Oliveira studying travel folders near the desk. Lou Bramely groaned.

"Jesus Christ!" he muttered. "She's just waiting. She knows and she's waiting."

&

On Friday Charlie arrived at the hotel at six-thirty and went straight up to their room where Constance was waiting for him. He kissed her fervently.

"You had me worried," he said then, holding her at arm's length, studying her. "Have you looked at your nose?"

She had; it was shiny and red as a plum tomato. It was also hot.

"You know what he's running away from?" she asked.

"I think so. He needs to confirm it; I don't have a stitch of proof."

"If he doesn't, we have to kidnap him or something. We can't let him go through with it, Charlie. I like him, he doesn't deserve that."

"And I like his wife a bunch too. We'll see. Now, what about that mystery woman?"

"I wish I knew. Look, Bramley hasn't left his room all day. He's waiting for that phone call. He was supposed to get a package to me for safekeeping, and he hasn't done that either. It's that woman. She's got some kind of control over him. I know, I know . . ."

Charlie watched her pace to the window, back. He had seen her like this before, but not for a very long time. He tried to pull her to the sofa next to him; she was too restless to sit down.

"Charlie, you'll have to get him out of here to talk to him. Tell him he's insured. Tell him you have to have something to eat, say in the coffee shop, that he has to sign papers and can do it there. She'll follow. In the lobby I'll distract her and that's when you have to get him out. There's a place down the road, south, Jake's Fish House. I'll meet you there. You rented a car, didn't you?"

"Yes. You told me to, remember? Constance, what is all this? You're nearly hysterical, you know?"

"I'm not hysterical, but there isn't much time. There's an eleven o'clock flight out of Miami and I want him on it. Charlie, he won't talk here! That woman is hanging out on his elbow. Believe me."

He kissed her again and went to the door. "Okay. Jake's Fish House. It'd better be good, sweetie, real good."

He would have recognized Lou Bramley from the photographs,

but they had not prepared him for the muddy color of his face. He had blanched when Charlie said he represented the insurance company.

"You have the policy, Mr. Bramley," Charlie said. "There are some formalities, of course, a few things to sign."

Bramley sank into a chair, staring at him blankly; very slowly the mud color changed to a reddish suntan. He moistened his lips. "Something to sign?"

"Yeah. Would you mind going to the coffee shop? I got a lousy headache on that flight down here. Cup of coffee, and a couple aspirins, that's what I need. We can get the paperwork done there."

Bramley nodded and stood up. He went to a chest, opened a drawer, and withdrew a manila envelope. "I have to drop this off at the desk," he said, looking at the envelope.

The woman was standing at the elevators when they arrived. The Dragon Lady, Charlie thought, and nodded to her. At his side Lou Bramley had gone stiff. He looked straight ahead as if he had not seen the woman at all. No one spoke.

She got off before them, but was walking so slowly that they passed her within a few feet of the recessed elevator bank. They went to the desk where Bramley handed over his envelope and watched until the clerk deposited it in Constance's box. He took a deep breath.

"The coffee shop's over there," he said dully, turning from the desk.

The woman was less than fifteen feet away. Constance appeared and walked between them and when the woman stepped aside, Constance brushed against her.

"Hey, what are you doing?" Constance yelled. "She had her hand in my purse!"

June Oliveira started to move away faster; Constance caught her by the arm and turned her around. "I know you did! I saw you and I felt the tug on my purse. It's happened to me before, just like that."

"Let's get the hell out of here," Charlie said, taking Bramley's arm. There was no need to tug; Bramley was already nearly running for the wide entrance doors.

*

In Jake's Fish House they took a booth and Charlie ordered. "One Scotch on the rocks," he said, pointing to Bramley. "One very dry martini for me."

"Your wife said that's your drink," he said easily.

"You saw my wife? Why?"

"Routine."

"You told her about the policy?"

"Nope. Told her I was a headhunter scouting you out for a new job."

"She believed that?"

"She sure was trying hard to believe it. She showed me your computer. Neat. Real neat."

Bramley ran his hand over his lips. "Who are you?"

"Actually I really am doing a bit of headhunting for Jim Hammond."

Bramley looked as if he might faint. The waiter brought their drinks and Charlie said, "Drink up." He sipped his martini and knew he wanted another one very fast. Bramley drank most of his Scotch without pausing. They regarded each other. Bramley looked haunted, or maybe treed. Charlie had seen that look on other faces. Sometimes if the person with that look had a gun, he began shooting. If he was on a ledge, he usually jumped.

"If you've done what we think you've done," he said softly, "Jim Hammond wants to hire you, starting now, tonight, or next week, next month, whenever you can arrange it."

"He doesn't even know. No one knows."

"Five hundred thousand dollars' worth for openers," Charlie said.

"For openers," Bramley said. He finished his Scotch.

"Hammond wants you, you can work it out together. You found

a glitch in his foolproof gadget. You could even say he needs you." He signaled the waiter to repeat the first round and then leaned back watching Bramley. "Of course, it was the dumbest thing you could do, get a policy like that and take off, I mean. Like a neon announcement."

"I never claimed to be smart. I was desperate. It would have worked. Lucky would have paid the money back and would have collected fifty thousand from Hammond. His offer is still good, isn't it? The reward for anyone who cracked his system? I wrote out exactly what I did to prove . . . Oh, my God!"

"Now what?"

"I've got to retrieve that envelope from the hotel desk!" He shook his head, then asked, "How did you find out?"

"The old Sherlock Holmes method. If it's all that's left, it's got to be it. Or something like that. We couldn't find anything on you, so I looked up your company. Two years ago they got a new Hammond computer system. I read about the guarantee and the reward. As soon as I saw that computer setup at your house, I knew."

Their new drinks had arrived before Constance showed up. She came straight to their booth and sat down next to Charlie. Bramley looked completely bewildered by her arrival.

"It's okay," Charlie said to Constance, putting his arm about her shoulders and squeezing slightly. "You put on a good show. How did you get out of it?"

"I apologized and explained many times that I had been robbed in New York by someone who casually brushed against me. She was not happy."

"You two . . .? You're with him?"

"This is my husband," Constance said. "I have your envelope. I suppose you want it back?" She took it from her purse and slid it across the table.

He looked from her to the envelope, back to her. "You've been working these past couple of days?"

She nodded. "I had planned to kidnap you and make you see

how unfair you were being, if Charlie hadn't pulled it off."

"It's too easy to make judgments from the outside," Bramley said. "It would have ruined her life, too."

"And what about the load of guilt you were planning to dump on her? Wouldn't that have ruined her life? Ruin, despair, humiliation, those were your burdens, but you know she would have shared them. Who would have shared her guilt?"

"She would have grieved, but she would have got over it. It was going to be an accident. Everyone would have accepted that."

"She already knows," Charlie said. "I don't know how, but she does."

"Just as I'd know," Constance said.

"She would have tried to stop me if she suspected," Bramley whispered.

"Maybe she feels she can take the guilt trip better than you could stand the humiliation and ruin from whatever you did. Maybe she wanted to save you from suffering," Constance said coolly.

"Stop it!" His voice broke and he gulped his drink. "You've made the point," he said.

"Lou, there's an eleven o'clock flight out of Miami for New York. You can take my rental car and turn it in for me at Miami. You have a reservation for that flight."

"This feels like a bum's rush," he said, but his eyes gleamed, and there was a look on his face that she had not seen there: boyish, eager.

"The hotel knows you're going out fishing tonight; they won't think anything of it when you don't come back. Call them from New York tomorrow."

He was nodding. "I really don't have to go back there. I could drive over in a couple, three hours. What time is it?"

"Seven-thirty."

"I'd better get started."

"I got some sandwiches, and a thermos of coffee. They're on the front seat. Here's the agreement for the car, and the key." Constance handed them to him.

He folded the paper and stuffed it in his pocket and brought out another slip of paper. He looked at it, then let it fall to the table. "My receipt for the fishing trip. Paid in full." Now he stood up. He looked down at Constance. "I don't know yet what I think about you. I owe you a lot. Thanks." Suddenly he leaned down and kissed her forehead. He reached across her to shake Charlie's hand. "You don't really have anything for me to sign. That was all done a month ago. Right?"

"Right. Good look, Lou. Hammond's waiting for your call." He hesitated, then asked, "Fill me in on one thing, before you go. What do you think the Oliveira woman was up to?"

"I think she knew I was going to die and she was hanging around to watch," he said without hesitation. "She'll be disappointed. Keep out of her way," he added, looking at Constance. "She's a ghoul, probably crazy, and I think she's very dangerous."

They watched him leave, then Charlie turned to Constance.

"Okay. What was that all about? He's right, it was the bum's rush. Why?"

"I don't think he would have been able to leave again if he had gone back to the hotel. I don't know how or why but that woman does have some kind of power over him. I think he's right, Charlie. She knew. That's what she was waiting for."

Charlie took a deep breath, blew it out again in exasperation. "Tell me," he said.

When she kept it all very objective, as she did now, Constance knew there was nothing frightening about the woman. She repelled and fascinated Lou Bramley, nothing too unusual there; except, she told herself, both she and Lou Bramley knew it was more than that, even if neither of them could ever demonstrate it.

"Now, you tell me. What did he do? He's not a crook."

"Not in the usual sense anyway. His company got a big multi-million-dollar computer system two years ago, guaranteed safe against illicit access. And Bramley couldn't resist trying to break into it. It was a game, puzzle-solving. And he did it. Eighteen months ago he got his own computer at home, and it's been like having a mouse in the cheese cupboard ever since. God knows how much money he's diverted, where it is. Hammond, the computer company president, wants to hire him." He shrugged. "I think I got out of the crime business at a good time. I just don't understand things anymore. Hammond said half a dozen companies would hire him if he actually got access to that computer. And I guess he did."

Hours later when Charlie fished for his keys, he felt the receipt for the charter boat and brought it out also. "Let's do it," he said. "Let's go fishing."

"He's going to take off at high tide, at three or a little after," she said. She thought of the glassy water of the gulf. "We have to sleep aboard if we're going." They began to hurry, like children rushing to a picnic.

For a moment or two Constance was aware of another feeling, the same one she had felt years ago when she had looked out her kitchen window that Saturday morning. The same, but intensified, and also directionless.

"You know," Charlie said, driving, "this is something I've wanted to do all my life. Never thought the chance would drop into my lap like this. Freezing rain was falling when I left the city . . ."

Beside him Constance was caught up in his infectious gaiety; she pushed the intrusive feeling of dread and fear out of her mind.

II

At the docks she and Charlie went into an all-night diner to ask directions, and they met Dino Skaggs there, one of the brothers who owned *Dinah's Way*. He was a wiry brown man with sunbleached hair, his face so wrinkled it was hard to guess his age, which Constance thought was about thirty-five give or take a few years.

Dino scowled when Charlie showed him the receipt. "You sure he isn't coming?" he asked suspiciously, studying the receipt.

"I'm sure," Charlie said. "Look, if there's an additional charge because there's two of us, we'll pay it."

Dino bit his lip as he studied Charlie, then Constance. "Shit," he said finally. "Hundred per head, in advance. We shove off at three. No checks," he added as Charlie pulled out his checkbook.

"I have cash," Constance said. She counted out the hundred and handed it to Dino who recounted it.

He stood with the money in his hand, still frowning glumly. "Shit, I guess you won't be eating all that much." He peeled off five tens and thrust the bills back to her. "Don't bother to come aboard until two-thirty, and keep it quiet when you do. We've got a sleeping passenger aboard already." He slouched away.

"Well," Constance said. "You're sure about this?"

"Shit yes," Charlie said, grinning. "Want some coffee?"

Dino met them on the dock where *Dinah's Way* was moored. It was too dark to tell much about the boat, except that it looked small, and very pretty, sparkling white with blue letters, blue trim, gleaming copper rails. It looked less like a fishing boat than Charlie had anticipated.

"You'll want to watch the lights and all, I guess," Dino said morosely. "I'm going to settle you in the stern and you stay put. When you've had enough, you go on to your stateroom. And no talking in the galley. Inside your room with the door closed it's okay, just keep it low. Right?"

Charlie said, "Aye, aye," and Dino groaned. Constance felt a stab of impatience with Charlie. He was too eager, too willing to let this pipsqueak boss him around.

"I'll take her out from up on the flybridge," Dino went on. He led them aboard, and to the rear. The boat rocked gently. "Grandstand seats," Dino said, pointing to two fighting chairs. "Back through here," he said, motioning them to come to the cabin, "you go down the stairs, and turn right at the bottom. There's a yellow light over the door, that's your room. Light switch on the wall. Head at the far end. Bathroom," he added, glancing at Constance. "You'd better take your seats. I'll see you in the morning." He waved to a man who was leaning against a piling and vanished around the side of the boat.

Constance leaned toward Charlie. "What's a flybridge?"

"I don't know."

They sat back in their chairs and watched the gleaming black water laced with ladders and bridges and arcs of lights. The engines started up and Charlie found Constance's hand and held it; lights came on above and around them, running lights, Charlie thought with self-satisfaction, and then they were moving easily, backing away from the dock, out into the bay. Here and there other boats were moving, small boats with lights hardly above the water line, larger fishing boats, a yacht that made everything else look toylike. Charlie sighed with contentment.

When they finally went to bed, after all the lights had disappeared in the distance, they shared one of the bunks. Sometime during the night Charlie moved to the other one and fell asleep instantly again.

He woke up first and was amazed to find that it was nearly eight. The motion of the boat was very gentle, nothing like what he had imagined. He had never been on a boat before, except for a rowboat when he was a kid. He thought of the seascapes he had admired, always stormy, threatening. Another time, he decided, and was glad that today the gulf was like a pond, the boat's motion hardly noticeable. As soon as he got up and started toward the head, he realized the motion had been effectively concealed while he had been horizontal. He held to the bunk and groped for the door. He had just finished showering when he heard Constance scream.

He flung open the shower door and stopped. Standing in the open doorway to the galley stood June Oliveira staring at Constance.

"Where is he?" she demanded.

✿

"Why didn't you tell us she was aboard?" Charlie snapped.

They were in the galley where Dino was making breakfast. June Oliveira had gone forward, he told them.

"I don't recall that you asked me," Dino said, breaking eggs, his back to them.

"We have to go back," Constance said.

Now Dino turned. "Lady, get this one thing straight. This is my boat. I'm the skipper. I say when we come out and when we go in. I made a contract with Mr. Bramley, all signed, paid for, everything. You and your husband said you wanted to use that contract. That means we do it my way. And that means we fish until this afternoon. I pick up my brother Petie, and then we go back. That's in the contract, and I'm following it to the letter. You don't want to fish, fine. You can look at scenery. I'll fish."

"When did she come aboard?" Charlie asked, his voice easy now, his working voice, Constance thought.

"Last night. I was checking things out and there she came. What's this? What's that? I'm going, too, you know. I'm his guest, you know. He wants to pretend it isn't planned, so just don't say anything to him, so he won't have to lie about it. That's her story. How was I to know anything?"

Charlie nodded in sympathy. "I've seen her operate. But you could have mentioned it to us," he added reasonably.

"Yeah. I should have. I was afraid you wouldn't want to go, and I sure as hell didn't want to go out alone with her. She's . . . I don't know. Anyway, I had to go out to pick up Petie, and I'm sticking to the original schedule. Now let's eat." He motioned toward the table where there was a coffee pot. "Help yourselves."

The galley was sparkling with copper fixtures, everything so compact and well planned that in an area hardly more than five feet square there was a two-burner stove, a refrigerator, sink, cabinets. The table and a right-angled bench could seat half a dozen people. Behind it there was a wall separating off another stateroom, and beyond that the pilot's cabin. The boat was moving slowly, on automatic pilot while Dino did the galley chores.

Charlie began to wonder how much it all cost. Opposite the galley was what Dino called the saloon, with three chairs and a bench-sofa and coffee table. The walls were mellow, rich paneling. Teak? mahogany? It looked expensive.

Dino served up ham and scrambled eggs and fluffy cinnamon rolls.

"Are you going to call her?" Charlie asked.

"She said she'd have coffee a little later. I think she's mad as hell." He looked at Constance who was eating nothing, just drinking the coffee. "Look, I'm sorry. But the boat's big enough for four people not to get in each other's way. You and Charlie just stay in the stern, do a little fishing. I'll see that she stays forward, or up in the flybridge. I can run the boat from the pilot's bridge down here, or from up there, either way."

"He showed them the pilot's bridge. "Dual controls," he said, "for the two diesels. This is clutch, this is throttle. Midway, that's idle, forward for going ahead, back like this to reverse, down all the way to stop. That's all there is to that. And the wheel here, just like a car, only you allow for more time and space for everything to happen. Okay?" He glanced around at the instrument panel. "You won't need more than that. In case Charlie gets a big one, I might have you run us while I help him. Oh, yeah, here's the starter, just in case you need it. Just flip it on."

Again Charlie was struck by the simplicity and the beauty of the boat. He was very much afraid the Skaggs boys were running more than fish out of the gulf waters. And he told himself to forget it, he wanted no part of the drug business; he was retired.

Dino got Charlie baited up, urged Constance again to give it a try, then went below. In a few minutes, he said, they'd start trolling. Constance looked at the water, almost too bright to stand; there were long, smooth swells, and now and then there was a soft plop as water broke against the side of the boat. She had grown used to the lesser slaps of water; the larger sounds broke the rhythm. Something splashed out of sight behind her and she wondered, prey or predator? The sea stretched out endlessly, formless, exactly the same everywhere, and yet different under the lazy swells. It would be terrifying to be out there alone, she thought; they were so small and the sea was so big. Another splash sounded and this time she swiveled to see what it was. She could not even see ripples. Prey or predator? She caught a movement from the corner of her eye and turned farther and looked into the eyes of June Oliveira up on the flybridge. She's frightening because her expression never changes, Constance thought, and abruptly swung back around. She felt cold in the hot sunlight. She should have known that woman would be aboard. It had been easy enough to figure out that Bramley had planned his accident to take place at sea.

"Why didn't you argue with Dino at least a little?" she asked bitterly.

"Wouldn't have done any good. I'm afraid we're on a drug run, honey. So let's just play it real cool. I'm in the insurance racket and you're a housewife. Period. We don't know from nothing. Right?"

"Oh, for heaven's sake!" she muttered helplessly, and stared at the brilliant water until her eyes smarted.

Dino brought her a big floppy straw hat and a long-sleeved shirt. "You're going to cook," he said. "You're already burning. People as pale as you can get sun poisoning without ever getting warm."

"Thanks," she said and he ducked away quickly, back to the pilot's bridge. Soon the boat began to move a little faster through the calm waters. "He's hard to hate," Constance said, tying the ribbon of the hat under her chin.

Charlie nodded, and thought, but he's a drug runner. Sometimes he tried to sort out the criminals he hated most on a scale from one to ten. Usually he put arsonists first, but he knew that was prejudice. He had had to get transferred from the arson squad when he had started having nightmares, had smelled smoke where there wasn't any, and suspected smoldering rags behind all locked doors. Child molesters came next, then rapists, and drug pushers, murderers ... But he always changed the order even as he composed it because some of them obviously had to be second, and they couldn't all be. He glanced at Constance; her eyes were closed.

He woke up with a start. Dino had touched his shoulder. "Sorry," Charlie muttered. Constance was coming awake also.

"Doesn't matter," Dino said. "If you'd got a strike that would have waked you up pretty fast. Just wanted to tell you, might as well reel in. I'm taking us to a place to try some reef fishing. Might get something there. Good place for scuba diving." He looked at Charlie hopefully, shrugged when Charlie shook his head.

Dino sent June Oliveira down from the flybridge, and then the boat stood up and raced through the water. Charlie nodded at Constance. He had suspected there was a lot more power in the engines than they had witnessed before.

June Oliveira braced herself in the doorway to the galley; she looked terrified. Constance remembered what Lou Bramley had said about her: she did nothing dangerous. Obviously she thought what they were doing was dangerous. Constance was glad to see that she did have at least one other expression.

When Dino cut the engines and came down he looked happy, as if this was what he liked to do, open it up and roar, leaving a wide white wake behind them as straight as a highway through a desert.

"Lunchtime," he said cheerfully. "Then you'll get a snapper or two, Charlie. Bet you a ten spot on it."

He would have won. Charlie caught a red snapper within the first fifteen minutes of fishing over the reefs.

"It's a beauty," Dino said. "Catch its mate and that's our supper. Go ashore, build a little fire, roast them on a spit. That's good eating, Charlie. Just you wait and see." He was keeping an eye on the progress of the sun, evidently timing their day carefully. "You've got half an hour." He watched Charlie bait his hook, patted him on the back, and left with the first snapper, to put it on ice. The boat was again on automatic, moving slowly over the shadows of the reefs.

Charlie was excited and pleased with himself, Constance knew, standing close to him, watching the water. The live fish on his line went this way and that, and vanished. Charlie was muttering that it was pulling, maybe he had something, no, it was just the bait fish. Something splashed behind them. Charlie let out more line as his bait fish headed deeper. Constance was watching, looking down, when she caught a glimpse of a larger motion. She jerked her head around and saw Dino in the water behind them.

"Charlie! Look!"

He dropped his rod and grabbed at one of the life preservers clamped in place against the side of the cabin. "Get this thing back there!" he yelled to Constance as he moved.

She raced through the cabin, through the saloon to the pilot's bridge. Put it on manual, she thought clearly, and flipped the automatic control off. Pull the control back to reverse. She pulled the lever back, heard a slight click as it passed neutral, and then the engines stopped. She groaned and hit the lever back up to the neutral position, aligned the clutch control. She pushed the starter, nothing. She repeated it several times before she gave up and ran back to the stern where Charlie was standing rigidly, staring at the water behind them. Their momentum was pushing them forward slower and slower.

"I killed the engines," Constance said, tearing off her hat, loosening her sneaker with her other hand.

"What are you doing?" Charlie asked. His voice sounded strange, forced.

"I'm going in after him."

Charlie's hand clamped painfully on her arm. He was still looking at the water. Now Constance looked. There was the life preserver, nearly two hundred feet away, bobbing easily. There was no sign of Dino.

"I almost hit him with it," Charlie said in that strained, thick voice. "He could have reached out and touched it, caught it. He never made a motion toward it. He wasn't even trying to swim."

"I can still get him up," Constance said, jerking her arm, trying to get loose.

"No! He went down like a stone. He's on the bottom, already dead. He wasn't even struggling."

Constance felt her knees threaten to buckle. She turned to look at the flybridge: June Oliveira was standing up there facing the life preserver. Her eyes were closed.

"She did it," Constance whispered. "She killed him."

"Take it easy, honey," Charlie said. "She was up there the whole time." He turned away from the water now. "He must have had a stroke or something, couldn't move, couldn't swim. He didn't even yell. Maybe he was already dying before he fell in."

"You don't just fall overboard," Constance said, watching June Oliveira who hugged herself, opening her eyes. She looked at Constance; her expression was as blank as ever. She moved to the ladder and descended from the flybridge.

"I think I lie down now," she said.

They watched her enter the cabin. "Let's go up there and see if we can get this boat started," Charlie said. He sounded tired. Wordlessly Constance started up the ladder to the flybridge.

The flybridge was built over the main cabin; the front was enclosed, the rear open with another fighting chair. There were wrap-around windows and a control panel exactly like the one below, the same wheel, dual controls for the engines, automatic pilot. The same array of dials and indicators that neither of them understood. Charlie sat down behind the wheel and looked at the controls: the automatic was turned to OFF, it must have moved when Constance turned it below. The dual controls were both at midpoint, in neutral. He turned on the starter. Dead.

"I thought it might be like a car engine," Constance said. "Maybe I flooded it when I moved the throttle too fast." She knelt down and tried to see behind the control panel. It was all enclosed.

"What are you looking for?"

"A wire. She must have pulled a wire loose or something."

Charlie shook his head. "Knock it off, honey. I'm telling you, she was nowhere near him. Let's go find the engines. Maybe we can tell if it's flooded, or if a battery connection is loose."

"See if the radio works," Constance said.

Charlie had no idea what most of the switches and knobs were for, but he did know how to operate a radio. It was dead.

At three Charlie called June Oliveira to the galley. He had made coffee, and was drinking a beer. Constance watched the other woman warily when she drew near to sit at the small table. She said she wanted nothing when Charlie offered her a drink.

"We're in a spot," Charlie said. "I don't think it's especially serious, but still, there it is. I can't make this boat go. I don't know how and neither does my wife. Do you know how to run it?"

She shook her head. "It is the first time I am on a boat."

"I thought so. Okay. So we have to wait for help. We have no electricity, and that means no lights. Someone may spot us before dark; if not we'll have to take shifts and keep a watch. I'm afraid we might be run down, or we might miss a passing ship or small boat. I found a flare gun to signal with if we see anything." He poured more coffee for Constance.

"His brother, he is expecting us," June Oliveira said. "When we do not arrive, he informs the authorities. Yes? They come for us then."

Charlie shrugged. He was trying to place her accent. Not Spanish, not anything he had heard before. Portuguese? He did not think so; there had been some São Paulo students at the crime lab, eight, nine years ago, and they had not sounded like her. He said, "Eventually they'll come, but I doubt they'll hear from Petie right away." Little brother, he thought, would have to hide something first, bury it, sink it at sea, do something. Depending on where he was, little brother might have to be rescued also. "We'd better prepare for an all-night wait, and a daylight search tomorrow."

"If there is more beer . . ." June Oliveira said then.

He took one from the refrigerator and handed it to her. Already the ice was melting. They would have to eat before dark, before the butter melted, the other food spoiled.

"If you two will start keeping a watch now," he said, "I'll gather up everything I can think of that we might need during the night. I found one flashlight only, so we'd better have things in one place." He handed a pair of binoculars to Constance. "You take the flybridge. Yell out if you see anything. Miss Oliveira, you go forward and keep an eye open for a ship. Later we'll switch around, choose lots or something. Okay?"

Constance watched her go around the cabin to the forward deck before she started up the ladder to the flybridge. Charlie handed up the coffee and the binoculars to her.

"Be careful," she said softly.

Charlie felt a twinge of impatience with her. He nodded and turned to his task. When Constance got a notion, he thought, she played it to the bitter end, no matter how ridiculous it was. He scanned the water briefly before going back inside. He could no longer see the life preserver and he was glad even though he could not tell if the boat had drifted, or if the wind had simply taken the doughnut away. He was glad it was not there, a constant reminder that he had done nothing at all, and had prevented Constance from trying to do anything. She swam like a fish; she might have saved him. He did not believe it, but the thought came back over and over. He remembered his own feeling of terror at the idea of letting Constance go over the side after Dino: what if she got out there and just stopped swimming, as he had done? He knew he could not have helped her, he would have watched her look of incomprehension, fear, disbelief ... Angrily he jerked up a life jacket and stood holding it. Where to put things? Not on the table, which they would be using off and on. Not in the saloon, probably they would take turns sleeping on the couch. Finally he opened the door to the stateroom he and Constance had shared the night before. He put the life jacket on her bunk and went out to continue his search; a first aid kit, what else? He was not certain what they might need; he could make no list and then go search. All he could do was collect things he saw that looked useful. He felt the same helplessness now that he had experienced when Constance had said they did not even know what switch to throw to put out an anchor to stop their drift. He did not know where they were, how fast they might be drifting, or in what direction, not necessarily pushed by the wind, although they might be; it was also possible that they were in a current from the Florida straits. He simply did not know.

✻

Constance made a hurried scan of the horizon in all directions, and then a slower search. She saw birds, and she saw porpoises in the distance. A few hours ago the sight would have thrilled her, seeing them leaping; now it was depressing that only the creatures of the sea were out there. Charlie clearly thought Dino's death was the result of a seizure of some sort; she knew she would not be able to convince him of anything else. Up here, examining the problem logically, she agreed that it had been an accident, but she rejected the logic. She knew June Oliveira had been responsible even if she did not understand how she had done it. She knew, and accepted, that she would not have been able to save Dino. It would not have been allowed. She could not see the woman from on the flybridge, and she could not hear Charlie moving about. She bit her lip and strained to hear something, but there was only the slap, slap of water on the side of the boat, and a faraway bird call. She went down the ladder and met Charlie coming up from the cabin.

"What's wrong? Did you see a ship?"

"No. I just came down for my hat." She had left it in the saloon. She retrieved it and started up again. "Charlie, say something to me now and then, or whistle, or something. Okay?" His nod was perfunctory and absent-minded. He was tying a self-inflating rubber raft to the side rail, out of the way of traffic, but available if they needed it. A second raft was already tied in place. Constance returned to her post and did the entire search again.

The sun was getting lower; a couple more hours of daylight, she thought, and then the long night wondering what Oliveira would do next, if she could do anything as long as Constance was awake and watching her. She leaned over the side of the fly-bridge and called, "Charlie, is there plenty of water?"

"Yeah, I checked. And plenty of coffee," he added, as if reading her mind. She smiled slightly and looked at the sea.

They should eat something before it started to get dark, she decided a little later. Oliveira could come up here while she made something; she started down the ladder again. There was only the gentle sloshing sound of water. Charlie was still below, maybe swearing at the engines ... She took a step toward the cabin door, paused, and instead went to the side of the cabin and looked forward. June Oliveira was standing at the rail near the pilot's cabin windows, and beyond her, ten feet away, Charlie was swinging one leg over the rail.

Soundlessly Constance dashed the fifteen feet to the woman and hit her with her shoulder, knocking her flat. She kept going and grabbed Charlie who was hanging onto the rail, dangling over the water. She hauled on Charlie's arms and he pulled himself up, got purchase with his foot, and heaved himself back aboard. He was the color of putty.

June Oliveira was starting to sit up.

"You move another muscle and I'm going to throw you overboard!" Charlie yelled at her. He unfastened the inflatable raft he had secured to the rail and tied the rope to one of the loops on it. Holding it over the side, he pulled the release and then dropped it, keeping the rope in his hand, letting it out as the raft fell and settled.

"Now get up!" he ordered. "Over the side, down the ladder. Move!"

She shook her head. "I am hurt! Your wife attacked me! I think my back is broken."

"You'd better be able to swim, lady. You go down under your own power, or I'm going to throw you in and let you swim for the raft. Right now!"

"You are crazy," she said.

"Hold this," Charlie said, handing the end of the rope to Constance, taking a step toward the woman. She was on her knees, and now she scrambled up, clinging to the side of the boat, then to the rail. She looked terrified, the way she had looked when Dino had roared at full speed over the water. "There's the ladder," Charlie said, stopping within reach of her. She backed away, stepped up the two steps to the rail, and over it, down the ladder. Charlie maneuvered the raft closer and she stepped into it, clutching the sides. "Get down low," he said. "I'm towing you to the other side." He didn't wait for her to crouch down, but yanked on the rope and hauled the raft, bumping and rubbing against the boat hull, around to the other side where he tied it securely.

"Let's go below," he said to Constance then. "I sure God want a drink."

Silently he poured bourbon for them both, added some shrunken ice cubes, and took a long drink from his.

A long shudder passed over him and his knees felt weak. He sat down and pulled Constance to his side, put his arm around her shoulders, and held her tight against him.

"Oh, Charlie," she said softly, "I'm afraid we've caught ourselves a boojum."

He held her tighter. He still saw himself going into the water, not struggling, not trying to swim, going under, down, down . . .

"I think you're right," he said. His voice was so normal that few people would have detected the difference, the slight huskiness, the almost too careful spacing of words.

"Do you know what happened to you?" Constance asked. She drank also and welcomed the warmth; she had become icy cold now that the woman was in the raft, and she and Charlie were side by side.

"I was going to go over just as if I had decided to do it. I was doing it and I was watching myself do it. Watching her watching me, pushing me, not even trying not to go, not even trying to resist. I was just doing it."

She nodded. Neither of them said, like Dino. "What are we going to do?"

"Remember when I read 'The Hunting of the Snark' to Jessica? Remember what she said when I asked what she'd do if she caught a boojum?"

Constance nodded again. Jessica had said the only thing to do was cut it loose and run.

"It might come to that," Charlie said grimly. "It just might." He took the last swallow of his bourbon, then pushed the glass away. He got up and put the coffee pot on the burner to heat it. "Start with the first time you saw her, the first thing Bramley said about her," he said. "You were right, honey. I should have paid attention. Let's try to make some sense out of it now."

He stopped her when she told again how Lou Bramley had bypassed her to sit at a table with June Oliveira. "Exactly what did he do?"

"You know the wide doors? He stood there looking around until he spotted me and he started toward my table." She closed her eyes visualizing it. "Then he looked past me and he didn't look at me again. His face changed a little, became set, almost like a sleepwalker, or someone in trance." She opened her eyes. "She did it then too. I was blind not to realize."

"You couldn't have known," Charlie said. "Then what?"

"I waited a minute or two. Then I decided to spoil it for her, to join them. I got up and started toward their table..." She stopped, remembering. "I thought it was my decision to take a walk instead. Oh, my God, I wasn't even aware...I didn't even wonder about it!"

Charlie squeezed her shoulder. "Try to remember exactly how it was, honey, I think it may be important. What was he doing when you started to walk?"

"His back was to me. He was staring at the water. I got pretty close to them before I changed my...He hadn't moved, I'm sure. Then I turned right." She stopped, eyes closed. "I think he might have stood up, there was a motion. I just caught it from the corner of my eye, and I was thinking how hot it was on the sand. It was sunny, and I had been trying to avoid the hot sun. I went a little farther and decided I didn't want to walk after all."

"You were thinking it was hot, all that, close to their table?"

She nodded. "What is it, Charlie?"

"She couldn't hold both of you," he said. "She got you past the table and lost him, grabbed him back and lost you. What do you think?"

She considered it and nodded. "But we can't be certain. We can't count on it."

"No, but it's something." The other thing she had said, that the woman did nothing dangerous, alarmed him. No doubt she thought it was very dangerous out there on the raft with night coming on fast. She might even be right; it could be dangerous. He didn't know.

"I'd better start making sandwiches," Constance said. "We're all going to be hungry eventually."

"Okay, but keep talking. What else was there?"

She talked as she rummaged in the refrigerator and the cabinets. When she stopped again, Charlie was staring fixedly at the table top, deep in thought. She did not interrupt him, but continued to assemble the sandwiches.

It did not make any sense to him. If she had that kind of

power, to control people like that, why use it in such a perverse way? Murder was so commonplace, never really dull, but not exciting either; it was always sad, always futile, always the action of ultimate failure. It was the final admission that there was no solution to a problem, no human solution. But no one needed her kind of power to commit murder. A gun, a knife, poison, a brick, a fire . . . he had seen them all; death that looked accidental — a fall, car exhaust in a closed garage, a leaky gas stove, overdoses of everything that could be swallowed. All filthy, all irreversible, all committed by ordinary people for ordinary reasons: money, sex, revenge, greed . . . All committed without her kind of power. That was the puzzle. Why use such a gift for something so mundane? And why out here in God knew what part of the gulf? She could be knocking people off every day of the week — running them in front of trains, making them jump from high places, forcing them to put bullets through their brains. Who would suspect? Each and every one would go down as accidental, or suicide.

He remembered what Lou Bramley had said, that she had known he was going to die and wanted to watch. He nodded.

Constance, seeing the nod, stopped all movement, waiting, but Charlie continued to stare through the table top.

Bramley had been broadcasting death and she had picked it up somehow. She had planned to watch for whatever insane pleasure that gave her, and she had been cheated. Again Charlie nodded. She had had her death through murder, not suicide. And she planned to kill the witnesses. Now he shook his head. No one had witnessed anything. What could he or Constance say that could damage her? She could make a better case against them. Of course, if she was a psychopath, none of the best reasoning in the world would apply to her. He rejected that also. She was the boojum, an *it*, not like other people. He could not fathom her motives in either event — a whacko, or something inhuman. And, he thought, motives were not the issue. What she might try next was the only issue now. She had tried to kill him, damn near succeeded, and she no doubt would try again.

But she had not come out here to kill, he said to himself, and he held on to that one thought as the only clue he had about her, the only thing he was reasonably certain about. If the original plan had worked, Bramley would be dead now, a legitimate suicide passing for accident, and she and Dino would be back ashore. Their stories would have been accepted: Dino was well known; the insurance would have entered into it. Finis. Dino's death was a different matter. No one would believe he had fallen off his own boat in a dead calm, in the first place. And it was less plausible to suggest that he had not got back aboard even if he had managed to fall. Although no one could prove anything else, no one would ever believe that story. What if there were others, like her, who would know the story he and Constance could tell was true? His skin prickled all over at the thought that his people would never believe his story, but that this woman's people, if she had people, would.

He was certain she planned to be the sole survivor of a ghastly tragedy. No one knew he and Constance were aboard. If they vanished, no one would know that. The contract would be found with Bramley's name, and he was in New York, out of it. She could say anything to account for Dino's disappearance, and he was the only one she would have to account for actually.

Constance froze in the motion of cutting through a sandwich, Charlie lifted his head and listened. June Oliveira was calling them in a shrill, panic-stricken voice.

They went out together, staying close to each other. Constance still carried the butcher knife.

"There is a shark! I saw it! You can not keep me out here! I will stay in the little room. You lock the door. Please, I did not do nothing. You know I did not!"

In the west a spectacular sunset was blossoming; the light had turned deep pink making June Oliveira look flushed, almost ruddy, very normal, ordinary, and very frightened.

"Who are you?" Constance demanded.

"I see him starting to climb over the rail, and I am petrified. I cannot move. I am terrified of water. I can not to help him or call out or anything. I am coward. I am sorry."

"You don't just watch them die, do you?" Constance said. "You weren't watching Dino. Your eyes were closed. You feel it, experience it. Why? Why don't you feel your own people's deaths? Why ours?"

"She crazy," June Oliveira wailed to Charlie. "She crazy!"

"I saw you," Constance said. "You knew exactly when Dino died. We didn't, we couldn't know, but you did. You planned to experience Lou's death. You come here to feel death without dying yourselves, don't you? Do your people ever die? Just by accident, don't they? Isn't that why you're so terrified of water, of fire, of anything that might be dangerous?"

"Please give me jacket, or sweater. I am cold. So afraid," June Oliveira moaned.

"For God's sake," Charlie said and turned away. "I'll get her jacket."

"How many of you are there?" Constance asked furiously. "How many murders do you commit? How many accidents do you cause?"

The woman was huddled down, her arms wrapped about herself. Suddenly Constance realized what she had done; she had separated them. She turned to see Charlie in the narrow passage between the rail and the cabin, coming toward her, carrying the heavy gaff, the iron hook Dino had said they used on the big ones.

Constance put the knife to the rope tethering the raft. "Let him go or I'll cut you loose! You'll drift away. He can't bring you back, he doesn't know how." She began to cut.

She stopped the sawing motion and watched as if from a great distance as the knife turned in her hand, began to move toward her midsection. In the stomach, she thought, so death wouldn't be too fast. There would be time to feel it all, to know it was happening . . .

Charlie leaped at her, grabbed the knife, and threw it out into the water. His hand dripped blood.

Constance sagged, then straightened. "My God, oh, my God! You're hurt! Let's go fix it." Neither of them looked at the woman in the raft as they hurried away, back inside the cabin.

"What are we going to do?" Constance whispered. "Charlie, what can we do? We can't even cut her loose!"

"Get the first aid kit," Charlie said calmly. "You'll need the flashlight. The kit's on your bed. Bring a clean towel too."

Constance snatched up the flashlight and ran to the stateroom for the kit and towel. When she returned Charlie was washing the blood from his hand. She dried and bandaged it and neither spoke until she was done.

"I'm going to kill her," Charlie said. He reached out and gently touched the shirt Constance had on. There was a slash in it; she had not even noticed, had not realized how close it had been.

This was why some people murdered, Charlie thought, because there really was no solution, no human solution. How easy it was to step across that line. He felt as if he had always known that, had denied knowing it, had pretended it was not true when of course it had been true from the beginning. When he had transferred from the arson squad it had been because he had dreamed too many times that he was the one arranging the materials, pouring the oil or the gasoline, setting the match. The thrill of the pursuer, the thrill of the pursued, who could tell how different they were? Now that he had crossed that imaginary line, that arbitrary line that each cop drew for himself, he knew the thrill was the same, the desperation the same, the fear, it was all the same.

"We can't cut her loose," he said in that deceptively calm voice, "So we cut ourselves loose, We have to go out in the other raft, get the hell away from her. She'll try again, maybe soon. Before it gets much darker." He glanced about the galley. "Start packing up everything you think we might need for tonight and tomorrow. We might not be picked up for hours, maybe a couple of days. Fill whatever you can find with water."

Thank God she didn't argue, he thought, going into the stateroom. She knew their chances of escaping as well as he did, knew their only chance was in getting distance between them and June Oliveira. He lifted the mattress of his bunk; foam, he thought with disgust. There was a plywood board, and beneath it there were cabinets with linens. He nodded. It would do. He cut a circle out of the foam mattress with his pocketknife and tucked the extra piece under the pillow on the other bed. He had seen a can of charcoal starter in a cabinet in the galley; he went out to get it. He took the flashlight back with the can. He soaked the plywood board and let it air out before he replaced the mattress. In the hole he now put a folded towel and then added a layer of crumpled toilet paper, then another towel, this one folded in such a way that the paper was exposed in the center of it. He studied it for a minute and sighed. The fumes were gone, the odor so faint that he might not have noticed it if he were not sniffing. He had seen cigarettes somewhere, in one of the cabinets in the saloon. Dino did not smoke, but maybe Petie did, or their guests. He went to the saloon and found the new package and opened it, lighted a cigarette with the flame from the stove. Constance was filling a plastic water bottle, a collapsible gallon jug. There were two at the bottom of the stairs, already filled. She looked startled at the cigarette, but she still asked no questions.

"About ready?" Charlie asked.

She nodded. "It's getting dark fast."

"Yes. Come on, let's tell her our plans."

"Charlie . . ." She stopped; there was not enough time to spell it out. She followed him to the door.

Charlie went to the corner of the cabin and yelled, "You, you can have the goddamn boat! We're taking off in the other raft. Before we go I'm going to toss the portable ladder over your side so you can climb aboard. Just leave us alone and let us take off. Is it a deal?"

He puffed the cigarette hard. It was not yet dark, but within half an hour it would be. Already the water looked solid, impenetrable, and there were two stars in the deep violet sky. She must be calculating her chances of getting one of them before dark, making the other bring her aboard. He was not even sure she could make someone do anything as complicated as that; she was not a telepath. Her power was cruder, a total assault, a complete takeover. She could not read their thoughts, he said to himself, praying it was true.

"If you leave the flashlight. Put it on the flybridge, turned on so I can see it." She sounded calmer, and was controlling her accent and syntax better, but her voice was still tremulous.

He let out his breath. "Okay. We're taking provisions with us, water and stuff. It'll take us a few minutes, ten maybe."

He nodded to Constance. "Let's get the life jackets and other stuff over by the ladder."

As Constance began to carry things from the cabin to the railing Charlie entered the stateroom again. He lighted a second cigarette from the first and then put them both very carefully on top of the paper in the hole in the mattress. He pulled the sheet over it, and the bedspread, with ripples in it for air to pass through easily. For years he had known how easy it would be, how well he would be able to do it. He put the extra life jackets on that bed, and then he was through. He left the stateroom door open when he went into the cabin. One last thing he had to get, he thought, almost leisurely, and he went to the drawer where he had seen an assortment of thread and needles. He chose the largest needle, a darning needle, or a sail-mending needle; it was four inches long and only slightly less thick than an ice-pick. He stuck it through his shirt. Constance returned for the last of the items she had put aside, the bag of sandwiches.

"Listen," he said to her softly. "We'll put the raft out, make sure the paddles are in it, and then load. While you're putting the flashlight on the flybridge, I'm going to swim around the boat. The last thing you do is hang the ladder over the side, make sure it's secure and everything. We don't want her to get suspicious now. Then you get in the raft and start paddling to the front end of the boat. You pick me up there and we paddle like hell."

"What are you going to do?"

He pointed to the needle. "Puncture her escape route."

Constance shook her head and began to strip. "That's my department," she said. "You'd never make it in time, and you splash like a puppy. Same plan, different performers."

"No!" He saw her, arms crossed over her chest, sinking, sinking . . .

"Yes! Let's move!" She was making a bundle of her clothes. She had on only her bra. Now she reached out and took the needle and put it through the top of the bra. "You know the only way it'll work is if I do that part. You know that. We don't dare have her out in the water alive. We have no idea how far she can reach."

He pulled her to him and kissed her hard, and then they hurried to get the raft into the water, get it loaded. Only one quadrant of the sky was still light now; to the east the sky and sea merged in blackness.

"Arrange it any way you can," Charlie said, nodding to her, when they were through. She slipped from the raft soundlessly and vanished into the dark water. "That looks good enough for now. When I get in we can shift things around some. I'll put the flashlight up there, and then give her the ladder. You okay?"

It was all taking much longer than he had realized it would, he thought bleakly. What if smoke began to pour from the cabin? What if she got suspicious, caught Constance down there in the water? What if she took this as her last chance to get them both? He climbed to the flybridge and put the flashlight down, shining toward the stern, away from where Constance might be surfacing. What if there really had been a shark? He felt weak with fear; his hands were trembling so hard he could scarcely hold the rail as he left the flybridge to get the ladder.

Constance surfaced at the prow of the boat and waited. There was the ladder, and Charlie was running away to the other side. June Oliveira had to haul herself in hand over hand to reach the ladder; she started to climb. As soon as she started up, Constance sank below the surface again and swam to the raft. She lifted her face only enough to get air, then went under and pulled out the needle and stuck it into the raft. The raft bobbed and she stopped moving, afraid the woman would be alarmed, turn around. She stuck the needle in three more times before she had to surface for air. The next time she went under she began to swim toward the prow of the boat, praying that Charlie would be there by now.

When Charlie first started to paddle, he found himself moving away from the boat at right angles. Frantically he pulled with one paddle until he bumped the boat. Keeping against the hull, using one paddle only, he finally got to the front end. Where was she? She should be here by now, he thought with despair, and she appeared at the side of the raft. He grabbed her arm and hauled her in, and she began to pull on her clothes as fast as she could. She was shivering hard from the cold water, the chill night air. Before she got her shirt buttoned, Charlie was putting the life jacket on her. He was wearing his already. As soon as she had the life jacket tied, she took her place by him, took up the paddle, and they both began to row hard. The raft did not move through the water easily, it seemed to be mired in tar, but gradually they pulled away from the boat, and now Charlie could see the light from the flash bobbing in the windows of the cabin, then the pilot's cabin, stern. She was checking it out, as he had thought she might. She went to the flybridge and in a minute or two the boat's engines started up.

Constance groaned and pulled harder on her paddle. It was no use, she thought dully. She would run them down, watch them die anyway, feel them die.

"We have to stay behind the boat," Charlie said. "You know how to turn these things?"

"You push, I pull," Constance said, knowing it was no use. They could dodge for a while, but eventually they would tire, or she would make one of them stop paddling, or something.

Slowly they made the raft go astern. The boat was not moving yet, the engines were idling. Now the lights came on. Constance blinked as the light hit them. "Charlie, she can back up!" she whispered.

"Christ!" He had forgotten.

The boat began to move forward, not very fast; the wake shook the small raft, tilting it high to one side. The boat left them behind, then started to turn. Like steering a car, Charlie remembered. It was just like steering a car, except you need more room. She turned too wide and came out of it far to the right of the raft. She had switched on a searchlight now, was playing it back and forth, looking for them. She seemed not to realize how wide her turn had been; the light came nowhere near them. It stopped moving.

Constance watched fearfully. The boat looked so close. The engines were so loud. She felt herself go blank, felt sleep-heavy, immobilized. When it passed, in a second or two, the light began to move again, this time swinging around to focus on them.

"She reached me," Constance said tonelessly. "We can't hide from her."

Why didn't the damn boat start burning? He knew it had to burn. He visualized the fire that had to be smoldering along the bed board, in the cabinet under the bed. The towels should be blazing by now. The boat was turning slowly; she was being careful. She had all the time in the world, she seemed to be telling them, keeping them pinned by the blinding light, keeping them waiting for her next move. Charlie wondered if she laughed. If she ever laughed.

She was steering with one hand, holding the light with the other, not letting either go to increase her speed. The throb of the engines did not change, only grew louder.

Constance began to pull on her paddle. "At least let's make her work for it," she said grimly. Charlie pulled hard, sending them on the beginning of another circle. Then suddenly the light made an arc, swung wildly away, up, down, off to the other side.

"I'll be damned," he said, pleased. Smoke was rolling from the cabin windows. He began to pull on the paddle again, harder now. "We should try to get some more distance from it," he said.

Silently they rowed, not making very much gain, and they watched the boat. The smoke had lessened. Constance was afraid June Oliveira had put the fire out already. Charlie felt almost smug; he knew the smoldering had turned into blazing, there would be less smoke, more heat, more fire. When the first flame showed on the side of the boat, he said, "I think we should get down in the bottom of this thing, as flat as we can." It would blow, he knew, and he did not know how much of an explosion there would be, what kind of shock there would be, if they were too close. He hoped June Oliveira was tossing water on the flames, that she had not thought of the beautiful fire equipment on board, or of abandoning the boat. He had not seen her since the powerful spotlight had come on.

He and Constance curled up in the bottom of the raft. "Try to keep your ears covered," he said. He raised himself enough to continue to watch, his hands cupped over his ears. Flames were shooting out every window now, licking up around the flybridge. When the explosion came, it was not as loud or as violent as he had thought it would be. A fireball formed, and vanished almost instantly, and the boat erupted in a shower of fiery objects; the lights went off, and now there was only a low fire that was being extinguished very fast as the boat settled, began to slide under the water. They could hear a furious bubbling, then nothing, and the fire was gone. The sea was inky black.

Constance was on her knees clutching the side of the raft. She shuddered and Charlie put his arm about her, held her close. "Did she get off?" she whispered.

"I don't know yet."

They waited in silence as their eyes adapted to the darkness. Charlie could see nothing out there; he could hardly even see Constance. She was little more than a pale shadow. He strained to hear.

When it came, it sounded so close, he felt he could reach out and touch the woman. She sounded as if she was weeping. "Why do you do that? Why? Now we all die in the sea!"

He could not tell her direction, distance, anything at all. The voice seemed close, all around him.

Constance put her head down, pressing her forehead against the rounded side of the raft. "We should have slashed the other raft, scuttled it."

He had been afraid that if she had not believed she had an escape at hand, she might have used the impressive fire-fighting equipment. She might have been able to put out the fire with it. She might have known about the emergency hatch in the tiny engine room with the simple instructions: *Open in case of fire.* It would have flooded the engines and the fuel tanks with sea water; the boat would have been immobilized, but it would be afloat. Worse, he had feared that if she had been trapped, she might have reached out and killed them both instantly. She had been in the raft, she knew it was comparatively safe; she had to trust it again. How long would it take for the air to leak out enough? He did not know. He could hear a paddle splashing awkwardly.

"Do you remember where we put the flare gun?" he asked in a whisper. One to light up the scene, he thought; the next one aimed at her.

Constance began to grope for the gun. There was a loud splash close by. June Oliveira screamed shrilly.

"Sharks!" Constance yelled. She knew sharks did not make splashes, did not leap from the water. Perhaps the porpoises had come to investigate the explosion. Maybe a sea bird had dived. Her hand closed on the gun and she handed it to Charlie.

"First Charlie," the woman called out. "Constance stay with me until morning. You are good swimmer. I saw you in water. Is possible I need you to swim for me."

She was talking to still her terror of the water, the sharks she believed to be circling her, to break the silence. Constance recognized that shrillness, the clipped words; Oliveira was panic-stricken.

"Sometimes they come up under you and graze the boat," Constance yelled. "They're so rough, they puncture the rubber, and you don't even know it until too late. You can feel the sides of the raft getting soft, the top sinking in a little . . ."

Charlie was searching for the extra packet of flares. One was in the gun, he wanted a second to jam in and fire quickly before the light faded, while she was still dazed from the sudden glare.

"I've got it," he whispered finally. "Shield your eyes."

He fired straight up, and scanned the water. She was several hundred feet away, kneeling in the other raft, holding the paddle with both hands, stilled by the unexpected light. He rammed the second flare into the gun, and then pitched forward, dropping the gun, not unconscious, but without muscle tone, unable to move.

Constance snatched up the paddle and started to row as hard as she could. She was stronger than the other woman, at least she could outdistance her.

"Stop!" Oliveira called. "Stop or I kill him now. I do not like it at this distance, but I do it."

Constance put the paddle down. The light had faded already; again there was only darkness, now even deeper, blacker. Charlie lay huddled in the bottom of the raft unmoving.

"Stay very still," the woman said. "I come to your little boat. You are right about many things. During the night you explain to me how you know, what makes you guess, so I tell my people."

"Why Bramley? People are dying all the time. Why him?"

"Because I know him. We seldom know them, the people who are dying. It is more interesting to know him."

The water remained quiet around them; there were only the splashes of her paddle. She was so inept it would take her a long time to cross the distance separating them. Constance nudged Charlie with her toe. He did not respond.

"Why don't you just hang around hospitals? People die there every hour, every day."

"They are drugged. Sometimes it is good." Her voice was getting firmer, losing its fearful note, as she narrowed the space between them, and the water remained still.

Constance nudged Charlie again. Move, she thought at him, please move, get up. "You come here and murder, kill people. Watch them suffer for your own amusement. Do you torture them to death to drag it out?"

"We are not uncivilized," the woman said sharply. "We do not kill; we participate. It does no harm."

"You killed Dino!"

There was silence, her paddle slapped the water, then again. "I expect the other one. I have only until Sunday. I will be forgiven."

Constance shuddered. She reached out and touched Charlie's face. She wanted to lie down by him, gather him in her arms, just hold him.

The paddle hit, lifted, hit. And then it suddenly splashed very hard, and the woman screamed hoarsely. "My raft getting soft! It is punctured!"

Charlie stiffened even more under Constance's hand. *She* was using him as a beacon, homing in on him.

Constance picked up one of the water jugs and heaved it out toward the other raft. It made a loud noise when it hit the water.

"Sharks are all around us!" she yelled. The other paddle stopped and there was no sound. Constance groped for something else to throw, something heavy enough to make a noise, light enough to lift and heave. Her hand closed over the paddle. She lifted it silently and brought it down hard on the water. She screamed. "They're hitting our raft! Charlie, do something!"

Charlie began to stir; he pulled himself to his knees cautiously; the woman was letting go. Her terror was so great she could no longer hold him. From the other raft there were sounds of panicky rowing, she was simply beating the water with the paddle. Charlie and Constance began to row, saying nothing, trying to slip the plastic paddles into the water without a sound, pulling hard.

"It is sinking!" the woman screamed. "Help me!"

Constance screamed also, trying for the same note of terror. She screamed again, and then listened. The other woman was incoherent, screaming, screeching words that were not human language. Soon it all stopped.

*

For a long time they sat holding each other without speaking. Now and then something splashed, now close to them, now farther away. They could see nothing.

In a little while, Charlie thought, he would fire the flare gun again, and periodically through the night repeat it. Someone would see. Maybe someone had seen the fire, was on the way already. He would have to think of a story to tell them — a fire at sea, Dino's going back after getting them into the raft . . . He could handle that part. He had heard enough stories essentially like his, lies, excuses, reasonably enough put together to fool most people. He could do that.

And Constance was thinking: there would come a day when one or the other of them would start to doubt what had happened. What that one would remember was that they, together, had killed a crazy woman.

"She wasn't human," Charlie said, breaking the silence. And Constance knew he would be the one who would come awake at night and stare at the ceiling and wonder about what they had done. She would have to be watchful for the signs, make him remember it exactly the way it had happened. And one day, she thought, one of them would say what neither had voiced yet: that woman had not been alone. There were others.

Now Charlie thought: they would live with this, knowing what they had done, that there were others out there, maybe not as murderous as this one had been, or maybe just like her. They could tell no one; no one would ever believe. Constance had her proof of that uncharted part of the psyche, and could not even use it.

"I think I dislocated my shoulder when I threw that jug out," Constance said, shifting in his arms. "I'm aching all over."

And he knew his hand was bleeding through the bandage; it was throbbing painfully suddenly. He had forgotten about it. "In just a minute I'll see if there's a sling in the first aid kit. I need a new bandage too." He felt her nod against his shoulder.

"Poor little miserable, helpless, vulnerable, hurt people," she sighed. "That's us. Adrift on an endless ocean as dark as hell. With a terminal case of life. But I wouldn't trade with them." Knowing you were gambling eternity, you wouldn't dare risk your life for someone you loved, she thought, trying to ignore the pain in her shoulder, down into her arm. You wouldn't dare love, she thought. You wouldn't dare. Period. Not far away something splashed.

Neither of them moved yet. It was enough for now to rest, to feel the solidity of the other, to renew the strength the last several hours had taken from them. Quietly they drifted on the dark sea.

MOONGATE

I

WHEN ANYONE ASKED Victoria what the Go-
MarCorp actually did, she answered vaguely, "You know, light
bulbs, electronics, stuff like that." When her father pressed her,
she admitted she didn't know much about the company except
for her own office in the claims department of the Mining Di-
vision. She always felt that somehow she had disappointed her
father, that she had failed him. Because the thought and the at-
tendant guilt angered her she seldom dwelled on it. She had a
good apartment, nice clothes, money enough to save over and
above the shares of stock the company handed out regularly.
She was doing all right. At work she typed up the claims reports
on standard forms, ran a computer check and pulled cards where
any similarities appeared — same mine, same claimants, same
kinds of claims . . . She made up a folder for each claim, clipped
together all the forms, cards, correspondence, and placed the folder in her superior's in-basket. What happened to it after that she
never knew.

Just a job, she thought, but when it was lunchtime, she went
to lunch. When it was quitting time, she walked away and gave
no more thought to it until eight-thiry the next morning. Mimi,
on the other hand, boasted about her great job with the travel

agency, and never knew if she would make it to lunch or not. Victoria checked her watch against the wall clock in The Crêpe Shop and when the waiter came she ordered. She ate lunch, had an extra coffee; Mimi still had not arrived when she left the restaurant and walked back to her office. "Rich bitch, couldn't make up her mind how to get to Rio," Mimi would say airily. "I'm sending her by dugout."

Late in the afternoon Diego called to say Mimi had had an accident that morning; she was in the hospital with a broken leg. "You can't see her until tomorrow. They've knocked her out back into last week to set it, so I'll come by later with the keys and maps and stuff. You'll have to go get Sam alone."

"I can't drive the camper alone in the mountains!"

"Gotta go. See you later, sugar."

"Diego! Wait . . ." He had hung up.

Victoria stared at the report in her typewriter and thought about Sam. He had worked here as a claims investigator eight years ago. She had been married then; she and Sam had developed a close nodding relationship. He was in and out for two years, then had grown a beard and either quit or been fired. She hadn't seen him again until six months ago, when they had met by chance on a corner near the office.

His beard was full, his hair long, he was dressed in jeans and sandals.

"You're still there?" he asked incredulously.

"It's a job," she said. "What are you up to?"

"You'll never believe me."

"Probably not."

"I'll show you." He took her arm and began to propel her across the street.

"Hey! I'm on lunch hour."

"Call in sick."

"I can't," she protested, but he was laughing at her, and in the end, she called in sick. When she told Sam it was the first time she had done that, he was astonished.

He drove an old VW, so cluttered with boxes, papers, magazines, other miscellaneous junk, there was hardly room for her to sit. He took her to a garage that was a jumble of rocks. Rocks on the floor, in cartons, on benches, on a picnic table, rocks everywhere.

"Aquamarine," he said, pointing. "Tourmaline, tiger-eye, jadeite from Wyoming, fire opal . . ."

There was blue agate and banded agate, sunstones, jasper, garnet, carnelian . . . But, no matter how enthusiastic he was, no matter by what exotic names he called them, they were rocks, Victoria thought in dismay.

When he said he made jewelry, she thought of the clunky pieces teenaged girls bought in craft shops.

"I'll show you," he said, opening a safe. He pulled out a tray and she caught her breath sharply. Rings, brooches, necklaces — lovely fragile gold chains with single teardrop opals that flared and paled with a motion; blood-red carnelians flecked with gold, set in ornate gold rings; sea-colored aquamarines in silver . . .

A few weeks later he had a show in a local art store and she realized that Sam Dumarie was more than an excellent craftsman. He was an artist.

○

"You get off at noon on Good Friday," Sam had said early that spring. "Don't deny it. I lived with GoMar rules for years, remember. And you have Monday off. That's enough time. You and Mimi drive the camper up to get me and I'll show you some of the most terrific desert you can imagine."

"Let's do it!" Mimi cried. "We've both asked off until Wednesday. We were going to my parents' house for the weekend, but this is more exciting! Let's do it, Vickie." With hardly a pause she asked if Diego could join them. "He's a dear friend," she said to Sam, her eyes glittering. "But he wants to be so much more than that. Who knows what might develop out on the desert?"

Watching her, Victoria knew she was using Diego, that it was Sam she was after, and it didn't matter a bit. Hadn't mattered then, didn't matter now, she thought, driving slowly looking for a restaurant, remembering Diego's words:

"Get hungry, just pull over and toss a steak on the stove. Enough food for a week for all of us. Get sleepy, pull over, crawl in one of the bunks. That simple."

But there was no place to pull over on the highway, and no place to park and broil a steak. She spotted a restaurant, had dinner, and wished the motels had not had their no-vacancy lights on all down the main street of this small town. According to the map, she was about fifty miles south of Lake Shasta, and there would be campgrounds there, places to park and sleep. She climbed back inside the camper and started driving again.

Sam had given Diego explicit directions, and the more Victoria thought about them, and about the roads — everything from double green lines down to faint broken lines on the map — the more she wished he had taken Mimi's suggestion and called the Oregon state police. Sam had gone up to the mountains with friends who had left him there. The police could find him, she thought, or find his friends and locate Sam that way. They could give him a ride to the nearest town, where he could rent a car to drive himself home. Sam would understand why no one had showed up at the appointed hour. And she knew she had refused that way out because Mimi had angered her finally.

"Why?" Mimi had asked petulantly. She was very lovely, her hair black and lustrous, her brown eyes large as marbles. "After all, if you haven't snagged him in six months, why do you think this weekend will do it?"

❋

It was after twelve when she finally came to a stop, hit the light switch, and rested her head for several minutes on the steering wheel. She had been up since six that morning, had worked half the day, and she felt as if she had been wrestling elephants all evening. She neither knew nor cared where she was, someplace near the lake, someplace where the traffic was distant and no lights showed. She hauled herself up, staggered through the camper to the bunks, and fell onto one of them without bothering to undress. Presently she shifted so that the covers were over her instead of under her, and it seemed she had hardly closed her eyes before she was wakened by shouts.

Dazed, she pulled the shade aside. It was not yet light.

"This is a parking lot!" a man yelled at her. "Move it out of here."

It was bitter cold that morning and the sky was uniformly gray. She turned the radio on to the weather channel and nodded glumly at the report. Freezing level three thousand feet, snow in the higher passes.

All morning she crept along, sometimes in the clouds, sometimes in swirling snow, sometimes below the weather. At one o'clock she realized she had left the cold front behind her; she was east of the mountains, heading north in Oregon. The sun was brilliant, but the wind speed had increased enough to rock the camper, and she fought to hold it to forty miles an hour.

The rain forest had given way to pines on her left, and off to her right there was the desert. Later in the afternoon she turned east on U.S. 26, and after a few miles stopped at a rest area for lunch. This was the Juniper Wayside Park, a small plaque said, and went on to extol the virtues of the juniper tree. The trees were misshapen, no two alike. Some grew out sideways like shrubs, some were almost as upright as pines; none was over twenty feet tall. Beyond the small grove of junipers the ground was flat, brown, dotted with sagebrush and occasional clumps of wirelike grass. The wind screamed over the empty land. Shivering, Victoria got back inside the camper. She made a sandwich and studied the instructions Sam had written.

She had less than sixty miles to go; it was four-thirty. She should be there well before dark. A truck thundered past the park, and she jumped, startled. It was the first vehicle that had passed her since she had turned east. But, she thought, it proved other traffic did use this highway; she would not be totally alone on the desert.

When she started again, no one else was in sight. The road was straight as far as she could see in both directions, and it was a good road, but she had to slow down again and again until she was driving no faster than thirty-five miles an hour. Even at that speed the wind out of the northwest was a steady pressure against the side of the camper, pushing, pushing. When it let up, she rebounded. When it gusted, she was almost swept off the road.

To her left — she could not judge distance in this treeless country — there were hills, or mountains, and sharply sawed-off mesas. Now and then a pale dirt road appeared, vanished in the sagebrush. Her highway was sending out feelers, tendrils that crept toward the hills and never reached them.

Milepost 49. She shook her head. Those little roads were being swallowed by the desert. It was all a joke. Sam had not meant for them to drive on one of those go-nowhere roads. Milepost 50, 51 . . . She slowed down even more, gripped the wheel hard enough to make her hands ache. There was noplace she could stop on the highway, noplace she could pull over to consider. U.S. 26 was two lanes; there was no shoulder, only the desert. When Milepost 57 came, she turned north onto a dirt road. She felt only resignation now. She had to keep driving; the road was too narrow for two cars to pass. On either side there was only rock-strewn, barren ground, sagebrush, and boulders, increasing in size now. She could see nothing behind her except a cloud of dust. The sun had dipped behind the mountains and the wind now hurled sand against the windshield. The road curved and she hit the brakes, gasping. Before her was a chasm, a gorge cut into the land so deeply she could not see the bottom, only the far side where sharply tilted strata made her feel dizzy for a moment.

Some ancient river, she thought, had thundered out of the hills, an irresistible force that no rock could withstand. Where was it now? Gone forever, but its passageway remained. A mighty god, it had marked the land for centuries to come, its print cruelly raked into the earth. The forests it had nourished were gone; the bears and otters and beavers, all gone; the land was deserted, wailing its loneliness. She roused with a jerk. It was the wind screaming through the window vent. Soon it would be dark; she had to find a place where it would be safe to stop for the night.

She read the directions again before she started. Sixteen miles on this road, turn right, through a gate, a short distance to a second gate, twelve more miles. She glanced at the odometer frequently as she drove, willing the numbers to change. The cliffs on her left were already dark in shadows, and the gorge she cautiously skirted appeared to be bottomless. This narrow road had been blasted out of the mountain; it threaded upward in a series of blind curves.

Every step for six months, she thought, had led her to this: driving alone on the desert, miles from another person, miles from help if she should have an accident. Driving on a track that seemed designed to make any stranger end up at the bottom of a ravine.

She realized there was a wire fence on her right. She could not remember when it had first appeared. She had been climbing steadily, slowed to ten miles an hour on hairpin curves, with no attention to spare for scenery. Now the land was flattening out again. She almost cried out her relief when she saw the gate. She had to turn on the headlights to see how to open it; she drove through, got out and closed it again, and stood looking at the western sky, streaked with purple, gold, and a deep blue that almost glowed. The wind stung her eyes and chilled her. She turned around to study the track ahead. It could not be called a road here, she decided, and knew she would not try to drive another mile that day.

"I'm sorry, Sam," she murmured, climbing back into the camper. She humped and ground her way only far enough from the dirt road not to be covered with dust if someone else drove by, and then she turned off the motor. Without that noise, it seemed that the voice of the wind intensified, filled all available space. She closed the vent tight, and the high-pitched wail stopped, but the roar was all around her. Now and then the camper swayed, and she thought perhaps she should move it so that the wind would not hit it broadside. She sat gripping the steering wheel, straining to see ahead, until she realized how dark it had become; she could see nothing at all with the headlights off. Night had come like the curtain on the last act.

She pulled the shades tight, checked the locks, and thought about dinner, decided it would be more trouble than it was worth. Instead, she looked in the liquor cabinet, chose Irish, poured the last of the coffee into her cup, filled it with the whisky, and sat on a bunk sipping it as she pulled off her shoes. Her shoulders and back ached from her day-long battle with the wind. When her cup was empty, she lay down and pulled the covers over her ears. The wind roared and the camper shook and she slept.

*

She awakened and sat up, straining to hear; there was nothing. The wind had stopped and there was no sound except her breathing. A faint light outlined one of the windows where she had failed to fasten the shade securely. Wearily she got up, not at all refreshed by sleep, and very hungry. She went to the bathroom, looked at the shower, shook her head, and went to the refrigerator instead. Food, then a cleanup, then drive again. As she sipped her second cup of coffee she opened the shade and looked out, and for a long time didn't even breathe.

It was not dawn; the brilliant light was from a gibbous moon that had never looked this bright or close before. She stared at the desert, forgetting her coffee, forgetting her fatigue. There was an austere beauty that would drive an artist mad, knowing the futility of trying to capture it. Not color; the landscape was revealed with a purity of light and shadow from hard platinum white through the deepest, bottomless black that seemed for the first time to be a total absence of everything — color, light, even substance.

Slowly Victoria pulled on her coat and stepped outside. The sky was cloudless, the air a perfect calm and not very cold. The clumps of sage were silver — surreal stage props for a fantasy ballet; grasses gleamed, black and light. Nearby a hill rose and she started to walk up it. From the top she would be able to look out over the strange world for miles, and, she thought, it was a strange world, not the same one that existed by sunlight.

She walked with no difficulty; every rock, every depression, every clump of sagebrush was clearly, vividly illuminated. Light always symbolized warmth, she thought, comfort, the hearth, safety. But not this hard, cold light. She looked behind her at the camper, silver and shining, beyond it to the pale road, farther to the black velvet strip that was the gorge, the black and white cliffs, the sharp-edged mesas . . . For a moment she felt regret that she would never be able to share this, or explain it in any way; then she turned and continued up the hill.

She saw boulders on the crest of the hill and went to them and sat down. To the east the brilliant sky was cut off by high, rounded hills; far off in the west the horizon was serrated by the Cascade peaks. Closer, there were mesas and jumbled hills, a dry wash that kept reversing its ground-figure relationship, now sunken, now raised. She lost it in the hills and let her gaze sweep the valley, continue to the dirt road she had driven over earlier, the kinky black ribbon of the gorge . . . Platinum whites, silver whites, soft feathery whites, grays . . .

Something stirred in the valley and she shifted to look. What had registered before as a large shadow now had form, a hemispherical shape that looked solid. Suddenly chilled, she pulled her hood up and pressed back against the boulders. A patch of pale orange light appeared on the shape and something crossed before it, blocking the light momentarily. Then another shadow appeared, another . . . The shadows moved onto the desert floor where they reflected the moonlight just as her own camper did and, like her camper, they were vehicles. Campers, trucks with canopies, trailers, motor homes, station wagons . . . They lined up in a single column and moved toward the dirt road, without lights but distinct in the brilliant moonlight, too distant for any noise to reach her. More and more of them appeared, bumper to bumper, a mile of them, five miles, she could not guess how far the column stretched. Now they were reaching the dirt road. When the first one drove onto it, headlights came on; it turned south, and she could see the taillight clearly. The next one followed, turning on lights when it entered the road. The third one turned north.

"Of course," she breathed. "On 26 they'll divide again." Suddenly she began to laugh and she buried her face in her hands and pressed her head down hard against her legs, needing the pain. "Don't move," she told herself sternly. "They'll see you." After a few minutes she looked up. The hemisphere was a shadow again. The line of campers and trailers was halfway across the valley. Down the road she could see many sets of rear lights. Those turning north were hidden from view almost instantly by the cliffs.

Moving very slowly she stood up, keeping close to the boulders. She began to pick her way among the tumbled rocks. She had to stop often to fight off dizziness and the laughter that kept choking her as she stifled it. She could no longer watch where she was going, but groped and felt her way like a blind person. "The birthplace of recreational vehicles!" she gasped once and nearly fell against a rough boulder, then clung to it. "Biggest damn mother of them all!" she sobbed.

She was running and couldn't remember when she had started to run. They would train instruments on the surrounding hills, she realized, and they would come to eradicate any witnesses. They would have to. She knew she must not run over this ground, knew it and ran blindly, stumbling, seeing nothing, falling again and again. She screamed suddenly when something caught her arm and dragged her to a stop.

"Whoa now, honey. Just take it easy. You're pretty far from the nearest bus stop. You know?"

She struggled frantically and was held, and gradually she could hear the voice again. ". . . calm down. Steady now. Nothing's out here to hurt you. Coyotes, jackrabbits, seven head of the damnedest dumbest cattle . . ."

Then he was saying, "That's right, just take a look. Reuben's the name. Honey, you're as cold as a trout in snow water. Come on. That's the girl. Build up this little fire. Here, wrap yourself in this."

She was holding hot coffee, drinking it, and still he droned on, his voice warm and comforting, almost familiar. He was talking about cattle.

"Spotted them yesterday with the plane, but no way you're going to bring them in with no plane. Nope. Me and old Prairie Dog here" — a great pale dog lifted its head, then put it down on its paws — "we come up like we been doing forty years. Not him, a'course, he's only eight or nine, but only one way to get seven head a cattle back in the herd, and that's on a horse." He paused and leaned toward her. "You feeling a bit better now? Not shaking so hard?"

"I'm all right," she said. She glanced around. They were in a hollow with hills and boulders all around them. "How did you find me?"

"I was asleep," he said. "I heard this thing crashing all over the place and thought you was a coyote, to tell the truth. But old Prairie Dog didn't. He knew. Took me straight to you." He laughed, a deep growly snorting noise. "Thought at first I was still asleep and dreaming a pretty girl come to keep me company." He refilled her cup, felt her hand, then sat down again, satisfied. "You're okay, I reckon. Now you tell me what the hell you're doing out on the desert three o'clock in the morning."

He had been asleep; he could not have seen it, then. Victoria opened her mouth, looked at the fire, and instead of telling him about the thing in the valley, she said, "I woke up when the wind stopped and just walked out a little from my camper."

"An' saw something in the moonlight that scared the bejeesus outa you."

She looked at him quickly, but he was turned away, facing the cliffs.

"I know," he said, almost harshly. "When the moon's big and bright, you see things out there. It's when you start seeing them in daylight that it's time to hang up the saddle." He stood up. "You came through the gate back by Ghost River. Right?"

"I don't know the name. By the gorge."

"Not far," he said. "Key's in the thing?"

She nodded.

"I'm going to get it, bring it over here. You sit tight by the fire. Prairie Dog!" The dog jumped to its feet. "Come over here, boy, here. Stay, Prairie Dog." The dog sat down by Victoria. "He won't move till I get back. Won't be long." He took a step or two, then stopped. "Call it Ghost River 'cause nights like this some folks claim they can hear the water crashing down the rocks." Then he left and she was shivering hard again.

It wasn't like that, she wanted to cry out at his back. She had seen something! The dog put its head on her knee, as if in sympathy, and she whispered, "I did see it!"

The cowboy returned, took her firmly by the arm, and led her out of the hollow, through a second gate. "That's a mighty nice machine, Miss. Very fine. Just lock up tight and get some sleep. Going to be fine weather tomorrow, you'll have a nice driving day."

He opened the door and almost pushed her inside. "I'll be right down there, but you'll be all right now. Just lock it up and get some sleep."

She snapped the door lock, heard a distant "Good night," and shrugged off her coat and let it fall. She kicked off her shoes and fell into bed again and had no memory of pulling up the covers.

❧

"Why would I tell such a ridiculous lie?" Victoria cried.

"That's the right question," Sam said.

She had reached the designated spot at ten, and two hours later Sam had arrived. She had coffee and sandwiches ready, and as they ate she told him about Mimi's accident. Sam, she thought, had been impressed that she had driven here alone. Then she told him about the thing in the valley, knowing even as she started, while she still had time to back out, that she was making a mistake.

Sam started to unload his backpack, jerking things out with furious energy. He hadn't actually called her a liar. What he had said, snapped, was, "Storytime's over."

"Why do you think I'd tell any lie at all?"

"Maybe to pay me back. I know what kind of a drive that was. When that front came through I was prepared to wait three, four days. I can imagine how it was, bumping over rocks, sliding down gullies, hugging the cliffs over a thousand-foot dropoff, hating me for getting you into this. Fix old Sam. Tell him this cockamamie story, watch his eyes bug. You tried. It didn't work. No amusing little anecdote to hand over to your pals. Sorry."

"I didn't lie to you." She tried to keep her voice calm and matter of fact, but she heard the indignation in every word.

"All right! You dreamed it then. Or hallucinated. You were stoned, or drunk. I don't care what you call it, it isn't true!"

"Because I didn't get an affidavit or photographs?"

"Christ! Victoria, look, I know this country. There is no little hill back there. There are cliffs and mesas and chasms. No little hills you can stroll up in the middle of the night. That's point one. Two: do you have any idea in the world how scarce water is out here, how far apart the wells are? Too goddamn far to

take the old faithful dog along, you idiot! You carry water for
your horse, for yourself, if you have the room. You don't carry
water for a fucking dog! Your old pal the cowboy had a nice
fire blazing away, coffee on! What in Christ's name was he burning? You expect me to believe anyone would waste water making
coffee in the middle of the night, have a fire burning away while
he slept? And the seven head of cattle. That area's fenced off
to keep cattle the hell away from there. No water, larkspurs in
the spring — that's poison, Victoria, like arsenic or ptomaine.
There wasn't a gallant cowboy. No ghost river. There wasn't a
thing spewing out campers!"

He hit his palm hard against the now empty pack. "Let's get
started. I have two hundred pounds of rocks up there."

Angrily, in silence, Victoria pulled her pack on, adjusted the
straps, and waited for Sam to lead the way up the mountain.
Much later it occurred to her that Sam's fury had been all wrong.
If he had believed she was lying, or mistaken, he might have
laughed, might have been contemptuous or scornful. But furious?
Full of hatred? Why? She could feel the shivering start again
deep inside. When she looked up, Sam was watching. He turned
and walked on.

The afternoon was crystalline, the air almost still, the sun was
warm on her back. Every step they took upward revealed more
of the alien country. Land that had appeared flat and unbroken
turned into a series of mesas with sharp edges; a black pit
closed, became a barren lava flow; a cliffside of mud with a
sparkling waterfall became brown jasper with a thick vein of
blue agate. Deceptive, lying, deceitful land, she thought.

"Fifteen minutes," Sam said suddenly, and Victoria almost
bumped into him as she rounded a boulder as high as a two-
story building.

She sank to the ground thankfully. Her legs were throbbing,
her thighs so hot she was vaguely surprised that steam was not
rising from her jeans. Office work and a daily stroll to lunch
had not prepared her for this.

Sam squatted beside her and handed her his canteen. "It isn't much farther," he said. He pointed down the cliff. "Look. Poison Creek. Dry now, but sometimes there's water. Alkaline. Tomorrow we'll drive by it. You can pick up thunder eggs."

"This is all very beautiful," Victoria said. "I never knew that before."

"It can be, if you accept its terms, don't try to make it be something else. It fights back and always wins."

"The eternal desert, like the eternal ocean?"

"Something like that."

But he was wrong, she knew. The desert changed; she could see the evidence everywhere. It would change again and again. She did not doubt that the desert would win in any contest, but it would win by deceit. It would lull with a beautiful lie and then strike out. "No one would really try to fight a place like this," she said. "Only a fool."

Sam laughed. "Down there in Poison Creek there's gold. You'll see it tomorrow. It's no secret. A grain here, a few there, shining, laughing. The desert's little joke. It would cost more to ship in water and equipment to get it out than it's worth even today, or tomorrow, or next year, no matter how high gold goes. God knows how many men have died or been wiped out, have gone crazy, trying to get rich off that gold. One way or another the desert kills them. The ones who last are those who can pick up a handful of the sand, look at the shiny grains, and let it all sift back down to Poison Creek where it belongs, and then smile, sharing the joke. They're the ones who accept the terms." He stood up and offered her a hand.

"Can you do that? Leave it there, laugh at the joke?" Victoria asked. She tried not to grimace as her legs straightened out painfully.

"Sure. I'm not after gold. Come on. You're getting stiff. It's best to keep moving."

She wanted to ask him what he was after, but she knew he would not answer. The reason they always got along was that neither ever asked that kind of question. They liked the same plays, music, books sometimes, and could talk endlessly about them. They argued rather often about politics, economics, conservation, religion, but it all remained abstract, a game they played. No other lover had been willing to remain so impersonal, had kept himself as uninvolved as she was determined to remain. He had asked if she was still married and she had said no, and the subject had never come up again.

Never again, she had said after the divorce, and it had been fine.

She thought of the cruel, deliberately hurtful words she and Stuart had flung at each other, as if each of them had been determined not to leave the other whole, unscarred.

"You're some kind of creeping fungus!" he had yelled. "You're all over me all the time, smothering me, sucking the life out of me!"

She had believed she was a good wife; it had come as a shock to learn that her goodness was an irritant to him. She never lied, always did what was expected of her, never was late by a second, never demanded anything not readily and easily available. She had been like that all her life, and her father distrusted her, Stuart hated her. The only two people she had tried to please wholly, absolutely, had ended by abandoning her. Never again, she had thought, would she ask anything of anyone. Never again would she be willing to give anything of herself to anyone. If no one could touch her, then no one could hurt her. If she belonged to no one but herself, no one could abandon her again.

But, she thought suddenly, never again meant keeping such a distance that everyone else, every man, would forever be a stranger. And strangers could be dangerous, unpredictable. Sam's sudden rage and this return to affability made her uneasy. She knew it would be impossible to resume the careless relationship they had had only a day before. She tried to imagine herself again in his arms, giving and finding pleasure, and the images would not come.

She concentrated on climbing. When they got to the camp high on the mountain, Sam would not let her rest, but packed quickly and started down. "You'll freeze up, or get a charley-horse," he said cheerfully. "Then I'd have to backpack you out of here. I'll get the rest of this stuff tomorrow."

It was as if he had managed to erase everything she had told him, as well as his own reaction, but she did not have enough energy to worry any more about that. Doggedly she followed him down the mountain, seeing nothing now but the ground directly ahead.

❋

She dreamed of a swarm of fireflies winking on and off in an intricate dance that she could not quite follow. It had to be seen from the center, she realized, and she began picking her way carefully to the middle of them. Observing the rhythms from the outside had been charming, but as she drew inward, she began to have trouble breathing; they were using up all the air, sucking the air from her lungs. Off and on, off and on, off . . .

She woke up; Sam was shaking her hard.

"You were dreaming," he said. "Are you okay?"

She tried to sit up and groaned. "What time is it?"

"Midnight. Hungry?"

When they came back with the rocks he had made dinner, but she had been too tired to eat. She had stretched out on the bunk and had gone to sleep instead.

"What you need," Sam said, "is a cup of soup, which I just happen to have." He jammed a pillow behind her back and stepped over to the stove. He made the camper seem very small.

"Haven't you been to bed yet?"

"Nope. I was reading and waiting for you to wake up, starving and in agony. Soup first, then a rubdown, milk and aspirin."

"If you touch me, I'll die," Victoria said.

Sam laughed and dragged a camp stool to the side of her bed. "I'll hold, you drink." After her first few sips, he let her hold the mug of beef broth. "I've got this guaranteed snake-oil liniment, made by the oldest medicine man in the West out of certified genuine magic snakes. What we do, see, is haul off the jeans, pull the cover up to your fanny, and let me work on those legs. Ten minutes, and you'll walk tomorrow. A miracle."

"Hah!"

"Word of honor. If you misuse this potion, use it for anything other than what old Chief Calapooia intended it for, you will call down on your head, heart, soul, and liver the wrath of the sacred snake god, who then will do certain very nasty things to you."

He kneaded and massaged her legs and rubbed the liniment on them until they glowed, then he covered her again, tucking the blanket in snugly; he brought her milk and aspirin, kissed her chastely on the forehead, and before he could turn off the lights and get himself in bed, she was sleeping.

When she woke up in the morning she could remember that during the night Sam had shaken her again, possibly more than one time, perhaps even slapped her. She must have had a nightmare, she thought, but there was no memory of it, and perhaps she had dreamed that Sam tried to rouse her.

She got up cautiously; while she ached and was sore from her neck down, she felt better than she had expected, and very hungry. There was a note on the refrigerator door. Sam had gone up the mountain for the rest of his gear.

After she ate she went outside; there was no place to go that wasn't either up or down. It was only nine-thirty. Sam would be four hours at least; if he had left at seven, she had an hour and a half to wait. Time enough to drive back to the gate, locate the hill she had walked up, look for the thing in the valley by daylight.

The keys were not in the ignition. Victoria found her coat at the foot of the bed and searched for the single key Diego had had made — one for her, one for Mimi, one for himself, so no one would ever be stranded outside if the others were delayed. She searched both pockets, then dumped the contents of her purse on the bed. No key. Growing angry, she stripped the bed and searched it, the space between the mattress and wall, the floor around it. Sam could not have known about the extra keys; he had been gone when Diego had them made.

She made the bed again, then found a book and tried to read, until she heard Sam returning.

"Why did you take the keys?" she demanded as he entered the camper.

He looked blank, groped in his pockets, then turned and opened the glove compartment and after a moment faced her once more, holding up the key chain. "Pains me to see them in the ignition," he said. "I always toss them in there."

Silently Victoria began to secure the cabinets, lock the refrigerator, snap the folding chairs into place. She had known he would explain the keys. He would explain the single key away just as easily. She did not bother to ask. Soon they were ready to leave.

*

They stopped frequently; in the dry Poison Creek bed they picked up thunder eggs and filled an envelope with sand that Sam promised would contain some grains of gold. Once they stopped and he led her up a short, steep cliff, and from there it seemed the entire desert lay at their feet — brown, greenish-gray, tan, black. There were no wires, no roads, no sign anywhere of human life. The vastness and emptiness seemed more threatening than anything Victoria had ever experienced.

There had been no horse, Victoria thought suddenly. She could see the cowboy again — not his features, she realized. She had not seen his features at all. She visualized the fire, but not what was burning; the moonlight gleamed on the dog's pale coat. And there was no horse anywhere. The sheltered depression had been bright; if a horse had been tethered there, she would have seen it. The cowboy would have taken it into shelter, not left it out in the brutal wind.

Sam pulled her arm and she stifled a scream. She had not

heard his voice, had not felt his hand until he yanked her away from the edge of the cliff. He pulled her, stumbling and shaking, back to the camper.

Neither spoke of her near trance. Sam made dinner later; they played gin, slept, and, as before, she knew when she awakened that she had had nightmares. When Sam said he was taking her home, she nodded. She felt that the barren desolation of the landscape had entered her, that it was spreading, growing, would fill her completely, and the thought paralyzed her with dread.

II

Serena Hendricks met Sam at the back door of the ranch house.

"Stranger! Your beard is a bush! Does Farley know you're here?" She had the complexion of a Mexican, the bright blue eyes of her German mother.

Sam shook his head. "Where is he?"

"Out there. God knows. A hundred degrees! You know it's a hundred degrees? Gin and tonic. Lots of ice. Come on." She drew him into the house.

Serena's parents had worked on the Chesterman ranch, her father the foreman, her mother the housekeeper. Serena and Farley had grown up together and, Sam thought, they should have married, but had missed the chance, the time, something. She had married one of the hands instead and her three children ran around the yard whooping and playing rodeo, while Farley remained single.

Sam followed her to the kitchen. The air in the spacious ranch house was twenty degrees cooler than outside.

"We expected you and your friends back in April," Serena said as she sliced a lemon and added it to the ice cubes in a glass. She pursed her lips, closed one eye, and poured gin, nodded, added tonic, stirred, then tasted it.

"There were complications," Sam said. Sometimes he almost

wished he had asked Serena to marry him ten years ago, back
when anything was still possible. Serena rolled her eyes, drew
him to a chair at the table, dragged another one close to it, and
sat down by him, her hand on his arm. "That means a woman.
Tell me about it."

Sam laughed, gently put her hand on her own knee, and stood
up. "What I'm going to do is get my stuff from the camper, go
upstairs, and take a shower and a nap."

"Pig!" she yelled at his back. "You're all alike! Inconsiderate
pigs! All of you."

When he brought his pack in she handed him a new drink.
"Same room as usual. Supper's at six. Sleep well, dream happy."

Farley and Sam had been at U.C.L.A. together; they had
climbed mountains together; they had lived through an August
blizzard on Mt. Rainier together. Farley was slightly taller than
Sam and leaner, and his hair was graying.

They sat on the wide porch drinking beer at midnight.

"You haven't seen her since then?" Farley asked.

"I guess neither of us wanted to. She quit her job, moved.
Got another job. Dropped just about everyone we both knew."
He finished the beer and put the can down. From far off there
came a coyote's sharp, almost human coughing, yapping cry. He
waited. There was an answering call. Then another. They were
very distant.

"She must have had a good scare," Farley said. "There's no
Reuben in the territory, you know."

"There's nothing like she said."

"There's something, Sam boy. There is something. And I don't
know any way on God's earth for her to have known it. We used
to have a hand called Tamale. An old Mexican, one of Serena's
uncles. He died when I was five or six. It's been that long. He'd
tell us stories. Superstitious old bastard. He told me about Ghost
River, scared me shitless. Haven't heard that again since then.
Until now when Reuben comes along and tells your friend the
same thing."

Sam felt prickles on his arms. "So there was someone. Who the hell was he?"

"Reuben," Farley said. He stood up. "Can't take these hours anymore. Must be age. You want to ride out with me in the morning? I'm making the rounds of the wells. Lundy's had bad water up the other side of Dog Mountain. I'm collecting samples to have tested."

Water, Sam thought later, sitting at his window staring out at the black desert. Water was the only real worry out here. Dog Creek irrigated Farley's wheat. Dog Creek determined if Farley would succeed or fail. Years when the snow did not come to the mountains, when the winds drove the sparse clouds over too fast to release their rain, when the summer started early, ended late, Farley watched Dog Creek, and the reservoir his father had dammed, like a woman watching a feverish child at the climax of a serious illness. The fear of drought accounted for the gray in Farley's hair. There were a dozen deep wells on the ninety thousand acres of his ranch, most of them pumped by windmills, a few of them close enough to the power lines to use electricity. The water was pumped into troughs. If one of the wells started pumping bad water, or no water, if one of the troughs was shot by a hunter, sprang a leak in any way, that meant disaster. Days, weeks went by between checks of the troughs. In this country a lot of cattle could die in that time.

And she thought he would swallow that silly story about a cowboy and his dog!

❉

They drove the jeep cross-country to inspect the wells, and Farley drove places where Sam would not have attempted to go. At one o'clock Farley stopped and they sat on the ground in the shade of an overhanging cliff to eat their lunch. There was a valley below them; on the other side were more cliffs. Suddenly Sam realized where they were: this was the same valley Victoria was talking about, viewed from the other side.

"See that fence?" Farley waved his beer can toward the op-posite cliffs. "Three hundred acres fenced off. Tamale brought me out with him once, when I was five. I rode all the way, still remember. I asked him why this piece was fenced off and he told me about Ghost River. Said the cattle heard the water some-times and went off the cliffs trying to get to it. I believed him. Never gave it another thought for years. Then I was home from school one summer and Dad had me come out here to fix one of the gates. I knew by then cattle don't find water by sound, they smell it. I asked him about the three hundred acres. He said it always had been fenced because of the larkspurs that come up thick in there." He looked at the other side of the val-ley thoughtfully. "They do, too," he said after a moment. "Only thing is, they're on both sides of the fence and always were."

In the valley was a thick stand of bunchgrass, the sign of a well-managed range. No sage or gray rabbit grass had invaded there, no erosion scarred the land. No tracks flattened the grass, or made ruts in the earth. The valley was a cul-de-sac, a box canyon surrounded by cliffs. Where the valley narrowed, with a break in the cliffs, there was a dropoff of two hundred feet. The wire fence started at the gorge, crossed the ranch road, climbed the cliff, followed the jagged ridge around to the break. On the other side the fence resumed, still clinging to the crest, then turned, went down the cliffs again, recrossed the road, and ended at the gorge, several hundred yards from the other sec-tion. The area enclosed was an irregular ellipse. The irregulari-ties were caused by the terrain. Where heaps of boulders, or abrupt rises or falls, made detours necessary, the fence always skirted around to the outside.

Farley got back in the jeep. "Might as well finish," he said, and drove along the fence on the crest, then started the descent down a rocky incline, bumping and lurching to the two-track ranch road and the first gate. He drove fast, but with care and skill; turned around at the second gate and made his way for-ward, as Victoria had done.

"Probably stopped along in here," he said. "First curve out of sight of the road." The gorge was nearby, and there should have been a hill to the right, but the hill was nothing less than another steep cliff. Farley studied it a moment, motioned to Sam, and started to walk. Unerringly he turned and twisted and took them upward. They reached the top with little trouble.

"She could have done it," Sam said, looking down at the valley again, across it to where they had been a short time before. He looked about until he saw the boulders she had mentioned, where she had sat down. They started toward them. They were on the ridge of an upthrust, picking their way over the weathered edges of crazily tilted basalt, which would remain when everything about it was turned to dust. In some places there was less than a foot of space between a sheer dropoff on one side and a slope almost that steep on the other.

"Her guardian angel sure was with her," Farley said as they drew near the boulders. One of the mammoth rocks was balanced on the edge of the crest.

"I don't believe any of this," Sam said angrily. He stopped. Ahead of them, lodged in a crevice, something gleamed in the sunlight. Farley took several cautious steps and picked it up. He handed it to Sam, a single key. Without comparing it, Sam knew it was a key to his camper.

They made their way among the boulders, through the only possible passage, and came out on top of the ridge that now widened for several hundred feet. At the edge of it Sam could look down over the gorge; he could see the ranch road, and between him and the road there was a small sunken area, the sheltered spot where "Reuben" had taken Victoria. There was no sign of a campfire ever having been there. No sign of a horse, a dog, a camp of any sort. Silently the two men walked back to the road and the jeep.

Farley did not turn on the ignition immediately. "That was in April, three months ago. Why are you checking on it now?"

Sam looked at the gorge wall, imagined a river roaring below.

"Mimi, the girl who was going to drive up with Victoria, came to see me last week. She and Victoria were friends, but Victoria dropped her too. Mimi thought something happened out here between Victoria and me, that I raped her, or tortured her, or something. She told me Victoria is sick, really sick, in analysis, maybe even suicidal. Whatever is wrong with her is serious and it started here."

"You *have* seen her?"

"Yeah. For half a minute maybe. She wanted to see me like a rabbit wants to see a bobcat. Wouldn't talk, had to run, too busy to chat." He scowled, remembering the pallor that had blanched her face when she saw him. "She looked like hell."

"So you want to get her back out here to find out what she saw."

Sam grunted. After a moment he said, "I don't know what I want to do. I have to do something. I just had to check for myself, see if there's any way it could have been like she said."

Farley put the key in the ignition. Without looking at Sam he said, "She could have gone back east, or to Texas, but she didn't. She could have taken an overdose, slashed her wrists, gone off the bridge. She could have really hidden, but she kept in touch with the friend who could get to you. She wants you to help her. And you owe it to her for losing your temper because she had the vision you've spent so many years chasing." He turned the key and started to drive before Sam could answer.

✴

That night Sam said he would try to get Victoria to come back, and Farley said he would visit his parents in Bend to see if there was anything his father could or would tell him about the fenced-off acres.

Sam walked. If you really wanted to find a god, he thought, this was where to look. Such absolute emptiness could be relieved only by an absolute presence. Men always had gone to a mountaintop or to the desert, in search of God. Not God, he thought angrily, peace, acceptance, a reason, he did not know what it was he sought on the desert. He would be willing to settle for so little, no more than a clue or a hint that there was more than he had been able to find. After he had quit his job with GoMar, he had tried drugs for almost two years. Drugs and a personal teacher of the way, and both had failed. He had found only other pieces of himself. He had turned to asceticism and study, had become a jeweler. He had fasted, had lived a hermit's life for a year, had read nothing, denied himself music, the radio, had worked, walked, waited. And waited still.

He was out of sight of the ranch buildings, the spacious house with old oaks and young poplars sheltering it; the big barns, the small bungalows some of the hands lived in, the bunk house, machine shops . . . You stepped over a rise and the desert swallowed it all, just as it swallowed all sound, and existed in a deep silence, broken only by the voices of those few animals that had accepted its terms and asked for nothing but life.

And just having life was not enough.

❖

He waited across the street from her apartment until she entered and, after ten minutes, followed her inside. When she opened her door and saw him, she hesitated, then with obvious reluctance released the chain to admit him.

"Hello, Sam." She walked away from him and stood at the window looking out.

He remained by the door, the width of the room between them. He was three months too late. In those months she had turned into a stranger.

When they had returned to San Francisco in the spring, he had taken her bags inside for her, and then left. She had not invited him to stay, and he had not sat down as he usually did. "I'll call you," he had said.

But he had let the days slide by, pretending to himself that he was too busy sorting the material they had brought back, too busy with an order from a small elite store in Palm Beach, too busy, too busy. Every time he thought of calling, he felt an up-rush of guilt and anger. Finally, filled with a senseless indigna-tion, as if she were forcing him to do something distasteful, he dialed her number, only to get a recording that said her number was no longer in service. Furiously he called her office; she had quit, and left no forwarding address.

Relief replaced the anger. He was free; he no longer had to think about her and whatever had happened to her out on the desert. He could get on with his own life, continue his own search. But he could not banish her from his mind, and worse, his thoughts of her were colored with a constant dull resentment that marred his memories of the good times they had had, that quieted his sexual desire for her, that distorted her honesty and humor and made her seem in retrospect scheming and even dull.

Over the months they had been separated the new image he constructed had gradually replaced the old, and this meeting was destroying that new image, leaving him nothing. He had to start over with her, falteringly, uncertainly, knowing that the real changes were not in her but in himself. There were intimate things to be said between them, but intimate things could not be said between strangers.

Everything Sam had planned to say was gone from his mind, and almost helplessly he started, "I treated you very badly. I'm sorry." His words sounded stiff and phony, even to him. She didn't move, and slowly Sam repeated his conversation with Far-ley, all of it, including Farley's explanation of his rage. "It's pos-sible," Sam said, then shook his head hard. "It's true I *was* sore because you saw something I didn't. I can't explain that part. We both, Farley and I, want to find out what happened."

"It's true then!" Victoria said, facing him finally. She was shock-ingly pale.

Sam started to deny it, said instead, "I don't know."

"We have to go back there to find out, don't we?" She crossed the room to him.

"You don't have to now," Sam said quickly. "I think it would be a mistake. Wait until you're well."

"Thursday," she said. When Sam shook his head she added, "You know I won't get well until this is over."

Color had returned to her cheeks and she looked almost normal again, as she had always looked: quick, alert, handsome. And there was something else, he thought. Something unfamiliar, an intensity, or determination she had not shown before.

"Thursday," Sam said reluctantly.

✻

She had never been so talkative or said so little. Her new job, the people in the office, the changing landscape, a grade school teacher, sleeping in the parking lot, how easy driving the camper was . . .

"Mimi says you're in analysis," Sam interrupted her.

"Not now," Victoria said easily. "She was more Freudian than the master. Treated my experience like a dream and gave sexual connotations to every bit of it. The thing in the valley became phallic, of course, so naturally I had to dread it. Reuben was my father firmly forbidding my incestuous advances, and so on. I took it for several weeks and gave up on her. She needs help."

Too easy, Sam realized. She was too deep inside; all this was a glib overlay she was hiding behind. After dinner, she took two pills.

"Something new?" Sam asked.

"Not really. I used them when Stuart and I were breaking up. They got me through then."

"Bad dreams?"

"Not when I take these," she said too gaily, holding up the bottle of pills. She had changed into short pajamas; now she pulled a book from her bag and sat on her bed. "My system," she said cheerfully, "is to take two, read, and in an hour if I'm still reading, take two more."

"That's dangerous."

"At home I keep them in the bathroom. If I'm too sleepy to get up and get them, I don't need them. Foolproof. Hasn't failed me yet. Have you read this?" She handed him the book.

"Stop it, Victoria. What are you doing?"

She retrieved the book and opened it. "It's pretty good. There's a secondhand book store near the office . . ."

"Victoria, let me make love to you."

She smiled and shook her head.

"We used to be good together."

"Another time. I'm getting drowsy, floating almost. It's like a nice not-too-high high once it starts."

"And you don't dream? How about nightmares? You were having three or four a night last time I saw you. So bad you wouldn't even wake up from them."

She had become rigid as he spoke. She closed the book and let it drop to the floor, then swung her legs off the bed.

"What are you doing?" He felt the beginnings of a headache: guilt and shame for doing that to her, he knew.

"Water. More pills. Sometimes I don't have to wait an hour to know."

Presently she slept, deeply, like a person in a coma. She looked like a sick child with her brown hair neatly arranged, the covers straight, as if her mother or a nurse had only then finished preparing her for a visitor. He no longer desired her. That rush of passion had been so sudden and unexpected, he had been as surprised as she. He had not thought of her as a sexual partner for months. Their sex had been good, but only because each had known the other would make no further demands. It had been fun with her, he thought, again with surprise because he had forgotten. It had been clean with her, no hidden nuances to decipher; no flirtatious advance and retreat; no other boyfriends to parade before him hoping for a show of jealousy. If they existed she was reticent about them, as she was about everything personal. No involvement at all, that had been the secret of their success.

He had planned to surrender the camper to Mimi and Diego, and share his tent with Victoria, out of sight and sound of the others, with only the desert and the brilliant moon growing fatter each night. Even that, showing her the world he loved so much, would have been something freely given, freely taken, with no ties afterward. They both had understood that, had wanted it that way.

He turned off the lights but was a long time in falling asleep.

Toward dawn he was awakened by Victoria's moaning. He put his denim jacket over the lamp before he turned it on. She had the covers completely off and was twisting back and forth in a rocking motion, making soft, incoherent sounds. As he drew near to touch her, to interrupt her dream, she stiffened and he knew she had slipped into a nightmare like the ones she had had before. The first time he had shaken her, called her repeatedly, and after a long time she had screamed and gone limp. After that he had simply held her until it was over, held her and murmured her name over and over. She had not remembered any of the nightmares.

He slid into the narrow bed and wrapped his arms around her, whispering, "It's going to be all right, Victoria. We're going to fix it, make it all right again."

It went on and on, until abruptly she began to fight him. Then she wakened and, gasping, she clung to him as he stroked her sweaty back. He pulled the covers over her again.

"Sh, sh. It's over. Go back to sleep now. It's all right."

"No more! I want to get up!"

"You'll be chilled. No more sleep. Just rest a few minutes. It's too early to get up. Try to relax and get warm."

The drugs and the nightmares were battling for her; the nightmares waited for a sign of weakening in the pills, ready to claim her swiftly then.

What had she seen? What was she still seeing when her pink pills lost their effectiveness in the darkness before dawn?

●

"How sick is she?" Serena asked. She was watching Farley and Victoria going toward the reservoir for a swim.

Sam shrugged. "I don't know. Why?"

"I like her. I don't want to see her sick, maybe die. Farley likes her. Is she, was she your girl?"

"Not the way you mean," Sam said, laughing.

"What other way is there?" Serena raised her hands and let them drop, expressing what? Sam always knew exactly what she meant, yet could never put it in words.

After Serena left him on the porch, he wondered how sick Victoria really was. After six days on the ranch, she was tanned, vivacious, pretty. Maybe she was sleeping better. Farley was keeping her busy riding, hiking, swimming, whatever they could find to do out in the sun and wind, and her appetite was good again. By ten or eleven she was ready for bed. And sleep? He wished he knew.

Farley sidestepped every question about what he planned to do. "Don't rush," he said. "She's terribly tired. Let's get acquainted before we dance. Okay?" He said he had learned nothing from his father.

"Aren't we even going out there?"

"In time, Sam. In time. She quit her job. She tell you that? She's in no rush. No place she has to go."

She hadn't told him, and it annoyed him that she had told a stranger. It annoyed him that Farley and Victoria were having long talks that excluded him, that Farley had announced their swim after Sam had said he was expecting a long-distance call. Most of all it annoyed him that Serena evidently thought of Farley and Victoria as a couple. An hour later, his call completed, he walked over to the reservoir, but stopped on the hill overlooking the lake. Victoria and Farley were sitting close together under a juniper tree, talking. Sam returned to the house.

It was not jealousy, he knew. It was the delay. Victoria had something, could show him something that he needed desperately. Every delay increased his impatience and irritation until he felt he could stand no more.

After dinner he said coolly, "Tomorrow let's ride over to the gorge area and camp out."

Victoria leaned forward eagerly. "Let's. Let's camp out."

Farley's face was unreadable. He watched Victoria a moment, then shrugged.

"In that case," Victoria said quickly, "I'd better wash my hair now and get plenty of sleep." There were spots of color in both cheeks and she looked too excited. She hurried to the door, said good night over her shoulder, and ran upstairs.

Farley leaned back, studying Sam.

"There's no point in putting it off any longer," Sam said. He sounded too defensive, he knew. Sullenly he added, "I'm sorry if I upset your timetable."

"Not mine. Hers. She thinks she's going to die out there. We had an unspoken agreement, a pact, you might say, to give her a vacation and rest before she had to face that valley again."

"You know that's crazy!"

"I don't know half as much as you do, Sam. I seem to know less all the time. I don't know what's in the valley, don't know what it will do to her to face it again. I don't know why you think you can use her to see it too. Nope. I don't know nearly half as much as you do."

Sam had risen as Farley spoke. "Back off, Farley. I said I'm sorry. Let's drop it."

Farley nodded and left the room.

❖

Gradually the ranch lights went out, until only the dim hallway light in the main house remained; outside, the desert crept closer. From the porch Sam watched the darkness claim the barn area, the yard, the bungalows, until he could feel it there at the bottom of the porch steps. He had dug around one of the desert ghost towns once, where only a juniper mounting post remained. That was what the desert would do here it this small group of people let it. The desert would reclaim the ranch, erase all signs of the outsiders.

The moon rose, a half moon. Enough, Sam thought. It was enough.

That was what the old Indian had said. Sam had driven three hours over New Mexico desert roads, gravel roads, dirt and sand roads, to find the shack. It had a tin roof covered with sagebrush. An Indian woman had admitted him silently; inside, the temperature was over a hundred degrees, cooler than it would have been without the sagebrush insulation, but stifling. On a straight chair before one of the two windows sat the Indian man, one arm swathed in bandages where the stump was still not healed. There were a roughly sawed table, two chairs and several stools, a wood-burning stove with a cast-iron pot on it, a rope-spring bed and several rolled-up pallets. The walls were covered with newspapers, carefully cut and pasted up so that the pictures were whole, the stories complete. From outside there was the sound of children's whispers, a faint giggle. The woman scowled at the window on the opposite side of the cabin, and the sounds stopped.

Sam had seen many such cabins, many worse than this one. He pulled the second chair around to face the man, introduced himself, sat down, and drew out his report form. "I've been to the mine," he said. "What I need now is a statement from you so the company can process your claim."

The Indian did not move, continued to gaze at the desert.

"Sir . . ." Sam looked at the woman. "He was rambling when he was found. Did he suffer head injuries? Can he hear?"

"He hears."

Sam glanced at the preliminary report. There had been an explosion at the potash mine; an avalanche apparently had carried this man down a ravine where he stayed for two days before he was found. Two days on the desert, in the sun, no water, bleeding from an arm injury, possibly head injuries. "You haven't filed a claim yet," he said. He explained the company's disability pension, the social security regulations, the medical settlement. He explained the need for the claimant's signature before processing could begin. The Indian never stirred.

Sam looked from him to the woman.

"He won't sign," she said.

"I don't understand. Why won't he file a claim?"

"He says he should pay the company," she said, and although her face remained impassive, she spoke bitterly. "He says a man should be happy to give up an arm to see the the face of God."

"He's crazy!" Sam looked at the Indian for the first time. He had been looking at a claimant, a statistic, one like many others he had seen before and recognized instantly. Now he studied him.

"You have a right..." he started, then fell silent.

The Indian shifted to regard him and Sam thought, he *has* seen the face of God. Harshly he demanded, "Who's going to take care of your family? Hunt for them, earn money? Who will go up to the mountain to get firewood? You have only one arm!"

"It is enough," the Indian man said, and turned his gaze back to the desert.

Sam filled out the claim and the Indian woman signed it. He drove away as fast as the company truck could take him. That was the last case he handled; two months later he quit his job.

For seven years, he thought, he had searched for something that would give him what that son of a bitch had. They called him an artist now, and he knew that was a lie. He was a good craftsman, not an artist. He understood the difference. He was using the rocks he found, making something, anything that would permit him to survive, that would give him an excuse to spend days, weeks, months out on the desert. It amused him when others called him an artist, because he knew he was using a skill to achieve something else; he felt only contempt for those he fooled — the critics, the connoisseurs, the buyers.

He would have it, he knew, if he had to risk an arm, both arms, Victoria, Farley, anything else in the world to get it. He would have it.

III

Farley watched Victoria. She rode reasonably well, held her back straight and trusted her horse to know where to put his feet, but she would have to do a hell of a lot of riding before it looked natural on her. He planned to watch her and if she started to slump, or her hand got heavy on the reins, he would call a halt, walk her up a ridge or down a valley, anything to rest her without suggesting that that was his intention.

Watching Victoria, he thought of Fran, riding like a wild thing, so in tune with her horse, it seemed the impulses from her brain sped through its muscles, in a feedback system that linked them to create a new single creature. The last time she had come back, they had ridden all day.

When they stopped to water the horses at one of the wells on her father's land, he asked, "You aren't happy in Portland, are you?"

"I get so I can't stand it. Begin to feel I'm suffocating, there's no air to breathe, and a million bodies ready to smother me. So I come back and can't stand this either. Too much wind, too much sand, too much sun and sky and cold and heat. Too much loneliness. When I start wanting to scream I know it's time to go back to the big city. Heads I lose, tails I lose."

Fran was beautiful, more so now at thirty than she had been at fourteen, or eighteen, any of the lost years. He had loved her, and had left her when he went to school. A year later she had married a doctor from Portland. She had two children, and Farley no longer tried to sort out his feelings about her. When she came home they spent days together out on the desert. When she was gone they never corresponded.

"You should have told me you'd leave here with me," Fran said that day. She tossed rocks down a hole in the ground where an earthquake had opened a fissure ten thousand years before.

"We could have made it work, half the time in town, half out here."

He shook his head. "Then we'd both be miserable, not just one of us."

"Aren't you miserable? Aren't you lonely? Is this goddamn desert all you really want out of life?"

He had not answered. His life was his answer. He had tried to live in town, during, immediately after his college days, and he knew the city would kill him, just as a cage kills. His mother was dying in Bend where she had to remain for daily cancer treatments. His father was dying, too. The small town of Bend was killing him. He was like a caged animal, the luster gone, the sheen, the joy of living, the will to live, all leaving him as surely as her life was leaving her.

Fran was gone the next day. He might see her again in a month, or six months, or never. He continued to watch Victoria.

They skirted an old alfalfa field; it looked as dead as the rest of the desert this time of year. Even the deer passed it up for the greener range high on the mountains. But if the winter rain didn't come, if the summer persisted into fall, into winter, the cattle, deer, antelope, rabbits would all be here grazing, and they would bring in the coyotes and bobcats. There would be some ranchers who would start yelping about varmint control, bait stations, traps, and he would try to talk them out of it, as he had done before. Farley knew they could never control the coyotes and bobcats; only water or the lack of water could do that. In the desert everything was very simple.

They had reached the trail leading up Goat's Head Butte, and he called a brief rest to water the horses. He and Sam had inspected this pump and well only last week.

"There are trees up there," Victoria said, pointing.

"Snows up there just about every year, not much, but enough to keep them more or less green," Farley said. "We'll take it nice and easy. It gets a little steep and narrow up there, and, you'll be happy to hear, cooler. I'll go first and lead one of the pack horses, then you, Victoria, then Sam with the other pack horse. Okay? Just give Benny a loose rein and he'll stay exactly where he knows he should."

They zigzagged for the last hour of the climb; the curves became tighter, hairpin turns joining rocky stair steps that let them look directly onto the spot where they would be in a few minutes. Then suddenly they were on the top, a mesa with welcome shade and waist-high bunchgrass for the horses. The grass was pale brown and dry, but good graze. A startled hen pheasant ran across their path into the grass, closely followed by a dozen or more half-grown chicks. A hawk leaped from a tall pine tree into the sky and vanished, gliding downward behind the trees. From up here they could see other trails, most of them easier, but Farley would not bring horses up through the sparse woods and grasses. Such life was too precious on the desert, and horses were hard on trails. He had chosen the north climb because it was barren and rocky, and would suffer little damage from their passage.

"Do we get off now?" Victoria asked. She sounded strained.

Sam was already dismounting. He gave Victoria a hand. "Tired? Sore?"

"Tired and sore," she said, standing stiffly, hardly even looking around. "And scared. My God, I've never been so scared in my life! What if that horse had stumbled? We'd still be falling!"

Sam laughed and put his arm about her shoulders. "Honey, you did beautifully. You came up like a bird."

"I was afraid to move! What if I had sneezed, or coughed, or got hiccups? What if the *horse* had looked down?"

*

Serena had packed beef chunks and chopped vegetables, and within an hour stew was ready. They ate dinner ravenously and took coffee with them to the western end of the butte where they sat on rocks and watched the sunset over the Three Sisters in their chaste white veils.

No one spoke until the display was over and the streaks of gold, scarlet, salmon, baby pink had all turned dark. The snow on the Sisters became invisible and the mountains were simple shapes, almost geometrical, against the violet sky.

"They look like a child's drawing of volcanoes," Victoria said softly. Then: "Why do they call this Goat's Head Butte? It certainly looks like no goat's head I've ever seen."

"A mistake," Farley said. "The Indians called it Ghost Head, the source of Ghost River. A U.S. Geologic Survey cartographer got it wrong."

Victoria drew in her breath sharply. "It really is called Ghost River!"

She sat between Sam and Farley. There was still enough light for them to see each other, but shadows now filled the valley below; the moon was not yet out. For what seemed a long time no one spoke. Farley waited, and finally Sam said, in a grudging tone:

"I didn't know it then, Victoria, or I wouldn't have said what I did."

"Piece by piece it's coming together, isn't it?" Before either of them could respond, she said, "We're too far away."

"What do you mean?" Sam asked.

Helplessly Victoria shrugged. "I don't know what I mean. I think you have to be closer to feel anything. I don't know why."

Sam stood up, but Farley motioned him back. He put his hand lightly on Victoria's arm. "Tonight we observe," he said matter-of-factly. "Tomorrow we'll crisscross the valley and tomorrow night we'll camp down there. Relax, Sam. Just take it easy." Without changing his tone of voice he asked, "Victoria, what did you see in that valley that night?" He felt her stiffen and tightened his clasp on her arm.

"I told you."

"No. You told both of us your interpretation of what you saw. You translated something into familiar shapes. If you ask a primitive what something is that he never experienced before, he'll translate it into familiar terms. So will a child."

"I'm not a primitive or a child!"

"The part of you that interpreted what you saw, that has been reacting with terror, that part is primitive. I'm not talking to that part. I'm talking to the rational you, the thinking, sane you. What did you see? What was the first thing that caught your attention? Not what you thought it was, just how it looked."

"A black dome," she said slowly.

"No. Not unless you could see the edges beyond doubt."

"A black shape, domelike."

"Let's leave it at a black shape. Are you certain it had a definite shape?"

"No, of course not. It was night, there were shadows, I was on the hill over it."

He was silent a few moments, and finally Victoria said, "It was just black. I remember thinking it was a shadow at first, then it took on shape."

Farley patted her arm. "Then?"

"There was a door, when it opened, a light showed . . . That's not what you want, is it?"

"Just how it looked, not what you thought it was."

"A patch of pale orange light. No. A pale glow. Orange-tinted. I thought of a door, the way light comes through an open door."

They worked on it painstakingly, each detail stripped of interpretation, stripped of meaning. Victoria began to sound tired, and Farley could sense restless small movements from Sam.

"I knew they were vehicles of some kind!" Victoria cried once. "They reflected light, they moved like automobiles — in a straight line, gleaming, and they turned on headlights at the road."

"But what you described doesn't have to be vehicles," Farley said. "What you said was clusters of gleaming lights, like reflections on metal."

"I suppose," she said wearily. "They were spaced like cars on a road, and they moved at the same speed, in a straight line, not up and down, or sideways, or anything. Like cars."

"And when they turned on lights, could you still see the reflections?"

She sighed and said no, she didn't think so.

"You're getting tired," Farley said gently. "We should get back to camp, get some sleep. One more thing, Victoria. Look down there now, the moon's lighting the valley, probably not as brightly as that night, but much the same as it was then. If you had been up here that night, Victoria, would you have been able to see what you saw?"

Farley still had his hand on her arm. The moon behind them made her face a pale blur; it was impossible to see her features clearly, but he felt a tremor ripple through her, felt her arm grow rigid.

"No!" The trembling increased. "We're too far away. You can't see the road from here."

"Not because we're too far to see it," Farley said. "The road's lower over there than the valley is."

"You mean I couldn't have seen it from the hill either?"

"No."

Victoria rose unsteadily and stared at the valley, turned her entire body to look at the cliffs surrounding it.

"What is it?" Farley demanded. "You've remembered something, haven't you? What?"

"This isn't the right place."

"It's the place. You were over there. You can see the boulders, the pale shapes near the end of the ridge. Below that is the ranch road where you parked. It's the right place."

"It's wrong! It isn't the right place! I was on a hill. It wasn't like that!" She closed her eyes and swayed. "I was on a hill, and I could hear . . . I heard . . ."

"You heard what? You heard something and saw something and smelled something, didn't you? What was it?"

She shook her head hard. "I don't know."

Farley made her face the valley again. "Look at it, Victoria. Look! You're hiding among the boulders on that ridge over there. You know they might see you. You keep in the shadows, hiding. Don't move! Don't make a sound! What do you smell? What do you hear?"

She moaned and he said, more insistently, "You smell something. What is it, Victoria? You know what it is, tell me!"

"Water!" she cried. "Water, a river, a forest!"

"You're running," Farley said, holding her hard. "You're on the hill and you're running. Your eyes are open. What do you see?"

She tried to push him away. "Nothing! I can't remember that part. Nothing!"

"Look at the ridge. Look at it! You couldn't run up there! There's no place to run!"

"It's not the same place! I told you, I was on a hill, there was grass. I ran until that man, Reuben, stopped me."

"You're terrified they might hear you. You smell the river and forest. You hear the rushing water. You run. Where are you running to? Why?"

"The trees," she gasped. "Bushes under the trees. I'll hide in the bushes, in the mist." She pulled harder, her voice rising in hysteria. "There isn't any forest or river! Let me go! Let me go!" She began to sag. "I can't breathe!"

Farley and Sam half-carried, half-led her back to the campfire, which had burned to a bed of glowing ashes. Sam built up the fire and Farley held a drink to Victoria's lips, keeping one arm around her shoulders. She sipped the bourbon, then took the cup and drank it down.

"Better?" Farley asked. She nodded. "Sit down. I'll get a blanket to put around you." Wordlessly she sat down by the fire. Sam was making coffee.

No one spoke until they all had coffee. Then Farley took Victoria's hand. "We have to finish it," he said.

She nodded without looking at him. "I'm crazy," she said. "I would have killed myself that night if that cowboy hadn't been there to save my life."

"You saved yourself," Farley said. "You panicked and you ran. You knew there was no forest, no river, no mist, but they *were* there. You invented Reuben, you projected him, because you couldn't resist the evidence of your senses. You had to have help and no one was there to help you, so you helped yourself, through Reuben."

"I'm going to bed," Victoria said dully. She made no motion to get up.

Farley was not certain if she could accept anything he was saying. He could not tell if she heard him. "You acted out of self-preservation," he said.

"It was all just a dream or a series of hallucinations," Sam said. His voice was hard, grating. His angular face looked aged; his full beard made him look Biblical, like an old bitter prophet.

"You can't regard it all as one thing," Farley said. "That's the mistake you made before, the same mistake the psychiatrist made, that if part of it was false, it all was. Obviously the cowboy figure is right out of romantic fiction, but that doesn't make the rest of it false. I wondered if Victoria rejected the truth because she was convinced the truth was impossible, and accepted instead the illusions that could have been possible." He paused, then added, "Both in what she saw in the valley, and again in the cowboy."

Victoria stirred and shook her head. "I don't understand anything," she said, but with more animation now, as if she were awakening.

"I don't either," Farley said. "But you did see something, and you smelled and heard Ghost River. I bet not more than a dozen people today know it was ever called that, but you renamed it. That's what I keep coming back to."

"That's crap!" Sam shouted. "She saw something and ran. Probably she stumbled and knocked herself out. You know you can't run over that country, not even in daylight. She dreamed the rest of it." He had risen to stand over Victoria. "The only important thing is, What did you see in the valley?"

"Not what you want me to say!" Victoria cried. "It wasn't a god figure. Not a burning bush or a pillar of flame. Not good or evil. Nothing we can know."

Farley reached out to touch her and she jerked away. "You

said we have to finish it. We do! I do! Sam, you wanted to know my nightmare. Let me tell you. I'm wearing tights, covered with sequins, circus makeup, my hair in a long glittering braid. Spotlights are on me. I'm climbing the ladder to the tightrope and there's a drum roll, the whole thing. I know I can do this, the way you know you can ride a bike, or swim, or just walk. I smile at the crowd and start out on the rope and suddenly there is absolute silence. I look down and realize the crowd is all on one side of the rope, to my left: no one is on the right side. The audience is waiting for me to fall. Nothing else. They know I'll fall and they are waiting. They aren't impatient, or eager; they have no feelings at all. They don't care. That's when I panic, when I realize they don't care. And I know I must not fall on their side. I try to scream for someone to open the safety net, for someone to take my hand, for anything. Then I am falling and I don't know which side I'm on. I won't know until I hit. That is what terrifies me, that I don't know which side I'll die on." Her voice had become almost a monotone as she told the dream. Abruptly she rose to her feet. "I'd like some more bourbon, please."

Farley poured it and she sat down once more and drank before she spoke again.

"I came back here to see which side of the rope I'll land on. The next time I'll finish the dream and find out."

Sam reached for the bottle and poured bourbon into his cup. "A lousy dream," he muttered.

"Indifference, that's what made it a nightmare. Their indifference," Victoria said quietly. She sipped at her drink and went on. "It's the same way we might break up an anthill and watch the ants scurry. Or how we tear a spiderweb and maybe see the spider dart away, or not. We don't care. We watch or not, it doesn't matter. Like the bank camera that photographs me when I go to the window. Me, a bank robber, someone asking for information, it doesn't matter, the camera clicks its picture." She was starting to slur her words slightly. Her voice was low, almost inaudible part of the time. "It . . . they watched me like that. They didn't care if I went over the cliff or not."

Farley felt the hair rise on the back of his neck and wondered if she realized what she was saying. She wasn't talking about the dream any longer.

"They didn't care if I went over the cliff. They didn't care if I stopped, or ran, what I did." She drained her cup, then set it down on the ground with elaborate care. "That's inhuman," she said. "Not like a god, the opposite of what it would be like for a god. Beyond all idea of good and evil. No awareness of good and evil."

Sam sighed and said, "She's drunk. She never could drink."

Victoria pushed herself up from the ground. She nodded. "I am," she said carefully. "I'll go to bed now." Both men rose. She looked at Farley. "I know why I'm here. I have to see where I land. And I know why Sam's here. He's looking for God. Why are you here? What is your noble cause?" She was taking care to pronounce each word, as if speaking a foreign language.

"You're too stinko to talk any more tonight."

"I can't talk, but my ears are not drunk. My ears are not blurring anything."

"Will you remember?"

She nodded an exaggerated yes.

"It's my land. Over the years twenty-five or thirty head of cattle have gone over that cliff. Two people have vanished in that area. My land. I have to know what's there. I put it off and pretended it was just a superstition, wiped it from my mind, but I can't do that now. You won't let me do it ever again." He paused, examining her face. "Do you understand that?"

"No, but I don't have to." She began to walk unsteadily toward the tent. "Because it's not true," she said, then ducked under the flap of the low tent.

It was true, though. He wanted to exorcise a devil, Farley thought, sitting down again. And Sam wanted to find God. All Victoria wanted was to learn the truth. They'd both use her, and through her they might find what they looked for. Across the fire from him, Sam sat brooding, staring into the flames.

"I want to stay up tonight," Sam said abruptly. "Just in case there is something down there."

Farley nodded. "We'll take turns. You want to sleep first?"

Sam shrugged, then wordlessly got up and went to his sleeping bag spread on the ground a short distance from the fire.

Farley sat with his back against a pine tree and watched the shifting patterns of light and shadow as the moon moved across the sky. From time to time he added a small stick to the fire, not enough to blaze much, just to maintain a glow to keep the coffee hot. A fire during a night watch was friendly, he thought, nudging a spark into flame.

What was he doing here? What he had answered was part of it. Maybe all of it. He didn't know. For hundreds of years people around this area had known this piece of land was strange, not to be trusted. The Indians had shunned it for generations. His father had known it was not safe for cattle or men and had fenced it off. Easier to cross off three hundred acres out of ninety thousand than to pursue a riddle that probably could not be solved anyway. He would have done the same if Sam and Victoria had not forced him to examine it. He was examining many things suddenly, he admitted to himself.

"You have so many books!" Victoria had exclaimed. "Did you major in geology?"

There were four shelves of geology books. "Nope. That's why I have to keep reading. Can't find the one I'm looking for, I guess."

"And that is?"

"Life and death, desert style. Something like that. Someone who can relate the earth cycles to life cycles. I'm not sure, that's why I keep reading and searching."

"You'll have to write it yourself," Victoria had said.

And Fran had asked, "Aren't you lonely?"

He was sure he was not lonely in the sense she meant, but

there had to be more. A few months ago he had not known that. Every day he got up at dawn and worked as hard as any of the hands on the ranch, doing the same kind of work, doing more than any of them most days. Dinner at six, read, bed by ten. There were women in Bend, one in Prineville, all very casual, noncompelling.

He was evading again. Why was he here? He had come home because he could not live in the city. He had found strength in this harsh desert. But evil had followed him, had claimed his mother. Sometimes when the phone rang late at night, he found himself pausing, willing it to be his father telling him it was all over finally. Sometimes he found himself watching Serena playing with her children and he almost hated her for being able to find a good life so simply without any effort at all.

He could have married Serena. They had experimented with sex together; at the time they both had assumed they would marry when they were grown. Something in him had said no, and he had practically pushed her into the arms of Charlie Hendricks. And Fran. She would have gone to school with him. Their parents had expected it, and even discussed the financial arrangements. Instead he had decided he couldn't handle a bride and the university at the same time. Leave him alone, his mother had said, he'll find himself in school. But he had found nothing.

He had been drafted and at first he had believed he was finally going to do something worthwhile. He had discovered only despair and hopelessness. School again, sinking ever deeper, then the flight home to the safety of the land. Here, he had thought, was the only place he had been able to find any hope. Here nothing was unclean, nothing was evil. The coyotes, the bobcats, the summer frosts and the winter droughts all were proper here.

He had sought refuge in work on this healing land, only to learn that evil was here too. Not the land! he wanted to howl. And he knew this time there was no place he could go, no last refuge he could bury himself in.

Reluctantly, compelled by circumstances he could not understand, he accepted that finally, after years of flight, he would stand and confront the enemy.

IV

Victoria dreamed that her boss was coming, that he would rage at her for not doing her work better. "I'm doing the best I can," she cried. "Even a child could do it better," he stormed at her. And she woke up.

The light was as it had been the other night, perhaps not as bright, but almost. She didn't make any noise; she knew that either Farley or Sam would be up, and for the moment she didn't want to talk to anyone. She remembered the dream. No boss had ever raged at her in that way. A child could do it better, of that she was certain. Slowly she sat up and waited for the moment of terror to pass. It always overwhelmed her when she first awakened; then it receded, but never completely.

Now she could see Sam, a clear profile against the pale horizon. His full beard made his head look grotesquely oversized. He had aged. It was as if he had left Shangri-la and before her eyes were passing into the mundane world where age caught up. He looked old and tired. He looked frightened. She tried to imagine Farley frightened as Sam was, and somehow it was harder to picture him so. She didn't understand Farley. Something was driving him, and she didn't know what.

Something was out there that each of them needed to learn about. They had followed Farley's plan, had searched all day by sunlight, on horseback, then on foot, and had found nothing. But the moon changed the land; it made strange things possible.

"You should be sleeping," Sam said when she joined him.

"I know. The silence and the moonlight woke me up, I think. Has it been quiet all evening?"

"Yup. Not a thing stirring."

She sighed. "The desert is very beautiful at night, isn't it.

That's a surprise. I'd read that, but it's like reading that the ocean is beautiful, or that the sunset is beautiful. It's meaningless until you see it. I can almost understand why Farley wants to stay here."

Sam laughed. "Nobody understands why Farley stays here. He's a hermit."

"Sam," she said, "after tonight, then what?"

He shrugged.

"I mean, what if nothing happens?"

"Then I come back tomorrow night, and the next night, and the next night."

"But what if nothing ever happens?"

"Then you're crazy."

"That's possible."

"Vickie, don't talk about that right now. Let's watch the horse. Let's watch the desert. Watch the shadows on the face of the moon. They deepen as you watch. Let's not talk about anything else right now."

She sat down beside him. "May I smoke?"

Sam laughed irritably. "I wish you'd stayed asleep."

"I know. I'm just nervous. What if noth —" Suddenly she stopped. The horse had a listening attitude; its ears were straight up, poised. They were like the ears of a racehorse before the signal. It was sniffing the air. And now, coming from nowhere, Farley was there with them.

The three of them watched the horse as he sniffed the air and pawed. He was pulling at the tether, neighing. The other horses, hobbled on the safe side of the fence, answered sleepily. They weren't interested. Whatever it was that had wakened the one horse hadn't bothered them. Now he was acting wild, rearing.

Farley said, "You two stay here, I'm going to go get it." He ran to the gate and opened it very quickly.

Victoria closed her eyes. She didn't know what she expected, but she didn't expect him to return with the horse. Somehow that seemed too simple.

After a moment, Sam shook her and said, "Well, whatever it was we'll probably never know. That horse sure isn't going to tell us." Farley was standing before them with the horse. He led it to the others, hobbled it, and returned. He looked stunned, and bewildered, and he looked frightened.

"What was it?" Sam asked brusquely.

Farley said, "We — we'll all have to go across that fence and hear it. You can't hear it from here."

"The river!" Victoria cried.

Farley nodded. "You can hear the river over there."

For a moment no one moved as they listened to the still desert. Then they went through the gate together and stopped a few feet from the fence.

Victoria strained to hear, but there was nothing. Everything looked the same, yet different, the way it always looked unchanged even while changing. She thought Sam was cursing under his breath. He strode ahead, holding himself too stiff. Angry, she thought, and disappointed. Abruptly Sam stopped, gazing upward at the ridge.

"Farley, look!"

A woman had appeared on the ridge, making her way clumsily through the jumbled boulders. She glanced backward once and hurried even more. A flicker of light appeared around the rocks.

Victoria felt Farley clutching her arm too hard. "It's me," she breathed. His grip tightened.

The other Victoria ran wildly down the slope of a hill they could not see. She was dashing panic-stricken through the air, and behind her, gaining on her, came the cloud of lights. The cloud flickered all about her, like a swarm of fireflies. The light did not illuminate, it obscured the racing figure.

Now she was coming down the ridge, drawing near the edge of the cliff, stumbling, falling, rising only to stumble again. Suddenly she flung herself down and drew up her legs in a tightly curled position. The swarm of cold lights settled over her, seemed to expand and contract with her breathing. Minutes passed. The expansion was less noticeable, the lights more compactly together. Suddenly the woman stirred and rose, moving like a sleepwalker. She looked straight ahead and started to walk slowly, carefully down the side of the mesa. The swarm of lights stayed with her, but she was oblivious of them. At the bottom she turned toward the ranch road where Sam's camper was parked. Moving without haste, she passed the camper, opened the gate, returned to the vehicle, got in and drove through. Ten or fifteen feet from the gate the light swarm stopped, hovered in air for a few moments, then streamed back up the cliff, like a focused light beam that could move around curves with ease.

Victoria felt the frozen, supporting rigidity leave her. She sank to the ground.

"Me too," Farley muttered, his arm still about her. They sat huddled together.

"I'm going over there," Sam said. He started in the direction of the camper, stopped after a dozen or so paces. He came back to them and also sat down. "Gone. It's not there."

Victoria freed herself from Farley's arm and stood up. "We have to go up to the ridge," she said. She felt almost detached.

"Tomorrow," Farley said, and Sam muttered something unintelligible.

"Now." Victoria stood up.

"Okay," Farley said, "but first we go to camp and get flashlights and jackets. We may be out for hours, and it can get damned cold."

Impatiently Sam started back to camp; Victoria and Farley followed more slowly.

"Are you all right?"

"Yes." She really was, she realized. Since they had seen something, too, the strangeness must be in the land, in the valley, not in her; her relief made her almost giddy.

At the campsite, Sam already had his jacket on and his day pack slung over his shoulder. He handed Victoria her pack and tossed the third over to Farley, who knelt and started to rummage through it. Victoria snatched up her jacket. Farley moved to the big packs.

"Come on," Sam said. "You put flashlights in. I saw you do it." He turned and strode toward the gate again. Victoria hurried after him.

"I'm getting my camera," Farley called. "Be right with you."

"Ass!" Sam said. "Like a goddamn tourist."

The gate was still open and they left it that way for Farley.

"I think the best way up is —" Sam stopped, his hand on Victoria's arm. "Jesus!"

It was different. The crystalline light was changed: a pale mist dimmed the moonlight; the air was soft and humus-fragrant, the coolness more penetrating. To the right the Ghost River thundered and splashed and roared. Victoria looked behind them, but the gate was no longer there. The ranch road was gone. Underfoot the ground was spongy; wet grass brushed her legs. She looked to the ridge that had become a wooded hill, and over the crest of the hill streamed the light swarm, winding sinuously among the trees toward her and Sam.

V

Farley hesitated at the gate, then left it standing open; the horses were safely hobbled, and a quick retreat might be necessary. He was carrying his camera, his pack over his shoulder, not strapped yet. He began to hurry. He hadn't realized the other two had gotten so far ahead of him.

"Sam! Victoria!" His echo sounded as dismal and lonesome as a coyote's call. He stopped to study the cliff up to the ridge, and he felt a chill mount his back, race down his arms. The cliff was almost vertical, the road they had been on was gone; ahead the cliff curved, and the narrow terrace ended dead against the wall. He backed up a few steps, denying what he saw. He strained to hear the river, and heard instead a low rumble, and felt the ground lift and fall, tilt, sink again; the rumble became thunder. He was thrown down, stunned. The thunder was all around him. Something hit him in the back and he pulled himself upright, only to find the ground really was heaving and the thunder was an avalanche crashing down the cliff all around him. Frantically he ran, was knocked down again, ran, fell, until he was away from the cliff. He stumbled to the horses, groped blindly to untie them, and he fell again and this time stayed where he fell.

*

He dreamed he and his mother were having a picnic at Fort Rock. The Fort was a natural formation, an extinct volcano, the caldera almost completely buried; what remained formed an amphitheater where he was on stage, she his audience of one. He recited for her and she applauded enthusiastically; he sang and danced, and when he made his last bow she came to him with tear-filled eyes and hugged him. She was very pretty, the wind blowing her hair across her face, her cheeks flushed under the dark tan, her eyes shining blue and happy. She opened a beach umbrella and they stayed under it out of the sun, while she read to him and he dozed.

He dreamed he was in the hospital. He had taken her place, had released her. People kept wanting to talk to him, kept wanting him to speak, but he wouldn't because then they would learn they had the wrong patient.

He woke up and felt a terrible confusion because he *was* in a hospital bed; his father was sleeping in an armchair at the window. For a long time Farley didn't speak, hoping that if he remained perfectly still he might wake up again in his own bed.

He studied the peaceful face of his father. The late afternoon sun gave his pale face a ruddiness that had faded months ago. His father was fifty-seven and until recently had always looked ten years younger than he was. Relaxed now, he looked as he had when they used to go on all-day outings — like the trip to Fort Rock ... A memory stirred, a dream surfaced, and he realized why his father was here, in his room, not in hers.

He started to get up, and grunted with pain.

"Farl! You're awake?" Will Chesterman moved with such effortless speed that people often thought of him as a slow man, very deliberate. He awoke, crossed the room, and was leaning over Farley all in one motion.

"Dad. How'd I get here? Mother?"

"No talking. Supposed to call the nurse the second you open your eyes. No moving. No talking." He pushed a button on the call box and after a moment of muted static a woman answered. "My son's awake," Will said. The nurse said she would call the doctor, to please keep Farley quiet . . .

"Tell me about Mother."

"We buried her yesterday."

Farley shut his eyes hard. "Christ! How long have I been here? What happened?"

"Six days. Now Farl, I'm not answering anything else, so just don't bother. You got a concussion, ten broken ribs, dozens of stitches here and there, and you are a solid bruise. Nothing seriously damaged. Now just shut up until Lucas gets here and goes over you."

Then unabashedly he leaned over and kissed Farley on the forehead. "God, I'm glad to see you back, son. Now just relax until Lucas comes."

"I've been out for six days?"

"Awake and sleeping, not really out all that time. Lucas said you might not recall much at first. Don't stew about it."

Farley started to speak and his father put his hand over his mouth. "Any more and I'll go out in the hall."

Lucas Whaite arrived and felt Farley's skull, examined his eyes, listened to his heart, checked his blood pressure, and then sat down. "How much you remember now, Farley?"

"Being in here? Nothing. Or coming here."

"You remember what happened to you?"

"We camped out, by the gorge near the old road . . ." Suddenly it was all there. "Are they all right? There was an earthquake. Were they hurt bad?"

The doctor and Will exchanged glances. Will said slowly, "Listen, son. There wasn't any earthquake. You were talking about it before, and we checked. Farl, someone came damn near to beating you to death. Looks like they used four-by-fours on you, then left you for dead. Was it Sam Dumarie and the woman with him? What for, son?"

"Where are they?"

"Wish to God we knew."

Farley groaned and turned away. "They're missing? Is that what you mean?"

"No one's seen them since you all rode out together last week. The horses came back around noon Sunday and some of the hands scattered to look for you. They found you at the campsite, more dead than alive. Should have died too, I guess, out there in the sun bleeding like a stuck pig. Your friends were gone, their day packs and yours gone with them, nothing else. And they haven't lighted yet. Now you tell us what the hell happened."

Farley told them. Then a nurse came with his dinner and Lucas said he should eat and rest, and no more talk. He left, taking Will with him. The next day Lucas took out forty-nine stitches, from both legs, his back, his side, and right arm. "Been run through a goddamn mangle," he grunted. "Boy, there ain't no way you're going to lay where you ain't on something that's going to hurt."

"Where's Dad? What's he doing about Victoria and Sam?"

Lucas lighted his pipe. "He's sleeping, I hope. Told him we had hospital business to attend to this A.M."

"You don't believe me, do you?"

"Farley, I delivered you, took out your appendix, named your diseases as they appeared, wrote your prescriptions for ear drops, cough syrup, stitched you up from time to time. I know you don't lie, son. But I also know there hasn't been any earthquake in this whole territory for years. It's the concussion, Farley. Funny things happen when the brain gets a shock like that."

"You believe Sam Dumarie could do all this to me and be able to walk away afterward?"

Lucas tapped out his pipe and stood up. He lifted Farley's right hand and held it so Farley could see the knuckles — unmarked, normal. "No," he said slowly, "you'd have him in worse shape. We all know that. But he's gone, the woman's gone, and you're in here. Listen, son, I've held Tom Thorton off long as I can. Maybe there was a landslide, or maybe you fell off a cliff, but there wasn't any earthquake, and he'll know that just as sure as I do. Maybe you plain can't remember yet. I'll back you up on that. But no earthquake."

Over the next two days Tom Thorton, the sheriff, questioned him, a state trooper questioned him, the search was resumed in the desert, and no one was satisfied. Farley told Tom Thorton he had been caught in a landslide and Thorton came back with a map for him to pinpoint the exact location.

This was how it had been with Victoria, Farley thought. No one had believed her and she had come to doubt her sanity. Thorton returned again looking glum.

"Look, Farley, I was over every inch of that ground. There ain't been no slide or anything at all out there. You sure of the place?"

"You calling me a liar, Tom?"

"Hell no! But a man can make a mistake, misremember. I been reading about concussions. Down in San Francisco they been using a medical hypnotist, helping people remember things better. I been thinking —"

"No," Farley said. "Why would I be lying, Tom?"

"I been thinking," Tom Thorton said. "We all know this Dumarie's been digging around them mountains for years. What's he looking for? He makes fancy jewelry, right? So what does he need? Gold! Silver! What if he found it on your land and took you to show you, and you gave him an argument about it, being's it's on your land and all. Gold comes between brothers, fathers and sons. So he waits till your back is turned and knocks you over the head with a rock, then he takes you over by the gorge and rolls you down the cliff, him and that girl with him. He doesn't want you found anywhere near the gold."

"Jesus Christ! Just go out there and find them, will you, Tom? They're both dead by now, but they're out there, somewhere near the gorge, or down in it, or in the fenced-off valley."

The next day Lucas reluctantly agreed to let Farley go home. It had been ten days since they had made camp by the ranch road at the Ghost River gorge. On the way home Will drove by the small cemetery. It was wind-scoured; clumps of junipers, small groves in the barren land, were the only signs of the care given the burial ground where Farley's grandparents lay near Farley's uncle and a cousin; where his mother now was.

Standing at her grave by his father, Farley said, "I'm sorry I wasn't with you."

"I know. That last night she dreamed of you. She told me. You sang and danced for her, recited some poetry. She said she held her umbrella over you so you wouldn't get sunburned. The dream made her happy. She died without pain, smiling over her dream."

Both men became silent; the wind whispered over the tortured land.

✿

Farley sat on a rock, aching, hurting, unwilling to move again soon, and watched Fran ride up. She made it look so easy, he thought, remembering how Victoria had sat in the saddle climbing Goat's Head Butte.

Fran waved, but didn't urge her horse to quicken its gait; it was too hot to run a horse on the desert. She stopped near his jeep in the shade of a twisted juniper tree, tied her horse, then joined him inside the fenced area. No one ever brought animals inside if they could help it.

"They all said you look like hell," she said cheerfully, surveying him. "They're right."

"You just happened to be passing by?"

"I came when . . . I've been home awhile, thought I might as well hang around to see you. Want to talk about it?"

He didn't know if she meant his mother's death, or the landslide he had dreamed up for the sheriff. "No."

Fran nudged him over and sat by him. The sun was low; long shadows flowed down the gorge like cool silent lava.

"It was here, wasn't it?" Fran asked. She lighted a cigarette and pocketed the match. "Serena said you came out here right after breakfast. Been here all day?"

He stared morosely at the gate standing open. Here in the hot still afternoon it was just another ranch gate; no way it could vanish with a twist of the head.

"We all think you were lucky. If you hadn't been separated from them you'd be gone too."

Farley turned to look at her. "Tell that to Tom Thorton. And my father."

"We aren't a bunch of superstitious Indians," she said, "afraid of a curse on the land, or land claimed and held by a god. Tom will never admit anything so irrational, but he went over this whole area with half a dozen men at least twice. The rest of it, searching the desert, the bulletins, that's all for show. Your father, my father, if they knew we were sitting here, well, they'd probably lasso us and haul us out."

"Aren't you afraid to be in here?"

"Not during daylight."

Farley laughed and pulled himself off the rock, wincing as he moved. "And I was going to invite you to come back with me tonight."

Fran caught his arm as she rose. "You're not serious! Why? What good can it do if you disappear?"

"I don't know. That girl asked for help, and I told her to trust me. Now she's gone. I can't pretend it never happened."

Fran shook her head impatiently. "When you were found, they thought you were dying, because they couldn't wake you up. Dad heard about it and called me. He doesn't approve, of course. We've had scenes. But he called me." She glanced at him, then looked out over the gorge. She was speaking almost dispassionately. "I was having a dinner party, people were just arriving, and I forgot them. Forgot my husband, my children, my guests, everything. I got in the car and left, didn't change clothes or pack.

I just left. I outran a police car coming over Santiam Pass." She shuddered briefly. "Then they wouldn't let me see you. They wouldn't even let me look at you. It's a scandal, how I showed up late at night in a long dress, made a spectacle of myself." She lighted another cigarette. "Edward came down. It was all very loud and nasty. He's always known, but it was so discreet, he didn't have to admit it. I believe in your earthquake. It's shaken my world apart. I don't want you dead. I don't want you just gone, like your friends."

Her face shone — she used oil lavishly here on the desert — and she was tanned very dark, her hair sun-bleached almost white. She was beautiful; it seemed every year she was more beautiful than ever before. She continued to gaze at the deepening shadows of the chasm.

"It wouldn't work," Farley said. "You wouldn't stay here with me. I can't leave."

"Won't," she said; she dropped her cigarette and rubbed it out with the toe of her boot with exaggerated care. "Won't, darling." She shook her head at him. "Forever in love with the unattainable. It's the poor lost girl now, isn't it? Now you can live the ideal romantic dream, never have to make any tough choices. Come here and mope, prowl these hills all night, and finally one day your horse will come in alone and you'll have exactly what you're after. Complete nonexistence." She strode away from him.

"What will you do?" Farley called after her.

Without turning she waved. "Probably go home and fuck the devil out of my husband and talk him into moving to San Francisco, or Hawaii." She yanked her horse's tether loose and swung herself into the saddle smoothly. "And you can follow your goddamn Pied Piper right into the side of the cliff!" She rode away at a hard gallop.

✿

Tom Thorton was waiting for him when he got home. He charged off the porch, stopped when he saw Farley's face, and said, "Good God! You look like old puddled candlewax."

Farley concentrated on climbing the steps to the porch. Will stood watching.

"You eat anything today?" he asked quietly.

Farley sat down without answering, and presently Serena appeared with a tray. He drank the cold beer gratefully, then ate. He wanted a shower and clean clothes, but not enough to climb the stairs to the second floor.

"You can search those rocks till Doomsday. Won't find anything," Tom said. "I've been over that piece of ground three times myself."

Farley grunted. "That's the place. I'll find something."

Will opened a bottle of beer and poured it, watching the head form. "You came to the hospital and asked me about that piece of land," he said. "I told you it was poisoned, as I recall. When my father came out here in eighteen-ninety or about then, there were stone markers down there, put there by the Braddock Indians. They were still thick then. No one ever said how the Indians read the stones, but they did. Little piles, like dry walls, here a heap, a mile away another heap, and so on. Anyway, over the years Pa got to be friends with some of the renegades, sheltered them, hid them when the army was on their tail, and they warned him about that three hundred acres. One of them took him all around that piece and told him to keep clear of it. From nineteen-two when he actually homesteaded until nineteen twenty-four when he bought the west quarter, including that piece, two Klamath Indians disappeared over there; six or eight white men vanished. Course some of them could have just wandered on, but he didn't think so. Several dozen head of cattle went in and never came out. Soon as he got that land, he fenced it, been fenced ever since. Even so in nineteen twenty-nine two white men went in looking for oil and they vanished, left their truck, their gear, everything." He drank and wiped his mouth.

"Tom's been over it three times. I've been over it a hundred times or more."

"Why didn't you get help? People with equipment? Scientists?"

Will laughed, a short bark like a coyote's. "In nineteen-fifty when the hunt was on for uranium, we had a couple of geologists here with their Geiger counters, stuff like that. They heard me out and we went over. Nothing. They moved on. Who's going to believe you, son? You tell me. What's there to believe? How does it fit in with anything else we know?"

"We found something," Farley said angrily. "I heard that river! I smelled it!"

"And you're damn lucky to be sitting here talking about it," his father said quietly. "You're not the first to go in and see or hear something and come out again. But you're the first since my father began keeping a record in nineteen-two."

"Victoria came out."

"But she's not around to tell anyone."

Tom Thorton stood up then. "Whatever you say here don't mean I buy it. I can't put that kind of stuff in a report. People don't get swallowed up by the desert. And that girl's father is coming over here tomorrow. He says he's going to make you tell him what you've done to his daughter. I think you better have something ready to tell him. And you better be here. I've had my fill of him; I tell you that."

❀

Farley hadn't gone back to the gorge. When he made a motion towards the steps, his father had said very quietly that he would knock him out and tie him to his bed first, and Farley knew he could do it. He had gone upstairs and to bed. Now, waiting for Victoria's father to arrive, he was glad he had slept. He felt better and stronger, and at the same time much worse. It was as if his emotions, his mind had taken longer to wake up than his body.

He felt deep shame over his treatment of Fran; his father's grief and loneliness was a weight he wanted to share without knowing how. Most of all he kept remembering Victoria's trust in him, her faith. The past few days all he had been able to think of was getting back to the gorge, finding something, anything. Not enough, he knew now.

He needed to think, to plan. Whatever was in the valley was pure malevolence; it could kill, had tried to kill him, had tried to drive Victoria over the edge of the gorge. He no longer believed in the earthquake he had experienced. It was as false as Reuben. You couldn't believe anything you saw, felt, heard, experienced in there; and that made the problem impossible, he thought. If observers could have watched him that night, what would they have seen? He felt certain now that they would have seen him tumbling over the ground, falling repeatedly, running frantically, just as he had seen Victoria running and falling. But, he thought with a rising excitement, then she had risen, had ignored the lights and, like a sleepwalker, had simply left the area. That was the starting point. The clue to her escape that night lay in that action: she had walked away like someone in a trance, or asleep.

His thoughts were interrupted by the appearance of an automobile, or the cloud of dust from a car, at the top of the hill overlooking the ranch buildings. The car came down too fast, screamed around the curve at the bottom of the hill; the dust cloud increased.

"You want me out here?" Will asked from inside the screen door.

"No point in it. I'll talk to him." Farley watched the car careen around the last curve, screech to a stop. The driver was a thin, balding man wearing a pale blue sports coat, white shirt, tie, navy trousers. He made Farley feel hot. He went down the steps to greet Victoria's father.

"Mr. Dorsett? I'm Farley Chesterman."

The man ignored his hand and walked quickly to the shade cast by the house. "This is where she came to spend a week? In this hellhole?"

"You might as well come up and sit down," Farley said. He

went up the steps and sat in one of the canvas chairs. "You want a drink? Beer, Coke, anything? That's a long hot drive."

"I don't want anything from you," Dorsett said shrilly. "I just wanted to see for myself. A pack of lies, that's all I've had from your sheriff. Nothing but a pack of lies. You don't look like someone almost dead to me. And this sure as hell doesn't look like any resort hotel where my girl would spend even five minutes, let alone a week. I want to know what happened up here, Chesterman, why my girl came here, what you've done to her."

Farley told him the official story of the campout, the landslide. "I was found and taken to the hospital. They haven't been found yet."

"I'll take that beer," Dorsett said, wiping his forehead with his handkerchief.

Farley went in for it and when he came back Dorsett was sitting on the porch.

"Why did your sheriff send people poking around in my affairs? What's any of this got to do with me?" The belligerence was gone from his voice.

"I don't know. I guess he's trying to account for the fact that Victoria and Sam weren't found."

"Ha! Because she's just like her mother — follow anyone who whistles."

"It's hard to believe they'd leave anyone hurt, not try to help."

"Didn't her mother leave me in a jam? She ran off with one of my buyers, vanished without a word, nothing. Left me with a two-year-old baby girl. What was I supposed to do with a *girl*?"

"Did you ever find her?"

"I didn't look! She found *me* a couple years later when lover-boy ran out of cash and things got tough." He drank his beer and stood up. "As for Victoria, she'll show up again. If you have any pull with that sheriff of yours, just tell him to keep his god-damn nose out of my business. I haven't seen her and don't expect to. I wasn't sure if it was just him, or if you were making insinuations too. Now I know. If it's a shakedown, he's bucking the wrong man. I didn't get where I am today being intimidated by two-bit politicians. You tell him, Chesterman."

Farley didn't stand. Dorsett regarded him for a moment, turned, and went back to his car. He drove away in a cloud of dust as thick as the one he had brought with him.

Victoria had said her mother died when she was a baby. Maybe she did, Farley thought.

✿

Farley lay on his back, his hands under his head, on top of his sleeping bag, and listened to his father and Tom Thorton exchange stories. Tom was talking about his dude-rustling days for Leon Stacy, before he had been elected sheriff twelve years ago.

"He says to me right off, 'Mr. Thorton, I don't know a damn thing about horses, trails, desert country, nothing else I should know. All's I know is Egypt, history, pyramids, anything you want to know, I can more'n likely tell you. Now if I agree not to treat you like an ignorant slob because you don't know shit about my specialty, will you agree not to treat me like one because I don't know yours?' " Thorton poured himself more coffee from the thermos. "Real fine fellow. Teaches at the University over at Eugene. Came back every year, still does, more'n likely. Nice wife, kids. Questions! Never heard so many questions. And they all listened to the answers. Fine people."

Farley counted stars, lost track, and went over the steps again. In the valley there was enough dynamite to blow up ten acres. On the ridge was the detonator. He had already cut the fence up there, made a four-foot opening. They could step through, observe whatever was in the valley, get out, and set off the explosives. On the cliff and at the bottom gate there were powerful searchlights. "It *will* work," he told himself again.

But there was nothing to blast. Halfway through their second night the men had seen nothing, heard nothing. The horse tethered fifteen feet inside the area remained quiet.

"Three nights," Will had said. "If there's nothing for three nights will you give it up? Admit there's nothing you can do."

He had been so certain. Victoria hadn't waited. Her first night, there it was. When they came again, it was right there. He got up, walked to the gate, and watched the horse a few minutes. The starlight was so bright that if it acted up, they would be able to see it. He sat and poured coffee.

"You should get some sleep," he told Will.

"Intend to. Want to check the ridge again first?"

Farley shrugged. "No point. Not until the horse tells us."

Tom Thorton unrolled his sleeping bag. "Call me at three." He grunted several times, then began to snore softly.

"Me too," Will said. "If there's a sound, anything . . ."

"Sure, Dad."

The night remained quiet and Farley didn't bother to awaken either of the men. At dawn his father got up first, grumbled, and roused Tom, and when their relief came, two ranch hands who would guard the dynamite during the day, they returned to the house, where Farley went to bed.

The third night was the same.

"Farl, that was the agreement," Will said stubbornly. "You agreed."

"I didn't. I didn't say I would or wouldn't. I'm taking the camper up there and staying a few more nights. I'll hang around during the day. You won't have to send anyone up to relieve me."

"It isn't that, and you know it. If it was this easy don't you think someone would have done it years ago? That thing comes and goes when it gets ready. It might be quiet up there for months, years. You planning to wait it out?"

"Yes!" Farley stamped from the room, up the stairs. He began to throw his clothes into a pack.

His door opened and Serena slid inside and shut it. "Farley, why are you carrying on like this, giving your father more grief? What's the matter with you?"

"I'm crazy! Haven't you learned yet? I'm crazy! Get the hell out of here, Serena."

"You're crazy all right. Driving off Fran, driving your father beyond what he can endure. Why don't you stop all this foolishness and help your father now that he needs you."

"I can't help him."

"You can! Just let yourself instead of rushing off after ghosts all the time."

"There's something out there, Serena! I know because it almost killed me! Do you understand that? It almost killed me!"

"And it will kill you the next time! You think your father can stand that?" Serena's voice rose.

"You don't understand."

"*I* don't understand? You're the one who doesn't understand anything, Farley Chesterman! Right through the years everyone else's had enough sense to leave it alone."

Farley indicated the door. "Beat it!"

"You pig! You don't care, do you?"

"*All right!* There's something out there! A devil. You understand devils, you Catholic bitch! There's a devil out there and I'm going to get it off this land! That's what I have to do!"

"If there's a devil, it's not out on the desert! You're carrying it around with you all the time!"

"Shut up and get the hell out of here! What gives you the right to — "

There was a knock on the door. This time it was Will, who stuck his head into the room and said mildly, "I thought you two gave up screaming at each other ten, fifteen years ago."

Serena gave Farley one last furious look and ran from the room, down the stairs. Will regarded his son for a moment, then closed the door gently.

"Bitch," Farley muttered, and sat down on the side of his bed, suddenly shaking. *Bitch, bitch, bitch.*

*

Although the sheriff had collected Victoria's belongings to have them delivered to her father, no one had known what to do about Sam's camper, and it was still parked in the side yard. Farley loaded it, checked the water and food, added coffee to the stores, and left, driving slowly, unwilling to add to the coating of dust on everything in the valley.

At the gorge he told the two hands they could go back to the ranch. He chose a spot near the gate where the camper would have shade during the hottest part of the afternoons; then he climbed the cliff to check the detonator, and to scowl at the cul-de-sac below where something came and went as it chose.

His ribs ached abominably, and his head throbbed; fury clouded his eyes, blurring his vision. Somewhere down there, within the three hundred acres, he knew, the bodies of Victoria and Sam lay hidden. The packs they had carried, his pack and camera, it was all in there, somewhere. Unless, he thought, they had fallen over the gorge and the rushing river had carried them miles downstream. The desert shimmered with heat waves, and in the distance a cloud of dust marked the passing of a jeep or truck — it was impossible to see what had raised the cloud. No other life stirred in the motionless, hot afternoon; no sound broke the silence, and even the colors had taken on a sameness that was disturbing, as if a patina of heat had discolored everything, obscured the true colors, and left instead the color of the desert — a dull, flat dun color that was actually no color at all.

But he had smelled the river, he told himself, and then as if he needed more positive affirmation he said aloud, "I smelled the goddamn river, and I saw the earth move. I felt the rocks of the earthquake!"

And for the first time he wondered if that was so, if he really had smelled the river, really had been in an earthquake. And he wondered if maybe he *was* crazy. In the intense heat of the desert in August, he had a chill that shook him and raised goosebumps on his arms and made his scalp feel as if a million tiny things were racing about on it.

VI

Victoria watched the swarm of lights with rising panic, until Sam tugged her arm; then they both started to run blindly down the hillside. The lights swirled about them and Victoria stumbled, was yanked forward, stumbled again, and they both stopped, and now Sam was trying to brush the darting specks away.

The lights hovered around Victoria, blinding her momentarily, then left her and settled around Sam, who fell to his knees, then all the way to the ground, and rolled several times before he became quiet. Victoria could no longer see his body under the pulsating lights; instead, it was as if the shape was all light that gave no illumination, no warmth, but swelled and subsided rhythmically.

Victoria knelt beside him; they mustn't be separated, she thought. She reached for him, hesitating when her hand came close to the mass of lights; she took a deep breath, reached through, and touched and held his arm. The lights darted up her hand, paused, flowed back down and rejoined the others. Presently Sam stirred. There was a tightening in his muscles, a tensing before he started to sit up. The lights dimmed, moved away from him a little distance, and he got up shakily, Victoria still clutching his arm.

"Are you all right?" she asked.

"Yes. I think so." His voice was hollow, distant.

He began to walk aimlessly, as if unaware of her; she held his arm tightly and kept up. Tree frogs were singing, and there was a chirping call of a night bird, and, farther away, the roar of the river. A pale moth floated before her face; a twig snapped. A large animal scuttled up a tree, as if in slow motion. A sloth! she realized. It turned its head to look at her, then humped its way upward until it was out of sight in the thick foliage.

Still the lights hovered about Sam, not pressing in on him as they had done at first, but not leaving him either, and she remembered watching herself — the other woman — surrounded by lights, walking as if in a trance out of the fenced-in area. She began to direct their steps, keeping parallel to the wild river, and suddenly the lights stopped, as they had done before. She and Sam had crossed the dividing line. She jerked Sam to a halt and stared in disbelief. The soft moonlit rain forest continued as far as she could see. She turned, but the lights were gone. Hesitantly she took a step, and they surged toward her from the tree-covered hill. She darted back across the invisible line, and they vanished.

"Sam, sit down a few minutes. Rest. It's all right now," she said. Sam obeyed. Victoria began to arrange stones and sticks to indicate the beginning of the three hundred acres. She made a short wall, only inches high, a marker, not a barrier. Sam was still blank-eyed.

For a long time neither of them moved. Not until she began to shiver did Victoria realize how cold the night air had become. Reluctantly she stood up to look for sticks to build a fire. Hypothermia, Farley had said, could strike any time, summer or winter. She had watched him put several thick fire-starting candles in each pack. Deliberately she thought about the candles, not about Farley, who must be dead or lost.

After a smoldering start, the fire began to blaze. Victoria was still nursing it when Sam suddenly jumped up and shouted, "Come back! Wait for us!"

Victoria hurried to him and grasped his arm. "Who, Sam? Who did you see?" She peered into the forest.

"The Indian. Where is he? Which way did he go?"

"There isn't any Indian." But perhaps there was. He might have seen her fire, might have been attracted by the smoke.

"There was an Indian, Victoria! With one arm. He was taking me somewhere. You must have seen him!"

Abruptly Sam stopped and rubbed his eyes hard. "I saw something," he muttered more to himself than to her. "A path, a path of glowing light, and the Indian motioned me to follow him away from it. The path was the wrong way, that's it. It was the wrong way, and he was going to take me the right way. With one arm! You must have seen him too!"

She shook her head. "He's like Reuben. Your Indian, my Reuben."

For a moment she thought he was going to hit her. Then he slumped and his hands relaxed. "What happened?" he asked dully.

"I don't know. The lights came down the hill; you fell down, just like I did that other time. When you got up you were walking like someone in a trance, and I brought us out here." She stopped while Sam turned to stare at the forest all around them. "I thought it would be like the other time, that I would go back out, be where our camp was, but . . ." When she stopped there was only the sound of the river, a constant muted roar in the background. "I made a line to show where the gate was," she said, indicating it.

Sam hesitated only a moment, then took her hand and started over the stones. More afraid of their being separated than of whatever lay on the other side, she yielded and they moved into the strange area once more.

This time everything was different. The trees were skeletal, bone-white under the brilliant moon. No grass had grown here for many years; the ground was barren and hard, littered with rocks that made walking difficult. The wind was piercing and frigid; it was the only sound they could hear — a high wail that rose and fell and never stopped entirely. Suddenly Sam yanked her arm hard and she felt herself being pulled backward, back over the wall that no longer existed. She fell heavily.

Sam knelt by her and held her. "I'm sorry," he said. "Are you okay? I didn't want to hurt you. The lights were coming down the hill. I couldn't let them swarm over me again."

"I know," Victoria said. "I had nightmares about them."

"I didn't see them the first time," Sam went on. "I saw a path, wide, easy, glowing. I knew it led to . . . to . . . I don't know what I thought it led to. It terrified me and I wanted to get on it, follow it home, all the time thinking it would kill me if I did. Then I saw the Indian, and I knew he knew the way. I know that Indian. He *does* know the way."

"We can't be separated," Victoria said. "Farley was separated from us. He must be in there somewhere, lost, maybe he fell over the gorge. Maybe they drove him over the gorge . . ."

"*Sh.*" Sam's hand tightened on her arm. "Maybe he just came out somewhere else, like we did."

Victoria looked around. Everywhere it was the same, dead trees, no signs of life, and the bitter wind that tore through her jacket. "The fire's gone, the wall I made is gone. My pack. We can't put anything at all down and expect it to stay. We can't leave each other even a second, or one of us might vanish."

Sam nodded. "It's too damn cold," he said slowly. "Every time we've gone in and out, it's been different. Different climates, different scenery. Times." He stopped and when he spoke again, his voice was strained. "We're yo-yoing back and forth in time! That's it, isn't it! Come on, once more."

Victoria's ears were hurting from the cold and her toes were starting to go numb. "We should count our steps or something," she said. "The wall won't be there, no point in making another one. But we have to know how to get out again."

Sam nodded, and hand in hand they started forward. There was no sense of transition, nothing to indicate change, but one moment they were in the frozen air, and then the air was balmy and sweet smelling, not from a rain forest this time, but from thick lush grasses that crowded down the hillsides, and from tangled vines, creepers, dense bushes that made nearly impenetrable thickets to their right. The river was there, not a furious roar of a cascade, but rushing waters singing over rocks.

"Here they come," Sam muttered. "Out!"

The lights were coming in an elongated cloud, head-high, straight down the hill toward them. They took several steps, and the lights were no longer there. They had crossed the boundary.

They made a fire and huddled close together. "We need shelter," Sam said finally. "The moon's going down. While there's still enough light we have to arrange something." By the time the moon vanished over the mountains in the west, Sam had made a lean-to with the Mylar space blanket from his pack, attaching it from bushes to the ground, and Victoria had gathered armloads of grass that made their mattress. They wrapped Victoria's jacket around their legs, and Sam's around their torsos, and after a long time they fell asleep in each other's arms.

*

"We can't stay here!" Victoria cried late the next afternoon. They had bathed in the clear river, had portioned out their scant rations, had hunted for berries to supplement their food, and now the sun was setting and she was hungry and tired.

Sam was standing just beyond their marker stones, facing the hill. Together they had explored the hill, the valley, the entire area repeatedly. They had crossed and recrossed the barrier without effect; nothing had changed.

"It's not evil, not malevolent," Sam said softly. "This must be what happened to the others who disappeared. They weren't killed at all, just put out somewhere else, away from harm."

They would starve, Victoria thought dully. Grazing animals would find this a paradise, but not humans.

"Once more," Sam said abruptly and started up the hill again. Victoria didn't follow this time. There wasn't anything up there, nothing in the valley. It didn't show itself by daylight, she thought, and suddenly realized that the only times anything had happened, there had been brilliant moonlight. She started to call Sam to tell him, but he was nearly to the top out of hearing.

When Sam came back it was twilight. "Think of the power!" he said exultantly. "It's showing us what we can have. How many of those who vanished realized what was being offered? They probably came out and ran as far and as fast as they could and died out there on the desert, or in the cold, or of starvation.

But the power's there, down in that valley, waiting for anyone who has nerve enough to accept it. It's ours, Victoria! Yours! Mine!"

He wasn't hungry, he said, wasn't tired, just impatient. "There's a secret we haven't learned yet, about how to call it, how to make it manifest itself. We'll learn how to summon it."

He began to stuff things back into his pack. "Come on. I'm going to wait for it this time down in the valley. Hurry up before it gets too dark."

"It won't be there," Victoria said. "It's never there until after the moon is up. Both times the moon was up."

"Coincidence. Come on. The point is we don't know why it decides to come and when it will decide again. I intend to be there when it does, with you or alone."

They climbed the hill in the deepening, silent dusk, shadows moving among shadows.

"Unlimited power," Sam said hoarsely. "Omnipotent. It can move back and forth in time the way you cross a street."

But it was not omnipotent, Victoria protested silently. It was stopped by the invisible barrier. It had no power to control, only to observe. An observer, she thought, that's what it was, no more than an observer. It came only when the moon cleared the cliffs that were the eastern boundary of the valley, not when it wanted to. She had been able to get out in the right time, the right place once; it could be done again, if only she could remember how she had done it then. They were descending the hill now; it was a gentle slope, covered with waist-high grass, no rocks, nothing to impede their progress. They might have been out for an evening stroll — if only she were not so hungry and so tired.

"You want to think of it as some kind of mechanism," Sam went on, "subject to the same laws and limitations that restrict all the machines you're used to. It isn't like that. It's an intelligent being, a godlike being, testing us, for some reason we can't begin to grasp."

Each time they had talked about it, he had refused to hear

anything she said. Now she shrugged and they finished their
walk into the valley.

"Where was it?" Sam demanded. "Exactly where?"

"I don't know. Everything is changed again. The center I think,
but I don't know. Remember, we can't believe anything we see
or feel in here. Your Indian, my Reuben, the dog, none of it was
real."

He was no longer listening. He considered the valley for a few
moments, selected a spot, and spread his blanket on the ground.

"Here," he said. "We'll wait here. Don't speak now. Just concen-
trate on it, call it. Okay?"

Helplessly Victoria sat down also. The Indian and Reuben
were the clues, she thought. "Sam, before we start concentrating,
just tell me one thing. When your Indian was guiding you, why
were you zigzagging?"

"We were making our way among the rocks and boulders,"
Sam snapped. "Now just shut up, will you? Go to sleep if you
can."

"But . . ."

Sam caught her wrist in a tight grip and she became quiet.
After a moment he released her and they sat side by side in silence.

But there weren't any rocks or boulders then, she had started
to say. Not for her, she corrected. They had been together and
still had seen different worlds.

Sam had invented the Indian, just as she had invented Reuben; if she had not interfered, would Sam's Indian have led him
to the safety of his own time? It was as if within each of them
there existed a core of consciousness that would not be fooled by
the shifting scenery, a part of the mind that knew where they belonged and how to get back to it. *Come back!* she wanted to
cry. *Reuben, Indian, anyone. Please come back!*

The night had become very dark, and it was too hazy to see
the stars. Maybe it would be too cloudy for the moon to light
the valley later, she thought. What if there were weeks of cloudy

weather? They would die. The land would change, the forests grow, fall, be buried in rocks from earthquakes and landslides, and somewhere deep in the earth their bones would lie never to be discovered.

In a little while she put on her jacket, and still later she stretched out on the blanket and dozed. She was awakened by an exclamation from Sam. She sat up. The valley was moonlit again, brilliant, sharply defined, and Sam was walking away from her, his arms outstretched, oblivious of her, of the need to stay together.

"Sam!" she cried, but he didn't pause. From the corner of her eye she caught the flash of light coming down the hillside. She recoiled as the light dots touched her. Momentarily Sam was covered with them, a glowing crucifixion, and then he was gone.

"Sam!" She scrambled to her feet, and ran toward him, where he had been, and stumbled over rocks that had not been there only moments before. In panic she looked behind her: the blanket was gone, the pack; the valley was barren, with scattered clumps of desert grasses. In the distance there was a flare of light, and she thought of volcanoes, of earthquakes, and even as the thought formed, the earth shook beneath her, and she threw herself down, holding her breath. "No!" she said against the ground. "No!" She closed her eyes hard.

She didn't open them again until she could smell forests and leaf mold and pungent odors of mushrooms and mosses and ferns. She was wet from the grasses under her. Very slowly, concentrating on forests, she got up. She could see only a few feet in any direction because of the trees, and she no longer knew the way out of the valley. She walked, accompanied by flickering lights that she ignored, and then she heard someone else walking through the forests.

"Sam!" she called. "Farley!" There was instant silence and she held her breath, remembering the sloth she had seen before. There might be bears, or wolves, or wildcats . . . She eased herself around a mammoth tree, darted from its shelter to another one, then to a third, and was starting to skirt it when across an open area, she stood face to face with an Indian, a young man, not the one-armed Indian Sam had talked about. He looked as frightened as she, and the unquiet lights were hovering about him. Before he could move, she ran, and could hear him running behind her. Suddenly before her there rose a rock wall, the cliff, and she turned to see the Indian no more than twenty yards away. She watched, frozen, until he had taken several more steps, almost leisurely, and the lights that had been with him vanished. The barrier, she realized, they had both crossed the barrier without knowing it. She darted back toward the trees, and after only a few paces, the forest was gone, and the valley was frost-rimed, blasted by an icy wind shrieking like a witch.

She stopped, backed up until she felt the cliff behind her, then stepped forward again, into a different time, with warmer air and junipers and grass. Now she sank to the ground and sat hugging her legs hard, keeping her eyes wide open.

A flash of light caught her eye and she watched the swarm settle over something small, possibly a mouse; it moved erratically, stopped, moved again, and the lights withdrew, flowed back through the valley, up the cliff and disappeared.

She stared. *Up* the hill? She had assumed they came from somewhere near the center of the valley. She got up and began to walk toward the cliff. She could think only: there must have been a time before it was like this. Momentarily she was aware of a kaleidoscopic effect, of moving through layers of time, of ceaseless change. She paused, closing her eyes, then moved on.

A knoll rose like a gentle swell before her, and she began to ascend. When she stopped, it was because standing before her, filling her field of vision, was a glowing shape that was indefinable. Smaller shapes, higher than she, glided over the ground toward her, came to rest in the air a short distance away. They were oval, or nearly so, glowing as the lights glowed, without illumination; behind the glowing surfaces she could almost see other shapes, darker shadows. She blinked rapidly, but was unable to resolve the shadows within the ovals. From one of the shapes there came a swarm of the restless light dots, a cloud large enough to envelop her completely. She did not flinch when the swarm settled over her like a suffocating net.

She was aware that the large oval shape was sinking into the ground, and distantly she thought: they are placing it now, without trying to understand who they were or what they were placing. She was aware when the motion of the oval stopped, and she thought: they realize they already have me, wherever they store information — computers made of glowing dots?, an information pool in the ground? wherever. She was aware of a heavier blanket of lights all over her, inside her, draining her, using up the air so that she could no longer breathe.

"God Almighty!" She heard the voice, opened her eyes.

"Reuben!" He stood before her with his hands on his hips.

"You again? The little lost girl again. What in hell are you wandering out here for this time?"

"I've lost a friend. I'm looking for him."

Reuben scowled. "Bearded fellow? Some kind of religious nut?"

Victoria nodded. "Is he still in the valley?"

"Come on, I'll take you to him. Can't understand why in tarnation this part of the world is worse than a big city suddenly, people wandering about all night where they got no business being."

Victoria knew she didn't have to hold his hand, knew he would not leave her until she was ready. They started down the steep, dangerous cliff.

A motion caught her eye. Across the valley, silhouetted against the sky, she saw a man's figure, and recognized Farley. He was climbing down the opposite cliff. The lights flashed toward him and he turned and scurried back up. She took a step toward him and he was gone. In the valley she could make out boxes.

Concentrating on them, she let Reuben lead her across the valley until they stood before the boxes.

Dynamite! Farley was going to blow up the valley!

And somewhere within a few feet of where she stood, in another time, Sam sat and waited for something he could not even name. She blinked hard and saw Sam, almost hidden by the high lush grass. He was sitting cross-legged, his hands on his knees, staring ahead fixedly; he was covered with lights. He wouldn't hear her, see her, be aware of her at all, she knew; but the blast? Would the blast jolt him back into his own time?

She hurried back up the cliff that became a gentle slope under her feet. The large oval had not moved, was still partially in the ground; around it there were now a dozen or more of the smaller ovals. She stopped and was aware that from all sides the lights were streaming toward her. Before they reached her, she realized that she had lost them before; she had moved from one time to another and left them behind. Now she felt almost a physical assault as they touched her, thicker and thicker clouds of them settling over her, then entering her, becoming part of her.

She visualized mushroom clouds and lasers; moon-landing vehicles and satellites; the skyline of New York and a hologram of a DNA model; computers that extended for city blocks deep underground and missiles in their silos; undersea explorer crafts and a surgeon's hand inside a chest cavity mending a faulty heart . . .

A core sample, she thought, taken through time, to be collected at a later date, to be wandered through by beings she could not even see well enough to know what she had seen.

And when they came to collect their sample, a great gaping wound in the earth would remain and the earth would heave and tremble and restore equilibrium with earthquakes and volcanoes.

Her head felt hot, throbbing; it was harder and harder to hold the images she formed. If only she could rest now, sleep a few minutes, she thought yearningly, just let it all go and sleep.

Reuben's grumble roused her again. "This is going to take a hell of a long time if you lollygag like that. Come on, get it over. I got me a sleeping bag and a fire and I sure would like to get back to them sometime before morning."

She thought of men aiming polarized lights that were indistinguishable from moonlight, calling forth the lights that streamed out into nets that would contain them. She thought of men excavating the hillside, studying the energy source they found. She thought of low white buildings hugging the hills, high-voltage fences outlining the enchanted three hundred acres.

The large oval shimmered and started to rise. The small ovals clustered about it.

Victoria felt leaden, unable to move. She looked down at herself and saw that the lights no longer surrounded her, but had become part of her; she was filled with light.

"Give me your hand," Reuben said patiently. "Telling you, honey, it's time."

He led her to the boulders where she looked down at the valley and waited for the shifting landscape to become the right one, with high grass and the figure of a man, sitting, waiting.

The lights were streaking back now from the valley, the hills, abandoning the objects they studied. Farley would see them and know it was time.

❖

Sam waited. As random images formed, words sounded in his inner ear, he acknowledged and banished them. He might wait all night, all the next day, forever.

He no longer knew how long he had been there; he felt no discomfort or sense of passing time. When he heard his name called from behind him, up the hillside, he denied it, but the call came again and he turned to see.

And now his heart thumped wildly in his chest and he was overwhelmed by exultation and reverence. With tears on his cheeks, he extended his arms and moved toward the figure that burned and was not consumed by the flames, that was light and gave no light, that was motionless in the air above the slope he started to climb.

"My God!" he whispered, and then cried the words. "My God! My God!"

*

Victoria felt a wrench when the lights flowed out of her. She swayed and groped for the boulder; her head felt afire, and a terrible weakness paralyzed her; her vision dimmed, blurred, failed.

"Let's get the hell outa here," Reuben said, and his hand was warm and firm on her elbow as he guided her, blind now, up the slope that was rocky and steep.

The blast shook them, echoed round and round in the valley, echoed from the gorge walls, from rocks and hills and sky. It echoed in Victoria's head and bones. She found herself on the ground. The noises faded and the desert was quiet, the air cool, the sky milky blue with moonlight.

She waited for a second blast, and when none came, she pulled herself up. She was on the gorge side of the cliff, protected by the ridge from the force of the explosion. Slowly she began to pick her way up the cliff. At the top she paused.

Across the valley, on the cliff opposite her, she could see Farley in the moonlight. His gaze was upward, intent on the sky. Victoria thought: he has seen evil depart on giant bat-wings, recalled to hell from whence it came. She smiled slightly.

Midway down the cliff she could now see Sam getting to his hands and knees, shaking his head. He stood up slowly. And he, she thought, had come face to face with his god.

They made a triangle, three fixed points forever separated, forever bound together by what had happened here.

Farley had seen her, was waving to her. She waved back, and pointed down toward Sam. No one would believe them, she knew, there would be endless talk, and it wouldn't matter. They would reappear together and stay together, as they had to now, and the talk would subside, and people would even come to regard them as inseparable, as they were. She thought she heard a growly whisper, "No more little Miss Goody?" She laughed and held out her hand to Sam, who was drawing close; he was laughing too. Hand in hand they picked their way down the cliff to join Farley at the gate.

THE UNCERTAIN EDGE
OF REALITY

The Guest of Honor Speech
Delivered at the 38th World Science Fiction Convention,
Noreascon II: Boston, Massachusetts, 1980

THE TITLE of my speech is "The Uncertain Edge of Reality," and I think this weekend will demonstrate just how uncertain that edge is. It is appropriate, I think, to talk about reality at a science fiction gathering; it would be much harder with a general audience, because the concepts we take for granted would need lengthy explanations. But also it seems appropriate because it has become acceptable suddenly to speak of science fiction as reality fiction, and even to qualify it as the only reality fiction. I use the phrase quite often, and I must warn you now that I may not use it in exactly the same way that others do. This fact points to the difficulty we have with language — word associations and meanings. As far as I can tell some writers think that fiction that solves problems is reality fiction, and that it is the only fiction dealing with real problems. For example, suppose you have a sanitary engineer as a protagonist, and the problem is that the entire sewer system of a future city has stopped working. His problem is to unclog it. It's future, therefore it's science fiction. He has a problem that could be real, and certainly is serious, therefore it's reality fiction. In this kind of thinking, the grimmer the problem, the closer it has to be to reality.

I don't mind if others call that reality fiction, but I think of it as how-to fiction. How to build a better space station. How to manage a galactic empire. How to conquer the aliens. How to unclog sewers. And so on.

In each of these the author already knows the answer, the author already knows the reality of the fictional world, the author is God about to give a lesson masquerading as fiction.

There is another way the term reality fiction is used, this time by those who say it is fiction about us, here and now. But I have to object to this definition also. Any fiction worth talking about is about us and our culture. Sometimes it is heavily disguised, but for anyone seriously searching, we'll be there, our culture will be there, perhaps inverted, or a small part of it isolated, or somehow twisted, but you'll know it is our world being examined. That is what good fiction does. And that is saying that good fiction is reality fiction, which is nice, but not very informative.

When I use the phrase, I mean it very literally. Reality fiction, like mystery fiction, western fiction, nurse fiction, is self-defining. It is fiction about reality. This instantly sets up new problems, partly because most people think automatically that everyone knows what reality is, and it is this basic premise that I am testing. It is evident that we all draw different lines separating reality from fantasy; we all have different boundaries.

If you don't believe in water dowsing, you've drawn a line separating a small section of reality from fantasy. If you do believe in water dowsing but don't believe in map dowsing, you've drawn a different line, and if you believe in both water and map dowsing, your line is still different. It is no use for Joe, the nonbeliever, to say, I can prove that's wrong, because while Joe can prove it to his own satisfaction, he cannot prove it to Mary's satisfaction. And Mary, more likely than not, will turn around and prove that her beliefs are correct, at least to her satisfaction.

It is no good saying, let's ask the experts, the geologists. They are as divided as the general public on this, as well as other problems of defining reality.

❖

I live in Oregon and among all the northwest residents there is more than a passing interest in volcanoes these days. In other places, the interest is simpler; the volcano represents something exotic and remote, but we look on it as a near neighbor that has run amok. Think of the words we use to express stability, changelessness, security: terra firma, solid ground, steady as a rock, granite-faced, stony countenance, immovable as a rock. How easily they rise in the mind. I wonder what phrases the northwest Indians used. I suspect they were not like ours.

The Indian legends tell of the terrible chiefs of the under-world, chiefs of the air, hurling flaming boulders at each other, turning day into night in their wrath. They tell of two warriors who fought for the love of a beautiful, white-clad virgin; their strife filled the sky with smoke and dust, caused the ground to shake, and a natural bridge over the mightiest of all rivers to crumble in ruins. Finally wearied of the noise, the fire, the destruction of the land, the Great Spirit silenced them both, and turned them into the guardians of the river they had sullied. We call them Mt. Hood and Mt. Adams.

The prize they fought for has her own legend. An ugly, old, hunchback hag was magically transformed into the lovely, virginal maiden whose beauty was praised by all who saw her. She was perfection of symmetrical form, pristine and serene. In keeping with the legend, we could add the next chapter: the maiden waited for one of the warriors to claim her. She stood steadfast in the summer heat, the driving rains, the bitter snows, until at last a fear started trembling in her heart. No longer able to sustain the magic that had transformed her, she groaned aloud in a terrible voice that echoed over the land, that all might know her grief. Still no lover came to her side. With the death of love, the magic failed. Voicing a fearsome scream, she flung off the virginal robe, and the sorrow of the maiden became the fury of the hag who hurled fire and ash, scoured the land, and fouled the pure waters.

They stand thus: the two warriors silently guarding the river, the ancient hag revealed in her fury, trembling, breathing sulfurous fumes, spitting curses on the land, her love betrayed, her magic spent. But deep within, hidden from sight, the old witch is stirring her caldron again.

Magma, magmatic vents and plugs, caldera, pyroclastic flows, harmonic tremors, ash plume . . . We, like the Greeks, have a word for it, and this past spring we all acquired a whole new vocabulary.

Every age has its adepts who understand, predict, and try to control their environment. Priests, shamans, sorcerers, scientists. The Indian wise men who explained the smoking mountains were trying to do exactly what our scientists are trying to do: make mysterious and frightening events fit into their overall scheme of reality. We all know the priests, shamans, and sorcerers relied upon superstitions, magic, and revelations for their insights, and these proved false. Scientists base their findings on fact, experiential evidence.

In the case of Mt. St. Helens on Sunday, May 18, 1980, at ten in the morning, a group of people was due to arrive at Spirit Lake high on the mountain side to collect belongings, water plants, do whatever displaced people feel compelled to do on a brief visit home. U.S.G.S. scientists said there would be at least a two-hour period of grace after the first warnings of a major eruption; it was safe to go in. Less than two hours before the party was due, the mountain erupted with a two-minute warning. Everyone was surprised, and we've all been surprised together again and again since then.

In July, in fact, one of the guardians of the river, Mt. Hood, started to rumble with earthquakes — ninety within a one-week period — and no one has said yet if that means it too will erupt.

I suspect the Indian legend would give us a clue, if we would listen to it.

Let's go back for a moment to the natural bridge that was destroyed; it was called the Bridge of the Gods, and the fact of its historical existence is questioned. Geologists line up on both sides, each faction proving its case. Among the Indians it is known that before the destruction of the bridge, and a waterfall that divided the upper and lower Columbia, there was no salmon fishing upstream from that point. The salmon could not climb the falls. There was a trading center at the waterfall where the salmon fishermen met the high plateau Indians and exchanged wares, with salmon the chief item of barter. But legends from prehistory are not valid: science demands facts, and oral history is not acceptable. The geologic evidence lends itself to two interpretations. There was a bridge. There was not a bridge.

❀

This kind of split is evident in all the sciences. Jokes are made about opposing psychiatrists appearing in court, trying to prove the same person sane and insane. Handwriting analysts join in a similar battle. Meteorology is deeply divided between those who believe we are entering a new ice age, and those who think the climate is in a warming trend. Archaeologists date Machu Picchu either from the time of the Spanish conquest or back to about 7000 B.C., and anthropologists and archaeologists place Indians in North America 11,000 years ago, or close to 30,000 years ago.

In medicine iatrogenic illnesses account for almost one third of all hospitalizations. Iatrogenic means medicine-caused. This is sending a rift through the medical profession as nothing has done in many years.

None of these are hard sciences, it may be suggested. How about chemistry? Well, there are funny things in chemistry too. Until the middle of the nineteenth century it was known that glycerine would not crystallize. Many people had tried without success, and for that reason it was shipped in liquid form, harder to handle, more expensive, generally more inconvenient. Then one day a shipment from Germany arrived in England, and when the cask was opened, it was discovered that the glycerine had crystallized spontaneously en route. But, stranger than that, it is reported that glycerine in flasks on shelves also crystallized, and since then there has been no problem with it.

It's rather well known that researchers from one laboratory sometimes will go to another to set up an experiment that has been giving the second laboratory problems. This process of having the originators duplicate their own work, changing nothing in the second lab, which has followed instructions scrupulously, is often all that is needed and from then on the second group has no more trouble. Nothing changed, only now it works.

And, of course, chemists are in opposition concerning the effects of insecticides, defoliants, additives to food and to material that goes into clothing.

It is tempting to assume that those who don't think as you do, gung ho for banning Agent Orange, for example, are in the grasp of the evil corporations — and maybe some are — but it is also true that there is a very real difference of opinion. Different conclusions are drawn from the evidence.

One more example before I pass on to where all this is leading. In biology the arguments over nature versus nurture have never been stronger. Sometimes the gene is called immortal; the combinations are changed endlessly, but always the same genes are shuffled and redealt. There are people who believe all behavior can be traced directly to the genes, and since no one can be responsible for the particular genes that were passed on at conception, no one can be held responsible ultimately for behavior. But what can't be accounted for genetically is culture, religion, patriotism, true altruism, and a host of other activities that arise from ideas and are sometimes counterproductive genetically. No gene for lifelong celibacy has ever been transmitted to offspring. Here is where a many-branching chasm forms in the areas of biology, ethology, sociobiology. The scientists are climbing cliffs and are shouting across the abyss at each other, each group certain it has the key to the riddle of human behavior. Theories they are shouting about are: territorial imperative, innate aggression, a ghost in the machine (a split between the old and new brains), bicameral brain (a split between the right and left hemispheres), cytology, molecular biology . . .

*

It is true that without enthusiasm, without faith in your work, your work does not advance. This is especially true for all creative work, including science. It is also true that an observer has to be free to point out that opposing theories cannot both be right; science has made mistakes in the past and is not exempt from making mistakes in the present and in the future. Science needs its critics as much as any artistic group, and it is always best if the critics are aware of the real accomplishments as well as the goofs. It is the duty of a critic to point out that at the fork in the road a decision is needed. It's as simple as the formula: If A then not B. Since we are all pulled down the chosen road willy-nilly, it would be good to know on what basis the choice was made.

Today's scientists are the equivalent of yesterday's shamans: they point the way and the rest of the populace follows. And they are human with the same divisions that the rest of us have, the same uncertain edge of reality we all share.

It matters. All these differences between the experts matter. Eventually, current, disputed ideas find wide acceptance and become part of an ever-emerging conventional wisdom. Acceptance does not necessarily mean the ideas reflect reality any better than those not accepted, but it does mean they become self-perpetuating, and they can change our perception and understanding of reality. There is a word for such ideas that endure, much the same way that genes endure, by replicating themselves again and again for centuries, or even thousands of years. They are called memes. Moses and the Red Sea is such an idea, as is Plato's Atlantis, Aladdin and his wonderful lamp, much of what Aristotle wrote, long since proven wrong, but still alive. It would be a serious mistake to assume that only in the past did people accept without proof memes of this sort.

No one has proven to my satisfaction that UFOs are anything but what the name says: unidentified flying objects. Yet how many people have had their perceptions of reality altered by accepting the various ideas about UFOs? How many people now believe, and have had reality shifts to accommodate the beliefs, in the idea of chariots of the gods? How many people believed during Hitler's Germany that there is a natural superiority in the white, north European Aryan?

It matters because what you believe shapes the reality you experience and the way you behave. Subjective experience is very difficult to assess, maybe impossible. It is well known how psychological factors can influence expectations and bring about certain behavior. Self-fulfilling prophecies are all too common; it has been demonstrated that if teachers are told that some children are expected to do well, they generally do well, while if others are predicted failures, sure enough, they fail. Remember when Johnny Carson made a joke about a pending shortage of toilet paper, and a panicky public made it come true. Just like that people accept a twist in reality, asking for no evidence, denying their own experience, reacting in fear to something that does not exist.

You can see why science takes a dim view of subjective feelings, eyewitness accounts. Science wants and needs controllable experiments, but the real world is not a laboratory, and real people do strange, unpredictable, and sometimes wonderful things. Science subdivides reality into smaller and smaller units, in much the way that physicists have divided the atom, until one wonders how they can sell pieces so small. I keep waiting for the announcement of yet a new particle with no mass, no charge, and no duration. This is one way to look at reality, but there does come a time when one must ask: is this new piece of reality an artifact? And going from there: is all reality an artifact?

*

Let me tell you some of the things people widely believed at different times; some are still believed today. Stones could not fall from the sky. Look at the sky; you can see that water is up there, not stones. Everyone knows that water comes down, but show me a stone falling. Hah! Only when no qualified observer is around. Stones from the sky, what an insane idea.

Night vapors cause malaria. Close the windows at dusk, shut the doors, stay inside. It may become a little stuffy, but you won't catch malaria. If that had not changed we would not have drive-in movies.

Royalty exists through divinity. It is God's will that this man be king, or this woman queen. It is part of God's inscrutable plan that you were born to your status, kings born to theirs, and to attempt to change it is heresy.

A red-haired woman in the kitchen will keep butter from forming in the churn. There were, and are, a lot of food beliefs that you may or may not share: eating fruit and drinking milk at the same meal will give you a stomachache. Tomatoes are poisonous. Green beans have to be cooked at least two hours, or you'll get worms from them.

The list could be extended to fill a book. There is nothing so implausible and easy to disprove that someone won't accept it as a true reflection of reality. Imagine how the red-haired-woman belief came about. Sometimes butter just does not form during churning. Wrong butterfat, wrong temperature, the milk is too fresh, or something else goes wrong. But this day it happens that a red-haired woman passes through when the butter doesn't come. She is instantly suspect. Why? Were red-haired women so rare that this was the first time one had shown up in a kitchen during this particular chore? Where did she live as a girl? Was she a foreigner to wherever this belief arose? Why would others accept such a statement? You say a red-haired woman did it? I see. Well, keep her out of here the next churning day, you hear me!

That really isn't fair. We are so desperate in our search for reality, for something to believe in to account for our mysterious world, that we'll accept the red-haired-woman story, or something equally weird, if it seems to offer an explanation for the effect we are worrying about.

✿

Scientists are a tougher audience. They can dismiss the beliefs of others, past and present, by calling the observers incompetent. The incompetent observer is any eyewitness who reports something that contradicts an accepted theory. For example, all those who said stones fall from the sky obviously were incompetent. An incompetent observer is also a nonscientist reporting on scientific concerns. Geologists have a hard time accepting Indian legends — the observers, were, after all, incompetent. The people in New England who are studying megalithic structures very much like those in Europe are incompetent amateurs; the archaeologists know there were no megalithic dwellers or visitors in North America. A scientist studying and reporting in an area that is not his or her specialty is incompetent. Linus Pauling has no business talking about vitamin C, since he is incompetent in the fields of nutrition and diseases. But even the scientists who report within their own fields in a manner that is not judged acceptable by their peers suddenly become incompetent also. A discovery first reported on a television talk show or in a popular book must be false; a real scientist who has made a real discovery would not disclose it that way.

✿

Homo sapiens sapiens, that's us, has just been around and thriving for forty thousand years or so. If the biography of our ancestors would take a three-hundred-page book, we would be the last short paragraph of that book, but during our time we have effected more changes on earth than any life form that ever walked on land. When our first true ancestors appeared there wasn't a whole lot to separate them from Neanderthalers. They all lived in caves and ate what they could find, gather, kill, but then the first truly great discontinuity in the slow process of evolution happened. Language, and with it shared, abstract ideas, came about, and in a twinkling civilization arose, cultures formed, dissolved, re-formed. We, our ancestors, have tried many different reality systems to explain our world, and we are still doing it.

Homo sapiens sapiens builds mountains of information, data, knowledge, and abstractions. We stand somewhere on that mountain to observe our world and we think from this place alone can reality be revealed at last. We don't see that our mountain is but one of a chain, that we are surrounded by countless eroded mountains, that the ground below is uneasy, as if it were being undermined. Indeed it is; the mountain-building is a continuing activity. What we accept is little more than reality by consensus and compromise, and that's exactly what the Amazon Indians do, and the Australian bushmen, and every other culture that exists.

One of the Amazon tribes that was especially successful in achieving a stable life in the jungles, with extensive plantings and abundant game, found itself confronted with the new reality of the white civilization. The tribe went into an immediate collapse, and for two years did not plant anything at all, because the shock of losing their reality was so great. They would have died out entirely if the white newcomers had not fed them. Those Indians had built their own mountain and within minutes it crumbled to nothing under their feet.

That is one of the ways reality shifts, but there is another, slower, more subtle way, a way that is less dangerous. Imagine reality as the surface of a pond that we have dug and filled with water, we and our ancestors before us. It is our pond, and we can drop questions like pebbles into it, first here, then there, with each one setting up ripples, disturbing that surface. Eventually, so slowly no one even notices, the pond is filled with pebbles, but as the water is displaced, it flows out and makes a new pond further down the slope.

If what we have now is the ultimate reality, the universe is absurd. We, *Homo sapiens sapiens,* or Homo sap sap for short, have made, and are making, the reality we live in day by day, and we can change it. It is absurd and tragic, irrational and illogical for Homo Sap Sap to waste the finite resources of this world in armaments races. It is absurd and tragic for Homo sap sap to deny equal rights to all adults. It is absurd and tragic for Homo sap sap to accept as inevitable the incredible social injustices that endure — racism, sexism, famine, malnutrition, epidemics, pollution, illiteracy . . .

Our reality is failing us. We have to question it. We are on a dead-end track as surely as the dinosaur walked a dead-end track, as surely as the saber-toothed tiger did. But there is a vast difference. They were helpless, at the mercy of their genes, caught up in the slow evolution to extinction. We have the enormous advantage of being able to externalize our power and our weapons. Unlike the saber-toothed tiger that armed itself unto death, we can stop. It isn't our genes building neutron bombs and MX missile complexes. It isn't our genes building bureaucracy on bureaucracy, diverting basic resources and brain power from the real problems of the world in the name of corporate or government policy and profit. These things are the products of the reality we have created, and reality is fluid.

❖

What is perhaps most absurd, and possibly offers an explanation for the insane suicidal track we seem to have accepted, is that we don't know who we are or what we are. One third of our lives is spent in a state of unconsciousness — sleep — and we don't know why. Theories come and go, but we know as little now as Plato did when he asked why.

It requires as much intelligence to ask questions as it does to answer them, but we are not only not answering, we are pretending certain questions do not even exist. We know the dangers of fire, children learn this particular lesson very young, and yet throughout history there have been fire walkers who do not burn. Unless all the observers of this phenomenon are truly incompetent, it happens. Why? How? We don't know. Almost everyone has a story about synchronicity — the times when a real object appears that is the subject of a discussion, for example. Our story is about one Halloween evening when we were watching a "Star Trek" show about vampires and bats. Suddenly a bat flew through the room, and we all forgot television to chase it down and put it outside where it belonged. Most people get a phone call now and then from someone they have been thinking about with no expectation of hearing from, or a letter, or a visit. Some of these are so minor we shrug them off instantly, and we tend to lump them all together as coincidence, as if by giving them a name we have explained something.

We can try to explain how an entire symphony can spring to life in the mind of a composer, how a scientist will have an elegant solution to a problem in a flash, how a novel can suddenly exist, needing only to be written down, but our explanations sound hollow. We can talk about the intricacy of the mind, likening it to a high-speed computer with many millions of cross-connections, but we don't even know exactly what we mean when we say mind. Is it the by-product of the brain, a mechanical organ that throws off thoughts in passing? We don't know.

There is the whole range of ESP effects that most people have had some experience with, but that have no place in our reality. Why? To deny them because they are unpredictable and uncontrollable seems rather arbitrary; no one can predict or control a meteorite either. To deny them because they don't fit in with our orderly universe suggests that our theories, our containers, are too small, or the wrong shape.

Our reality forces us to deny our own experiences, to label them as unreal, or to be embarrassed by them and try to forget them. Our reality might work with mechanical people, but we are not mechanical. We are unpredictable, we sometimes know things we have no way of knowing, we sometimes demonstrate powers we have no business having — under hypnosis, under stress, we are super people. Our reality is as restricting as the ancient Chinese foot bindings, but we accept it and hobble along and try not to dwell on those moments when we flew. Why?

*

This is my subject matter when I write. I am asking, what actually do we mean by reality, and are we stuck with the one we have? This is what I mean by reality fiction, and usually it is also called science fiction. Science fiction, of course, is Star Wars, and the gore of Gor, but it can also be something else: it can be visionary, not as mystics looking crosseyed trying to focus on unreachable utopias. But visionary in the most mundane, ordinary sense. It can look at us in our culture honestly, and ask why. We are more than simple animals using sophisticated tools in our search for food, security, and mates. We are something new on the earth because we are all that and also we are dreams and ideals and intuitions. We can change reality with immaterial ideas and symbols — language.

Sometimes the best way to look closely at an object is to remove it from its natural surroundings, study it in isolation. We do that in science fiction; often we transport the here and now to somewhere else, another time. Sometimes we stay here and change the time, or change the background to get a closer, clearer view.

Some writers will look at our world and find it acceptable, even good, the highest achievement Homo sap sap can possibly accomplish. They are usually male, just incidentally. Many readers are constantly reassured by this affirmation. But there are other writers who will look at the world and cry out, but it's absurd, tragic, unjust, arbitrary. Why? Who did this to my world? Using the metaphor of the pond one more time, I say here and now that it is my intention to ripple its surface; my aim is quite deliberate. The reality is on the surface; I want to disturb it, to question it. I want to demonstrate that the pond is artificial. We made it, you and I, our ancestors before us, and we failed. We didn't make it big enough, or deep enough. Too much is left out. We can't even be certain of where the edges are, where the bottom is. Any of you can join me in throwing questions like pebbles into it. Register for the draft? Why? Whom are we going to fight and why? How good will our cause look in a hundred years? What kind of reality is it that says every generation has to fight a war? Why? Why? Why?

❋

There was probably a day when the fate of the saber-toothed tiger depended on the generation born that year. A trained zoologist could have predicted the outcome when the baby tigers shed their milk teeth and grew the saber teeth. We look at their fossils and marvel at the experiment in evolution that failed. The doomed animals had no choice; they could not know an eighth of an inch more tooth would betray them. They could not have prevented it if they had known.

I maintain that we deserve better. We have the wisdom of hindsight, and the magic of foresight. We know, if we will only admit it, that we are capable of truly magnificent things on the face of the earth. We are capable of creating a just world, but not within the framework of the reality we have accepted.

I intend to keep throwing my pebbles.